Acclaim for

CATHRYN ALPERT's
ROCKET CITY

"Alpert beautifully weaves two stories together [and] creates characters you care about. They are gutsy, feisty, crude, rude, mean, dumb, gross, sensitive, loving, wistful, smart, sexy, blunt, but never, never boring. . . . A very good and very unusual first novel." —*Malibu Times*

"What a first novel should be: energetic, quixotic, different, devilish, eccentric and revelrous. . . . It's a hot, quick yarn that keeps the reader in stitches." —Stephen Dixon, author of *Interstate*

"A magnificent debut . . . a quirky, eccentric novel that will have you laughing and crying from first page to last." —*Bookviews*

"Full of twists and turns, with more surprises than on a roadside diner menu, and characters much fresher. With its lustrous prose, we can feel the desert heat." —*La Gazette*

"*Rocket City* merges the farcical detachment of Tom Robbins with the gentle humanity of Barbara Kingsolver." —*Santa Jose Metro*

"Hilariously funny and wickedly cynical. . . . The author keeps her multiple story elements moving at breakneck speed and makes the absurd believable. It's a blast." —*Books of the Southwest*

CATHRYN ALPERT
ROCKET CITY

Cathryn Alpert's award-winning short stories have appeared in numerous anthologies, including *O. Henry Festival Stories, Best of the West 5*, and *Walking the Twilight: Women Writers of the Southwest*, as well as many literary magazines. Formerly a stage director and teacher of theater, she lives in northern California with her husband and two sons.

ROCKET CITY

ROCKET
CITY

A Novel by

CATHRYN
ALPERT

VINTAGE CONTEMPORARIES

Vintage Books

A Division of Random House, Inc.

New York

FIRST VINTAGE CONTEMPORARIES EDITION, APRIL 1996

Portions of *Rocket City* have appeared in *O. Henry Festival Stories 1989* (Trans-Verse Press, Greensboro, North Carolina) and *Puerto del Sol*, Vol. 26, No. 2, and Vol. 27, No. 1.

Library of Congress Cataloging-in-Publication Data
Alpert, Cathryn, 1952–
Rocket city / Cathryn Alpert.—1st Vintage contemporaries ed.
p. cm. — (Vintage contemporaries)
ISBN: 0-679-77016-X
1. Man-woman relationships—New Mexico—Fiction.
2. Hitchhiking—New Mexico—Fiction.
3. Dwarfs—New Mexico—Fiction.
I. Title.
[PS3551.L69R63 1996]
813'.54—dc20   95-45868
CIP

Printed in the United States of America
10 9 8 7 6 5 4

For Marco

CONTENTS

ROCKET CITY

ALAMOGORDO

Three melons and a dwarf sat in the front seat of Marilee's '72 Dodge, but the cop was not amused. "I'd get rid of that bumper sticker if I was you," he said. "Folks 'round here, they're proud of their history." Marilee's bumper sticker said, "One nuclear bomb can ruin your whole day." Wrong place, wrong time. This spot on the road crossing White Sands Missile Range was fifty miles southwest of Alamogordo.

"You two traveling together?" the cop asked.

"Might say," said Enoch.

The cop's lips drew together like a drawstring purse. It was midnight and he wore sunglasses. "I'd like to see your license," he said, shining his flashlight at the little man riding shotgun.

"No can do."

"You have any I.D.?"

"Nope."

"What's your name?"

"Enoch Swann."

"Where you from?"

"Des Moines."

The cop gave Enoch a hard look. Enoch stared back at the cop. Marilee dug her fingernail into a tear in the upholstery. Surely it was not against the law to share the front seat of a woman's car with two honeydews and a casaba.

"Those melons come with you from California?" the cop asked Marilee.

"Near Bowie. Little road stand," said Enoch.

Marilee's body stiffened. The cop had to know Enoch was lying. There'd been nothing near Bowie—no road stand, and certainly not at night. Marilee wondered if they could be arrested for lying about fruit.

"Step out of the car," the cop ordered.

Enoch opened his door and lurched toward the rear of the automobile.

"You too, miss. Both of you stand over there," he said, aiming his flashlight into the space between the cars' bumpers.

Marilee did as she was asked, telling herself that none of this was happening.

"Put your hands on the trunk, spread your legs, and lean over. I'm going to search you."

The cop searched Enoch, then Marilee, patting them down from shoulders to feet. The patrol car's headlights shone up between their legs as they stood spread-eagled against the trunk of the Dart. "I'm going to search your car now."

For what? she wanted to ask him. On what grounds? For speeding? Was any of this legal? The cop climbed inside her car. "Is he going to find anything?" she whispered to Enoch.

"I'm not psychic."

"You shouldn't have said we bought the melons in Bowie. Don't you know it's against the law to take fruit across state borders? That's why they ask you about fruit. You lied. You told him we bought it here in New Mexico."

"Bowie's in Arizona. If he knew his geography, he still could've nailed you. But he doesn't know jack. Look at him. He's an asshole."

The cop sat in the backseat of the Dodge, rifling through the contents of Marilee's purse. He flipped open her compact, ran his finger over the powder, sniffed, then tasted it.

"What's he doing?" she asked.

"Couple of lines," said Enoch.

■

What was it that had compelled her that afternoon to go back for the dwarf? Her mother had taught her never to pick up hitchhikers, a lesson she hadn't needed to learn. Always shy, she'd never had the inclination to extend herself to strangers, especially to someone as different as Enoch. Perhaps it was the look on his face as she drove by him the first time, a look that said he'd been standing out on the road since dawn and hers was the first car that had slowed. Or perhaps it was the way he pulled his thumb in when he saw she was a woman alone. Or maybe it was nothing more than his obvious helplessness. Where he stood, alongside the interstate between Aztec and Sentinel, was nowhere; he'd been abandoned in the middle of the Arizona desert. As she passed him, the late-September sun reflected up off the asphalt so that his face seemed lit from all angles, open, devoid of shadow and threat. How dangerous, she asked herself, could a dwarf on crutches be?

At the first rest stop, Marilee turned the car around and drove west, back toward where she had seen the dwarf. She passed him again, on the other side of the highway. The dwarf followed her with his eyes. It would be crazy to pick him up, she knew, but now she felt obligated since he'd seen her drive by twice. She couldn't pass him a third time.

Marilee crossed over the unpaved median and again headed east. She slowed as she approached him, tensing at the crunch of pebbles under her tires. Closer now, she studied his features. He was a clean dwarf. His brown hair was tidy; his face, newly shaven. He stood about four feet tall and carried a backpack. He wore cowboy boots, a red shirt, and jeans.

Marilee reached over to open the door as he hobbled toward her car. He tossed his backpack and both crutches into the backseat. They landed on her suitcase with a thud.

"Obliged," he said in a normal voice as she pulled back into the slow lane. Was it just midgets who sounded like Munchkins?

"Been out here long?" she asked.

"Not too."

So, she hadn't saved him from near death. No matter. She liked his voice and she liked his face: a cleft chin and a nose cocked slightly to one side. His skin was tanned; his teeth clean; and when he raised his sunglasses to rub his eyes, she saw a glint of intelligence.

"I'm Marilee."

"Enoch," he said, holding out his hand. She shook his fingers. They felt like a handful of Vienna sausages.

"Enoch's an unusual name." How typical, she thought. Dwarfs always have oddball names, like Eylif or Egan. Or Bror. A band of motorcyclists passed them in the oncoming lane. Enoch squirmed and put his feet up on the dashboard; his stubby legs extended fully. Marilee fixed her eyes on the road and pretended not to have noticed, determined neither to stare nor to appear intrigued. "So," she asked, "where you headed?"

"Same place you are."

She didn't like the way he said that. It sounded ominous, as if he saw their destinies about to overlap.

"Where are you from?"

"Kingfield. Kingfield, Arizona. Couple hundred miles north. Big fire a few years back. That's when I split."

"Where you living now?"

"Here and there. In the desert."

Great, she thought. A weirdo.

"Take some melons," her mother had insisted, heaving three of them at her at once. "So in case the car breaks down, you'll have something to drink." It would never occur to her mother to send something direct, like a thermos. "And take this knife, too," she'd said. "You never know when you might need it." The kitchen knife lay hidden in the glove compartment of her car. Marilee wondered if she'd have the guts to use it, if necessary, and whether she'd be able to reach for it in time. Enoch shifted in the seat next to her. The honeydews rolled toward his thigh.

"My mother's idea," said Marilee, gathering the melons back into the space between them on the seat. "So if the car breaks down, I won't die of thirst. My mother's kind of out there sometimes. Of course, if anything happened, I could always drink radiator water. I brought a knife, too, so if I had to, I could hack up a cactus."

"Or a camel," said Enoch.

Definitely weird.

"So, where are we off to?" he asked. Again, her insides jumped. The highway stretched before them, a colorless slab dissolving into a blurred horizon. Save for the sun, the sky was bare. No clouds floated by. No birds flew. In other cars, people looked half-sedated, as though hypnotized by the strobe of disappearing broken lines and the hum of tires on asphalt, the white noise of the open road. Marilee was glad to have gotten it in about the knife.

"Alamogordo," she replied. "To get married, but he doesn't know that yet. Well, he does and he doesn't. I mean, he asked me to marry him, but he doesn't know I'm on my way." Oh God, she thought, she shouldn't have told him that.

"Roll it down?" Enoch pointed to the window.

"Sure. It sticks sometimes. You have to really crank it."

The dwarf turned the handle, but the window didn't stick. He then stood on the seat and reached for his backpack on top of her suitcase. What was he reaching for? A knife? A gun? Why in God's name had she picked him up?

A small bag of granola materialized from his backpack's zippered pocket. "Have some," he offered.

Marilee considered her options. What if it were drugged? Was he going to eat some too? She took a small handful. It tasted like a clump of dried weeds.

"What's his name?" asked Enoch.

"Who?"

"Mr. Wonderful."

"Oh, Larry. He's this guy I've been going with a long time. Since high school, really. Funny how you can end up with someone you knew back in high school. I mean, I don't know anyone I knew back in high school. Except him, of course." She was babbling.

"Larry what?"

Why did he want to know? "Larry Mitchell," she said, plugging in the first surname that came to mind.

"Boring," said Enoch. "Larry Mitchell. Mr. and Mrs. Larry Mitchell. Dull as dust."

Marilee studied the stretch of desert around her. Cactus. Tumbleweeds. Dirt for miles. A few rocks, not many. Probably insects under the rocks.

"What's he do, this guy, Larry?" Enoch offered her another handful of granola, but she declined.

"He's in the military. Holloman Air Force Base."

"Does he fly jets?"

"He's a flight instructor."

"So," said Enoch, "you're going to roll into Alamogordo so you two can get hitched?"

"That's right."

"And he has no idea you're on your way?"

Heat rose off the pavement and warped vision, not unlike the aura of an impending migraine. "Well, he does, sort of. I mean he expects me. Soon. But he doesn't know when, exactly. I was going to be a surprise."

"Sort of, 'Here I am. Let's find a church,'" said Enoch.

"Sort of."

"Sort of, 'Hi, I'm moving in. Hope you don't mind.'"

"No. Not like that at all. He's going to love it when I show up. He's been wanting this for a long time."

"And you?"

"I want it," she said. "I've thought about it. It makes sense that we get married."

"Why?"

"Look, are you hungry? I'm starving. I get cranky when I don't eat. What's the next town?"

"Casa Grande."

"Let's look for a restaurant."

"Yo! Casa Grande!" Enoch shouted, raising his fist in a power salute and stomping his feet on the dashboard. A toothbrush fell out of his pants cuff.

He was definitely one weird dwarf.

■

"Let's play a game," said Enoch, as soon as they'd ordered. "I'll ask you a question, then you ask me one. Whoever loses pays."

"Okay," said Marilee, although she was not sure at all that it would be okay.

"Can an irresistible force encounter an immovable object?"

"Sure." She was glad his question had been nothing personal.

"Which one gives?"

Marilee thought about it for a moment. "Well, it's really just a matter of semantics."

"Not at all," said Enoch. Two middle-aged ladies in the next booth eyed them with curiosity. Enoch's chest was level with the edge of the table; Marilee was glad the waitress hadn't offered him a booster seat.

"Okay," she said. "I guess it's impossible to answer."

"Bingo. One to nothing. Your turn."

Marilee took her time thinking of a question. She turned down the corners of her paper place mat. She traced her spoon over the outline of a hobo eating pancakes. He looked a little like Enoch. Sipping coffee, she stared out the window at the filling station next door. The attendant scratched himself when he must have thought no one was looking.

"All right, I've got one. Which came first, the chicken or the egg?"

"Impossible to know," said Enoch. "And a cliché."

"Think again." Two could play this game.

A group of teenagers erupted in laughter from across the room. They sneaked occasional glances at Enoch.

"Impossible," he said again.

"The egg," said Marilee. "It's obvious. At some point there had to be a mutation. But by the time the egg is formed, it has all its genetic material intact. It's a potential chicken. So the responsible gene, the gene that made the critical difference, had to have mutated inside the hen before it became part of the fertilized egg. And something had to pass on that altered gene. Something that was not quite a chicken but gave rise to a mutant egg that was destined to become the world's first chicken."

Enoch's face brightened. "Yes, that's logical. Very good." Their waitress appeared with their dinners. She wore a red ruffled skirt and an embroidered hat that said, "Doreen."

"I've got another."

"My turn," said Enoch, dipping a french fry in the Thousand Island dressing that ran out the side of his Hoboburger. "If God is all powerful, can he build an object too heavy for him to move?"

"Another paradox."

"Are you certain?"

"Positive."

"I win," said Enoch. "If God is all powerful, he can transcend paradox."

"What makes you so certain God's a he?"

"Different question. Stick to the point."

Marilee thought about the point. "Interesting," she said, forcing a smile; secretly, she was pissed. "Now it's my turn. A man is walking down a road. In order to take a step, he must first travel half that distance. A half-step. Then, in order to take a half-step, he must first travel a distance half the length of that. Will he ever reach his destination?" She bit into her club sandwich and hit a toothpick.

"Zeno's paradox. The answer is no."

"Wrong," said Marilee, with her mouth full. "Faulty premise. People don't move in half-steps, do they?"

"Then again, some people don't move at all."

What was that supposed to mean? She pinched a blister from the end of her bacon and buried it under her carrot twist. "All right. How many angels can dance on the head of a pin?"

"Box-step or hora?" said Enoch.

They ate the rest of their meal in silence. When Doreen brought their check, they agreed to split it. Marilee took the money to the cashier while Enoch went in search of a bathroom. She'd gone earlier, while the hostess was seating Enoch, because she didn't want to be seen walking through the restaurant with a dwarf.

Marilee paid the bill and sat on the brown vinyl seat by the coffee shop's front door. Five minutes passed. Then ten. What was he doing in there? she wondered, then asked herself if she really wanted to know. And why, come to think of it, was she sitting there waiting? This was her chance. She'd never have to see him again.

Her keys jangled as she made her way swiftly through the parking lot. But as soon as she opened the car door, she saw that Enoch had left his backpack. Now what? She could leave it on the ground, but what if somebody stole it? No, she'd have to take it into the restaurant and leave it for him there. She started the engine and steered the Dart toward the entrance. As she pulled up, an elderly woman held the door open for Enoch.

"That's nice," he said, resuming his seat next to the melons. "Bringing the car around. Thanks."

"Sure," said Marilee. She knew what it felt like to steal from an invalid. Strike a child. Throw a kitten off a bridge.

■

"So," said Enoch, as soon as they were back on the highway. "What does this Larry guy do for kicks?"

Not again, thought Marilee. "Well, mainly he likes to jog, work out with weights, that sort of thing. He's into fitness. Poetry. Books about the Civil War."

"That's it?"

"Sometimes he has friends over and they rent movies."

"Porno flicks?"

"Oh, God no, he'd die." Marilee laughed. "I bet he's never even seen one."

"Have you?"

She looked over at the little man in her front seat cleaning his fingernails with the corner of a Hobo matchbook.

"So show me this guy," he said. "A picture. I want to see."

She rooted in her purse for her wallet, wondering at the same time if this were a good idea. Couldn't he just grab it out of her hand? That's silly, she thought. Where would he go? She opened her wallet with one hand and dug out a photo of a young man in camouflage fatigues. She handed it to Enoch. The man in the picture had blond hair and a weak chin. The badge over his pocket said, "Johnston."

Enoch tossed the photo faceup on the dashboard. "So, you and Larry planning to have kids?"

"Why do you keep asking me about Larry?"

"Fine. Let's talk about me."

Marilee wondered what she should ask him. She wanted to ask what it was like to be a dwarf, but the words stuck in her throat. "Okay. Tell me about the fire. In Kingston."

"Kingfield," said Enoch. "Another time." A bug spattered against the windshield and left a yellow-green smear like the feathered tail of a comet. "I've got one," he said. "If a tree falls in the forest and nobody's there to hear it, does it make a sound?"

"Talk about clichés."

"Yes, but does it?"

"It's a moot question. Without a witness, there's no way to know."

"I think it does," said Enoch.

"Based on what?"

"Track record. All trees that have ever fallen in the presence of people who can hear have made a sound. That means something."

"But one that falls in a deserted forest might fall silently. You can't prove that it doesn't. That's not logic."

"Then you rely on faith."

"What's faith got to do with it?"

"Where logic fails," said Enoch, "that's where faith steps in. Sometimes that's all you've got. You've got to have faith in the laws of physics and you've got to have faith in people. Remember that line?" he asked, turning to face her across the front seat. "At the end of *Manhattan*, remember? Mariel Hemingway says that to Woody Allen. 'You gotta have a little faith in people.' Great line. Sums up the whole movie."

They continued east on Interstate 10, through Tucson, past Benson and Willcox. The sign at the border said, "Welcome to New Mexico. Land of Enchantment." Enoch curled up beside the melons and fell asleep as darkness consumed the landscape. He slept through Marilee's stop for gas in Lordsburg. He slept through the convoy of trucks that rumbled past them just east of Las Cruces. When he awoke, hours later, they were near White Sands Missile Range. Red and blue lights flashed in the rearview mirror.

Enoch stretched his legs and bolted upright. What he said startled her. He said, "You're a woman and I'm a dwarf. Woody is neither. I've got to pee."

∎

The cop crawled out of the backseat of Marilee's car. "We got a speed limit here, miss," he said. "Try and stay under it." He tore the ticket from his pad and handed it to her with a smile.

"Thanks," said Marilee.

"For what?" asked Enoch.

As the cop drove west, Enoch went in search of a bush. He didn't use his crutches, and he wobbled as he walked. Marilee leaned against her front fender and stared off into the distant lights of Alamogordo. She hated getting tickets, hated cops almost as much as she hated herself for having been so accommodating. She tried to think of a reason why this had been Enoch's fault but couldn't. In a moment, he returned.

Marilee opened her driver's-side door. When the interior light came on, she saw it down in her footwell. It was a pale scorpion, translucent almost, with two dark stripes running the length of its body. She drew back and motioned for Enoch to come over. How did it get there? How could it have crawled inside a car ten inches off the ground? Had the cop somehow brought it in? Or had it been hiding in some cranny of Enoch's backpack? Perhaps it had been there the whole time, down by her feet as she drove east from Los Angeles.

"Get it out," she whispered.

"Easy," he cautioned. He reached down into the footwell and gently prodded the creature. It crawled onto his stubby fingers. Marilee froze. Was this guy stupid or just plain crazy? She wondered, for a moment, if Enoch might try something funny like flinging it at her or insisting she touch it. She took another step backward.

The thing crawled into Enoch's palm. He lifted it out of the footwell, but instead of tossing it into the desert, he held it in his hand. Enoch looked at the scorpion. The scorpion looked back. Its legs seemed bulbous and awkwardly hinged, as if the result of some miscue of nature. It uncoiled its tail and rose up on its legs. Marilee felt she was going to throw up.

"Get rid of it," she whispered. A trickle of sweat ran down between her breasts.

"In a minute."

The scorpion's tail arched high over its head, its stinger suspended like a hooked needle; its pincers cocked, front and open. Standing in the light of the car's doorway, Enoch studied the creature, staring it down as if daring it to strike. A passing semi whipped dust in their faces, but neither of them flinched. Each stood poised for battle. Each bided his time, eyeing the other as though they shared some indelicate secret with which Marilee could presume no intimacy.

Finally, the scorpion lowered its tail. Enoch placed it in the dirt by the side of the highway, where it crawled to safety beneath a broken Styrofoam cup.

■

They continued east toward Alamogordo. In less than an hour they would arrive and she would say goodbye to Enoch, dropping him off at the Y, perhaps, or maybe at a shelter. Then she would get out her map and find Larry's street. She would knock on his door in the middle of the night, and he would open it and take her into his arms.

Marilee stepped down harder on the accelerator. Her muscles ached from driving; her lips tasted of salt. Brown dirt lodged in the cracks between her toes. "I could use a shower," she said, more to herself than to her companion.

"A pool!" said Enoch. "I know a place. On the road to El Paso. It's not far. I'll show you."

A pool sounded wonderful. Clean water in which she could bathe. Cool water in which she could float away under the stars. But it was out of the question. "I didn't bring a bathing suit."

"Swim naked."

Marilee felt a tightness grip her stomach. So this was it. This was where he'd jump her. Where he'd slip his little thing into her like a snake gliding into wet moss, and she'd end up with a little dwarf child she'd have to name Elwyn. And why not? Hadn't she picked him up off the side of some road? What jury would believe her? They'd say she'd asked for it, wanted it even.

Yet a pool sounded wonderful. It was after midnight. Her hair stuck to the back of her neck like a clump of seaweed. It would be a shame for Larry to see her like this. Besides, she was bigger than Enoch. Stronger, probably, too. A pool was just what she needed. She would swim in her underwear.

"So tell me about the fire," she said.

"No."

"You said you would. 'Later,' is what you said. I'd like to hear." Marilee glanced across the seat at Enoch. His nose looked thicker in the darkness, and his face showed the first signs of stubble. "I told you about Larry," she reminded him.

"Fire!" shouted Enoch, so startling her that she nearly swerved over the center line. "Burst of light! Fireball! Like a bomb going off! Butane. Storage tank. Erupted. Too much heat!" He was sitting on the edge of his seat, breathing hard and painting the fire with his hands. "Blowout! Exploded! Whole sky on fire!" His hand hit the rearview mirror. "Twelve people died. Twelve. Firemen," he said. "Too much heat."

Enoch stopped for a moment. He rubbed his eyes and scooted back on the seat so that his legs stuck straight out over the edge. "Rumors started," he continued, his voice lower now. "Children. You know how it is. Kids talk. Adults listen. Always the same. You're bound to be suspect if you're not like them. Grew up in that town. Guess they needed me."

Enoch stared silently at the oncoming headlights.

"I'm sorry," said Marilee.

"For what?"

"For what you went through. That's just awful. It's unfair."

"Who said life is fair?"

He had her there.

They drove the next twenty miles in silence. Then Enoch spoke. He said, "Larry's not good enough for you." It annoyed Marilee the way he said this, as if he'd been thinking about it for years. As if this dwarf had a corner on her dreams.

■

"VACA CY," said the sign above the Trinity Motel, a crumbling, one-story adobe that squatted upon the earth like a venerable Indian. The motel lay on the outskirts of Alamogordo, a few miles south of the city, near the base of the Sacramento Mountains. Trinity Site, according to Enoch, was actually northwest.

They sneaked into the motel courtyard through an unlocked wooden gate. The courtyard was centered around the pool, a kidney bean with a slide in the middle. No lights were on in the rooms. The moon hadn't risen, but the stars shone so brightly Marilee could see Enoch clearly.

He propped his crutches against the back of a plastic chaise. Then, as if no one else were around, he took off his clothes. Marilee could not tear her eyes away from his body. Deformed. Hunched. Contorted. One hip jutted out like a knot on a tree. His legs twisted at the knees. A concavity hollowed his chest as though he'd been punched in the sternum at birth. She'd had no idea. When he stripped off his undershorts, she saw that his genitals were the size of a full-grown man's; they looked huge by comparison. How, she wondered, could a person live in such a body?

Yet Enoch seemed unbothered by his nakedness. He walked without crutches to the edge of the pool, wobbled really, heeling to the left with every other step. On crutches he'd appeared less awkward, more in control of his ungainly self. Marilee watched as he lowered his body into the water. There, he swam with ease, as though he were at home in his element.

Enoch did not look at Marilee as she undressed. Or maybe he saw her out of the corner of his eye, she couldn't tell. She removed her jeans and cotton blouse and hung them over a chair. But starting for the pool, she hesitated at the sight of Enoch's twisted body floating on the water's surface. Open. Vulnerable. Unsuspecting. He looked more insect than human, with his large torso and disjointed limbs. A water bug. Easy prey. It seemed wrong, suddenly, to feel self-conscious in the presence of someone like Enoch. She unhooked her bra and stepped out of her underwear.

When she glanced up, she saw that Enoch was now watching her. This time he made no effort to turn away. She stood motionless by the edge of the pool and let him take in the sight of her. He stared shamelessly, as if he knew she wouldn't mind. As if he sensed this were exactly what she wanted. Her heart pounded. What would it be like, she wondered, to make love to a dwarf?

She shook out her hair and stepped down into the cool water. Enoch studied her every move. It felt strange and wonderful swimming nude, a freedom she had never known. She dove beneath the surface and let the water caress her skin, fan her hair, swirl all around her. She made waves in the water, turned somersaults, rolled onto her back. Spread her legs wide open.

What would Larry think if he could see her now? She laughed out loud at the thought of it: Larry in his loafers and button-down collar pacing at pool's edge, hissing through clenched teeth so as not to wake the occupants. Larry tossing her his jacket, remembering too late the wallet in its pocket. Larry swearing at Enoch, ordering him out of the pool, fists clenched and lip curled—a smoldering absurdity.

And Enoch—how might he respond? Slither out of the pool, tail between legs? (If he had a tail, which wouldn't much surprise her.) More likely tell Larry to go fuck himself. Splash water on his loafers. Thumb through his wallet. She smiled, a sad smile. Larry was only three miles north, in Alamogordo, yet he seemed farther from her now than the stars in the sky.

Marilee glanced over to where Enoch floated on his back. She swam to the deep end and floated next to him. What would he do with her body so close? Look at her? Reach out and touch her skin? She arched her back so her breasts broke through the water's surface. If he touched her now, would she push away or roll into his arms?

But he didn't touch her. Nor did he look at her breasts. Rather, he seemed content to float next to her and stare up into the night. The Milky Way cut a brilliant swath across the sky's blackness. She had never seen so many stars. Thousands of stars. Millions. Stars in number beyond her comprehension. Marilee listened to the faint drone of traffic from a distant highway. She felt light-years from anything familiar.

"I read a story once," said Enoch. "Science fiction by Asimov, called, 'Nightfall.' About this planet with six suns, so there's always daylight. But every couple thousand years, an eclipse throws the planet into total darkness. And when all those stars come out—stars nobody knew were there—all the people go insane."

Marilee gazed up into the desert night—so many stars it would take a lifetime to count. She felt Enoch's gnarled body bobbing close to hers in the water. So close, yet separate. Different, and alone. A strange silence took hold of her. Night silence. Water silence. Star silence. She threw her head back and let the water wash over her face, fill her eyes, stream out the corners of her mouth. Liquid smooth as desert sand. Liquid cool as starlight. She felt intoxicated by the water, the darkness, the explosion of stars. This is crazy, she thought.

Crazy, and real.

EAST IS WEST

Her lipstick tasted like rhubarb. This was all Figman remembered of the woman, this small detail and a question she had asked: "Why is it people go to New York to be discovered? Shouldn't a place like that be where people go to disappear?" Figman smiled into the woman's soft shoulder; he was not a man to bed down with dummies. "If you want to be discovered," she said, "go to Idaho."

But he didn't go to Idaho; he went to New Mexico. One western state seemed as good a graveyard as the next, and New Mexico was where his Aion dropped its axle. In Artesia, to be exact—a nothing little town between Carlsbad and Roswell, two other nothing towns, only bigger. How he'd ended up here he couldn't figure, nor at what point his course had gone astray. Dying, thought Figman, must inspire wanderlust.

But wanderlust alone could not explain what had drawn Figman to this bleak outpost. Perhaps it was luck; more likely it was destiny. Figman questioned, at times, his belief in destiny, but of this one thing he was certain: Nothing ever happened without a reason. If his car had delivered him here, then here was where Figman was meant to be. At least until he had his new axle.

Figman ordered a taco at the Burrito Box and waited for Ewell P. Durham to fix his Aion. If Artesia held anything, it held possibility. He knew only one detail about this place: *The Man Who Fell to Earth* had been filmed here. Figman could see why. Its landscape was lunar: dust, oil fields, endless horizon. Some moon cows in the distance. Artesia. Its name implied water. He was a fan of irony.

Figman guessed he had a year or two at best before the sickness overtook him. Time would become more precious as his symptoms worsened, but a solid year of work could lead to fame, and fame (albeit posthumous) was what he'd come looking for. He finished his taco and ordered up another. It was good he still had an appetite.

He'd begin his painting as soon as his car ran well enough to get him to Dodge City. Or Amarillo. He felt confident he'd find someplace where the air was clean and the light shone just right on his easel. Durango, perhaps, or some little town on the outskirts of Abilene. Grease from his taco rolled into his shirt sleeve. Trucks rumbled by on the highway. Figman gazed down Artesia's dusty strip of asphalt and wondered where it would eventually lead him.

Louis T. Figman was a man who, like planets in retrograde, had to go east to find West. Born in San Fernando, he'd grown up in Sepulveda, a city of concrete and neon, rusted sheet metal and yellow-brown haze. Its heat and its noisy grind of traffic belied any hint that nature had ever visited the Valley; early in his life, Figman vowed he would someday leave it.

Some thirty years later, fate served up the opportunity. "On death's doorstep," he explained to his boss, flailing instantly in the backwash of his own pretension. Patterson chuckled, then handed him some papers and told him to go talk to Rosemary in Human Resources. The man's look said, "Coward—nobody dies before forty." But Figman had always acknowledged the truth in cliché. Death's doorstep. It was a threshold. He liked that idea.

In Artesia, Figman finished his second taco, then spent the next eleven weeks waiting for parts to arrive from Germany. He took a room at the Starlite Motel, biding his time in contemplation of how he would make a name for himself and where (Texas? Montana? Utah?—No, not Utah.), all the while weighing the possibility that his doctor may have been right: Perhaps he was not dying—at least not yet. Though still violent, his headaches had become less frequent, and the blob in the corner of his vision had all but disappeared. As his health had improved, his general outlook had grown noticeably brighter. So after nearly three months of waiting for death and/or Germany, Figman concluded 1) Germany was faster, and 2) his stay in Artesia had been beneficial in some way.

Perhaps it was something in the water (for there *was* water in Artesia), or in the makeup of its atmosphere. He liked the smell of the place. Oil. Cattle. The creosote scent of its snow. The townsfolk were friendly; the prices, cheap. If he played his cards right (a cliché he never should have used, as he hated card games), his money might stretch two—perhaps three—years. Thus, Figman concluded that in Artesia he was not at all on death's doorstep but merely on death's windowsill. He took a house out on the highway.

The house was owned by a widow named Verdie Hooks. She had lived in it for almost three decades but now rented it out to supplement her income. At least that was the story she'd told Figman, who suspected the house simply held too many memories. He'd worked with widows; he'd even dated one once. She'd been a frail young woman who drank herb tea, took endless bubble baths, and often wept for no apparent reason.

Figman's new house was modest by anyone's standards: a living room, kitchen, two small bedrooms, and a single bath. Its doorways consisted of arches through which one room led to the next without benefit of hallways, a look that reminded Figman of the stucco bungalows of thirties Hollywood. Just ten yards beyond his kitchen window stood Verdie's grotesque pink and green trailer. He wondered whether a row of trees might help to disguise it.

At first, Figman worried that having his landlady living so close might impinge upon his privacy. But Verdie Hooks seemed reasonable—not high-strung like some women in menopause. "I'm fifty-two," she told him, the gold in the back of her mouth flashing. "A full deck." Figman had assumed she was at least ten years older. Her skin had that baked look that women sometimes acquire spending too many hours poolside. Small-boned and skinny, she had heavy lids and an overbite. She reminded Figman of a turtle.

When the Pontelle sisters finally vacated the house, they left their keys for Figman in the mailbox. He picked them up on a Thursday morning in early February. Snow had fallen the night before, and the metal mailbox door had frozen shut. Standing out on the edge of the highway, he hit the top of the contraption with his fist, then yanked the door open. Inside, he found two sets of house keys and a letter to Verdie from a hospital in Denver.

At once, Figman realized that his house and Verdie's trailer shared a single mailbox. He thought about the mail he was likely to receive and the likelihood of his landlady sorting through it, a prospect that made him feel uneasy. He'd be receiving nothing to be ashamed of: mostly letters from his mother and a flier or two. But mail was a private matter. Years earlier, he'd broken up with a girlfriend who'd opened a shoe-store advertisement addressed to him. Though she'd claimed she was only curious about the dates of an upcoming sale, Figman had seen her action as an indication of character. First store fliers, then MasterCard bills. Next, she'd be opening his paychecks.

Figman's new house was dirtier than he remembered. The carpet was soiled and mildew grew in the bathtub. White rectangles dotted the walls where pictures had hung from the now-yellowed plaster. In the closets, the smell of mothballs; throughout, the sour-sweet stench of menthol cigarettes. Burn holes pocked the sofa and armchair. The draperies, torn and sagging from bent, paint-chipped rods, lent testimony to years of closely guarded privacy. In the kitchen, the olive-green linoleum bore layers of accumulated food and dirt buffed to a dull patina by what had to have been an infantry of shoes. Scuff marks, black and heavy, suggested the former presence of a man. Dust was everywhere.

Figman hated dust. Before unloading his possessions, he set out to the local grocery. But Bulldog Superette, where he usually shopped, was clean out of Windex. Abandoning his cart half full, he headed over to Lester's E-Z Mart on Main Street. Lester's had plenty of Windex. Also rags, sponges, brushes, brooms, bleach, cleansers, floor wax, a mop and bucket, rug shampoo, a sewing kit, air freshener, and Lysol. At the checkout counter he added two jars of aloe to the stockpile in his basket.

"You from California?" asked the checker. Figman glanced up from his magazine at the woman standing before him. She was heart-stopping beautiful: pale complected with thick auburn hair pulled loosely into a ponytail. She looked about twenty. "Well?" she said, punching numbers faster than Figman could think. The badge over her breast said, "Oma."

He'd forgotten her question. "I shop here," he said.

"Hmm," said the woman. She had the most sensuous lips Figman had ever seen: pouty and full, with corners that turned sweetly upward. He looked for a wedding ring. There wasn't one.

"I live here, too," said Figman. "Do you live here? Of course you do. That was stupid."

Oma stopped her number punching and turned to face him. One of her eyes was blue; the other, violet, an anomaly that made her face all the more alluring. A shame, thought Figman, for such beauty to be squandered on a pit-town like Artesia. And then Oma smiled, a devastating smile, and the blob in his field of vision materialized.

Figman's headaches took a predictable course. First the blob, quivering, then a twenty-minute respite before agony set in. When the pain came, it came suddenly. Vomit-inducing and continual, it lasted five hours and no medicine could touch it. Figman had long since given up searching for a remedy. He'd tried them all at one time or another—Ergomar, codeine, Percocet, as well as other drugs whose names he could no longer remember—all to no apparent effect. Now, he simply endured his pain. It was a trial, he figured, something Zen and challenging and necessary to the evolution of his soul. A final test before dying. Dr. Feldstein had told him it was migraine.

Figman paid cash for his groceries and left the store quickly. His house was five miles south of town, on the highway to Carlsbad. If he drove about eighty, he'd make it home in time to close his bedroom draperies and take refuge under the covers. As he slipped his key into his car's ignition, he thought of Oma. Her mystifying eyes. Her tragic smile. Her smile was tragic because her two front teeth were broken into an inverted V that hinted boyfriend or father—some male with an attitude. She was otherwise perfection. The blob grew bigger.

■

The next day, in misery's afterglow, Figman scoured his house from one end to the other. It took him ten hours (twice the duration of his headache) and seemed, somehow, its logical extension. When in late afternoon he grew hungry, he drove into town for a quick bite at Eileen's Tac Olé. He picked up a copy of *Men's Health* at Batie's, then hurried back home to unpack his Aion.

At thirty-nine, Louis T. Figman was a man who owned little. Dying, and in need of what little redemption he could cultivate, he'd sold his house in Encino and most of his possessions. What he couldn't sell, he'd given to his gardener. He'd packed only clothes, his cassette player and tapes, some business files, and a box of personal articles. In El Paso, he'd picked up a book on oil painting. It was big and heavy and filled with pictures. He'd read the book cover to cover while waiting for his axle.

Ceremoniously, he placed the book on the highest shelf in his living room. It looked small up there, and appropriately lonely. Figman saw it as a metaphor. If art (and subsequent fame) were to become his sole purpose, he'd need to eliminate all life's other distractions. Painting would have to become his everything. Such singular devotion might even sustain him longer than fate intended, a happy thought that drew Figman to his refrigerator.

Uncapping a bottle of Dos Equis, he sat down at his kitchen table and thought seriously about his future. He would need to be mindful of his drinking; artists, he knew, had trouble with alcohol. At night only, he promised himself, once his day's work had been completed. Leaning back in his chair, Figman hit the light switch by the doorway and let his eyes adjust to the darkness. He kicked his feet up on the wooden table whose crevices and gouges, just that morning, had been filled with years of accumulated dust and grime. Outside, clouds threatened; Figman wondered whether Artesia might be in for another snow. A light came on in Verdie's trailer, illuminating her three ugly windows, two small half-circles and a center rectangle. It looked like a face staring back at him. First thing tomorrow, he vowed, he would buy kitchen curtains before setting about the business of becoming famous.

What Figman failed to realize was that he'd already had his fifteen minutes. They had started ticking one Friday morning in early spring on his way to work at Goetschke Life and Casualty. An adjuster in Accidental Death and Dismemberment, he had always prided himself on his ability to remain emotionally detached from his claimants, no matter how sad or grisly their predicament. AD&D was a heavy business, a job not everyone in the company could handle. It took a person like Figman—spiritual but not religious—to reach beyond the immediacy of life's tragedies and grasp the bottom line.

Traffic on the Ventura Freeway crept dismally through a heavy downpour. In nasty weather, it sometimes took Figman an extra forty minutes to get to work as slick roads played havoc with bald tires and engines stalled in the fast lane. Red taillights were all he could make out for miles ahead; behind him, the watery blur of headlights through rain. Cars jerked forward like the staccato movement of a symphony: Start, stop. Start, stop. Stop, stop, stop. Occasionally, they'd get up to speed, then come to a dead halt within seconds. Frequently, they sat idle for minutes. There was no logic to the traffic in L.A.

Bored more than annoyed by his delay, Figman pondered the Flechteau claim. He would have to be tougher next time he visited Flechteau at his home and not allow himself to be affected by the sight of the man's stub. His stub came into view whenever Flechteau's blanket slipped from his lap, an event that seemed regularly to coincide with Figman's explanation of limits of liability. He could have sworn, once, he'd even seen Flechteau give it a little shove when it had gotten hung up on the brake of his electric wheelchair. Then Flechteau, who'd been a pole setter for the phone company before his accident, asked Figman if he wouldn't mind helping him with his fallen blanket. This ploy ensured that Figman got a closer look at Flechteau's injury, a horrible sight with its whitish bulge where his severed femur pressed against his taut red skin, and its one remaining stitch, all black and waxy, which never seemed to fall off or be absorbed into his scar as normal stitches are absorbed but protruded from his wound like the single black hair that protruded from Jeff Goldblum's back in *The Fly*, a hair so thick and resilient that Geena Davis had to snip it off with kitchen shears. It was this terrible stitch that Figman was thinking about when the Pinto full of Mexicans cut directly in front of him and came to a halt just thirty feet from his windshield.

Figman liked Mexicans. He saw them as a proud, ancient people who had as much right to California as did he (if not more). On principle, Figman refused to refer to them in politically correct terms such as Hispanics or Latinos. They were Mexicans, an identity in which he believed they should take pride. He loved their food, their art, the lyricism of their language. Velasquez, his gardener in Encino, he'd hired solely because of the majesty of his name. Figman had first seen it on a business card left inside his mailbox:

ALEJANDRO ARTURO CUEVAS DE VELASQUEZ
Lawns   Trees   Shrubs

There was history in that name. Conquistadores. Proud Aztecs defending their cities. In his childhood living room in Sepulveda, Figman's mother had kept a book about Aztecs on the coffee table. In it were pictures of golden cities, exotic parrots, and men in armor on horseback. Alejandro Arturo Cuevas de Velasquez. It was right out of the index.

There was history, too, in the name Figman, but not the kind one reads about in coffee-table books. The name spoke of tallithim and mezuzahs and dark shops in the back streets of Eastern Europe. His first name, Louis, had been his great-grandfather's, and while he liked the name intrinsically, people frequently mispronounced it as Louie. Occasionally, someone would shorten it to Lou, a choice that made Figman wonder if they didn't see him as some crotch-scratching lug with a plumber's wrench.

Since mid-childhood, Figman had gone simply by the name Figman. It stemmed from an age (around ten or eleven) when boys referred to each other by surname alone. Later, when his buddies reverted to their given names (around the same time they discovered girls), Figman opted to remain just Figman. It seemed easier that way. Still, he wished he'd been blessed with a name like Alejandro.

Alejandro Arturo Cuevas de Velasquez was, however, nothing like the moniker that announced him to the mailbox owners of Encino. Fat as a potato bug, he had a fondness for cheap tequila and expensive women. His face, brown and gnarly, reminded Figman of a gourd he'd seen hanging from a fruit stand on Olvera Street. Fine black hair grew down from his sideburns, a maddening fuzz that Velasquez refused to shave despite Figman's gift one Christmas of an electric razor.

Velasquez managed to sustain himself in the Encino community until he was caught fooling around with Sugar Tildeman, the wife of a well-known sitcom producer—something to do with jute net and a garden hose, a scene Figman could hardly imagine. Bernie Tildeman subsequently sent a letter to the entire neighborhood asking anyone who employed Velasquez to fire him. Several of Figman's neighbors complied, having had scripts or daughters in the man's office at one time. Figman, however, who had neither script nor daughter and who hated all things Hollywood, could hardly bear to see a man named Alejandro Arturo Cuevas de Velasquez lose a good-paying job. Furthermore, he found it a miscarriage of justice for some big-shot producer to use his power and influence to exact revenge on the weak and downtrodden of California, a populace whose ancestors had once owned the very land Tildeman now paid men like Velasquez to fertilize and weed.

Letter in hand, Figman watched as a shirtless Velasquez squatted in his flower bed. "Velasquez," Figman called from his dining room window. The gardener went about his pruning. Figman opened his French doors and stepped out onto his patio. The bricks felt cold beneath his bare feet. "Señor," he called, but still the man did not answer. In the driveway, Velasquez's primer-gray pickup blared music, something up-tempo and decidedly Mexican. Velasquez rocked on his heels to its catchy rhythm.

Approaching him from behind, Figman placed his hand on his gardener's back, brown and soft as a rotting pumpkin. The man twitched and gazed up at him. "Velasquez, have you seen this?" Figman leaned over to show him the letter.

With his shirtsleeve, the gardener wiped at his great winter squash of a face. "Qué?" he asked. His breath smelled faintly of tequila.

"Have you seen this letter? From that asshole, Tildeman?" Figman hoped that by calling Tildeman an asshole, he would let Velasquez know he was not about to be fired.

Velasquez smiled briefly (perhaps remembering Sugar), then frowned, his thick brows melding into a Frida Kahlo winged line. The down on his cheeks held beads of sweat. "No read," he said, waving his hands in that universal gesture meaning *Don't talk to me about this.* Figman had no way of knowing whether the man was telling him he hadn't read the letter, didn't want to, or didn't possess the ability. Velasquez muttered something in Spanish and resumed his pruning, a little more urgently than before. Returning to the house, Figman swore he would do two things: He would ask his friends to find work for Velasquez, and he would one day look up Sugar.

All this (and more) raced through Figman's mind as his Aion bore down on the idling Pinto. He knew about these swoop-and-squat scams. Aaron Litvak usually handled them and had explained to Figman how they worked. An economy car crammed with Mexicans (How many were in the Pinto? Eight? Ten, maybe?) would swerve in front of a car or truck and slam on its brakes, guaranteeing injury to all of its occupants. The Mexicans, illegal, illiterate, and desperate for money, would each be paid one thousand dollars by some con artist who would subsequently file insurance claims on all their behalfs. Usually, the con man would pose as an employer or relative; less often as one of the so-called victims. The injured would then be expected to limp back to Mexico one thousand dollars richer, while the fraud-mongering scumbag hung around to collect the big money. There were variations to this game, but this, basically, was how it was played. Figman knew it to be a dangerous business. Sometimes people were killed in these "accidents," and sometimes the dead weren't Mexican.

Knowing these facts did not make it any easier on Figman as his car sped, seemingly in slow motion, toward the motionless Pinto. He checked his rearview mirror for a possible route of escape, but traffic on both sides of him was moving faster than he. A lane change now might cause a series of accidents as cars swerved consecutively to move out of each other's way. The truck directly behind him was traveling slowly and at a reasonable distance, leaving Figman no choice but to remain in his lane where he was certain to hit the Pinto.

Lifting his foot off the accelerator, Figman moved it over into the space above his brake pedal. His muscles clenched. Litvak had told him never to clench in an accident. It was reflex, he knew, but one to be fought with every brain cell he could call to action. The dead branch snaps in the hurricane. In rear-enders, drunks and druggies walk free, while the sober man bites the big one. It had happened in the Triggs claim. Randy Triggs, high on Old Crow and sinsemilla, had skidded fender first into the back of a late-model Lincoln. Two children on their way home from nursery school had burned to death, while Triggs suffered only a scalp wound.

The thought of flesh burning made Figman realize, for the first time, that the car into whose rear he was directly headed was a PINTO. What year was it? '69? '70? Had its fuel tank been converted? He might never know.

His own first car had been a Pinto, a gift from his mother upon his having graduated high school. He'd sold it years ago, as soon as he'd learned about the problem with its fuel tank. Figman was a man who took few chances in life. Now, absurdly, he appeared to be on a collision course with his own destiny. He thought of Oedipus on the road to Thebes. He thought of Laertes. He clenched tighter, still running on instinct and adrenaline. It was hard fighting instinct, a point he vowed he would take up with Litvak if he lived to see him. As his foot slammed down on the brake pedal, he felt his torso strain against his seat belt. The rear of the Pinto grew ominously larger. Rain fell harder. Water sheeted off his windshield faster than his windshield wipers could sweep it away, obscuring completely the blur of cars in front of him so that the only thing Figman's brain could process in the micro-moment before impact were his car's headlights making sense of the Pinto's bumper sticker: FATE HAPPENS. And indeed it did, for here was a concept whose synchronicitous irony caused every muscle in his body to relax, a second and wholly unexpected reflex that Figman later came to realize had both saved his life and bought him a morsel of fame.

■

The nightly news called it a miracle. Six Mexicans had been killed in the explosion, and here was this guy, Figman (an insurance adjuster of all things), with nothing more than a cut finger. His Aion had been totaled, its front, rear, and passenger sides crushed like an empty beer can. The Pinto (a '71 as it turned out) was unrecognizable, melted, as footage showed, into a 911 roadside call box. From his hospital bed, Figman explained to one reporter after another how he'd watched in horror as the car full of Mexicans had balled into flames. His Aion (whose left front brakes had locked, thus twisting his trajectory) had deflected off the Pinto's left rear bumper, first jerking right, then spinning one hundred eighty degrees in the opposite direction while skidding backward and sideways across three lanes of traffic. California lane change. Amazingly, no other vehicles had been in his way.

When his Aion struck the center divider, Figman's head jerked right, then left, hitting hard against the door frame. But he didn't black out or even bleed. He sat for a moment behind his steering wheel, astonished to find himself alive. The right front end of his Aion had been shoved up into its engine, its hood bent up like a steeple. Its rear suspension and trunk had accordioned into the back seat. The only section of Figman's Aion left undamaged was the place where he sat, dumbstruck and shaken. Through his shattered windshield, he saw smoke rising from the burning Pinto—black, thick, and stifling. He wondered, then, if he were dead and undergoing one of those out-of-body experiences he'd read about in his doctor's waiting room. But his chest hurt and his heart pounded. Glass chunks fell from his shoulders and hair. His legs felt weak and soon there was this fellow at his driver's-side window, banging on it with the palm of his hand, shouting at him, frantic, asking him if he were okay. Figman's window had stuck and his door had jammed; it took the Jaws of Life to pry it open. When lifted, an hour later, from his Aion's wreckage, he cut his knuckle on a piece of metal.

"Let's see it," said the cameraman beside his hospital bed.

Figman held up his middle finger.

■

By the time he was released from Valley Memorial, Figman had given no less than a dozen bedside interviews. His doctors, doubtful that a person could come through such carnage unscathed, had detained him twenty-four hours for observation, a day that, despite the dull pounding in his head, had proven to be the most exciting Figman could remember. It had been a day filled with lighting equipment, minicams, and pert young reporters scribbling furiously on notepads. That evening, he had dedicated himself to the nightly news, clicking avidly from one channel to the next, searching for his own sound bites. By eleven o'clock, the TV had called him a miracle so many times that his roommate, Bigler, suffering from bleeding ulcers and an irritable bowel, told him to turn the fucking thing off. Figman did as the man requested. He slept fitfully, not because of the day's excitement (for by this time he was truly exhausted) but because Bigler snored like a walrus. The next morning, the *Los Angeles Times* featured his picture on its front page. There he was, beneath the headline MODERN-DAY MIRACLE: Louis Figman in his hospital gown, giving all of L.A. the finger.

The following Monday, when he returned to work, Figman found himself a hero. By his fellow adjusters, his survival was seen not at all as a miracle but rather as proof that most accident claims were bogus, a conclusion that reinforced their strongest suspicions and boosted, temporarily, the gross profits of the company. Patterson patted him on the back and invited him into his office. Once seated, his boss leaned conspiratorially over his desk and informed Figman of the company's intention to file suit against the Ford Motor Company. This it planned to do not only on Figman's behalf but on behalf of all six of the dead Mexicans (once they had been forensically identified). An aggressive stance at this point, explained Patterson, would preempt a move on someone else's part as well as mitigate whatever liability their own company might incur. Not coincidentally, this might help garner publicity for Goetschke Life and Casualty. Mr. Goetschke himself was determined to smoke out the sleazebag behind the scam and publicly expose him as the scum-sucking dirtball they all knew him to be.

But in truth, there had been no swoop-and-squat scam. Instead of having been pawns in some elaborate scheme, the six dead Mexicans turned out to have been a crew of office janitors coming off the night shift. With their Speedy-Kleen van in the shop with a blown fuel pump, they'd collectively had the misfortune to have let Luis Rivera drive them home in his Pinto. In all likelihood, Luis Rivera, blind in one eye and unlicensed, had never even seen Figman's Aion.

This revelation, carried on Tuesday night's local news, threw Figman into anguished self-reflection: Had he done everything in his power to avoid the accident? If he'd known these men were janitors and not instruments of some insidious plot to defraud his insurance company, might he have reacted differently? Was it racist of him to even ask himself such things? Yes, no, and probably, he concluded. Still, these and other questions gnawed at his conscience. Why had he been chosen to survive and not the six Mexicans, all of whom had wives and children? What kind of world allowed six hard-working family men to burn to death in an automobile whose potentially fatal design flaws had been known all along to its manufacturer? What kind of God, if there were a God, would allow such evil and inequity?

Later that same night, Figman had his first in a series of violent headaches. It frightened him, with its vision distortion and excruciating pain. When, the following Friday, he suffered a similar attack, Figman put in a call to Dr. Feldstein. In the next two weeks, he endured four more of these episodes; by the time of his appointment in mid-April, Figman had convinced himself he was not quite the miracle the media had made him out to be.

Feldstein put him through a month of testing and found nothing. At a loss for any other explanation, he diagnosed Figman's problem as chronic migraine. The doctor gave him a list of foods to avoid, wrote him prescriptions for Ergomar and Vicodin, and sent him home to manage his pain.

Figman dutifully followed his doctor's advice. He cut out chocolate, cheese, and all forms of alcohol. Still, he was neither relieved of his pain nor convinced he was not suffering the effects of some rare and deadly malady. An aneurysm, probably, buried so deep inside his brain no machine could detect it. An aneurysm pressing on his optic nerve, hence the blob in the corner of his vision. An aneurysm that one day would pop inside his skull like a ruptured garden hose and blind him, or leave him paralyzed or in a state so vegetative that beautiful young nurses would have to change his diapers and suction out his feeding tube. He knew car accidents could cause such things. The Braverman claim. And now the poor woman was dead, her three children in foster care. He'd been stingy with their settlement.

During the next two weeks, Figman's headaches worsened, increasing in both pain and frequency. By the second week of June, he had used up most of his year's sick leave. Desperate for a real diagnosis, he went to see Litvak's neurologist.

Dr. Julie Mercer was very beautiful, a detail his friend had failed to mention. She put Figman through all the same tests Feldstein had administered. For a second time he was X-rayed, sonogrammed, CAT scanned, and MRIed. Again, he was relieved of his blood and urine. As before, all test results came back negative.

In her examining room, Dr. Mercer scooted prettily on her little stool-on-wheels over to where Figman was sitting. She leaned in close to him and on her prescription pad wrote the name of an acupuncturist who specialized in herbal remedies, an action that caused Figman to abandon simultaneously all lust and a goodly measure of his little remaining hope.

Figman's headaches persisted into the summer. One Friday in early August, his boss called him into his office to question him about his all-too-frequent absences. Figman explained about his headaches, omitting the part about his aneurysm. Patterson glanced down at the work sheet on his desk and shook his head. It didn't look good, he said. The company couldn't function properly without full-time AD&D. Figman would have to find some way to come in to work more often. Figman promised Patterson he would make an effort. That was good, said Patterson; Figman could start by putting in overtime that evening. Figman had a date that evening, someone new, he explained to Patterson. His boss shook his head and wrote something on his work sheet. Figman told him he would cancel his date. That was good, said Patterson. He erased what he had written and looked up at Figman. He wasn't smiling. There was something else, he said. The families of the six dead Mexicans had cross-complained against the Ford Motor Company, Speedy-Kleen Janitorial, Goetschke Life and Casualty, and Louis T. Figman.

Figman drove home late with a pounding headache. The next morning, from his desk at work, Figman called the acupuncturist. She was not your usual loony in a turban. She looked normal, almost, an older woman with hair to her waist and sensible shoes. Her name was Mrs. Smith. She jabbed at Figman with short, thin needles, then left him alone for an hour. Her method was not painless. When his treatment was over, he handed her cash amounting to seventy-five dollars. She in return loaded him down with herbs, aloe, and a small bottle of viscous red fluid called Essence of Chicken. "For your color," she explained. It was important he drink it all.

Figman went home and boiled his herbs. The tea it made tasted bitter, but he drank it faithfully for a week. The aloe resembled distilled water; this, too, he downed in his healer's prescribed quantities. Essence of Chicken, however, remained in its bottle on his kitchen windowsill, too vile-looking for him to actually consider drinking. (What did one do with it, anyway? Take it straight? On the rocks? Nuke it and pour it over brown rice?)

A week after his first visit, he returned to Mrs. Smith. "You look better," she said, examining his tongue. "I can see it in your color." Figman didn't feel any better but was pleased in some small way to have been told that he did. He endured another puncturing, then carted home his herbs, aloe, and fresh bottle of Essence of Chicken. He added it to the one on his windowsill.

When his collection of bottles grew to six, Figman stopped going to Mrs. Smith. Her treatments were doing him no good. Her herbs tasted terrible (he could hardly swallow them now without gagging), and all that Essence of Chicken was costing him plenty. He doubted acupuncture could cure anything, let alone an aneurysm.

By the end of summer, when Figman went looking for Rosemary in Human Resources, he had come to suspect he didn't have an aneurysm at all, that the pain in his temples was not the result of his auto accident but of something worse and darkly inevitable. Throughout autumn, his suspicion grew larger. And by the time he sold his house and drove east in search of West, Figman knew without question he had finally developed the brain tumor he so richly deserved.

ROCKET CITY

For breakfast they ate the melons. Enoch carved them up with Marilee's knife and made fruit salad inside one of the hollowed-out rinds. They sat Indian style in the New Mexico sand, eating the slimy chunks of flesh with their fingers. Juice ran down their arms and dripped off their elbows.

They had spent the night in Marilee's Dart, parked in a turnaround on Dog Canyon Road, about ten miles south of Alamogordo. The night had been an exercise in frustration. Enoch had taken the front seat because he was smaller. He'd laid his crutches lengthwise in the footwell, fashioned a pillow out of his backpack, and promptly fallen asleep. Marilee, who had moved her suitcase into the trunk, curled up with a sweater in the back. Her five-foot-ten-inch frame was longer than the width of the car's interior and her knees buckled out over the seat's edge. Restless for most of the night, she'd listened to the rhythmic murmur of Enoch's snoring. When Larry snored, he heaved and rasped; Marilee would have to nudge him into a new position in an often futile attempt to get him to stop. But Enoch's snoring was soft and steady, like an engine idling. Eventually, it lulled her into an uneasy sleep, during which she had a number of disturbing dreams. In the only one she could remember, she was in her mother's backyard eating honeysuckle off the vines that grew over the tall back fence. Perched on top of a clothesline pole, she pulled the long pistils from their blooms and sucked the sweet nectar. She was content, thinking about what she would make Larry for dinner, when a bee flew into her mouth.

Marilee awakened with a start. She sat upright, disoriented, still able to recall the unnerving sensation of the insect buzzing against her tongue and cheeks. For a moment, she didn't remember why she had slept in her car or that there was a dwarf in her front seat. She peeked over the headrest; Enoch was still sleeping. A tiny rivulet of drool flowed from the corner of his mouth onto the blue upholstery.

Marilee looked out the window at her immediate surroundings. They had parked near the Oliver Lee General Store, a small wooden structure that looked new, yet recently abandoned. Its windows were boarded up. A sign read, "No cash left overnight." Rusty wagon wheels leaned against a tall picket fence. Marilee checked the clock on her dashboard; it was half past eight. Even with the windows cracked, the air inside the car had become stifling. She cranked down her window and squinted into the bright sunlight. The desert shimmered. A few puffs of clouds dotted the sky.

A camper rolled by them, kicking up clouds of brown dust behind it. Enoch mumbled. His face looked sullen in the light of day. Skin moist. Eyelids puffy. Cheeks covered with heavy black stubble. He could have been a character right out of one of her forgotten dreams. She nudged his shoulder. "Good morning," she said tentatively.

"Hmmph," he answered back. He sat up, looked at her, and grinned. Marilee smiled back, a queasy smile. Gathering his crutches from the footwell, Enoch flung open his door and stepped out into the bright morning. Marilee climbed out of the car after him, her back stiff from sleeping most of the night in one position.

"Gotta pee," said Enoch. He hobbled around to the rear of the building, cutting between a cistern and a windmill that appeared to have come off an assembly line. Marilee leaned against the trunk of her car and shielded her eyes from the glare. The place looked desolate: On the western horizon, plains stretched clear to the Organ Mountains. Behind her, the sheer, near-vertical cliffs of the Sacramentos stood in shadow. To the north, a few ramshackle houses hovered under a pale sky. South, toward El Paso, two faintly visible structures—huge and shaped like inverted Mayan temples—rose up from the desert floor. Marilee had no idea what they could be.

As soon as Enoch returned, they carved and ate the melons. "What's next?" he asked, toweling the juice from his stubby arms with a spare shirt from his backpack.

What was next indeed? The night before, in the motel pool with Enoch, she'd felt her life transformed as though she *had* been in some land of enchantment and not some blighted state with dirty toilets, greasy cafes, and state troopers who got off on badgering women and the deformed. Floating in cool water, she'd felt her life detour down a strange and dangerous road, with potholes and curves and dark cracks a person could fall into. It was Enoch's road, lonely and seductive as a two-lane desert highway.

For an hour they'd floated, staring up into the endless sky. They'd said nothing to one another, just taken in the strange silence of the desert night. In starlight, Enoch's face had seemed less awkward: intelligent, kind, and oddly familiar. But now, in the glare of morning, Marilee found herself squinting into the thick, artless features of a dwarf.

A dwarf! She had spent the night in her car with a dwarf. A little man with stubby legs that stuck out over his seat like the stiff plastic legs of a doll. She had picked him up on the side of the highway. Swum naked with him in some seedy motel pool. Driven with him to an isolated road out in the middle of nowhere. Slept with him in her car. She must have been crazy.

And yet, it had all been so innocent. They had traveled south on Highway 54, following the tracks of the Southern Pacific Railroad toward El Paso. They'd turned east onto a narrow road, crossed over the railroad tracks, and driven a few miles to a turnaround. They'd locked their doors, cracked open their windows, switched off the lights, and said goodnight to one another like an old married couple, grown tired and too familiar.

She had listened to Enoch's steady breathing, aware of the exact moment that sleep had overtaken him like a wave washing him out to sea. And she had listened to him dream—dwarf dreams, she imagined, of tall women, taller men, and Goliath dogs who could topple you with their exuberance. She'd listened to his noises, his muffled sputters and sudden snorts, the soft clicking of his uvula, and she'd wondered what her life would be like with a man such as Enoch.

Now, she was wondering still. Part of her wanted to run away with him, to take him as her lover and lose herself in the desolate Southwest. To travel without direction, swim naked in motel pools, have reckless sex with a man half her size, and sleep out under the stars. Yet, how could she? She was Marilee Levitay, an art teacher from Sherman Oaks coming to New Mexico to get married. Nothing in her twenty-five years had prepared her for such insanity.

Enoch watched as she traced concentric circles in the sand. "I don't know what's next," she said. "What exactly did you have in mind?"

"Well, we zip into Alamogordo. Clean up. Gas up. Get some food for the road. Then head up north, toward Albuquerque and Santa Fe. Do some pueblos. See the Jemez. Camp in the Sangre de Cristos."

He had her life all planned. "I don't know," she said, looking out into the desert. "I just don't know." He offered her his spare shirt. She took it and wiped the juice from her hands and forearms. "How are we going to live?" she asked. "What do we do for money? I don't have very much. I was planning to get a job."

"I have money," said Enoch.

He didn't look as though he had money.

"I get a check once a month."

She'd heard about these things: the government paying the disabled when they couldn't work—or didn't want to. She wondered if there weren't something Enoch could do for a living, advertising, maybe, or phone sales. "I need to think," she said. "Let's drive up to Alamogordo. I want to change my clothes and brush my teeth."

"Yo!" said Enoch. "Alamogordo!"

■

At first glance, the town was not unusual. Clusters of fast-food restaurants lined White Sands Boulevard, the main drag through the western end of the city. Downtown, drab, blocky storefronts merged one into the next, their facades weathered by years of sun and sandstorms. Women in big American cars sported hairdos from the previous decade. Men strode by in ten-gallon hats, boots, and jeans—the business suit of the Southwest.

The town looked like any other she'd seen in the high desert plains, with one startling exception: Everywhere there were rockets. Rockets on top of buildings, rockets mounted on trucks, a whole configuration of rockets on the lawn in front of the Chamber of Commerce. They passed the Rocket Lounge on White Sands Boulevard, the Rocket Motel, Rocket Mobile Village, and Rockette Hair Styling. They passed a sign for Rocket Van and Storage, and a rocket on top of a sign having nothing to do with rockets. Like icons of some techno-god of the twentieth century, images of rockets dominated the city. They rose up from grass and stone; sprouted heavenward from storefront walls, restaurant doors, and the streets of Alamogordo.

"Check it out," said Enoch. "This place doesn't have soil, it has erectile tissue."

"What's that white thing?" Marilee pointed to a wing-like projection in the distance rising up from behind a mountain. It, too, looked like a rocket.

"Sunspot. Solar research lab."

"And those temple-like buildings out in the desert?"

"Haven't a clue."

There was something strange about this city, something not quite right. It was more than just the omnipresence of rockets. It was something larger and intangible. At first glance, the town had looked quite ordinary. Upon closer scrutiny, however, one saw that things were different. Odd. It were almost as though, having lived so near the first atomic test site, the town itself had mutated and grown things.

Off in the west, two fighter jets from Holloman Air Force Base wove their silvery trails high above the Tularosa Basin. They were too far away to be heard, too dramatic not to be noticed as they swung back and forth, in and out, like twin pendulums suspended from opposite points high above the cumulonimbus.

"Something's going on out here," said Marilee. "Something weird."

"Bingo," said Enoch. "You win the prize."

"And what might that be?"

He thumped his chest with his stubby hand. "Me."

They pulled into a gas station on White Sands Boulevard, where they took turns using the bathroom. Marilee washed her face in the sink and brushed her teeth, then changed into clean underwear, a blouse, and a pair of shorts. She returned to her car to put on makeup because there had been no light in the bathroom. When she opened her compact, she saw that her powder had a groove in it where the cop had run his finger. From her car, she watched through the open door to the men's room as Enoch stood on top of an overturned trashcan to shave at the sink. He looked like a five-year-old playing grownup with his father's razor.

When he'd finished cleaning up, Enoch filled her car with gas. Fumes rose from the nozzle as he pumped, wafting in through Marilee's open window. She'd always loved the smell of gasoline. As a child, sitting in the backseat of her mother's pink Buick, she would roll down her window to inhale deeply whenever the attendant pumped gas. The fumes made her dizzy, eliciting in her an indefinable yearning she later identified as sexual.

Larry's ROTC photo was still on the dashboard, faded and curled from the morning sun. His face smiled up at her, a sweet face the way his eyes squinted when he smiled and one incisor overlapped the other as though his two front teeth were bashful. She had always gone for blondes. Or maybe they had gone for her—she wasn't sure. Across the street, a rocket pointed skyward in front of an outdoor car lot. Where in this strange town did Larry live? So far, the houses all looked alike: stucco tract homes from the post-war building boom and cottages from the thirties. Where were the apartments? The condos? Where was Tomahawk Trail?

Marilee smoothed Larry's photo as best she could and slipped it back into her wallet. Leaning back against her headrest, she closed her eyes and drew in the heady odor of gasoline. She'd missed sleeping with Larry; in the seven months since he'd left L.A., Marilee had slept with no one.

She'd first met Larry Johnston when she was seventeen. Theirs had been a large high school in the San Fernando Valley in which a student could easily remain anonymous. But not Larry Johnston. Even before he turned up in her German class, Marilee knew of him as a loner, an odd boy who occasionally exhibited unconventional behavior. Once, he'd pinned a calcified praying mantis to the lapel of his sweater. Another time, he'd consumed a handful of salt pills before a track meet, a dose that had caused him to faint halfway around the field.

Weird was the word most commonly used to describe Larry. He wore penny loafers without socks, and suspenders before they came back into fashion. He sang in the hallways. He wrote poetry. Marilee and Amanda Wiggins would watch him from the lunch quad: his shoulders butted against the trunk of some tree, his blond hair swept straight back, a copy of *Howl* propped up on his knees. The two girls would laugh as they ate their sandwiches and gossiped about couples, parents, teachers, and what Mary Ellen Kazloff was planning to do about that baby growing in her womb.

Larry, though bright, was a poor student. Occasionally, his teachers could be overheard discussing his wasted potential as if they were talking about some stock market tip they should have taken or a house they'd sold before the market boomed. Marilee thought school must have bored Larry. He got A's in English and C's in most everything else including German II, where he sat in the back corner directly behind Marilee.

"Achtung," he whispered in her ear on the second day of class. "Marilee, wie geht's?" Frau Göckermann, pert in her gingham shirtwaist dress and patent leather spike heels, stood face to the blackboard conjugating endless tenses of irregular verbs, which, when spoken in succession, had all the sonance of a Hitler rally.

Larry's voice had startled Marilee. She glanced over her shoulder, but he motioned for her to face forward. Robby Franz, who sat in the seat next to him, whistled softly through his fat lips. Robby thought himself cool. He played lead guitar in a band called Spew, did ecstasy every weekend, and was the reason Mary Ellen Kazloff cried in the hallways.

Later, when Frau Göckermann once again had her back to the class, Larry parted Marilee's hair with his fingers. She felt his breath on the back of her neck like whiffs from a horse's nostrils. Her nipples stiffened. "Wer bist du, Marilee?" he whispered. The down on her arms rose; her heart pounded. Larry leaned farther over his desk and muttered again into her mass of red curls. "Marilee, du bist ein schöner Schmetterling. Ein Blümchen. Ein Stern in der Nacht." She froze, not knowing if he were being serious or making fun of her. Robby smirked. Frau Göcker-mann conjugated the verb, to click.

Convinced, after the first two weeks, that she was not the butt of some joke but rather the object of his true affections, Marilee Levitay began looking forward to sixth period. Larry's whispering had become a daily ritual she'd come to anticipate with ever-mounting states of arousal. Soon she began carrying heavy sweaters to school. On rainy days, when the windows were closed and the radiator knocked and spit with a vex-ing precision, Marilee would feel the warm, dry air; the heat from her body, rising; the rhythmic pulse of Larry's breath on the nape of her neck, and she'd feel dizzy and hot as a cat trapped in a spinning drier.

That semester she did not learn much German. Indeed, all her grades suffered. During periods one through five, she spent her class time writ-ing Larry's name on endless snippets of blue-lined paper, which she popped into her mouth, sucked beyond recognition, and collected in a ball in the zippered compartment of her notebook. Each night, after her mother left for work, she flushed the offensive wad down the toilet.

She did other childish things. She phoned Larry at home just to hear his voice, hanging up as soon as he answered. On the weekends, she spied on him at his job at Mojo's Books and Coffee Beans. From the sanctuary of the pizza parlor across the street, she watched him through the cof-feehouse window, making cappuccino, slicing fruit pies and carrot cakes, microwaving bagels and lemon poppyseed muffins. At night, in bed, she mouthed her passion into her pillow in much the same way he directed his, by day, at the back of her head.

"He's a geek," said Amanda. Wearing an old pink bathrobe, she sat rolling her hair on empty jumbo-size cans of Swanson's Chicken Broth. Her face was covered in green cleansing masque. "Have you ever seen his poetry?" Marilee had to admit she hadn't, whereupon Amanda pulled open the bottom drawer of her dressing table and produced a stack of old *Guardians*. She tossed them onto the bed next to Marilee. "There's a real howler in there, toward the end of last year."

Marilee thumbed through the stack of school newspapers, somewhat wary of what she might encounter. She came upon pictures of the foot-ball team and the Home Club Bake-Off. She relived the crowning of

Victoria Van Antwerp as prom queen and the Drama Club's production of *Billy Budd*. She leafed through articles about Spring Fair, college recruiters on campus, and National Merit scholars. Finally, in the May 23rd issue, she came upon a poem by Larry:

> MY SPIRIT
> *by Lawrence H. Johnston*
>
> tortured twisted thoughts
> spin their web around my muddled mind
> twisting, constricting
>   will there always be this darkness?
>
> am I free to be
> or am I caught
> between the crumpled pages of a time-worn novel?
>
> and yet, from some far-reaching destiny
> a pure white ray of light
> filters in between the masses and the gases
>   swirling 'round
> the tortured twisted visions
>   of this slumbering child
>   it is the ray of Hope

"It's not *that* bad," said Marilee.

Amanda swiveled on her stool and glanced at Larry's poem, wrinkling her nose as if she were opening a thermos that had been left in her locker all summer. "Read it out loud," she said to Marilee. "I dare you."

"I don't need to read it out loud."

"I want to see you keep a straight face when you get to the part about the masses and the gases."

"All right, okay," said Marilee. "So it's not Dylan Thomas. It's not dog doo either. There's some nice lines here, like this part about the pages of a time-worn novel. I like that."

Amanda shot her a tortured look. With her hair set on soup cans and her face the color of strained peas, she looked as if she might have stepped out of a first-season episode of "Star Trek."

Marilee walked home briskly that evening, annoyed that her friend could, at times, be such a brainless snot. The truth was, Marilee hadn't found Larry's poem all that objectionable, although she had to concede that the part about the masses and the gases was pretty awful. Still, he had a way with words, a sensitivity to the natural rhythm of language. She resented Amanda's making fun of him as if he were some tormented soul drowning in the quagmire of his own angst. That wasn't Larry at all.

But then, what was? For fifty minutes, five days a week, he whispered into her neck in German. This was strange, she had to admit. Stranger still was his habit of slighting her otherwise. Each day when the final bell rang, he was out the door before Marilee could even rise up out of her seat. If she passed him in the hall between classes, he'd refuse to acknowledge her. His behavior was baffling. Marilee understood his intentions to be sexual, but his style was so different, so utterly unnerving, that she was at a loss as to how to respond. She considered joining him at lunch some day, or milling about his locker, but realized she was simply too timid to carry through with either plan. So she played the game his way, pretending not to notice him when their paths crossed, ignoring him each time he whispered his guttural soliloquy.

"Mein süßes schönes Täubchen," Larry said into her hair one cold, drizzly Monday. Marilee scratched through her sweater at the trickle of sweat that ran down the length of her ribcage. "Mein Liebling," he whispered, then kissed the back of her neck. Marilee gasped. Robby snorted. Frau Göckermann spun on her heels, glaring toward the back corner.

"Who laughed?" she demanded. The room became abruptly silent. "All right," she said. "No one is leaving until I get an answer."

"I did," said Larry. Robby Franz relaxed in his seat.

"Please see me after class," said Frau Göckermann, who promptly assigned the class six pages of homework, which they were to begin immediately. Cindy Burris pivoted in her seat and shot Larry an evil look. Frau Göckermann said nothing until the bell rang. "Marilee, I'd like to talk to you as well. Please wait for me outside in the hallway."

"Shit," mumbled Marilee, as Larry passed her on his way to the front of the classroom. She stalled until most of the others had left, arranging and rearranging the papers in her notebook. Occasionally, she sneaked glances at Larry as he stood in front of their teacher's desk, his weight balanced on one leg, thumbs hooked in his pockets the way she imagined James Dean would have stood before a woman who wore patent leather spike heels and spoke German. Marilee strained to hear Frau Göckermann, but the woman's voice was drowned out by the din from the hallway. She got up slowly and left the room.

The hall was buzzing. Students swarmed the stairwells, slamming books into lockers, switching on radios, calling to one another from the building's opposite ends. She leaned back against the wall, her neck and shoulders tight and aching. Eau de School Bus permeated the air, a heavy mingling of diesel fuel and road grime that wafted down the corridor like slow poison. Cars sped by in front of the flagpole, splashing rainwater as they screeched out of the parking lot, running on high octane and testosterone. Kevin Thacker asked Marilee if she wanted a ride home, but she declined. In a few minutes, Larry emerged from the classroom.

"As ye sow, so shall ye reap," he said, holding the door wide open. They were the first words he had ever spoken to her in English.

She brushed past him into the room. Frau Göckermann sat at her desk. "You have an admirer," she said with a tight smile. "Don't think I'm not aware of what goes on in my classroom."

"I'm sorry," said Marilee.

"Don't apologize, dear. But do be careful. I've seen his type. I know what a boy like that can do to a young girl. Take my advice, dear, forget about him."

Marilee was speechless. She hardly knew whether to be insulted by the woman's presumption or flattered by her concern. She looked down at the desk, hoping to be dismissed.

"At any rate," Frau Göckermann continued, "it's time to break up your little tea party. I've moved Herr Johnston (she pronounced it Yonschton) to the front of the class, where, I hope, he will be less inclined to be disruptive."

Marilee's heart sank.

"Das ist Alles," said Frau Göckermann, turning her attention to the papers on her desk.

Marilee walked out of the classroom. She trudged down the empty hallway and outside into the rain, her books heavy in her arms. "You missed your bus," said a voice behind her. Larry stood leaning against the red brick wall of the building, much as she imagined James Dean would have leaned against a red brick wall. "I'll take you home," he said. He walked her to his car, talking to her about Hemingway. About big game hunting. The running of the bulls at Pamplona. Existential suicide. He said nothing about having kissed the back of her neck.

"Why'd you do that in there?" she interrupted, once they were seated in his red Pinto.

"I like Robby," he said, misunderstanding. He jammed his Pinto into gear and squealed out of the parking lot.

On the way home, he told her about his car: '71. A good year. Four on the floor. Twenty-five miles to the gallon, a real gem. You couldn't buy cars like that anymore. Pulling into her driveway, he threw his stick shift into neutral and pulled up on the emergency brake. The Pinto screeched to a halt. "She's old, but she's loyal," he said, running his hand along the steering wheel. Guys were weird about their cars.

"Thanks for the ride," said Marilee, flinging open the passenger door.

Larry shrugged. "Frau G. changed my seat."

"I know."

"So, I'll pick you up tomorrow morning around eight," he said, as if one thought led naturally to the other.

"Quarter to eight," said Marilee, gathering her books, trying to remain cool.

"Sehr gut," said Larry.

"See ya," said Marilee. As she stepped out of his car, her skirt rose up high on her thigh; she made no effort to pull it down.

■

"It's all yours," said a voice at her driver's-side window. She opened her eyes. Enoch thrust the stick end of a windshield scrubber at her.

"Excuse me?"

"Can't reach across the windshield. Sorry."

Marilee smiled weakly, then took hold of the dripping apparatus.

"I'll go pay," said Enoch. "Want anything?"

She shook her head no.

Enoch entered the building awkwardly on his crutches. Marilee stepped out of her car and went to work scraping bugs from her windshield. Occasionally, she sneaked glances at Enoch standing in line for the cashier. He stood no taller than the two little boys in front of him, one staring, the other giggling, both holding tightly to their father's hand. The man wore cowboy boots and an orange Broncos hat. Enoch smiled at the boys. The smaller one said something back, and the man whisked him into his arms.

When she was finished with her windshield, Marilee wetted some paper towels and wiped road grime from her headlights. Old as it was, she was fond of her Dart, a gift from her mother after Larry had left L.A. Ramona Levitay had picked up her daughter after work one day and driven her down to Aspromonte's. Ramona knew Nick Aspromonte from the club where she worked as a coat checker. Nick had a brother, Philly, who owned a car lot down on Van Nuys Boulevard.

Philly cut Ramona a sweet deal on the Dart. The car was unique, he said, because it had a clock on the dashboard. This model Dart never came with a clock, but the previous owner had installed one, special. She could have it for three-fifty. Marilee knew nothing about cars, but she liked its shade of blue. Amazingly, the Dart ran like a dream. It got twenty miles to the gallon and its clock kept time.

Both boys in his arms now, the man in the Broncos hat emerged from the building and headed toward a white pickup truck with a gun rack mounted in its rear window. Enoch moved up to the counter, barely tall enough to see over its edge. He pulled his wallet out of one of his socks and handed the cashier some bills. Having finished cleaning her headlights, Marilee polished her side mirror, then resumed her place behind the wheel.

Enoch struggled to open the glass door. A woman in line studied him as he propped the door open with one crutch, then hobbled through on the other. It would always be this way, thought Marilee: People staring, too absorbed in Enoch's awkwardness to avert their eyes. Too ill at ease to lend a hand. Too self-contained in their safe little spaces to make contact with a dwarf. And they would wonder about her. Were she and Enoch friends? Lovers? What weird things did they do in bed?

A Tootsie Pop came flying through the open passenger-side window. Marilee caught it between her knees. "Jack up your endorphins," said Enoch, tossing his crutches into the back and reclaiming his seat next to her. "Like heroin. Or being in love."

Marilee looked over at the small stranger sitting next to her, white stick protruding from his mouth. She wondered if he had ever been in love, or if anyone had ever been in love with him. She started her engine, pulled out of the filling station, and headed north on White Sands Boulevard. She had no idea where they were going. Annoyed, she tossed her Tootsie Pop on the seat between them where the melons had been. Enoch picked up the sucker, unwrapped it, and inserted it between her lips.

"Thanks," she mumbled, working the stick with her tongue.

"My pleasure," said Enoch.

It was grape, a flavor Marilee hated.

■

They headed north toward Albuquerque. A few miles out of town, just past North 54 Salvage, Marilee pulled over to the side of the road.

"I can't do this," she said. She took the Tootsie Pop from her mouth and switched off the car's motor. "I can't just take off like this. This is crazy."

"Okay," said Enoch.

"I've got to go back," she continued. "I'm sorry. This has nothing to do with you. It's just that I can't walk out on Larry like this. He's—"

"No problem," said Enoch, reaching for his crutches and his backpack.

"Look, you don't have to get out here. I'll drive you back into town."

"Fine," said Enoch.

"I'm really sorry. I just can't—"

"You done with that?" He was staring at her Tootsie Pop.

"You don't *want* this?" said Marilee. She was just getting down to the good part.

"Only if you're finished."

Marilee handed him her half-eaten sucker and restarted her engine. She made a U-turn and headed in the opposite direction, just as she had the day before when she'd first spotted Enoch on the highway. Enoch twirled the sticks in his mouth and hummed "Moon River" as she drove back to Rocket City.

"Where would you like me to drop you off?" she asked, as soon as the highway had once again become White Sands Boulevard. She was tired of Enoch's humming; irritated by his casual indifference.

"Anywhere," he said.

"Do you want me to take you downtown, or drop you off here?"

"Whatever."

His attitude annoyed her. She wished he would yell at her or call her names. On Tenth Street she turned left, then made a quick right onto New York Avenue. "How's this?" she said, stopping suddenly beside a bench on the sidewalk. It wasn't a bus stop as far as she could tell; there was no sign or special lane leading up to it. It was just an ordinary, lime-green bench sitting next to the curb in the middle of the block. Weird, she thought. And appropriate.

"Excellent," said Enoch, opening the door. Cars backed up in the lane behind them. A man in a Cutlass tooted his horn until he saw Enoch struggling with his crutches.

"Well, I guess this is it," said Marilee.

"I guess so," said Enoch.

"It's been fun, really," she said, then hated herself for having said that. Enoch slung his backpack over his left shoulder and maneuvered the door shut with one crutch. "Bye," she called through the open window.

"Thanks for the ride," said Enoch.

"Take care," said Marilee.

"Have a good life," said Enoch.

"Let's go!" yelled the man in the Cutlass.

"Fuck you!" shouted Enoch.

The man in the Cutlass honked loudly as Marilee accelerated. She watched Enoch in her rearview mirror. He didn't try to hitch a ride or get up and walk away. He just sat there on the bench-from-another-planet, watching Marilee drive down the street and out of his life.

She signaled to turn left at the first intersection. She had no idea where she was going or what she would do once she got there. It would be hours before Larry arrived home, hours she would have to kill. She glanced again in her rearview mirror at the small lump that was Enoch. He sat alone on the bench, staring in her direction. He waved. She winced and pretended not to have seen him.

A group of blind children stepped off the curb and started to cross the street in front of her. She had not seen them waiting. There must have been twenty of them, shuffling en masse in a tight swarm, tapping their way across New York Avenue. They tapped slowly. As soon as the last of them had cleared the intersection, Marilee rounded the corner, and Enoch passed out of her sight.

The clock on her dashboard said quarter past ten. It was Tuesday in Rocket City.

DEATH'S WINDOWSILL

The morning after he cleaned his house from top to bottom, Figman drove to Roswell for art supplies. He took his painting book with him and bought everything it said he would need to become an artist. He purchased oil paints in a sketch box, assorted brushes, three canvases, and an easel. He bought a palette, a palette knife, turpentine, a brush washer, and rags. He picked up a notebook to keep a painter's journal. He considered, also, buying a beret, thinking that it would keep the hair out of his face while he painted. But Figman, who did not have sufficient hair to justify the need for restraint, ultimately rejected the notion as clichéd.

He would also require food, a necessity his book failed to mention. Passing up Furr's in Roswell, he headed back south on Highway 285. It was Saturday, and Lester's E-Z Mart was crowded.

She was there like a dream waiting to be reentered. Figman shopped for two days' worth of groceries, lingering in each aisle, pretending not to have noticed her. "Still shop here?" she asked as he moved through her checkout line.

"No," said Figman. "I went back to shopping at Bulldog Superette."

Oma laughed, a warm laugh. Figman felt the tension at the base of his neck subside. "No aloe?" she asked.

"Not today."

"That's too bad. It's on special. Two for eight ninety-five."

"Really?" said Figman. "That's a good price." He drew four bottles out of the box on the rack and placed them on the counter in front of her. He'd continued taking aloe, the least offensive of Mrs. Smith's remedies, as a hedge against the possibility that the woman's method had some actual legitimacy.

"What's okra this week?" Oma yelled to the checker next to her.

"Eighty-nine," the woman yelled back.

Oma punched in the numbers. "You like okra?" she asked.

"I thought I'd try it."

"I hate okra. Too slimy. Even breaded and fried, it feels like snot." She rang up Figman's bottles of aloe. "What do people do with aloe, anyway?"

Figman contemplated confessing his terminal condition. "Experiments," he told her.

"Experiments? What kind?" Her right hand raced over the keypad while her left emptied his basket.

"Plant experiments," he said. "I study its effect on plant growth."

"You some kind of scientist?"

"Sort of. Listen, would you like to go get some coffee? I could tell you more about it."

"I'm working," said Oma.

"Well, yes, of course you are. I can see that. I meant when you get out of here." He'd been careful not to buy anything frozen in hope of her being available.

Oma emptied Figman's basket and punched more numbers into her register. "I don't think so," she said. "That'll be sixty-one thirty-two."

The bagboy eyed him. He was a tall, well-built football type Figman had failed to notice. His badge said, "Dino." Figman reached into his wallet and handed Oma two tens and a fifty.

Her fingers flew. "Sixty-one thirty-two," she said. Oma counted the change into his palm. "Sixty-one thirty-three, thirty-four, thirty-five, forty, fifty, seventy-five, sixty-two, sixty-three . . ." Would she ever get there?

"Need some help out with these?" asked Dino. He had slits for eyes, and the left corner of his mouth curled upward. He looked too old to be boxing groceries.

"I've got it, son," said Figman.

Dino's mouth uncurled and his eye slits narrowed, something Figman would not have imagined possible. Figman gathered up his three bags as if he'd purchased nothing but cottonballs. "Think about it," he whispered to Oma.

Oma shrugged.

Figman walked briskly to the store's nearest exit. Behind his back he heard Dino ask, "What the fuck's aloe?"

■

Having loaded his groceries into his trunk, Figman drove the five miles to his house on the highway. The day after his car accident, a representative of the Aion Corporation had contacted him before he'd checked out of the hospital. Off the record, the man had offered him a deal: Figman would be given a brand-new Aion in exchange for his refraining from any further mention to reporters of that insignificant detail about his car's locking left front brakes. Figman readily agreed. When he left the hospital shortly before dinner, the discharge nurse brought him his clothes, his wallet, and a new set of car keys. They fit the ignition of the vehicle of his dreams: a red 2SXT, replete with climate control, electronically adjustable sport seats, and black leather interior.

The flag of his and Verdie's mailbox had been lowered. Figman parked in front of his house and walked the short distance back to the highway. His boots crunched through the melting snow. Soon, he imagined, grass would be pushing up through the soil and the landscape would turn green.

Their mailbox held eight items: seven letters addressed to Verdie and a typewritten postcard from Figman's mother:

Dear Louis,

How's the new house? The new job? I'm so glad you've settled in somewhere and gotten away from that motel. Motel rooms can be so depressing.

I still can't believe you're not here anymore. New Mexico seems like such a lonely place, but if that's where the company needs you, I can understand your having to go. You've always been such a good employee. Virginia came to lunch yesterday and showed me pictures of her granddaughter. A real doll. And Dee called. Can I give her your address and phone number now? Running out of space. Send me a picture of your new home. I miss you oodles.

Love, Mother

He was glad to have intercepted the mail before Verdie got to it. Occasionally, his mother sent postcards; he would have to ask her not to do this anymore. Figman thumbed through Verdie's letters before placing them back in the mailbox. She'd received what seemed to be an awful lot of mail for a woman living alone. There were two envelopes he couldn't identify, an electric bill, a phone bill, a notice from the I.R.S., a statement from some doctor in Carlsbad, and a handwritten envelope addressed to Mrs. V. C. Hooks. Its postmark said Albuquerque.

"Anything for me?"

Figman jumped. He had neither seen nor heard his landlady approaching.

"Scared you, didn't I? Well, I'm sorry about that. How's the house? Find everything okay?"

"It's fine. Nice place," said Figman. "The heater puts out a lot of heat."

"Lordy, yes," said Verdie, laughing. "Ruby—she was one of them sisters I told you about—she used to say the heat from that heater made the back of her throat itch." Verdie's laugh was more like a cackle. She wore a pink-purple lipstick that exactly matched the color of her trailer.

"These are for you," said Figman. He handed over her assortment of mail.

"Thank you kindly," said Verdie. She had that west Texas accent that sounded like a coil wound tightly around a tomcat. Verdie tucked her mail up under her armpit and just stood there, squinting up at Figman, looking more turtle-like than he'd remembered.

"So," said Figman, starting down his driveway. "What's to do around here?"

Verdie followed him. "Well, I golf," she said.

That explained the problem with her skin.

"Then there's the caverns. Skiing up at Cloudcroft. Horse racing at Ruidoso, but they're closed all winter."

A semi whipped by them, heading north. As soon as it had passed, a chubby little boy about seven darted across the highway toward Verdie's ugly trailer. He carried a yellow bucket and a large metal spoon. Figman had first noticed the child the day he moved in. He'd been digging in the dirt out behind his kitchen window.

"Who's the kid?" asked Figman.

"Oh, that's Bobo. Rodriguez's boy." She nodded at the house across the highway, a white clapboard farmhouse with a side-yard clothesline. Figman knew the place. It was an eyesore, perfectly framed by his living room window.

"Don't his parents care if he crosses the highway?"

"Naw," said Verdie. "Bobo's got more sense than both folks put together. You want some help with them groceries?"

"Thanks, I can manage."

"Well, let me know if there's anything I can do for you," she said, continuing down the gravel driveway toward her trailer.

"Do you know how to fix okra?"

"Depends what's wrong with it," said Verdie.

■

Figman unpacked his groceries, then set about the heavy business of becoming famous. Figman liked fame. His brush with notoriety had been brief but gratifying beyond anything he'd previously known. He wanted more of it. And now that dying had proved more chronic than acute, Figman had to consider the possibility that fame might not come to him posthumously. Living in Artesia, with its good air and water, he would have more time to devote to his painting, more time to send his work out into the world, more time for the world to take notice. Dying was a time for fame. A time to make a name for himself. To do something to set himself apart from all the other Figmans of the world.

Months ago, in L.A., Figman had decided that what little time he had left would not be spent in courtrooms and hospitals. He would go somewhere obscure, not only to paint but to avoid being found in the meantime. He'd sold his house below market value. He'd sold his brand-new 2SXT. Then he'd bought a used Aion identical to the one he had totaled in his accident, a model known for its numerous mechanical defects. No one, he'd figured, would expect him to make the same mistake twice, even when that mistake was the reason he was still around to make it.

Figman had paid cash for the car and registered it in his mother's name. He'd told no one where he was headed (he himself had not known), and as soon as he'd settled on Artesia had informed only his mother. His goal was to become renowned while remaining anonymous, a concept whose irony was not entirely lost on him and whose prospect motivated him to assemble his easel.

An hour later, Figman had erected the contraption minus one bolt on its canvas holder that had been missing from its package of hardware. The art supply store in Roswell would be closed now. Figman constructed a makeshift fastener out of a large bobby pin he'd found under the toe kick in his bathroom, an implement sufficiently old and corroded to have belonged to Verdie and not one of the Pontelle sisters. He was handy with these things. He twisted the bobby pin and attached it to the canvas holder so that it held it to the upright without interfering with the support of the canvas.

After getting himself a beer, Figman returned to his living room to admire his work from all angles. It was a fine easel that would serve his art well. He moved it into the space beside his large front window. The light was best in his living room, both his bedroom and kitchen having northern exposures, and his spare room's windows being covered by tall hydrangeas. His living room's only drawback was that it looked directly at the Rodriguez house, a ramshackle structure whose paint peeled from its walls and whose front porch had slipped from its foundation. Figman eyed the house disparagingly between swallows of beer. Tires and rusty box springs leaned against its southernmost wall next to oil barrels, car doors, and assorted engine parts. Laundry sagged from its side-yard clothesline: old sheets and women's underwear, torn and starchless as overboiled zucchini. Birds nested beneath its eaves. Bobo, the family prodigy, squatted in its front yard, digging.

In college, Figman had been given an A in Watercolor. He'd received A's in most of his subjects, but the one in Watercolor had made him especially proud. He'd taken the class reluctantly because he'd needed an elective in the one-to-two-thirty time block on Tuesdays and Thursdays. Convinced he had no talent, Figman had entered the class believing he was, at best, destined for a C. But he'd received the best grade possible. The teacher had even told him he had promise.

In the fifteen years since, Figman had not lifted a paintbrush. Though it had been his intention to pursue painting as a hobby, L.A. afforded no time for hobbies, no time for anything but the bare necessities. His social life he considered a bare necessity, a pun that occurred to him one night while he was fondling the breasts of a woman named Renee.

It was hard for Figman to imagine how he could live without the breasts of a woman. There was nothing more comforting than the way the soft mound of flesh melted into the palm of his hand; few things more stimulating than the response of a woman's nipple to the flick of his tongue. He wondered what Oma's breasts looked like beneath her shapeless uniform. Figman had forgotten to notice her breasts, a realization that, in retrospect, surprised him. He noticed breasts and had long ago perfected discreet ways to regard them while not offending the person to whom they were attached. He felt a stirring inside, a familiar longing that he assumed to be sexual but soon identified as hunger. He had not eaten since his Chicken Fingers breakfast at Tastee Freez.

It was time Figman fixed his first home-cooked meal. Until now (indeed, for the entire three months he'd been living in Artesia) he'd eaten all his meals in restaurants. He was sick to death of restaurants. He gagged at the thought of another Big Mac or Whopper. He was bored with Kwan Den, the Town House Cafeteria, and Eileen's Tac Olé. Even La Fonda, which drew people from Carlsbad and Roswell for its chile rellenos and hot sopaipillas, no longer held any appeal. But mostly he was sick of cigarette smoke.

Figman had never lived in a place where people smoked so indiscriminately. Few of Artesia's restaurants had non-smoking sections; more often than not, Figman was forced to choke down his meal amidst the noxious fumes from somebody else's filthy habit. In New Mexico, people smoked in stores, in elevators, in markets, and in theaters. They smoked walking down the street. Sometimes they didn't smoke at all, just held on to their burning cigarettes or placed them in ashtrays while they ate. Figman was unaccustomed to such rudeness. In L.A., one would sooner enter a restaurant naked than holding a cigarette. In L.A., people cared about whom they poisoned.

Figman, who had located a frying pan for his steak and a small saucepan for his instant mashed potatoes, soon realized he had no suitable pot in which to cook okra. He'd bought a half-pound of the stuff. It was green and pointy and looked as if it wanted to be boiled whole. (Boiling was what Figman assumed one did with it, though he wasn't entirely sure.) The metal drawer beneath his oven contained a few pans of the wrong size, either too large or too small. Okra, he figured, required a medium-sized pan. Figman was hungry. His potato flakes were measured, and his saucepan of water and milk stood waiting. His steak sizzled over a low-to-medium flame.

When Verdie opened the door to her trailer, Figman was struck simultaneously by its foul odor and the presence of a man. He'd expected her to be alone. There'd been no car in the driveway but her green Impala; he'd seen no one tread past his windows. But here was this fellow in a plaid shirt and bolo tie seated at her kitchen table.

"Well, hi there," said Verdie. "Come over for a drink?" Her breath smelled of Scotch whisky. She wore a pink sweater over white slacks and the same pink-purple lipstick as before. The man looked up at them.

"I'm sorry to bother you," said Figman, standing on the top step of her trailer. "Do you have a saucepan I could borrow?"

"Sure, hon. Come on in while I hunt for one." She handed Figman the drink she'd been holding. The glass was sweaty.

Figman stepped through the doorway of the single-room trailer. It was a hurricane on wheels. Clothes and unwashed dishes were strewn everywhere. In the kitchenette, trash overflowed onto linoleum that looked as if it hadn't seen soap or wax in a decade. The sink was full of dishes in brownish-gray water. Paint peeled from the two cabinet doors that still clung to their hinges; fingerprints marred their button handles. Verdie's dinette, a formica table wiped surprisingly clean, was encircled by three matching metal-frame chairs, their plastic seat covers cracked and grimy. The place stank of mildew, fried onions, and unemptied ashtrays. And he'd thought the Pontelle sisters had been dirty.

Verdie dug around in her kitchen, hunting in corners, opening and slamming shut drawers, rummaging into the backs of doorless cabinets. Beyond the kitchenette lay Verdie's living room, dark and depressing as the living room of any thirty-year-old trailer could be. Its walls were covered in fake wood paneling that Figman thought must certainly absorb whatever daylight managed to seep through the curtains of her weird little windows. The carpet, which looked like a remnant of his own, was soiled and covered with pink fuzzballs the color of Verdie's sweater. She had no TV. The corner revealed a tiny bathroom. A sofa sleeper, opened and unmade, filled almost the entire width of the trailer's far wall, blocking access to a second external doorway. Directly over the center of her sofa bed, a red Christmassy fixture hung suspended from an extension cord looped twice around a screw-hook in her seven-foot ceiling. Verdie's entire trailer was not much larger than Figman's bedroom. He wondered what terrible necessity had forced her out of her house and into such a trash heap.

Verdie cussed as she ransacked the insides of a high cabinet. The man at the table eyed Figman. He and Verdie obviously had been playing poker. Plastic chips lay in a pile in front of her empty seat. The man cleared his throat. Verdie stopped her foraging. "Jeez Louise, how tacky can a body be? Poe Titus, this is Louis Figman. Louis, this is Poe."

Poe Titus? What was it with the names in this town? The man tipped his cowboy hat. "Nice to meet you, Louis."

"Likewise. But people call me just Figman. It's sort of this thing I have."

"Well, nice to meet you, Just Figman," said Titus. Verdie broke into fractious laughter, a rooster crowing to greet the dawn. Figman felt the veins in his neck swell.

"Well, I ain't calling you Figman," said Verdie. "I don't call nobody by their last names."

"That Jewish?" asked Titus, fingering the tidy stack of chips in front of him.

Figman ignored the question. He leaned back against the refrigerator, an old Amana with dust on its top and jelly smeared on its pull-down handle. He studied Verdie's companion. He looked like a man suffering from unrequited life. Tall and gaunt, he appeared to be a few years older than Verdie, which, as Figman remembered, was as many years as there were cards in a deck. Smoke rose from the cactus ashtray on the table.

Figman, who had never seen Verdie with a cigarette, assumed Titus to be the current source of the trailer's rank odor. He wondered whether the stench in his own house, which had yet to air from his drapes and furniture, had come from this Titus fellow. He wondered, too, if Titus were responsible for his kitchen floor's scuff marks. Figman checked out the man's shoes. He wore red leather cowboy boots with two-inch wooden heels.

"Eureka," said Verdie, producing a pan the size of a washbasin.

"Oh, no. I'm sorry," said Figman. "I should have been more specific. I need one a little smaller. Something medium. To boil okra in."

"I hate okra," said Poe Titus.

"Well, let me see," said Verdie, getting down on all fours. "Hand me that flashlight there, Louis." She motioned toward the countertop. He looked for a flashlight amidst all the clutter but couldn't see one. "It's right up there," said Verdie, "just behind them dishes."

Figman walked the two steps to the half-moon window above her sink, the window that comprised the left eye of the face that stared at him across his backyard. Sure enough, directly beneath its sill in a pool of standing water lay an old metal flashlight. It felt heavier than Figman remembered flashlights ever feeling. He wiped it dry on his 501 jeans. "You ought not let this thing get wet," he said, handing it to her.

"Oh, hell," said Verdie, laughing. She shone it into the dark cavern beneath her corner counter, then crawled halfway into the space as she banged around, hunting for just the right size saucepan for Figman's okra. Poe Titus reached for the bottle next to his ashtray and poured himself another drink. Figman, who wished he'd chosen a less elaborate vegetable, stared down at the glass he was holding, slender and covered with multicolored dots. Its ice was half melted and its rim was smudged with Verdie's fuchsia lipstick. He wondered what flavor it was, and how vile it must taste mixed with cigarettes and Scotch whisky.

Figman remembered women from the taste of their lipstick. Few women wore the same brand and color, and Figman was able to separate them in his mind this way. Lipstick tasted like nothing else, its flavor waxy and ersatz—not truly cinnamon or genuinely peach, but something not quite cinnamon or almost peach. Dee, his last girlfriend, wore sort of a licorice flavor, though its color had been pink. She'd cried when

Figman announced he was leaving, so he'd given her his stereo and bed, the two things he'd thought would most remind her of him.

Aside from Dee, few women stood out in Figman's memory. There was Lizzie, a bank officer who talked too much but enjoyed making love in parks and on the beach. There was beautiful Gwen, who hated sex but was thrilling to be seen with. There was Mary Ellen—not such a beauty, but sweet. She'd had a child in high school, and her father had once offered Figman ten thousand dollars to marry her. And then there was Sandy, a petite brunette who liked to give Figman head while he drove the streets of the San Fernando Valley. She had, unfortunately, been the woman who'd once opened his mail.

These were the women whom Figman remembered apart from the flavor of their lipstick. Occasionally, he'd kiss someone new, taste her lipstick, and recall some detail about a woman he'd once dated: the shine of her hair or the curve of her hip as they walked, arm in arm, about the city. He wondered sometimes if he didn't mix them up, so that what he thought he remembered of a particular lover was not a true memory at all but a fragment of some larger female composite whose features he culled from the melting pot into which all women had been poured.

"This is the mediumest pan I have," said Verdie. "You can keep it. I never use it, 'ceptin' holidays."

"Sorry it was so much trouble," said Figman. He took the pan and returned her drink.

"Sure I can't get you one?" she asked.

"Thanks, but I have to get back," he said.

Poe Titus stood up and extended his hand across the table. "Good meeting you, Figman. Good luck with that okra." Figman shook the man's hand. It felt beat up and scratchy as a fifty-year-old fence post.

"Now, remember, don't undercook it and use lots of butter and salt," said Verdie.

Figman had no butter. He'd forgotten to pick some up at the E-Z Mart but decided not to mention this lest Verdie go digging for some underneath her kitchen sink. He said good-bye and walked the thirty feet back to his spotless kitchen. His steak had burned. He yelled, "Fuck," and "Shit," and threw it into the sink, pouring water on it to lessen its smoking. It looked like some horrible fungus the Pontelle sisters had left for him to discover.

When the room finally aired, Figman whipped up his mashed potatoes and boiled his half-pound of okra. He set his kitchen table, poured himself a beer, and sat down to his first home-cooked meal in New Mexico. Without butter, his potatoes tasted starchy; his okra went down like snot. He dumped the whole lot of it in the sink on top of his mutant steak. Outside, the night was dark and windy. The lights went off in Verdie's trailer.

■

Figman awoke at daybreak to a clap of thunder. As this was the first thunder he'd heard in New Mexico, he took it as an omen, an auspicious beginning for his life as a famous painter. It was a Sunday in early February. Figman looked outside his bedroom window and saw the first signs of the changing seasons. The sky revealed clouds and wind, but not the same kinds of clouds or the same direction of wind to which he had grown accustomed. Surely these departures signaled spring.

Figman brewed himself a cup of coffee and pulled his book on oil painting down from its perch in his living room. He started reading at the beginning. His book told him to first pick a subject. He looked out his window; the Rodriguez house beckoned to him from across the highway. That was easy. Next, his book told him to study his subject in terms of light and composition. It was morning light, the best light in which to paint the east-facing Rodriguez house. The structure itself was nothing more than a box, but its drooping clothesline offset its otherwise static form. Best not to start with something too complicated, thought Figman. The Rodriguez house would make for a fine beginning.

The canvases he'd purchased had come ready-stretched and primed, but Figman would need to lay down an imprimatura, a thin layer of paint on top of the primer to tone the work surface. It was not unlike washing one's paper before beginning a watercolor. Reading further, he discovered that famous artists often used an imprimatura: Constable preferred red; Holbein, dark blue. Figman admired the work of Holbein. He squeezed Thalo blue onto his palette.

Figman had chosen oil as his medium because all great painters painted in oil. He knew of no famous watercolorists, but museums were full of masterpieces in oil. As his book suggested, Figman diluted his Thalo blue with turpentine. With a squared-off brush, he applied a thin coat of paint, completely covering his canvas. He was careful to check for any buildup; many canvasses whose imprimaturas were applied too thickly later cracked.

Once his underpainting was completed, Figman checked his book for the next step in the process. It said, "Wait twenty-four hours to let dry." He'd forgotten that detail. Outside, thunder rumbled off in the distance and the sky grew darker. There was nothing to be done about it. His art would have to wait a day.

Figman fixed himself breakfast, then sat down at his kitchen table to write a letter to his mother. Figman loathed letter-writing; his words were brief:

Dear Mom,

Got your card. Thanks. Things are going well. I like working in the field, especially not having to deal with L.A. traffic. My work is highly confidential, so it's still important not to tell anyone my whereabouts. There are even people at Goetschke who don't know what I'm doing out here.

My new boss is terrific—a regular guy who's already given me some pretty intense assignments. Sorry I can't be more specific. Please give my best to Dee if she calls again.

Got to dash. Say hello to Virginia. That's great about her granddaughter.

Love, F.

P.S. Next time please write to me in a letter. My landlady and I share the same mailbox and any postcard you send is likely to be read by her.

Figman had never asked his mother to call him Figman. She, alone, he allowed to call him Louis, but only because she had given him the name. Still, he had trouble signing "Louis" so he wrote just "F." He knew she would understand, for understanding was what his mother did best. She'd understood him when he lost his father at the age of three. When he was caught stealing eight years later. When he dropped out of college at nineteen. When he reenrolled at twenty-three. She'd even understood when he moved to New Mexico the year before he turned forty.

His mother was the person Figman trusted most in the world not to abuse his emotions. Still, he'd had difficulty informing her that he was leaving his job, his girlfriend, his home town (and her) to drive to some obscure western state to make a name for himself. So he'd concocted a small falsehood. His company was transferring him and there was nothing he could do. A lot of his friends were being laid off. If he didn't go, he'd lose his job. Besides, it was a better position, in fraud investigations. More money and more responsibility. He'd grown tired of AD&D.

It was the first lie he had told his mother since he was seventeen, and though he'd forgotten what that lie had been about, the guilt from having told it still lingered. He felt terrible about having to lie to her again and wished she would stop inquiring about his work. Outside his kitchen, the clouds were an angry swirl. Verdie stepped outside her trailer. She was alone. Perhaps Titus had left during the night, or maybe he was still asleep on the sofa bed in her living room. Figman watched from his window as Verdie climbed into her green Impala and drove off down the driveway. He wondered where she was headed.

When the dust from her tires settled, Figman noticed a small, hunched figure at her trailer's far corner. It was Bobo Rodriguez with his bucket and spoon. Figman watched as the child filled his bucket with dirt, then emptied it into a pile a short distance from the flower bed. Bobo worked meticulously, first excavating, then carefully refilling each of the holes he had made. He dug with intensity, with a sense of purpose Figman had rarely seen in adults, let alone children. When he'd filled his last hole, Bobo gathered up his spoon and bucket and headed back across the highway. He was followed by a large orange cat that Figman had not previously noticed. It was nice for a boy to have a cat, especially one that followed you around. Figman wondered what to do for the rest of the day; he knew what Bobo would be doing.

He decided to go see Oma. He'd buy another steak, a different vegetable, and tell her how right she'd been about okra. Figman stamped and addressed his envelope, then dropped it off at his mailbox on his way into town. The flag was up; Verdie had left an outgoing letter face down inside the box. Figman resisted the urge to turn it over. He tossed his letter in on top of hers and headed north on the highway.

At Lester's, Figman bought top sirloin and a head of fresh broccoli. Oma was not there. Instead, he found Gert behind the counter, a woman whose name said it all. It was an omen, he concluded, his second that day. If his time in this life were indeed limited, he should not be wasting it on women. If he couldn't paint today, he'd draw. He headed over to K-Mart on Main Street and bought sketching paper and charcoals.

On his way out of K-Mart, Figman ran into Verdie. "Well, hi there," she said. "How'd that okra turn out?"

"Not too well," he responded.

"Did you fix it up with lots of butter and salt, like I told you?"

"Damn," he said. Once again, he'd forgotten to buy butter.

"You gotta listen to me. I've been fixing the stuff for over forty years."

"I guess I'm not the okra type," said Figman.

Verdie looked him over. "No, I reckon you ain't," she said.

Figman wondered what she meant by that. He excused himself and drove home quickly, anxious to begin his afternoon of sketching.

Figman thought about what he should draw. He looked around his house, but few of his possessions called out to him. At a loss, he dug through a box in his spare bedroom's closet. Halfway down, he came upon an album of photographs. Surely it contained a wealth of subject matter, snapshots from which Figman could sketch portraits of the people he had known. But when he lifted the album, he discovered his six bottles of Essence of Chicken. He remembered having packed them despite his promise to scale down his possessions. Essence of Chicken was too weird to throw out; too wonderfully surreal to keep packed away. Perhaps their rediscovery was yet a third omen.

He carried all six bottles to the counter in his kitchen. Essence of Chicken had not aged well. Thick and red, it looked like the blood that Drs. Feldstein and Mercer had extracted from his body. When he shook one bottle, he saw particles. Beaks maybe, or chicken toes. It was foul, this rediscovery, but not insignificant, for Figman knew that in life there were no accidents. He stored five of the bottles on a shelf in his pantry. The sixth, he decided to keep in plain sight as a curiosity. And as a reminder. He wiped the bottle clean, tightened its cap, and centered it on his windowsill.

HAM AND EGGS

After dropping off Enoch at the lime-green bench, Marilee found herself in a residential neighborhood. Ahead of her, a group of teenage boys played Frisbee in the street, sailing their orange disc over cars as they drove by. The Frisbee grazed Marilee's antenna and bounced off her windshield with a slap. "Sorry," she heard one of them yell as she drove on without stopping.

She turned right, then right again at the next street, which took her back to White Sands Boulevard. She headed south to a Texaco station she had seen on her way into town. In the office, she requested a map of the city.

"What are you looking for?" asked the attendant. He was taller than she, rail thin, and carried a greasy rag in his hip pocket.

"Tomahawk Trail."

"You don't need a map. Just head north on White Sands till you get to Tenth Street and turn right." He indicated the direction with his hand. "Tomahawk's about halfway up the hill, couple of blocks past the hospital."

"Thanks," said Marilee.

"I'll take you there, if you like. I'm on a break." The attendant was young, about eighteen. He didn't look as if he were on a break.

"I'm sure I'll find it," she said. She hated it when guys came on to her.

"Nice hair," he said as she swung open the door. She pretended not to have heard him. Marilee's hair was the color of rust. Thick and naturally curly, it was her nicest feature, if one discounted the opinions of those who admired her freckles.

Tomahawk Trail turned out to be a wide avenue lined with mesquite trees. She located Larry's apartment, a pink, two-story stucco duplex with a Spanish tile roof. A flight of stairs ran up the right side of the building alongside a trio of palms. The apartment had a name: "The Mescalero Arms" was written in florid cursive between its two stories. Marilee had the odd sensation that she could have been on any street in the San Fernando Valley.

From Larry's letters, she knew he lived on the ground floor. The upstairs unit was rented by a man from El Salvador who wore wooden clogs and played Latin music at all hours of the night. Larry had twice complained to him about the clop, clop, clop keeping him awake—long dissertations about the properties of sound, the body's need for sleep, and the virtues of house slippers. Señor Escamilla, who'd nodded and smiled broadly throughout Larry's speeches, had turned out not to understand a word of English.

The curtains in Larry's apartment were closed. Marilee figured he would not be home at this hour, that he'd be at Holloman doing whatever it was he did there. Flight instruction is what she'd told Enoch; the truth was, she had no idea what Larry did for the Air Force—civilian work of some kind, but he'd not been specific. His letters had spoken only of restaurants, parties, picnics at White Sands, and Señor Escamilla. The only mention he'd made of the base itself was its rule about not carrying loose items beyond the flight line: one ballpoint pen sucked in at high speed could ruin a jet engine.

Marilee rolled down her window. From the apartment above Larry's she heard music, something Latin with a lot of hand clapping and ay-yi-yi-yies. A breeze billowed the curtains. It was ten forty and getting warmer by the minute.

Marilee drove back to White Sands Boulevard and looked for something to do. It was too early for lunch, and she was still full from having eaten so much melon. As she passed New York Avenue, she glanced to her left. The lime-green bench stood empty. Returning to White Sands Boulevard, she drove slowly, alternately checking out both sides of the highway. On the left, she saw a long, narrow park with picnic benches and barbecue pits; on the right, a used car dealership called Street Toys.

Farther up the block, she came upon the Chamber of Commerce with its rockets and airplanes elevated on poles like giant winged insects mounted for display. Next, a Mexican restaurant, a 7-Eleven, another car lot, a beauty shop. A lady emerged with a bouffant hairdo similar to the style her mother had worn for the last twenty years. Nowhere along the boulevard did Marilee see a dwarf.

Continuing north, she passed the New Mexico School for the Visually Handicapped. That at least explained the entourage tapping its way around town, but the rest of Alamogordo remained a mystery, a strange outgrowth of the nearby mountains not unlike a bunion on some otherwise normal foot.

At the northernmost end of town, Marilee came upon the White Sands Mall. Not in the mood to window shop, she drove back to the Chamber of Commerce with its panoply of phallic projectiles. Inside, a woman sat on a three-legged stool, knitting a patchwork of multicolored yarn. A cigarette smoldered noxiously in an ashtray on the counter. "Can I help you?" the woman asked. Her eyes, sunken and turned inward, told Marilee she was blind.

"I'm looking for some brochures. About things to do in town."

The woman used one of her knitting needles to point to a spindle of pamphlets behind the front door. Marilee thanked her and picked through the offering. The pamphlets had names like "Reach for the Stars" and "Have a Blast in Alamogordo," a pun Marilee found less than amusing. Most featured pictures of rockets. "How much for just two?" asked Marilee. Smoke rose from the woman's ashtray and found its way to Marilee's nose as smoke always seemed to do, especially in restaurants as soon as her meal had arrived.

"Oh, they're free, hon," said the woman. "Some heat wave we're having."

"Tell me about it," said Marilee, stuffing a few more brochures into her purse. "Is it always this hot in September?"

"Could be," said the woman. "Then again, maybe not." She knitted quickly, never missing a stitch.

Marilee thanked her and returned to her Dart, leaving her car door open for air. She sat behind the steering wheel and thumbed through her material until she came upon "Reach for the Stars." Its cover displayed a picture of the International Space Hall of Fame, a modernistic cube of concrete and glass in front of which stood a small assembly of rockets. It was located on State Road 2001, in the northeast corner of town. The building looked air conditioned.

The Space Hall of Fame was smaller than Marilee expected. In addition to the satellites, rockets, and space capsules suspended from its ceilings, it housed an array of space-flight paraphernalia: photographs of astronauts, engineers, physicists, and missiles; models of the earth, the sun, and the moon; models of the planets and their orbits; moon rocks and space suits; charts of rockets and their trajectories. Marilee started on the top floor, fascinated by the exhibit of space food and personal hygiene. She saw gray-looking substances labeled "chicken and gravy" in clear plastic bags, chocolate pudding in squeeze tubes, and cheese spread with directions for use: "Knead package before opening." She wondered how hungry she would have to be to eat any of it.

One level down, she paused in front of a Plexiglas display case. Inside, a model of a chimp in a green and white restraint suit stared out at her. It was a replica of Ham, the first monkey in space. The model looked amateur at best, a papier-mâché figure that looked less like a chimp than one of the bad makeup jobs in *Planet of the Apes*.

Descending the ramp to the next level, Marilee gazed out through the building's rear window. On the ground lay what could only be described as a rocket graveyard, missiles strewn haphazardly like felled trees upon the rugged hillside. She was about to look away when she noticed something stirring behind one of the rockets, a small animal—or was it Enoch? She stared down at the embankment, studying the spot where she thought she'd seen movement. Cupping her face to the glass, she studied the ground closely, but saw nothing.

An hour into her tour, Marilee grew hungry. She returned to her car and drove to El Ratón, a Mexican restaurant located directly across the street from the bench where she'd deposited Enoch. Two men held the door open for her. They wore turquoise and silver string ties and looked about thirty. One of them had a gold tooth. "¡Qué linda!" he said, as Marilee brushed by.

"¡Y las pecas!" said the second.

"Mi amor. Mi corazón," said the first, and laughed, the sun glinting off his gold tooth like headlights off a fender. Marilee smiled and wished she hadn't taken German.

In the dining room, serapes and brightly colored ponchos hung from dark, wood-paneled walls. A hostess in a ruffled skirt approached Marilee, who asked to be seated at a table next to the window. Marilee didn't know why she expected Enoch to return to the bench, or what she would do if she saw him there—run across the street or simply spy on him from the dark asylum of the restaurant.

She studied the menu. In a few minutes, a waitress came by with chips and salsa. "Just one today?" she asked Marilee.

"Just me. Is it okay if I order now?"

"Sure enough," said the waitress, pulling out her pen and pad. She was a middle-aged Chicana who wore stretch pants, a white blouse, and a coin apron around her waist. Her absence of any Spanish accent led Marilee to conclude the woman had spent her whole life in Rocket City.

Marilee ordered the lunch special because it was cheap: a beef enchilada and a stuffed sopaipilla for three twenty-five. She ordered iced tea because in the Southwest, restaurants will refill your glass for free. Enoch had informed her of this fact at the Hobo restaurant in Casa Grande. She thought about Enoch, how he had appeared to shovel his food into his mouth because his head had been not much higher than the table.

Marilee dipped a chip into her salsa and stared out the window. A man in brown pants and a work shirt sat down on the green bench. He pulled a pack of cigarettes from his pocket, flipped one into his mouth, lit it, and watched traffic go by.

"Expecting someone?" asked the man at the table next to Marilee. She'd hardly noticed him behind his open front section of the *Alamogordo Daily News*. He sat with his back to the window, facing her. For as long as Marilee could remember, she'd felt awkward sitting next to strangers in restaurants. Still, at first impression he seemed pleasant enough.

"No, I'm alone today," she said.

"Alcie Britton," said the man, extending his hand. "Obstetrics and gynecology."

"Marilee Levitay." She grasped his fingers lightly. Doctors made her hands sweat; gynecologists made her sweat all over.

"You look familiar. Have I seen you in here before?" His face looked slightly off-center, as if half of it were asleep.

"No," said Marilee.

"At the clinic, then?"

"No, sorry." She could imagine what he was thinking. "I'm new in town. I just arrived this morning."

"Really?" said Dr. Britton, folding his newspaper and placing it beside his glass of beer. He looked about fifty, with thinning brown hair swept up over his bald spot. He pulled a pack of cigarettes from his breast pocket, shook one out, and offered it to Marilee.

"No thanks," she said.

Dr. Britton returned his pack to his pocket without taking one for himself, a gesture Marilee found unusually considerate. "I've tried to quit," he said, laughing out one side of his mouth. "It's embarrassing when your patients lecture you, which is, of course, what I should be doing to them. But I just can't seem to shake it. It's harder than it looks."

"I quit when I was twenty-two. I thought it might be causing my migraines."

"How long have you had migraines?"

"Since I was twelve."

"Did quitting help?"

"No. But it was still good I quit."

"How'd you do it, if you don't mind my asking? Cold turkey, or did you taper off?"

"Cold turkey. With rubber bands."

He raised one eyebrow.

"Next best thing to electric shocks. You put a rubber band around your wrist and give yourself a good thwap every time you want a cigarette. You'll be into whips and chains in no time."

She couldn't believe she had said that. Dr. Britton looked vaguely amused; Enoch, she thought, would have laughed out loud.

"So, where are you from?" he asked, scooping salsa onto a chip. His gold elastic watchband cut into the flesh around his wrist like a tourniquet, causing the veins in his hand to bulge.

"L.A."

"Where in L.A.?"

"Sherman Oaks. Out in the Valley. Do you know L.A.?" She didn't know why she was making small talk with this stranger except, perhaps, that it made sitting next to him less awkward.

The waitress brought Dr. Britton's order: huevos rancheros with a side of guacamole. "Another Dos Equis?" she asked him.

"No, I'm fine, thanks."

"Yours'll be right up," she said to Marilee, her coin apron jingling as she moved.

"I did my residency at UCLA, back in the sixties," said Dr. Britton. "Rented a house up Glen Canyon and hitched a ride down to Sunset each morning. Nice two-bedroom with a view for three-twenty a month. Guess it would cost a fortune now."

"I went to UCLA," said Marilee. "Got my bachelor's in art."

"So, what brings you to these parts?" he asked, taking a bite of his huevos rancheros. "Art?" Egg yolk dripped off his fork and onto his lap like some primordial jelly. "Whoops," he said, dabbing at it with his napkin. "Excuse me."

Marilee preferred not to launch into her history with Larry. She would much rather tell him about Enoch, but how could she admit to this stranger that she'd picked up a hitchhiking dwarf? "I came here to get married," she said flatly.

"Really?" Dr. Britton's face brightened. "So, who's the lucky fellow?"

Marilee twisted her napkin and glanced out the window. The lime-green bench was once again empty. "Look, have you seen a dwarf this morning? He'd be right here in this area. He's on crutches. You can't miss him."

"A dwarf?" Dr. Britton put down his fork and stopped chewing. "You're marrying a dwarf?"

"Oh, no. No, of course not. He's just someone that I met. When I got here. And I wondered if you'd seen him, that's all. Because he forgot something. He left something with me, and I just wanted him to have it back. So I thought that maybe you might have seen him, that's all, being that he's . . ."

"A dwarf." The doctor leaned back in his chair and smiled out of the corner of his mouth. "I'm afraid I haven't seen any dwarfs today."

"I know it sounds strange," she continued. "I mean, it's not every day one meets a dwarf. At least not for me. In fact, I've never met one before. But I guess you see them all the time, being a doctor and everything." She hoped the waitress would hurry with her order.

"Not at all," said Dr. Britton, returning to his enchilada. "I delivered one once, but she died when she was three."

"She?"

"Yes. Does that surprise you?"

"Not really," she lied. For some reason, Marilee had always thought of dwarfs as male, which, now that she thought about it, made no sense genetically.

The waitress appeared with her lunch special, which she set in front of Marilee with a warning that it was hot. She handed the doctor a basket of hot sopaipillas and his check.

"Thank you, Maria," he said.

"This looks good," said Marilee, grateful for the opportunity to change the subject.

"So, if you're not marrying the dwarf," he continued, "then who are you marrying?"

"It's a long story. Sort of complicated."

"Ah, a woman of mystery," said Alcie Britton. "I do like a woman of mystery." He reached for a sopaipilla, bit off the corner of it with the side of his mouth that wasn't slack, and poured honey into its center.

Bell's Palsy. That's what he had, Bell's Palsy—a temporary condition in which one side of the face droops as though its nerves had been severed. She'd read about it in *Health* magazine. Dr. Britton's must be a mild case, perhaps already in remission. "Are you married?" she asked, then wondered whether he would misinterpret her question.

"Twice," he said. "You know how it is in small towns. Well, maybe you don't. Anyway, the first wife gets everything, the second wife bitches and moans. The whole town has an opinion about it—who did what to whom, and so forth. Well, I don't mean that as bad as it sounds." He wiped his mouth with his napkin and took another bite of sopaipilla. "It's just that in small towns, what you do with your private life is everybody's business. It was harder on Lucie—she's my ex. The woman always gets thrown the blame."

"That happens everywhere, not just in small towns," said Marilee.

Dr. Britton smiled warmly and finished off the last of his beer. "I'm sure it does," he said. "But small towns probably make it all the more insufferable. Anyway, that was years ago. There's new people to talk about now."

"Do you and your new wife have children?" she asked, although she didn't care at all whether Dr. Alcie Britton, OB/GYN and resident sociologist, had children, or pets, or a house with a three-car garage, or anything else she questioned him about in an effort to fill the gap that yawned between them like a desert arroyo. She preferred to let him do the talking, a task he seemed happy to perform. Her enchilada was soggy, and her sopaipilla was stuffed with a meat she could not identify, but she ate hungrily, sneaking occasional glances at the bench outside the window.

"Well, back to the salt mine," said Dr. Britton, as soon as he had finished his story of little Toby's visit to Sandia Peak. When he pushed his chair back and stood up, Marilee saw what she could not have known while he was sitting down: Alcie Britton was short. Painfully short, perhaps five foot two at the tallest. Marilee tried to conceal having noticed.

"Good luck with your wedding," he said, extending his hand. "It was nice sharing lunch with you. I do hope I see you again."

"Thanks. You too," she said, remaining seated. He had a firm grip on her hand and gave no indication that her release was imminent.

"And I hope you find your little person."

Marilee smiled. Enoch, she was quite certain, would never have referred to himself as a little person.

"Come visit the clinic," said Dr. Britton, finally releasing her. Marilee assured him that she would, although she had no intention of ever setting foot inside a clinic where this man, who was now someone she *knew*, would poke cold metal instruments into her vagina.

Knowing that it might be some time before her next meal, Marilee ate the rest of her chips. She waited for Maria to bring her her check, but the waitress was nowhere to be seen. Marilee stared out the window at the empty lime-green bench on New York Avenue. Enoch had not returned.

Where was he? Walking around town? Hitching a ride somewhere out on the highway? In the back of a pickup on his way to Amarillo? She left the table to go visit the ladies' room, a dark cubicle that contained no toilet paper and smelled like bubblegum. When she returned, she discovered her table had been cleared.

Marilee stood in front of the cash register and waited to be noticed. There was no sign of the cashier and only a few patrons left in the dining room. Busboys cleared dishes and wiped down tables, smacking dishrags across taut vinyl seats. Marilee grew increasingly impatient. A busboy brushed past her on his way into the kitchen, a tub full of dirty dishes up under one arm. "Excuse me," she said to him. "Could you find somebody to ring up my bill?"

The busboy disappeared into the kitchen. Moments later, Maria appeared through the same door. She looked puzzled and not at all apologetic, as Marilee would have expected. When Marilee asked for her check, the waitress informed her that her meal had already been paid for by Dr. Alcie Britton, the mayor of Alamogordo.

■

By now, it was two thirty. Since it was still too early for Larry to return home, Marilee decided to drive around town to get a feel for the place. First, she traveled the circumference of the town clockwise, up Indian Wells Road, out Scenic Drive, down First Street, then back along White Sands Boulevard. Next, she meandered through residential neighborhoods and up into the business district along Tenth Street. She drove past the rodeo grounds, the high school, the local cemetery, Alameda Park, and Champion Memorial Hospital, where, presumably, Dr. Alcie Britton delivered babies when he wasn't busy being the mayor. She traveled north to the fairgrounds, then out again to White Sands Mall. She drove south, to the poorer section of town, where people lived in trailers on dirt roads in the flight path of the airport. In the end, she felt she had seen all there was to see of Rocket City.

It all looked bleak. Gray. Depressing. She wondered how she'd ever adapt to this strange outpost where businessmen dressed like cowboys and warheads stood as shrines. L.A. had diversity in its landscape and in its people. But Alamogordo all looked the same. Concrete boiled up from colorless soil, merged with gray-brown desert, dissolved into endless sky. The townsfolk, a seemingly indistinguishable lot, emerged in low relief against a featureless background. Marilee wondered how she would blend in here, with her tall stature, red hair, and West Coast accent.

She returned to the Mescalero Arms. Perhaps because it was Larry's building, or perhaps because the architecture reminded her of home, she felt safe in its proximity. She drove beyond his apartment, made a U-turn at the intersection, and parked across the street. There, in the shelter of a full mesquite, she waited for Larry to come home.

She waited a long time. Hot, dry air filled the car; Marilee hoped she wouldn't look wilted by the time Larry arrived home from work. She studied her face in the rearview mirror. Dark circles rimmed her eyes, and her freckles seemed blotchier than usual. She switched on her car's radio before applying powder to her forehead, chin, and the small bump on the bridge of her nose. A rock station played "MacArthur Park," one of Larry's all-time favorites. In the car, he would always pump up the volume and sing along with Richard Harris, some nonsense about leaving cakes out in the rain. Marilee turned it off, curled up in her front seat, and promptly fell asleep.

At four forty-seven, she was awakened by the sound of somebody's loud muffler. She peeked over her headrest and her heartbeat quickened. It was Larry at the wheel of a blue Mustang. When had he bought *this* car? Larry turned into his driveway and parked on his front lawn, a spot he never would have chosen in L.A. He stepped out of the Mustang wearing a pair of tan slacks and a blue striped shirt. He popped open his trunk, lifted three grocery sacks out of it, then nudged it shut with his elbow. At the front door, he balanced the bags on one knee and inserted his key in the lock.

The door swung open. He left it ajar, affording Marilee a view of his apartment's kitchen and hallway. She watched him as he played back the messages on his answering machine, always the first thing he did upon returning home. She could almost hear his lame message on the recorder: "Hello, you've reached the home of Larry Johnston. You may embarrass yourself after the beep." Larry pushed buttons and jotted notes next to his telephone. She wondered if any of his calls were from women.

Marilee deliberated getting out of the car. Larry's open front door bothered her; she did not want him to catch sight of her as she approached his house. Rather, she wanted him to answer his door and discover her standing on the other side of his threshold. That was how she had planned it: He would open his door, see her standing on his doorstep, and take her into his arms.

Content to wait for just the right moment, Marilee studied her boyfriend from the safety of a car he would not recognize. She watched as he disappeared down his hallway and, minutes later, emerged wearing blue shorts and a green polo shirt. Moving around the shadowy interior of his kitchen, he unpacked bags and loaded groceries into his refrigerator, his gait familiar the way he lumbered when he walked. He disappeared from view, and a moment later his front curtains drew apart. Larry opened his windows; half of them appeared to stick. He'd have to get an air conditioner if he wanted her to live here.

With his drapes open now, Marilee was able to view the entirety of Larry's living room. It was smaller than their one in L.A. but immaculate as ever. As before, he'd fashioned bookshelves out of bricks and boards, and a coffee table out of egg crates. His desk faced the front window. A Navaho-print couch stood against the side wall; above it hung Larry's favorite painting, an oil rendering of an old Indian. Marilee found the work embarrassing. In L.A., she'd made him store it in their closet, a trade-off for his being allowed to leave his moronic message on their answering machine.

Larry walked outside and ducked into a space under the stairwell, emerging a moment later with his mail. Back inside, he tossed it on his kitchen counter before folding his empty grocery sacks. Marilee studied his every move. It was clear he had no intention of closing his front door.

Once again, Marilee scrutinized herself in her rearview mirror. Her face looked worse than before, powder and sweat having congealed during sleep into an oily lamina. She applied more powder, then, disgusted with the result, wiped the whole mess off with a balled-up Kleenex she ferreted from the bottom of her purse. She ran a brush through the matted hair at the base of her neck. She studied her eyes. Broken capillaries variegated the whites, listless and yellow in contrast to the green of her irises. Her eyebrows had grown stubble and her eyelashes stuck together in black, gooey clumps. Larry would take one look at her and send her straight back to California.

What *would* he do when he saw her? Would he want to talk? To catch up on the seven months they'd spent apart? Would he fix her a romantic dinner at home, or take her out to a little restaurant where they'd order Châteaubriand and a bottle of Jordan Cabernet? Or would he kiss her and take her into his arms? Carry her off to his bedroom, lay her gently on his bed and caress her all night, the way he used to, years ago, when they first started making love?

Marilee stepped outside her car. It felt good to stand up, good to throw back her shoulders, stretch her legs, lift her hair off her damp neck, let the breeze cool her skin. She tucked her blouse into her shorts, the way she knew Larry liked it, took a deep breath, crossed the street, and headed toward his open door. Her underarms felt clammy. She held her arms out, away from her sides, hoping her armpits would dry in the fifteen seconds it would take to reach his doorstep. But just as she started to cut across his lawn, an orange Camaro roared down the street, pulled into Larry's driveway, and parked on the grass beside his Mustang. Marilee shifted her direction and walked straight past Larry's apartment. Timing had never been her forte.

With her head high, Marilee hurried to the end of the block as though she were headed toward some matter of importance. Glancing over her shoulder, she saw a man about thirty step out of the Camaro and bound into Larry's apartment. Marilee turned the corner and debated what to do.

The neighborhood was pleasantly middle class. Cats lolled on front porches, licking their coats in the merciless afternoon heat. Children ran through sprinklers and squirted each other with garden hoses. Old men in suspenders sat in folding chairs on porches, sipping cold drinks out of orange-frosted glasses, watching traffic go by. They nodded to Marilee.

She continued around the block, taking in the sounds and smells of late afternoon in Rocket City. The peppery scent of fried chicken from a white cottage with a green roof. From a brick house, the velvety aroma of chocolate cake. Somebody's backyard barbecue. The sweet, earthy smell of freshly cut grass. She heard pots banging against stoves, rotisseries turning, egg beaters whirring, fat popping in frying pans. She listened to the sounds of cars pulling into driveways, screen doors slapping, televisions airing the evening news, field crickets tuning their wings. Everywhere, she heard the chorus of children. It was Norman Rockwell with mesquite. Marilee could see herself fitting in here, getting to know the neighbors, making friends with the local children, setting cookies out for the paper boy on Christmas Eve.

Rounding the corner of Tomahawk Trail, she continued toward Larry's apartment. Midblock, she came to a halt. *Five* cars now sat parked in front of Larry's duplex. In addition to his Mustang and the orange Camaro, she saw a white truck, a VW bus, and a yellow diesel Rabbit. Larry was having a party; Marilee returned to the sanctuary of her Dart.

Pained, she watched as more guests arrived. A man and a woman in a maroon Honda. Two guys in a Chevy. A woman alone in a car Marilee couldn't identify—something foreign, red, and sporty. Was this Larry's new girlfriend? Had he replaced her so soon? His letters had mentioned nothing about a new girlfriend, but then, Marilee would not have expected them to. The woman fussed with her hair in her rearview mirror before stepping out of her car. She had long legs, chestnut hair, and the tiniest butt Marilee had seen on any female beyond the age of ten. She strode straight into Larry's living room and into the arms of the owner of the Camaro, who kissed her on the mouth and squeezed what little he could grab of her scrawny bottom. Marilee's heart rate subsided.

More cars arrived, blocking the driveway and spilling out into the street. More people crowded into Larry's apartment. They brought pretzels, chips, cookies, ice cream, and baking dishes covered in foil. They carried wine, Cokes, coolers, and six-packs of Bud and Coors and Miller Lite. Music came on: James Taylor, the high priest of wimp rock. She thought she heard Larry singing.

Marilee sat in her Dart. She knew she could never walk into that room full of strangers who would certainly think she was crazy, showing up from California completely out of the blue. Larry would be embarrassed.

His guests would leave, and he'd be angry with her. She blinked hard to fight back tears. A silver van with its stereo blaring "Stairway to Heaven" pulled into the parking space behind her. It was time to go, but where?

Marilee started her engine, slammed her foot hard on the accelerator, and sped off down Tomahawk Trail. The Dart squeaked and groaned, bouncing on its coil springs. A woman pushing a baby stroller motioned for her to slow down, but Marilee flipped her off and drove faster still. What did she care? What did anything matter? And who the fuck gives a party on a Tuesday afternoon?

■

In the glow of evening, Rocket City looked even more depressing than it had earlier that day. Shops had closed for the night, their awnings rolled up, window blinds drawn closed. Traffic through the center of town had thickened. A late-afternoon breeze brought relief from the heat but also kicked up dust, which, when mingled with low-angle sunlight, cast an orange-gray pall over the city.

Marilee drove east to the foothills, then clear back to White Sands Boulevard. She parked in front of Alameda Park, a narrow stretch of grass and trees she'd passed several times earlier that day. The park had a zoo, an attraction she would have investigated earlier had it not been so hot. Now, she walked the length of it, studying the animals in their cages. She saw porcupines, great horned owls, and Mexican gray wolves. Pheasants, falcons, roadrunners, and hawks. Bears, lions, monkeys, and baboons. Emus, ostriches, kangaroos, and deer. She walked from the zoo's south end to its north, then back again, stopping at each cage, searching for answers. There were none. Just bored-looking creatures staring back at her, eyes hungry, faces expressionless as the bars that kept them caged.

At the southernmost end of the zoo, Marilee came upon a picnic ground. Men in plaid cotton shirts and denim jeans sucked stubs of cigarettes and tended barbecue pits while their women watched the children and set picnic tables for dinner. The women laid out condiments on red-and-white-checked tablecloths, set out piles of plastic silverware and paper plates; platters of onions, lettuce, tomatoes, and cheese; jars of

pickles and packages of buns; olives in Tupperware tubs. Marilee smelled
hot dogs charring on grills and the smoky aroma of chicken fat dripping
onto burning coals. She smelled the animals, too: the dirt-like scent of
the lions and black bears; the fetid wafts from the birds and monkeys.
She was hungry now, and the peculiar admixture of smells made her
stomach rumble.

She picked a spot some distance from the others and sat on a knoll facing the toddlers' jungle gym. She watched as children rolled and tumbled
in the sand, laughing, squealing, throwing handfuls of grass onto a yellow
metal turtle. Children, brown and white, with young mothers who wore
halter tops and smoked Marlboro cigarettes. Toddlers with jam on their
faces and soggy diapers hanging heavy around their knees. She observed
the children as they ran to and from their mothers' arms—a moment of
courage, a moment of defeat—bravado's ebb and flow, which, unbe-
knownst to them, would carry them through a lifetime.

When she watched the children, her tears came. With her head on her
knees, Marilee wept into her arms. She wept because she was tired and
hungry and feeling half ill. Because she'd wanted to surprise Larry but
had lacked the courage to carry through. Because she'd left the city
where she was born—her friends, her job, her only parent. Because she
knew, now, she could not go back. She wept because her back hurt. Because her money was running low. Because she'd driven for two days on a
few hours' sleep only to end up in some lousy park in front of a cage of
turkey vultures, sobbing like a fool into the space between her knees. She
cried for a long time, letting her tears rain down upon the dry grass. Her
chest heaved and her nose ran; she wished she had brought more Kleenex.

When she was done crying, Marilee pulled her shirttail out of her
shorts and used it to blow her nose. She wiped away her tears, smearing
mascara down her cheeks with the heel of her palm. Inhaling deeply, she
let the air run out of her lungs, slowly, steadily, as if to convince herself
she was still in control of some small part of her being. She glanced up at
the children climbing on the wooden structure. They were a multicolored blur. Marilee blinked and rubbed her eyes, swollen and scratchy
from crying, but still the world looked shapeless, odd, devoid of form
and boundary.

Once again, sadness overcame her. This time, Marilee simply turned away from the children, back toward the animals, who would understand her pain. A child stood at the corner of the bear cage, regarding her with benign interest as she sniffled and heaved and snorted into her shirt-sleeve. Marilee waved him away, hoping he would join the others and leave her to her misery. But the child stood firm, an eight- or nine-year-old munching something out of a bag. She wiped her eyes and squinted to bring his image into focus.

"You look like shit," he said. "Have a cheese ball."

It was Enoch.

CAT LIPS

The Gerson claim. Six high school boys crammed into a '65 VW, wearing nothing from the waist down. Mooning old ladies on Wilshire Boulevard; hanging their stuff out the window on Sunset. Shorts, jeans, and shoes tucked up under their seats, they collide with a Bentley full of television producers and their girlfriends during rush hour. Sunset and Doheny. Half-naked bodies and twisted metal. Blood, glass, and jockey shorts. Cussing executives. Hysterical girlfriends.

It would have been funnier had no one died. Three of the high school boys did. Two of them escaped with cuts and bruises, but the driver, Lenny Gerson, was impaled on his stick shift and instantly paralyzed in that half of his body that had not been clothed. One of the television producers received a nasty case of whiplash.

The parents of the dead boys filed a wrongful death suit against the Gersons and Goetschke Life and Casualty. Figman was assigned their claim. He visited Lenny Gerson in the hospital. The boy was as depressed as any seventeen-year-old paraplegic could conceivably be, and Figman had trouble getting him to talk. When he did talk, he broke down crying before Figman could extract any meaningful information. Then the nurse or one of Gerson's parents would ask Figman to leave, and he would have to come back the next day and try again.

Figman dreaded these visits. The boy lying in traction, dead from the waist down. The nurse changing his I.V. His mother feeding him tapioca while his father stared distractedly out the window. Figman asking the boy questions about weather conditions and cross traffic in the intersection. The boy confused, then in tears. His mother breaking down; his father holding his wife by the shoulders, pretending to be brave. Making stupid comments like at least their son was still alive. Telling them both they were lucky.

They were not lucky. Lenny Gerson would never walk, use a toilet, or give his parents grandchildren. The Gersons would lose in court. The jury's award would exceed their amount of liability coverage, and they would end up having to sell their furniture business to cover the remainder due. They would subsequently forfeit their house and life's savings to pay for their son's legal and medical bills. Mrs. Gerson would be forced to return to work after twenty-three years; Mr. Gerson would lose himself in alcohol. Their daughter, fifteen at the time of the accident, would never go to college.

Goetschke Life and Casualty would refuse to renew the family's auto insurance, citing claims history, for this had not been Lenny's first accident. It had been his third, each having involved increasingly larger quantities of alcohol. The judge would have no recourse but to revoke the boy's driver's license, an irony that would impel Lenny's mother, stoic through most of her son's trial, to rise up out of her seat and call the judge a motherfucker. The judge would not send Mrs. Gerson to jail.

In terms of its potential for human suffering, the Gerson claim had been Figman's worst. On the misery meter, it registered a ten. It was hard to blame the boy, lying motionless in his hospital bed, and harder still not to. Lenny Gerson was an asshole. Cocky and self-pitying, he'd tried to blame the accident on the driver of the Bentley, a version of the truth repeatedly denied by the accident's many witnesses and all five of the Bentley's survivors. He bullied his nurses. He bullied his parents. He tried to bully Figman, but Figman was not about to go away, or fetch his water four times in a single visit, or feel all that sorry for the boy once he'd figured out his game. He had no use for crybabies. Figman knew things happened for a reason. Life was school, and there were lessons to be learned. Assholes, more than any other people, needed to learn those lessons.

Lenny's parents, however, were not assholes, and here was where Figman ran into ideological trouble. Above all, AD&D required emotional distance. Yet it was hard to remain detached in the face of this couple's suffering, nearly impossible to see them daily and not be affected by their pain. The Gersons were nice people. They deserved their fate no more than they deserved a putz for a son, yet there was absolutely nothing Figman could do. His hands were tied. And while he understood that life wasn't fair, and that sometimes good people suffered while assholes got off scot-free (an inequity he attributed to some divine plan whose complexity was too staggering for the comprehension of mere mortals), he still had trouble reconciling this couple's pain. The Gerson claim bothered Figman as no other claim had ever bothered him. Following his own accident, which he'd survived unscathed and after which he'd been dubbed a miracle, he turned the Gerson file over to Litvak.

Figman was lying in his bed five miles south of Artesia, reminiscing about the Gerson claim, when his thoughts turned to Oma's teeth. Why hadn't she had them fixed? It was a simple matter of enamel bonding. (The Yablonski claim.) Figman thought it a shame such an otherwise stunning woman should go through life marred by so fixable an imperfection. He wondered if she'd be receptive to the suggestion she see a dentist.

Figman caught himself. He was not supposed to be thinking about Oma's teeth, or any other part of her anatomy. He was supposed to be painting. He jumped up out of bed and took his morning shower.

Skipping breakfast, Figman sat down in front of his blue-undercoated canvas. It had dried nicely. He consulted his book for the next step in the painting process. The book said he was to squeeze colors onto his palette and begin the outline of his subject. He peered across the highway at the dilapidated Rodriguez house. It looked just as it had the day before, and Figman congratulated himself on having chosen so immutable a subject. He applied dollops of oils in a semicircle around the thumbhole of his palette and selected a brush with which to begin.

Figman studied the Rodriguez house for composition. This is it, he thought, filling his brush with titanium white: the very moment he would embark upon the road to fame. With a decisive stroke, he sketched in the house's southernmost wall. He peered again across the highway. The brushstroke he'd made was too high on his canvas; he would have to remove it and start over.

Figman took a rag and wiped at the mark he had made. It left a white smear on his canvas. He opened his book to the index and looked up "erasure," but there was no such listing. Then he remembered what he was to do. He cleaned his brush, dipped it in Thalo blue, and painted over the white smear.

Again, he attempted the house's south-facing wall. This time he placed it too far left on his canvas. He painted it out and tried once more. His third wall was crooked. On his fourth attempt, Figman finally achieved a south-facing wall he felt he could live with, but by this time he'd grown hungry.

Figman fixed himself an enormous breakfast of eggs, toast, and sausages; took his daily dose of aloe; then cleaned up all his dishes. His sink still held the remnants of his previous night's dinner. Not wanting to risk clogging his disposal, he dug his steak out from under his okra and discarded it in the trashcan on his back porch.

Verdie didn't appear to be up yet, which was unusual, as she'd proven an early riser. Her car was in the driveway, and her curtains were closed. As it was already past ten o'clock, Figman worried that she might not be well. Aside from Poe Titus, she'd had no other visitors.

Figman returned to his kitchen and scoured his sink. With his breakfast dishes washed and neatly stacked, he looked around the house for any chores that might need his attention. The place felt dusty. Surely it was not a good idea to paint in a dusty house; one sneeze and he'd contaminate his oils. He dampened a rag and set about the business of dusting.

By two thirty, Figman had dusted. He had also vacuumed, cleaned his bathroom, mopped and waxed his floors, laundered his sheets, and washed all his windows. Occasionally, he'd glanced across his backyard to check for signs of activity. Verdie had neither emerged from her trailer nor opened her curtains, and by the end of his cleaning Figman had come to the conclusion she was either dead drunk or dead. Hoping to obtain a peek inside, he ventured over to her trailer. He walked its circumference, but her curtains were all closed too tightly to see in. He would wait a day and, if he still hadn't seen her, call the police.

At three o'clock, Figman returned to his easel. When he picked up his palette, he realized he'd forgotten to clean his brush and cover his paints.

He would have to start over, scraping the old oils from his palette, reapplying new, rinsing out his brush with turpentine. By four twenty, having completed his setup, Figman was ready to resume his work.

The light had changed. The east-facing Rodriguez house looked entirely different in the afternoon. Its facade now stood in shadow, its white borders difficult to distinguish against the sun's low-angle glare. He would have to paint in the mornings or choose a different subject entirely.

Just then, Figman heard a crash out on his back porch. Had Verdie finally awakened and come staggering over to his place? He ran to his kitchen window; her trailer looked just as it had all day. Curious, he ventured outside. There, on his back porch, he discovered his trashcan overturned and Bobo's huge orange cat attacking his forsaken meat. The cat took one look at Figman and darted into the foundation crawlspace.

He would paint the cat! Here was a charming scene, regional and picaresque: the planks missing from the dilapidated porch, the gravel driveway with its yawning potholes, the rapscallion cat (a scurvy-looking thing) looting the dregs of his discarded dinner. He would need a camera, film, and some cat food as a lure.

Oma was at Lester's, her fingers working their miracle on her cash register keys. Figman bought lamb chops (for himself) and hamburger for the cat. He bought apples and a bag of peas. He also picked up a box of Grecian Formula, a purchase he debated making in front of Oma. But he was dying, he reminded himself, and had resolved not to waste his precious time on women; it didn't matter what she might think. He tossed the box into his basket and stepped into her checkout line. Dino stood behind her bagging groceries. "Hello," Figman said, ignoring him.

"Hi," she said back. She smiled with her lips together, unnaturally. She must smile like this, thought Figman, to conceal her broken teeth. "This be it today?" she asked.

"That's it," he said. "Unless you carry cameras."

"We have film," she said. "Aisle nine."

"I need a camera first. Know where I could buy one?"

"K-Mart," said Dino.

Figman turned his attention to the boxboy. "No, I'm looking for a really fine camera. A Canon EOS 1 or a Nikon F4. Know anywhere in town I can pick one up?"

"Shit," said Dino.

"Excuse me?" said Figman.

Oma glared at Dino, who pretended to ignore her. "I think you'll have to go to Roswell," she said. "Mack's Camera on Main Street."

"Thanks," said Figman. He resisted the urge to invite her along. He resisted the urge to punch Dino.

"How much is this, did you notice?" She held up Figman's box of Grecian Formula.

"No, I'm sorry I didn't."

"Dino, will you run and get a price on this?"

The boxboy looked at Figman and his lips curled. It was not quite a sneer, not entirely a smirk, but something disturbingly in between. A snirk, thought Figman. Dino swaggered off with Figman's Grecian Formula in hand.

"What's a nice-looking man like you doing buying that stuff anyway?" asked Oma.

Figman felt himself blush, an infrequent reaction that usually compounded itself most embarrassingly. Her question had caught him off guard. If she'd been serious, he would have thought her too shy to make so bold an overture; if she'd been toying with him, he would not have imagined her to be so cruel. He thought fast, relieved to find no other customers in line behind him. "Keeps little dipsticks like Dino from calling me Gramps," he said.

Oma laughed, an ambiguous laugh, eliciting in Figman a twinge of discontent. Perhaps it was the sight of her teeth. "So why do you want a camera?" she asked.

"For my experiments," he said. "Plant growth, remember."

"I remember," she said, almost seductively. Was she coming on to him? Could it be she found him attractive? He was almost forty—not ancient, but not young to a woman half his age. His hair was thinning, and though he was tall and boyishly lean, he had never considered himself handsome.

"Seven twenty-five," said Dino, brushing behind Figman through the checkout line.

Oma punched in the numbers and rang up the total. "Fourteen fifty-seven," she said. Figman handed her a five and a ten.

"You want this in a bag?" asked Dino with a snirk. He had already bagged Figman's produce and meat.

"No, I thought I'd just tape it to my forehead."

"Fuck you, man," said Dino.

"Look, what is it with you?" said Figman.

"Guess I don't like old farts trying to pick up on my sister."

"Knock it off," said Oma.

"Well shit, what would Dad have said?"

"You're not Dad."

"I'm your brother."

"So what?"

Dino stuffed the Grecian Formula into Figman's bag, pushed it toward Figman, and swaggered off to the deli.

"I'm sorry," said Oma. Her blue and violet eyes were rimmed with tears.

Figman thought he had never seen a face more beautiful. "I'll apologize," he said.

"For what?" Oma handed him his change, not bothering to count it out.

"For talking like that to your brother. He's just doing what brothers do," said Figman, an only child but not a stupid one.

"Whatever." A tear slipped down her cheek. She wiped it away and stared at the counter.

"Listen," said Figman, "I don't suppose you'd like to get some coffee?"

"I can't. I have to work until ten."

"At ten, then."

Oma hesitated, glancing in the direction of the deli. "I better not," she said. "But thanks."

"I'll catch Dino next time," said Figman. "Give him time to cool."

Oma smiled at him, her lips parting softly to reveal her dreadful teeth. Figman noticed the quivering blob gathering dimension just above her eye that was blue.

■

His headache lasted a full ten hours. It was as painful as two headaches and just as unrelenting. Once released from its tyranny, he slept a full twelve hours, not waking until afternoon.

The day was shot. By nature, Figman's headaches left him disoriented and weak. He spent the afternoon in bed reading *Men's Health;* at sundown, he wandered into his living room. Figman looked at his painting. He had a blue canvas with a single white line—all he'd depicted of the Rodriguez house. All he had to show for half a week's work. He felt disgusted with himself. Though hungry, he crawled back into bed and fell asleep.

The next day it rained. Neither able to paint the Rodriguez house nor entice Bobo's cat, he drove to Roswell and bought a Minolta 7xi, all the camera that prudence would allow. He brought it home and tinkered with it, taking several snapshots of Verdie's horrible trailer. Though he'd yet to see his landlady, her wide-open curtains lent him reasonable assurance that she was still alive.

After lunch, Figman drove to Bulldog Superette and bought several days' worth of groceries. Returning home, he stopped at his roadside mailbox. He'd forgotten about his mail. So had Verdie, by the looks of things. He found their box crammed with letters, junk fliers, and a small package. He sorted through the lot of it, separating his mail from hers, weeding out the fliers and packets of store coupons. He'd received the usual supermarket ads, a Valentine's promotion from Love Bud Floral, and some sporting catalog forwarded by his mother. Verdie had received the same advertisements, plus two bills, a letter from the I.R.S., a legal-sized envelope from an attorney in Roswell, and a package from a mortuary in Santa Fe. There was trouble in her mailbox.

■

The next day it was raining still. Figman spent the morning sketching cats from memory. When the mail came early, he hurried out to retrieve it. He'd received nothing that day, but Verdie had received a letter from a collection agency in Albuquerque. It sat atop yesterday's stack of mail, which he'd left for her in their mailbox. To his surprise, Figman found himself worrying about Verdie. Coarse, hard drinking, and eccentric, she was not the type of person he'd ever choose to spend time with. Still, there was something about her he respected. Perhaps it was grit.

Figman stuffed her letters up under his jacket and jogged to her trailer. Her curtains had stood open since early morning. He knocked on her door, and in a moment she opened it. She wore a pink bathrobe, her hair in curlers, and her usual pink-purple lipstick. Poe Titus sat at her kitchen table.

"Louis," she said. "Good to see you." Her figure didn't look half bad in terrycloth.

"I brought you your mail. I noticed you hadn't picked it up in a few days."

"Look Poe, it's Louis."

"Howdy," said Poe Titus.

"Hello," said Figman. He waved at the man, stupidly.

"Well, don't just stand there. Come on in out of the rain. I was just fixin' to make us some sandwiches. Spam and avocado. Want one?" She took a step backward into her kitchen. Her leg slipped out the opening of her bathrobe, a scrawny appendage with flesh sagging above the knee.

"I can't," said Figman. "I have an appointment."

This was, of course, a lie. He wanted nothing more than to talk to Verdie. Her mail hinted at problems, and Figman was curious to see if there might be something he could do. But mostly he was just lonely. Here he was, a thousand miles from home, out in the middle of some high-plains desert with no family, no girlfriend, no friend-friend even. He wanted someone to talk to. But not Poe Titus.

"Another time," said Figman, handing Verdie her package from the mortuary. "Sorry if it's a bit wet."

"Pfft," said Verdie. She took her letters and package and tossed it all on top of her dish rack.

"Well, bye," said Figman.

"See you around," said Verdie.

"So long," said Poe Titus.

Figman got in his Aion and drove to Lester's E-Z Mart. He found Dino bagging for both Gert and Lester Meany, a man he recognized from the picture on his advertisements. Oma was nowhere to be seen.

"Got a minute?" he said to the boxboy.

"I'm working," said Dino.

"Take a break," said Figman.

"Oh, do," said Gert. "That would be nice. We're not busy." She was sixtysomething and had watery blue eyes.

"Ten minutes," said Lester.

Dino glared at Figman, then walked out the market's front door. Figman followed him. Dino was big, and Figman was relieved to discover other people walking along the sidewalk.

"There's a place we can go," said Dino. "A warehouse. I've got a key."

"What about right here?" asked Figman. Cars splashed rainwater up onto the pavement.

"We'd get arrested," said Dino.

Suddenly, it made sense. "Look, Dino, I don't want to fight you. I came here to talk. I want to apologize."

Dino stopped in his tracks and stared back at him. Rain beat down on his face, an angry mesh of stubble and frown lines.

"First of all, let me introduce myself. Figman's the name." Figman extended his hand to the boxboy.

"Figman what?" said Dino, hands in his pockets.

"Louis Figman, but people call me just Figman. I came here today because I wanted to tell you that I'm sorry about the other day. For being sarcastic. I didn't mean any harm."

"So what are you driving at?"

Figman shifted on his feet. "Just that. It's an apology. What do you say we just forget about it and go on?"

Dino looked at him as though the very notion of forgiveness were beyond his comprehension. His lip curled. "I know what this is," he said, taking a step toward Figman. "This is a suck-up."

Figman shifted on his feet but stayed his ground. "I don't have any reason to suck up to you, Dino."

"This is a suck-up because you want to dick my sister." His eye slits narrowed. "Don't you, Lou?"

Figman couldn't deny the partial truth in what Dino was saying. "My name's Figman," he said. "People don't call me Lou."

"Well, you're not going to dick my sister, Lou. You're not even going to think about dicking my sister. 'Cause if you do . . ."

A meter maid pulled up to the curb, an angel.

"What, Dino? What are you going to do to me if I think about it? Tell me, Dino. I'd like to know."

Dino glared at him, the vein in his forehead bulging. "Don't push me and find out," he said, knocking past Figman and swaggering back into the store.

Figman was sure he had never met a kid so hostile. He reminded him of Gerson, a petulant bully in need of a little paralysis to knock out the half of his body that was making him such an asshole.

■

At last, Figman awoke to sunny skies. The Rodriguez house looked magnificent, as though lit by a glow from heaven. Bobo squatted in the side yard, digging, but by now Figman was more interested in painting the boy's cat. He placed a wad of hamburger out on his back porch, over-turned his trashcan to set the scene, and waited for the beast to appear. As if on cue, the creature materialized. Figman took it as an omen he was indeed destined to be an artist.

He took as many pictures of the cat as his ration of meat permitted, then drove the film to Roswell for one-hour processing. His photos came out splendidly; Figman could hardly wait to return home and begin his life's work.

He would paint in the abstract. This he'd decided after struggling to recreate the south-facing wall of the Rodriguez house. Compared to re-alism, abstraction would afford him greater artistic latitude. Stylistically more sophisticated, it would reduce his work time while placing him squarely on art history's continuum. He lived in abstract times; his art, he reasoned, should reflect his milieu.

Clipping his best cat snapshot to the top of his upright, Figman painted over the single white line that adorned his canvas. He started in on the trashcan, a sketchy thing once he'd finished it. Next, he focused on the porch—just an outline; he would come back to it later. Figman then turned his attention to the cat itself. Mixing colors on his palette, he studied the exact hue of the animal's fur.

He'd selected a photo in which his subject squarely faced the camera. The creature had its mouth open, with a chunk of hamburger dangling from its lips. Though the majority of his painting would be abstract, Figman had decided to portray the meat as realistically as possible, a single departure he hoped would lend an element of naturalism to his work.

All day Figman attempted to interpret Bobo's cat. Though pleased with the shape and color of the body, he struggled to capture its face. He had suggested the animal's ears, and its eyes and nose were progressing nicely. But even in the abstract, he had trouble suitably rendering the cat's gaping mouth.

In his photograph, the cat's top lip appeared to curl upward (much like Dino's), revealing half-eaten hamburger and several of its teeth. But each time Figman tried to delineate the lips, the results left him less than satisfied. He tried dozens of times, dabbing paint onto his canvas, then wiping it off with a rag and painting over it. Sometimes in the process, he'd smear some other feature he'd previously been pleased with. Then he'd have to go back and try to recreate what he'd previously mastered.

As the day wore on, Figman grew increasingly impatient. If only he'd taken art lessons as a child. Painting was like playing the piano, or dancing, or speaking a foreign language—much harder to learn as an adult. Figman set down his paintbrush and made himself a sandwich. He did his daily exercises, then dusted. Hadn't he just dusted his entire house? Still, dust was everywhere. It must seep in through the windows when the wind blew, which in February was often. There was dust on his furniture, dust on all his countertops, dust in the corners of his windowsills. The top of his refrigerator was black with the stuff. New Mexico seemed to be an ocean of dust.

As Figman rinsed out his dustcloth, he thought about his problem painting cat lips. Lips were line and color, just like anything else, but for some reason their execution had eluded him. He wondered whether he'd have trouble painting the lips of a woman. He thought of Oma's lips: so full, so sensual, so shiny with lipstick. The last time he'd seen her she'd worn orangish-red, a color that beautifully complemented her long auburn hair.

He was standing in his kitchen envisioning Oma's lips when Verdie drove up in her Impala. At first, Figman thought he saw Poe Titus in the front seat but soon discovered him to be a set of golf clubs. He watched as Verdie unloaded them, swinging the bag up over her shoulder and toting it into her trailer. He wondered whether the mail had come.

It had. He'd gotten a flier from Abo Thriftway and a letter from Litvak, forwarded by his mother. Verdie had received the flier from Abo Thriftway, a MasterCard bill, and a letter from the Cancer Fund of America. It was hand addressed, which Figman found troublesome; this was not your usual bulk solicitation.

He rapped lightly on her trailer door. After no response, he rapped again. He walked around to the far side of her trailer and heard water running. She was probably in the shower. Figman returned to her front steps and read his letter from Litvak:

Dear Figman,

Things are strange around here without you. People keep asking where you are and even your mother claims she doesn't know. That was hard for me to believe, so I sent her this letter hoping that she might forward it to you.

The reason I'm writing is to update you on the situation with your accident. Goetschke has denied the families' claim, as did Ford, Aion, and that janitorial service. Their lawyer (a woman—did I call that one?) has threatened to file suit if their demands aren't met by the tenth of this month. It's my understanding that you're to be named as a defendant, even if they can't find you. As you know, they could get a judgment in absentia, and you wouldn't have had a chance to defend yourself.

I guess what I'm trying to say is that you might think about letting your whereabouts be known, if only to protect yourself. Things like this have a way of catching up to you. They'll hire a private investigator and find you in no time, and that won't look very good.

Figman, I'm only telling you this as a friend. It's your life, and I don't want to butt in where I don't belong. But if I were you, I'd get a lawyer and start making some contact.

Enough of the fatherly advice. News: Sue in accounting had her baby, a boy she named Eli. (I don't understand this modern propensity for farm names.) Bill is dating Cheryl Messersmith. We had another earthquake—five-point-six and centered on some undiscovered fault in Glendale. Wherever you are, I hope you're on firm terra.

Please think about what I've said. If you choose to stay in hiding, it's best not to let me know where you are. I may have to testify.

Keep the faith, *Aaron*

P.S. Get yourself a woman attorney. Two can play that game.

Figman returned his letter to its envelope and gazed out across the highway. Bobo stooped in his side yard, digging. What was it with that kid? All day he just dug and filled, dug and filled. It was almost spooky, the intensity with which he focused on so meaningless an activity, shutting out the rest of the world as though he were on some divine mission that he alone understood. Bobo Rodriguez was starting to work his way under Figman's skin, this seven-year-old with his bucket, his spoon, and his cat with unpaintable lips. Figman knocked loudly on Verdie's door.

This time, she answered it. "Mercy Maude, Louis! What in heaven's name is it?" She wore her pink bathrobe; her hair was wrapped in a turban.

"I brought you your mail," said Figman. "I hope you don't mind."

"Lordy, I thought the house was on fire," she gasped, raising her arms to the sky like a Holy Roller. When she stepped back, her bathrobe split open a bit; Figman prayed she was wearing underwear. He handed over her envelopes and stepped up into her kitchen, not waiting for an invitation. Verdie's trailer looked and smelled as it had before except that there was no old cowboy at her table.

"Sounds like you could use a drink," she said.

Figman thought about it. "Sounds good."

"Scotch okay?"

He hated Scotch. As a teenager he'd gotten sick on the stuff. "Do you have something else?"

Verdie dug inside one of her two cabinets that still had doors. "I got some gin," she said. "I could mix it with a little soda."

"That sounds fine," he said, sitting in Titus's chair.

"I sure don't see much of you," said Verdie.

"I paint most of the day."

"You working for Elmer-Lloyd Cunningham? He's got that slaughter-house project out by Hagerman."

"No, actually, I paint in oils." Verdie cocked her head. Her face was beginning to take on a certain familiarity that Figman found appealing. "Art," he said. "You know, oil paintings."

"No shit?"

"Do you know much about art?"

"Hell," said Verdie. She handed him his drink and sat across from him at the table. "I don't know nothing about nothing. 'Ceptin' golf. You know golf?"

"No," said Figman. He sipped his drink. It tasted good, surprisingly.

"Then we're even," she said, laughing. Without lipstick, her lips reminded Figman of sundried tomatoes. He wondered if he'd have trouble painting them.

"There's something I've been meaning to ask you," he said.

"Shoot."

"You don't happen to know this woman who works down at Lester's? She's young and she has this . . . problem with her teeth."

"Oma?"

Figman heard her name pronounced for the first time. It sounded bovine. "Yeah, Oma," he said. "Do you know her?"

"Honey, everybody knows everybody in this town. I can remember the day she was born. Poor thing."

"Were there complications?"

"Not until the boys got a look at her."

"Ah," said Figman.

Verdie's eyes twinkled. "You interested in Oma?"

Figman shrugged.

"She's a sweet thing, but her luck ain't good, if you know what I mean."

"It doesn't matter. She won't go out with me. I've asked twice."

"Horsefeathers. Handsome young fellow like you?"

Figman felt himself blush for the second time in as many days. "Listen . . . I . . . Are you okay?" he asked.

"Me?"

"I couldn't help noticing some of the mail you've been getting. I.R.S., mortuaries, cancer societies—that sort of thing."

"Pfft," Verdie said, a sound Figman imagined was easy to make with protruding teeth. "You want another drink?" She held up her empty glass.

"No, I'm fine," he said. "I should be getting back to work."

"And I should be doing something with this hair." She pulled off her turban to reveal thin, wet locks in overpermed ringlets. Figman took it as his exit cue.

"Thanks for the drink," he said.

"You haven't finished it."

"That's all I care for. But it was good," he said as an afterthought.

"I ain't never left a drink unfinished," said Verdie, laughing.

Figman stepped over to her door. "Look, I hope I didn't offend you. With my last question, I mean. I didn't mean to pry."

"Pfft," said Verdie, running her fingers through her hair as if trying to shake out lice.

"It's just that I was concerned, you know."

"That's real sweet of you, Louis."

"And I'd want you to tell me if there was ever anything I could do."

"Oh, I would," she said.

"I mean anything. I'd want you to feel free—"

"Oh, hell," said Verdie. She was grinning, so he figured he hadn't really made her angry. Her gums showed and her hair was a snarl.

"Well, I guess I'll be going," said Figman. "I've got to go jump in the shower."

"Well, be careful," she said. "We're not insured."

■

NOT INSURED. The words rang in Figman's ears all the way back to his easel. He knew all too well the dangerous implications: fire, damage, theft, liability. Figman wondered whether they lived in a flood zone. He would have to figure out some way to take out an insurance policy, but not in his real name. The process could be tricky.

As for Verdie, he felt thwarted by her furtiveness. Still, he had to respect her privacy. Being a private person himself, he understood her need to establish boundaries. Indeed, he found admirable her reluctance to burden him with her day-to-day concerns. In many ways, Verdie Hooks was a pleasant diversion from the people with whom he was used to dealing. Still, he wished she had at least explained that package from the mortuary.

As for Litvak's letter, he realized he would have to be more careful in the future. Figman was not a man to run away from life's consequences. But he knew in his heart he'd done all he could to avoid the accident, a tragedy that certainly would have been exacerbated had his car not malfunctioned. Furthermore, he was dying of a brain tumor. From the severity of his last attack, the malignancy seemed to be growing. It was inconceivable that he spend what little time he had left mired in the slough of litigation.

Let them hire a private investigator! They'd have to find him first, and Figman was determined not to be found. His utilities were all in Verdie's name. He'd canceled his credit cards and now made each of his purchases in cash. His car was registered to his mother in California. Once he'd sold his house, he'd added his equity to her life's savings. She paid his insurance premiums and once a month sent him cash parcel post, an unusual procedure he explained as vital to his job's secrecy. He'd even used an alias to register at the Starlite Motel: William J. Forbes. It was an ordinary moniker, but strong.

Figman dabbed his brush to his palette. He'd been painting for the last twenty minutes, and his cat lips were coming along nicely. At last he was beginning to get the hang of them, refining their curl and fleshing out their three-dimensionality; perhaps all he'd needed was a drink and a little company.

He blended Indian red with burnt sienna, then added a trace of cerulean blue to the glop of paint on his palette. Carefully, he applied it to the space between the cat's two rows of teeth, hoping to portray (naturalistically) the visceral quality of the meat. He stood back to admire what he had achieved. The result was glorious; he'd captured brilliantly the very nuance of ground beef.

Figman got himself a Dos Equis and stood in his living room, savoring his work from every angle. He downed most of his beer, then returned to work on the cat's cheeks. He'd let his oils dry a bit before adding in the whiskers. When he had drawn in three of them, his elbow (quite by accident) knocked the upright, and his canvas holder's bobby-pin fastener sprang free. Figman's cat, eyes hungry, lips exquisitely curled, tumbled sideways off his easel and landed face down on his carpet.

DIRTY LAUNDRY

"And the mayor's a gynecologist." Marilee laughed and rolled down her window as she and Enoch headed north out of Alamogordo. It was cooler now that the sun was setting; with her air conditioner off, Marilee hoped they could make it all the way to Ruidoso without having to stop for gas.

They drove north to Tularosa, then headed east on Highway 70 up into the Mescalero Apache Reservation. The landscape looked strangely mythic in the blue-gray shadows of evening. The tall pines and meadows reminded Marilee of the California Sierras, where she and Larry had spent their last winter vacation.

She was happy to have Enoch back for a while, happy to see his awkward face smiling up at her from across the worn-out seat of her Dart. After recognizing him in the park with his bag of cheese balls, she'd realized she'd actually missed his company.

They were quiet for most of the drive to Ruidoso, a contented and mutual silence unlike the silence they had shared on their way to Rocket City. They took a room at the Tomahawk Lodge, a one-story colonial with pink columns and a painted frieze. Enoch waited in the car while Marilee registered. She signed in as Mr. and Mrs. M. Levitay and charged the room to her MasterCard. The man behind the counter handed her a key. "Number eighteen, to your right," he said. Marilee felt too exhausted to consider the ramifications of sharing a motel room with a dwarf.

Room eighteen was artless and overheated, with a linoleum floor and cinder-block walls. The double bed (the only size available) was draped with an orange bedspread that looked and smelled as though it once had been the nesting place of a small but incontinent dog. Marilee stripped the bed of its spread and blanket, then lay on her back while Enoch opened the window. With her body sprawled on top of the sheets and a cool breeze blowing in the scent of pine, Marilee fell into a deep sleep from which she did not awaken until morning.

When she opened her eyes at a quarter till eight, Enoch was nowhere to be found. She sat upright, taking in her spartan surroundings: bare walls, minimal furnishings. She listened to the sound of cars on the road, birds singing, a pair of voices passing by her window. Perhaps Enoch had risen early and headed out for a morning paper. Then again, perhaps he'd left her for good, having only needed a ride to the next town.

The room was chilly. Marilee leaned over the foot of the bed to reach for the blanket on the floor; only then did she discover Enoch wrapped inside it. She did not disturb him. Kicking her feet under the top sheet, she contemplated the coming week with Enoch.

Seven days. That was all the time she had given herself to figure out what she wanted, an amount of time dictated as much by her dwindling funds as by her desire to see Larry. On the drive to Tularosa, she'd informed Enoch of her intentions as best she understood them: to get some sleep, clear her mind, and feel rested by the time she returned to Alamogordo.

Enoch suggested they drive on to Ruidoso. Ruidoso, he said, was in the mountains. It had lakes, trails, and a racetrack open in summer. There was a lot to do there: art shows, craft fairs, golf courses, restaurants, horseback riding, fishing, camping, and hiking. There were motel pools to swim in at night. The two of them could spend the week in Ruidoso or, if they got restless, move on to another city.

She welcomed having company for the week. Enoch, she suspected, would give her space to think and possibly lend her a sympathetic ear. At the very least he would be entertaining. Larry, she hoped, would understand her brief excursion, as it would all be quite proper. She wanted Larry to like Enoch, so that Enoch could visit them whenever he passed through Rocket City.

She peeked again over the foot of the bed. Enoch looked childlike with his eyes closed. She was liking his face more and more: the cleft in his chin, his curled dark lashes, his cheeks covered with stubble.

She tiptoed from the bed, retrieved her makeup from her suitcase, and made her way into the bathroom. After washing her hair as best she could under the showerhead's trickle, she blotted it with a towel and combed out its tangles. She took her time plucking her eyebrows and applying fresh makeup. When she emerged from the bathroom clutching a towel around her middle, Enoch had awakened.

"Good morning," he said. He sat on the edge of the bed with the blanket wrapped around him, reading an issue of *Rolling Stone*.

"Good morning," said Marilee, tightening her grip on the towel. "I left my clothes out here. I thought you'd still be sleeping."

"I'm up."

"Yes. I see."

"Sleep well?" He returned to his magazine.

"Fine," she said, crossing to her open suitcase on the dresser. With one hand, she wrested free her jeans, bra, underwear, and a clean blouse. "And you?"

"Like a stiff on a sack of kittens." Enoch slid off the bed and hobbled into the bathroom. He was stark naked.

■

They ate breakfast at the Whispering Pines' buffet. Marilee piled her plate high with fried eggs, sausage, biscuits and gravy, and hash browns, then went back for three strips of bacon, a waffle, and a bowl of sliced pineapple. She'd eaten nothing but cheese balls since her lunch with the mayor of Rocket City.

"So, what should we do today?" she asked, hoping Enoch would suggest nothing that required energy. It was right before her period, and she felt like a lump.

"Let's go to the races. They have the best chili you'll ever eat."

The races sounded like a good idea. She could sit. "Did you get right to sleep last night?" she asked, downing the last of her orange juice.

"Went for a walk. Got some dinner. Came back. Watched you sleep."

"Watched me sleep?"

"Nothing on TV."

Marilee felt the blood rush to her face as she stared down at her half-eaten waffle. Syrup ran from one toasted coffer to the next, like water in an ice tray searching for equilibrium. "I don't like being watched," she said. "It makes me nervous."

"How could you be nervous? You were sleeping."

"That doesn't matter."

"Why?"

"I don't know, it just doesn't." She pushed her plate toward the center of the table and stared out the window. "I guess I'm kind of shy about some things."

"You weren't shy the other night. In the pool," he added, as if she needed to be reminded.

Marilee reached for the check on the table, perhaps a bit too aggressively.

"I'll get it," said Enoch. His fingers brushed hers as he lifted the slip of paper from her hand and set it on the table in front of him.

"Then I'll get the tip," she said, rooting for change in her purse, a testament to her life's current disorder. By nature, Marilee was organized, preferring all things be in their rightful place. At home, she had even sectioned and labeled her sock drawers: knee-highs separated from socks, separated from pantyhose, separated from nylons. Sheers separated from regulars. Sandal feet separated from demi-toes. Her fingers found a dollar fifty.

"Keep your quarters," said Enoch. "We'll need them for laundry."

Enoch unrolled his wallet from his right sock and tossed a five and a ten on top of the check. "Let me pay for things," he said. "This week's on me."

"I can't let you do that." She had purse grit under her fingernails.

"Why not?"

"It wouldn't be fair."

He raised one eyebrow.

"Right," she said, dropping her quarters back into her purse.

Enoch smiled and nodded. Marilee thought he would get up to go, but Enoch remained seated, staring at her from across the table with his intelligent brown eyes. "I think you're pretty," he said.

Marilee laughed nervously. "Don't embarrass me."

"No, you are. I like looking at you. Even when you're asleep. But I won't do it again if you don't want me to."

"Thanks." She glanced up at the man across the table, no bigger than Disney's dancing dolls from *It's a Small World*.

"Marilee, you don't have to worry about me." Enoch leaned across the table as far as his body would allow. "I'm four-foot-one. I weigh a hundred and fifteen pounds, and I can't run. Besides, I'm not like most men."

He was right about that. "Do I look worried?" she asked.

Enoch smiled but didn't answer.

■

They walked out into the morning air. It was cooler than down on the plains. Sunlight filtered through the pines and cast shadows over the parking lot. A toddler on his way into the restaurant pointed to Enoch and said, "Look, Mommy!" The woman yanked him by the hand. Enoch ignored them.

"Does it bother you when people point and stare?" Marilee asked him once they were headed out to the racetrack.

"Nah," he said. "I'm used to it." He rolled down his window and let the wind blow through his hair. The air smelled of pine, bacon, and horse manure. "Does it bother *you?*"

"A little," she admitted.

"You'll get used to it. If it gets on your nerves, stare back. Makes them squirm."

"What about kids, when they point and say things?"

"No, the kids—they're great. They'll walk right up to you and say what's on their mind. I like that." He laughed. "I once had this boy—I guess he was about five—ask me if I had to stand on my tippy-toes to hit the urinal. I wish adults would ask questions like that." Enoch put his hands behind his head and glanced over at Marilee. He looked weirdly handsome.

"Well, what was your answer?"

Enoch laughed. "I told him it wasn't a problem. That dwarfs' penises grow out of their belly buttons for just that reason."

"You didn't!"

"You should have seen the look on his face."

Marilee pulled into the racetrack parking lot, which was deserted. The sign in the ticket booth said, "May through September." It was still September, but the racetrack was unmistakably closed. "Now what?" she asked.

"Laundry," said Enoch.

They drove back to the pink motel. Together, they crammed their dirty clothes into Enoch's backpack. Marilee grabbed her car keys and headed for the door.

"Let's walk," said Enoch. "It's just down the street."

"You don't want to drive?"

"No, I'm fine," said Enoch. "I've been navigating on crutches my whole life. Since I was two. I have calluses in my armpits and on my palms. See?" Enoch held out his hands in front of Marilee. He had thick pads on his palms, worn shiny and smooth.

They set out on foot down Sudderth Drive, Marilee toting the backpack, Enoch keeping pace with her on crutches. Drivers craned their necks while other pedestrians hugged the curb and stared down at the pavement. At a 7-Eleven, they bought a small box of laundry soap, then set out again, trudging slowly up a hill at the top of which was the Laundromat.

Marilee loaded the free-standing washer and inserted two quarters. Enoch leaned against the driers. "Can I ask you a personal question?" she said, once the machine had started to fill. They were alone in the room, which was steamy.

"No, I don't have to stand on my tiptoes."

"Oh, thank God!" she said, clutching at her breast.

Enoch laughed, then leaned his crutches against the folding table. "Ask me anything you like," he said. He smiled at her with the earnest intensity of a schoolboy; Marilee was struck by how sweet he could be when he wasn't being irascible.

"What's it like," she asked, "being a dwarf?"

Enoch chuckled and shook his head.

"I'm sorry," she said. "I shouldn't have asked you that."

"No, I like your question. Surprisingly, it's one that few people ask. Let's see." Enoch grabbed a chair from the folding table, stepped up onto it, and sat atop the churning washer. He was more agile than Marilee would have expected.

"What's it like?" he asked rhetorically, drawing his legs up under him Indian style. "Well, it's all the things you'd expect, I guess. It's being a man in a child's body and having to buy clothes out of the kiddie section of department stores. It's having to sit on your knees in some restaurants. And seeing the world at crotch level—which has its distinct advantages but at times can be quite revolting."

Marilee laughed. She pulled the chair away from the washer and sat down on it backward. For the first time since she'd met Enoch, she looked up at him, a perspective she found appealing.

Enoch fingered the frayed cuff of his jeans and continued. "It's not being able to see over other people. That can be frustrating if you're in a large group and can't get your bearings. Sometimes I get turned around. A couple of times, I've gotten lost in a crowd and had to ask someone for help." Enoch was silent for a moment. "It's having to stand on overturned trash cans to see yourself in restroom mirrors. It's people not making eye contact. You're pretty good about that, but most people look the other way when they talk to me."

Marilee smiled. It was not as easy for her as he thought.

"And then there's the usual bullshit. People staring. Men calling you 'Sonny' and 'Boy.' Women always assuming you're some kind of pervert—or no pervert at all." Enoch's face twitched. "And it's looking up people's noses. God, some of the junk you see up people's noses!"

Marilee laughed, then wondered whether she had anything up her nose. A woman toting two small girls pushed open the door to the Laundromat. When she caught sight of Enoch sitting on top of the washer, she steered her two children back to their car.

"And it's crap like that. People being afraid of you, as if you're going to hurt them or do something socially inappropriate." Enoch ripped a string off his jeans cuff, balled it up, and flicked it onto the floor. "What else is it like?" He thought for a moment, looking away from her at some indistinguishable spot on the Laundromat's far wall. "It's not being able to do normal things, like riding a roller coaster or driving a car. It's not being taken seriously by most of the people you meet. It's wanting things you can never have. It's masturbating a lot."

Marilee wanted to reach out to him, to squeeze his hand or put her arm around his shoulder—anything to let him know she understood (as much as any normal-sized person *could* understand) what it was like to be a dwarf. She would have kissed him if, in so doing, she would not have risked his misunderstanding. Instead, she stared down at the scuffed tile floor.

"Sound bitter?" he asked, hopping down from his perch. He landed on his feet, startling her. "I don't want to sound bitter, or sorry for myself, because I'm not." Enoch was eye level with her now, leaning back against the washer as it vibrated and hummed.

"No," she said. "Resigned, maybe. But not bitter."

"This may sound strange to you, Marilee, but I like being a dwarf. I've lived thirty-eight years in this body. I'm comfortable in it—probably as comfortable as you are in yours. Maybe more." Enoch grabbed his empty backpack and tossed it to her. "Let's blow this joint," he said, reaching for his crutches. "Too much heat."

Marilee held the glass door open for Enoch. "You really *like* being a dwarf?" she asked. "I mean you don't just tolerate it, but you actually *like* it?"

"Yeah. I do."

"So, what's so great about it?"

"Weeds out the assholes," he said, smiling.

■

They headed back to the 7-Eleven and picked up some snacks for the motel: Doritos and apples for Marilee, a bag of pork rinds for Enoch. Returning to the Laundromat, they flung their wet clothes into a drier. The machine ate one of Marilee's quarters, and Enoch had to bang on its side with one of his crutches to get it to spin.

Strolling up the road a bit, they came to a sidewalk cafe. There, they sat in the shade of a leaning pine and waited for their laundry to dry. A waitress approached, a young woman in skin-tight turquoise pedal pushers and a red tube top. "Would you like to see a menu?" she asked Marilee.

"Please," she said.

The waitress handed her two menus and disappeared inside the building. In a few minutes she returned to take their order.

"What'll it be?" she asked Marilee. Enormous silver and turquoise earrings hung suspended from her earlobes.

"I'd like a large iced tea with extra lemon."

"And your friend?"

"Why don't you ask him?" Marilee could hardly believe she had said that. Enoch squinted up at the waitress.

"I'm . . . sorry," said the woman.

"I'll have a lemonade," said Enoch.

"We don't have lemonade."

"Some orange juice, then."

"Sorry, we don't have orange juice, either."

"Do you have apple cider?"

"Nope. Sorry." Her earrings swept at her collarbone.

"What do you have, besides iced tea?"

"Pepsi, Diet Pepsi, root beer, Sprite, orange, Dr. Pepper, milk, tea, cherry Calistoga, lime Calistoga, and pear nectar," said the woman.

"Pear nectar? You don't have lemonade, but you have pear nectar?" Enoch's eyes were dancing.

"Is that what you want, a pear nectar?" The waitress started to write it down.

"I'll just have water," said Enoch. "You *do* have plain water?"

"Large or small?"

"Large, please. With ice."

The woman walked away from their table, her earrings pendulating. She whispered something to the busboy, who, in due course, brought Enoch a pear nectar and a flex straw.

■

After finishing their drinks, Marilee and Enoch rescued their laundry. They folded it, stuffed it into his backpack, and walked the distance back to their motel. Upon entry, Marilee retreated to the bathroom to check the inside of her nose, which was, to her relief, devoid of anything that might have disgusted Enoch.

Their large breakfast and Ruidoso's seven-thousand-foot elevation had made them both sleepy. Marilee located an extra blanket on the top shelf of the closet. She spread it over the bed and crawled beneath it. Enoch curled up with a pillow and blanket in the same spot in which he'd spent the night. She felt bad about Enoch sleeping on the floor but said nothing.

Marilee fell asleep quickly. When she awoke, Enoch was reading in an armchair. She felt relieved he was not watching her.

"Well, hello," he said, flipping the pages of his *Rolling Stone*.

"Hi." She fluffed her pillows and sat up in bed.

"Sleep well?"

"Too well. I'll probably be up all night."

Enoch raised his eyebrows, a gesture that made her feel uneasy.

"So what should we do now?" she asked.

"I'm game for anything." He tossed his magazine onto the floor.

Marilee ripped open a bag of tortilla chips and pondered the options. There was nothing she wanted to do.

"We could go out for something to eat," said Enoch.

"I'm not hungry," she said, munching.

"We could drive up to Eagle Lake. It's nice in the summer."

Marilee shrugged.

"We could go see a movie."

Marilee scrunched up her nose.

"Well, I guess we could stay here and read. Stuff our faces with junk food. Be totally degenerate and check out what's on TV."

"Let's do that," she said, eying the *Rolling Stone* at his feet. Enoch tossed her the magazine and pulled a book out from his backpack, Spalding Gray's *Sex and Death to the Age 14*.

They spent the rest of the afternoon snacking, reading, and watching Oprah Winfrey, Marilee finishing her Doritos and Enoch making an awful mess with his pork rinds. At seven o'clock, they walked to dinner at Casa Blanca. They ordered combination plates and Coronas while the couple at the next table did their best to keep their daughter from staring. After dinner, they walked around town. Ruidoso reminded Marilee of Lake Tahoe, with its quaint shops, cozy restaurants, and wooded-wonderland motif. They stopped for coffee at a small cafe, then hiked down to the Villa Inn next to K-Bob's.

By now it was ten fifteen. The motel pool was empty, and most of the room lights were out. Hurriedly (for the night was cold) she and Enoch stripped off their clothing and slid into the deep end of the pool. The water was warm; the sky, clear. The moon had not yet risen. They floated, and they looked up at the stars, much as they had that first night together on the outskirts of Rocket City. They floated for a long time until Enoch's voice broke the silence.

"Ever notice that a man can be an asshole, but not a woman?"

"What?" said Marilee.

"Men. You can call them assholes."

"I often do."

Enoch laughed. "But what do you call a woman who acts just like a man acts when he's being an asshole?"

Marilee thought about it. "This isn't one of your paradoxes, is it?"

"No, I'm just curious. Women get called bitches, but that doesn't really describe them when they act like assholes. When they're not being malicious, just jerks."

"Is this the sort of thing that keeps you up all night, staring at sleeping women?"

"I was just thinking of this guy I knew back in Kingfield. Chester Chittibaugh. This guy had his head so far up his butt he could have eaten his own eyeballs."

"Lovely," said Marilee.

"Used to write his initials 'Ch. Ch.' What a geek. He had this younger sister who was my age. Cherry Chittibaugh, who also wrote her initials 'Ch. Ch.' She was almost as big an asshole as her brother, but you wouldn't really call her that. Bitch didn't quite fit, either. So I don't know what you'd call her. Maybe an assholette."

"You're weird," said Marilee.

"Yeah," said Enoch, grinning in the watery darkness. He paused for a moment, then continued. "In the fifth grade, I was in love with her. Don't look surprised."

"I'm not," said Marilee, lying. "I'm just not used to you being so chatty."

"At eleven, she was no bigger than most six-year-olds. I guess I took it as a sign. You know, like maybe God put her on the earth, in Kingfield, Arizona, in Mrs. Lindecott's fifth-grade class, so I'd have somebody to marry when I grew up. She wasn't much to look at. Stringy brown hair that hung down to her butt. Nose full of blackheads. Big, ugly teeth that looked like Stonehenge. But I didn't care, because when I stood next to her I was looking at her face and not at the spot where half her lunch had landed."

"Appetizing."

"We used to line up for recess tallest to shortest, and Cherry Chittibaugh was always right in front of me. I'd try to smell her shampoo. I'll never forget the smell of her shampoo. Coconut or something. After recess, we lined up the other way, so I was in front of her. Cherry would try to zap my crutches. If you step on one just right, the rubber tip comes off and I go flying." Enoch sank under the water, then resurfaced, pushing the hair back off his forehead. "She got me dozens of times. And to think I actually looked forward to her doing that."

"You're right," said Marilee.

"About what?"

"Definitely an assholette."

"That was nothing compared to what she did to me in high school."

Marilee waited for Enoch to continue, but he didn't. "Where is she now?" she asked.

"Still in Kingfield, I imagine. She married Chester's best friend, this drug burnout we called Lucid Moments. His real name was Doug Glasgow. I doubt he was ever in love with her. Got her pregnant a couple years out of high school. Guess when Cherry married him, she had to change her initials to Ch. G."

"Ch. M." said Marilee.

"Oh, that's good," said Enoch. She could see his eyes light up in the darkness. "Cherry Moments. God, that's wonderful. You don't know how wonderful that is."

"I take it she was not destined to become one of the Sisters of Perpetual Abstention."

"Cherry Moments," said Enoch, his mind lost down a thousand ancient avenues.

"Look!" said Marilee, grabbing Enoch's arm under the water.

"What?"

"Shooting star. You missed it."

"Good luck for you, though," he said.

She stared up into the sky, hoping to spot another meteor. The light went off in the room nearest the shallow end of the pool.

"So tell me about this guy, Lucid."

"Lucid, he was pretty fucked up. He'd been in Nam, and his dad was the local sheriff. Got him a job on the force when he got back from overseas, but he was never the same as before he went to war. Maybe it was the fighting, maybe just the drugs."

"Maybe both," said Marilee.

"Maybe. Old Lucid stayed stoned most of the time. Got his supply by busting kids going two miles over the speed limit. Most everybody knew they could buy their way out of a ticket with the right stuff. Getting your hands on it was the problem. Sometimes you'd have to drive all the way to Flagstaff."

"What was he into?"

"Acid. Coke. Mescaline. Grass, of course. Uppers. Downers. You name it. He'd pull you over for some minor infraction of a law you'd never heard of, then give you three days to come up with the stash. If you couldn't, next time he saw you, he'd write you out a nice fat speeding ticket, even if you were just sitting there picking your nose waiting for the light to turn green. He chewed tobacco, and his teeth were all brown. And his breath—when he leaned in the window . . ." Enoch shivered.

"I didn't know you drove."

"I don't. Never have. But these buddies of mine—we used to go cruising up and down Stockton Hill Road in Norm Feinberg's old Lincoln."

"A Jew in Kingfield?"

"There weren't many. One less, now."

"What do you mean?"

"He was killed. In that fire I told you about."

"Oh. I'm sorry."

"Let me tell you what we'd do—now, this was funny. After pulling you over, Lucid would give you three days, max, to score whatever you could get your hands on. But sometimes he'd remember, and sometimes he wouldn't, his brain not being what it used to be. So you'd always test him the next day, just to see if he remembered having messed with you. You'd park on the main drag, and pretty soon old Lucid would cruise by in his squad car, and you'd wave and yell, 'Hey Doug, what's happening?' And he'd either yell back, 'You got two more days, fuckhead,' or he'd play cool and adjust his sunglasses, completely unaware of the deal he cut you the night before out on Highway 66. But it had its flip side. Sometimes, after three days had gone by and you'd busted your ass to pay him off, he'd give you a ticket anyway, just to let you know what a mean son-ofabitch he was. That's the guy Cherry married. Six-foot-four inches of solid dick."

"Maybe it's a good thing you didn't drive."

"I never would have bought off the sonofabitch."

"That's what I mean," she said, laughing.

Enoch smiled.

Marilee's fingers were getting wrinkled. "So, tell me about this brother of Cherry's."

"Chester? God, that's another two hours. And I *am* being overly chatty."

"Not overly."

"Could you handle the *Reader's Digest* version?"

"Shoot."

"Chester was two years older than Cherry, and he used to tease me about being in love with his sister. In grammar school I guess he thought it was pretty funny, me being a dwarf and all. But by the time we got into high school, he was definitely not seeing the humor in the situation."

"You were in love with her that long?"

"No. I was never really in love with her. I think I was in lust. She got a little prettier once her teeth got fixed and she started doing something about her skin. But she never grew taller than four foot nine, which is still a lot taller than me."

"Have you ever been in love?" asked Marilee. "I mean, real love?"

"As opposed to fake love?"

"Yeah."

"Once," said Enoch.

Marilee wanted him to tell her about it, but Enoch just floated on his back in the middle of the pool, gazing up at the stars, waiting, it seemed, for the sun to rise. She had a thousand questions: Who was she? A dwarf? Not a dwarf? Did she love him in return? Did they ever get married? Was it over now? If so, how had it ended, and why?

"So tell me the truth about Larry," he said.

Marilee felt a quickening in her stomach. "What do you want to know?"

"Let's start with his real name."

Marilee took a deep breath. "Johnston. Lawrence Hurd Johnston. No relation to Peter Hurd."

"How do you know about Peter Hurd?"

"I have a B.F.A. in art. I wrote a paper on him."

"I think he lived somewhere near here," said Enoch.

"Hondo."

"Right, Hondo. We should go there."

"Why?" asked Marilee, but Enoch ignored her question.

"So what does Larry really do for a living?" he asked.

Marilee was nonplussed. She knew Enoch had seen Larry's ROTC photo with his name above the pocket, but how had he known she'd also lied about his job? "Well, he's not actually in the Air Force," she admitted. "He just works at the base. As a civilian."

"Doing what?"

"I don't know. He won't tell me. I guess that's why I lied and said he was a flight instructor, because I'm embarrassed. I have no idea what he does."

Enoch looked over at her, his face cast in shadow.

"Honestly. I don't have a clue."

"I believe you," he said. "And what do you do?"

She was surprised to realize this topic had never come up. "I teach art as therapy. In nursing homes. Well, I used to."

"Sounds interesting," he said.

"It can be."

Enoch dove to the bottom of the pool, then resurfaced, shaking the water from his hair.

"Look, I'm sorry I lied to you," said Marilee. "I promise I won't do it again."

"Do you love this guy?" he asked.

"Of course I do."

"Are you sure?"

"Yes."

"Well, then, I guess you've got it all figured out."

"I guess so," said Marilee. She swam to the ladder and pulled herself out of the water. Enoch was getting testy. "It feels good to be clean," she said, stepping into her underwear. "And it'll feel even better to put on fresh clothes when we get back to the motel."

"Yes," said Enoch. "It's important to stay clean." Marilee shivered, hunting for her bra in the darkness. "You look great like that," said Enoch.

She felt the blood rise to her face and pulled on her T-shirt. "Are you coming out?" she asked.

Enoch swam to the ladder. "So, why'd you lie to me about Larry's name?"

"I don't know. I said I was sorry."

He stared up at her from the edge of the swimming pool. "Forget it," he said, finally, kicking off from the pool's side wall and floating on his back toward its center. "I lied to you, too, so we're even."

Marilee stopped buttoning her jeans and looked down at Enoch bobbing in the water. She could hardly imagine him lying. He seemed so candid and straightforward, so unabashedly wedded to the truth. "About what?" she asked.

"There are times," he said, "when I do have to stand on my tippy-toes."

THE FIGMAN CLAIM

A week after his cat lips kissed the carpet, Figman received another letter from Litvak forwarded by his mother.

Dear Figman,

I shouldn't be writing to you, but I had to let you know what's going on. The families of the accident victims have filed suit and you've been named as a defendant. Their lawyer has hired a private investigator to find you. Goetschke has hired one too. I overheard Patterson talking about it with Roger Beale.

Yesterday Aion cross-complained against you and Goetschke. Ford and Speedy-Kleen are expected to file suit against you by the end of the week. It turns out the Pinto *had* had its fuel tank converted, so that wasn't a factor. They're claiming it was the force of the impact that caused the explosion, and that you were following too closely in the rain.

Sorry—there's more. The district attorney is now involved. Seems he's talking involuntary manslaughter. One of the guys who died has a cousin in his office. Tough break, huh?

I'm sorry to be the bearer of such bad news. But I did want you to know what's going on so you can make an informed decision about what to do. Again, I urge you to hire a lawyer.

If you get this letter (again, I sent it to your mother for forwarding), please don't tell anyone I've written to you. Patterson's been pumping me for information, and I've told him I have no idea where you are—which is true for now. Let's keep it that way.

I can't be writing to you anymore. It's just too risky. Good luck to you, Figman.

Best, Aaron

Figman's mailbox held other worries. Verdie had received her telephone bill, another letter from that collection agency in Albuquerque, and a statement from the Hospice Caring Project of Alamogordo addressed to Verdeen C. Hooks. The pieces of the puzzle were beginning to fit. Verdie was dying of cancer and running out of money to pay for treatment. This would also explain why she'd rented out her house and moved into her abominable trailer.

Figman returned her letters to their common mailbox; he'd had enough of other people's problems for a while. Back in the sanctuary of his kitchen, he sat down and wrote a letter to his mother.

Dear Mom,

Please burn this as soon as you get it. Some people may try to contact you regarding my whereabouts. Please do *not* tell them anything. For reasons I am not at liberty to discuss, it is vital that you maintain my secrecy.

People you know and trust may ask you questions about me. The police may even get involved. You must not tell anyone—even the police—where I am.

I want you to know that I am a good citizen and not in any trouble, despite what others may imply. They may tell you any number of frightening things in an effort to get you to talk. They may try to intimidate you. But I don't want you to worry. Just know that by telling them nothing, you are doing what's best for your son.

Someday this will all make sense, I promise. Until then, I must ask for your patience. And your trust.

Love, F.

P.S. I am using the alias William J. Forbes. Please use this name when writing to me. I'm sorry I still don't have a telephone. To open an account requires personal identification.

Upon reading Litvak's letter, Figman's first thought had been to pack up everything he owned and leave town. He'd head north, maybe, to Taos or Durango. But no sooner had that thought crossed his mind than he saw the inherent pitfalls in such a scheme. Travel could be dangerous; there was always the chance he would pick up some cop and leave a paper trail behind him. Anyway, where would he go? One hick town was as good as the next. And what were his odds, really, of finding another house where the owner didn't insist he carry the utilities in his name? No, he'd have to stay right here. It was clear Figman was destined to live (and die) in Artesia, New Mexico.

Figman drove to the post office and mailed his letter, using a phony return address and his new name. He was beginning to like the sound of it: William J. Forbes. Figman wondered what the J. might stand for. John sounded too ordinary with William and Forbes; Jameson, too prissy. Jed and Jeremy were both farm names that Litvak would have found amusing. Justin was nice, as were Jason and Jackson, but much overused of late. Figman contemplated names until his thoughts drifted to Oma. It was then it came to him: William Justice Forbes. The name was strong, masculine, and a metaphor.

On his way home, he stopped at T-Bird Home Center and bought new lettering for his mailbox. Twenty minutes later, its aluminum sides said V. C. Hooks/W. J. Forbes. He stood back to admire his accomplishment, realizing he'd have to think of some explanation to tell Verdie. Figman gathered up her mail and headed toward her trailer. Poe Titus's GMC truck was parked next to her green Impala. It was good she had someone to look after her, Figman thought, especially in her decline. Figman decided he would find a way to start liking the man.

He knocked on her trailer door. The afternoon had turned windy and cold, not the best day for painting. In fact, no day in the last seven had been a good day for painting. Exactly one week earlier, it had taken Figman an hour to clean up the mess on his carpet and another fifteen minutes to repair his easel. After that, he'd lost all momentum. His painting had been ruined. He'd have to start his feral cat from scratch.

Poe Titus answered Verdie's door, wearing pink rubber gloves up to his elbows. Figman peered into the room beyond him; his landlady was nowhere to be seen.

"I brought the mail," he said.

Titus wiped his brow with the back of a gloved hand, leaving a wet smear across his forehead. "Right kind of you," he said. "Come on in."

Figman thought about it for half a second. "Happy to," he said. "Where's Verdie?"

"Doctor's appointment up in Roswell. Want a beer? I could use me a break."

"I'd love a beer," he said. The trailer looked less filthy than usual, and it dawned on Figman that Titus had been cleaning.

Titus pulled off his gloves and opened the door to the refrigerator. "Jeez, will you look at this?" The inside of the refrigerator was disgusting: meat that had turned green, milk that had dripped down the side of the carton and congealed into a yellowy pool, spoiled tomatoes, plastic bags filled with blackened bananas, mildew growing on the gasket. The smell was riveting. "Coors or Miller?" asked Titus.

"Miller, I guess." Figman would have killed for a Bass Ale.

"So what are you up to?" asked Titus.

"The usual. Painting. Living. You know."

"You working for Elmer-Lloyd Cunningham?"

"No, I paint pictures," said Figman, a little sheepishly.

Poe Titus hunted in Verdie's kitchen for a bottle opener. He gave up, finally, and opened both bottles with his teeth. "Don't worry. I ain't got cooties," he said, handing one of them to Figman.

"Thanks."

Titus sat in his usual seat at Verdie's table, looking taller and thinner than Figman had remembered. "Take a seat, son," he said. Figman did as he was told.

"So what sorts of pictures have you been painting?"

"A cat. And a house, but it didn't turn out the way I'd wanted."

"How was that?" asked Poe Titus.

"Finished," said Figman, laughing.

"Ah."

The two men looked at each other. Figman downed a large portion of his beer. "So, Verdie's at the doctor's?"

"Yup."

"I thought I saw her car out in the driveway."

"She took the bus."

"Ah," said Figman. He thought about it: After her treatment, she'd undoubtedly be in no shape to drive, and Poe obviously hadn't wanted to spend the whole day up in Roswell waiting for her. Figman looked around the kitchen. "You're doing a great job on this place."

Titus broke out laughing, a sharp rasp that sounded oncological. Perhaps he and Verdie had met at some clinic. "The only great job that could be done on this place would be to drop a bomb on it."

Figman laughed and drank some more of his beer. This guy might be okay after all.

"Verdie's great at some things, but keeping house ain't one of them," said Titus.

"What things?"

"Beg pardon?"

"What things is Verdie good at?"

"Oh, golf, for sure. And poker. And making tamales. She makes the best chipotle tamales you'll ever eat. Her mother was a Mexican. Taught her to cook real good."

So that's what Figman liked about her face. It was Mexican. Or Indian. Or Mexican Indian. Why hadn't he seen it before? "Do you know what time she's due back?"

"Well, let me figure," said Titus, glancing at his watch. It was silver and studded with turquoise. "It's three thirty now, and she left around eleven, so I reckon she'll be back around suppertime."

"Ah." Figman calculated the timing in his head. Allowing an hour each way for travel, that left Verdie at the doctor's for roughly five hours. That seemed a reasonable length of time to receive chemotherapy, although he had no firsthand knowledge of the procedure. Figman wondered where her cancer was located and how many months she had left to live. Titus stared at him across the table, a penetrating look that made him feel self-conscious.

"I've been meaning to ask you something," said Figman.

"Ask away," said Titus.

"Do you know a young woman in town named Oma?"

"Twigg or O'Malley?"

It was hard to believe there were two of them. "She's a checker at Lester's E-Z Mart."

"That would be O'Malley. What about her?"

"Well, nothing really. It's just that . . . I was wondering . . . well, I was curious if you knew why she's never had her teeth fixed."

Titus's eyes narrowed; he took a long, slow swallow of beer. "Can't say as I do," he said.

"I know it's none of my business, but it's hard not to notice a thing like that. I mean, she's such a pretty girl, and all. So, I was just sort of wondering, you know. Rhetorically."

"That it is," said Titus, slipping a rubber glove up over his watch.

"Is what?"

"None of your business, son."

"Well, you're right, of course," said Figman. He pushed back his chair and stood. "None of my business at all. Hey, thanks for the beer."

"Anytime," said Poe Titus. "Just drop on in. Always look forward to a little company."

Figman walked the thirty feet back to his house. Who was this guy? Verdie's lover? Friend? Did he live with her? Figman had seen nothing in her trailer to suggest the permanent presence of a man, but a man's permanent presence was sometimes harder to detect than dry rot. What was it with that condescending attitude of his? Figman had already learned that small towns were vastly different from large cities; Artesia was a tight-knit community with social ties that went back a full century. But this guy acted as if he owned the whole town and everybody in it. He decided not to like Titus after all.

Figman plunked himself down on the couch in his living room. Across the highway, Bobo hunkered under his clothesline, spooning dirt into his yellow plastic bucket. The kid bugged the hell out of him.

So did Litvak's letter, especially that part about the Aion Corporation suing him. It was preposterous. A travesty. They'd paid him off, for Christ's sake. What possible grounds did they have for suing him? For not steering his car directly into the back of the Pinto? For buying a model of Aion that malfunctioned? The whole idea was ludicrous. Figman, who'd worked in the insurance industry for eleven years, was hardly

naive about such things. He understood fully that in cases involving liability, everybody sued everybody. It was part of the game, something
Americans did for sport. But now that he'd inadvertently become one of
the players, he was beginning to see that the game itself was not much
fun and that, in the process of playing it, people's lives could be ruined.

Figman felt anxious and depressed. This was not how he'd envisioned
the end of his life. His headaches were worsening and increasing in frequency. He hadn't had a date in months. He hadn't painted in a solid
week. And as if this weren't bad enough, now people were suing him.
Treating him like some criminal. Hiring private detectives to track him
down. He'd been forced undercover. Compelled, even, to change his own
name. And now he would have to live forever in this godforsaken town
where people were named Bobo and Poe, and the most upscale shopping
was the local K-Mart.

Figman glanced across his living room at his only work of art, a bleak
smudge of a cat sitting dejectedly on his easel. He entertained, briefly,
the idea of creating a new artistic genre. Smudge painting. He would
paint a dog or a house, drop it face down on his carpet, and pop it into a
frame. It would be up to the viewer to determine what it had been orig-
inally. He could have fun with it. Paint blobs of nothing, fling it across
his carpet, then eavesdrop on gallery patrons convincing one another it
had once been a rooster.

Figman laughed at the idea. And then he cried, a reaction that astonished him. He could not remember the last time he'd actually shed tears.
Not after his car accident. Not when he told his mother he was moving.
Not even when he realized he had a brain tumor. But here he was, looking up at his smeary cat, bawling into his couch pillows.

Figman sobbed for a good half-hour, then washed his face and drove
into town. He was lonely, he realized, and in need of some female com-
panionship. Oma was working. He waited for her line to clear, then came
through it with a head of lettuce, a salami, and a loaf of Jewish rye. Lester
Meany stood at the next register; a boy named Santos bagged groceries.

"Hello," said Figman, placing his purchases on the counter.

"Hi," said Oma. She smiled her closed-mouth smile.

"Oh, darn," he said. "I forgot pickles. Where would I find a jar of pickles?"

"I'll get it for you," said the boxboy. "Sweet or dill?"

"Dill," said Figman. "Thanks."

Santos ran off down aisle two.

Figman looked directly into Oma's blue and violet eyes. "Go out with me," he said.

"What?" She laughed, revealing her broken teeth.

"Go out with me. Right now. Drop everything and let me take you out to dinner."

"Don't be silly," she said.

"Tell them you're sick. Make up something. Tell them you've come down with a terrible headache."

"I never get headaches."

"Think of something else, then. Cramps or something." Oma blushed noticeably; Figman could have kicked himself. "Or not cramps. Maybe heart palpitations. A peptic ulcer. Toxoplasmosis."

Oma laughed as she pulled a wilted leaf off Figman's lettuce and tossed it in the trash beneath her counter. "I don't even know what that is."

"You get it from cats," said Figman.

"I'm allergic to cats."

"Well, there you go," he said.

Santos appeared with a jar of dill spears. "Oh, I'm sorry," Figman said to the boxboy. "I need the sliced kind. You know, for hamburgers. I should have told you that."

"No problem," said Santos. He hurried back down the aisle.

"So how about it?"

Oma hesitated a moment. "How old are you?" she asked.

"Thirty-four. Look, I know you don't really know me, but how else am I to try? We can go out of town if it makes you feel better. Carlsbad or Roswell. No one will ever see us." He saw Santos hurrying toward the register. A woman with a full shopping cart stepped in line behind Figman. He lowered his voice. "I'm going to go out to my car and wait for you. It's a white Aion 2FD. I'll wait an hour, so they'll have plenty of time to find you a replacement." He glanced at his watch. It was stainless steel and studded with nothing. "If I don't see you by five thirty, I promise I won't ever bother you again. I'll even go back to shopping at Bulldog Superette."

Oma frowned and ran her hand through her long auburn hair. Santos handed her a jar of sliced dills. "I hope the size is okay," he said. "All we had left was medium."

"That's great, thanks," said Figman. "So?" he asked Oma.

"You're crazy," she said, totaling his purchase. "That comes to four fifty-seven."

Figman handed her a five.

She counted out his change, dropping coins into his hand one by one. "Four fifty-eight, fifty-nine, sixty—"

Figman wrapped his hands around hers and swept the coins into his palm. "White Aion," he whispered, and left the store.

■

At five-o-seven, Figman watched Gert drive up in a blue Rambler and knew he was home free. Oma emerged from Lester's eighteen minutes later. She'd changed out of her badge and uniform and wore jeans and a tight yellow sweater. She walked quickly to Figman's window.

"I'm going to have to move my car," she said. "I told them I was going home."

"I'll follow you," he said. She looked stunning dressed as a real person.

Oma drove a few blocks to Dallas Avenue and parked her white Corvair. Unsafe at any speed, thought Figman.

"This is nuts," she said, sliding into the front seat of his Aion. "I don't even know your name."

"Figman."

"What kind of name is that?"

"It's Jewish."

"That's not what I meant. I mean, is that your first name? Figman?"

"It's my last, but it's the only one I use."

"You're weird, Figman. And I'm insane. They're going to find my body up at Lake Arthur in a week, and no one will ever suspect it was you."

"Your brother will."

Oma laughed. "Maybe I should call him and let him know who I'm out with."

"And maybe I should just take a hammer and break my kneecaps now, to save him the trouble tomorrow."

Oma laughed. "You *are* crazy."

"It's the aloe," said Figman. He started his engine. "Where to?"

"There's this place about an hour from here. Tinnie Mercantile. It's just before Hondo. I don't think we'll be seen. You go up through Roswell, then head out west on Highway 70."

Out west. Just the sound of it made Figman feel better. He eyed the pink stucco bungalow in front of which she had parked. "Is this your house?"

"Yeah. Me and Jesse's, before he died. He was my husband."

"I'm sorry," said Figman.

Oma shrugged and said, "Don't be."

It was an odd response; Figman chose not to press her for details. Instead, he told her about his life in L.A. (where she'd never been) and described to her the nature of his aloe experiments. He was glad to have remembered a smattering of freshman botany, though it wouldn't have mattered, as Oma seemed not to understand much of it anyway.

Oma seemed not to understand much of anything Figman talked about on the drive to Tinnie Mercantile, a provincialism he attributed to her limited upbringing and the school system in Artesia. Not planning on marrying her (and thus making her a two-time widow before her twenty-fifth birthday), he figured the education factor would not have to come into play. Indeed, as a dinner companion Oma proved warm and engaging, and Figman congratulated himself on having chosen so perfect an antidote to his depression.

"So, Figman," she asked, once they had ordered dinner, "what brought you to Artesia?"

"My Aion," he said.

"What do you mean?"

"Never mind. That was stupid. What brought me here? Well, a lot of things," he said. He debated how much of the truth to tell her. "There's this feeling I have about the Old West. You know, the solitude. The adventure."

Oma laughed. "I don't think you'll find much adventure in Artesia."

"You never know," said Figman. His chair felt as if one leg were shorter than the others, an annoyance Figman decided to overlook in the interest of keeping the conversation rolling.

"I've lived here all my life," said Oma, "and I can't say as I've ever seen anybody have an adventure. Except Sue-Jean Pittman. She got lost for five days in some back part of the Carlsbad Caverns. When they found her, she'd busted her leg. Took three men the better part of a day to carry her out. But that wasn't anything she went looking for."

"Well, it wasn't just adventure that brought me here. I also came here to paint."

"I thought you said you were a scientist."

"I am. But I'm a painter, too."

"I heard Elmer-Lloyd Cunningham was hiring about a week ago."

"Not that kind of painter. I'm an artist. I work in oils."

"Good. Elmer-Lloyd doesn't pay very much, anyway."

Their waitress arrived with bread, Figman's glass of cabernet, and the 7-Up with grenadine Oma had requested.

"Can't people make oil paintings in Los Angeles?" she asked.

"Well, yes," said Figman. "But it's a hostile environment. Not conducive to putting in a lot of hours. And the subject matter . . . well."

Oma ran her finger over the rim of her water glass. "So, how many paintings do you finish in a day?"

Figman shifted in his chair, which wobbled. "It's not that simple," he said. "It takes time. Weeks."

"Well then, how many hours a day do you paint?"

"Eight to ten," said Figman. "Sometimes more."

"I have shifts that long on the weekends. Gets real tiresome standing around on your feet."

"Beats standing around on your nose," said Figman. Oma laughed. Her teeth looked like angry scissors. Figman focused on her eyes, relieved that this time she'd gotten his attempt at humor. "It's unusual, isn't it, to have two eyes of different colors?"

Oma looked stricken.

"Don't get me wrong," said Figman. "I think they're beautiful. I think *you're* beautiful, but I've never seen eyes quite like yours."

"I hate them." She ripped off a hunk of bread and shoved it into her mouth.

"Why?"

"It makes me feel different. I got teased all through school."

"I love your eyes," said Figman. "I think they're your best feature." Oma blushed; Figman gathered she was one of those people who embarrassed easily.

"I'm thinking of getting a contact lens. Just one, you know, to make them both the same color."

"Oh, don't," he said, pitching forward on his chair.

"I'm tired of looking like David Bowie."

"You don't look anything like David Bowie."

"You know, he was here when I was little. Filming *The Man Who Fell to Earth*. My mother got me his autograph."

"I've always liked David Bowie."

"Not me," said Oma. "I grew up hating the guy. If it hadn't been for him, kids might have left me alone."

"I doubt it," said Figman. "Kids will find one way or another to be cruel."

Their waitress brought Figman's steak with mushrooms and Oma's fried chicken with coleslaw and french fries.

"They used to call me Majorette Tom," said Oma, as soon as the woman had left.

"I'm sure they were just jealous."

"I never liked that song. But I like 'Changes,' and 'Suffragette City.' And 'Fame,'" said Oma.

"I like 'Fame.' And 'Sorrow'—that's a great one." Figman sliced into his steak and watched the juice run onto his plate.

"I don't know 'Sorrow.' Anyway, I'm more into country than rock. Do you like Billy Ray?"

"Who?"

"Billy Ray Cyrus."

Figman had to admit he had never heard of him.

"Garth Brooks? Travis Tritt?"

"Country's not all that big in L.A." Figman worried their age difference might not be their only obstacle. Still, he reminded himself, he was not planning on marrying Oma.

In truth, Figman was not planning on marrying anyone, a sentiment that went far beyond the knowledge of his impending demise. He wondered, at times, if despite what his mother had told him, his parents' marriage had not been all that happy; if he hadn't retained some vestigial memory of their life together that had irreparably soured him on the institution as a whole.

His father had died when Figman was only three. He retained no overt memory of the man, no fuzzy recollection of the sound of his voice, or the feel of his lap, or the scent of his aftershave. When he was a child, his mother had often shown him pictures of a short man with reddish hair and a stubby mustache. This, she'd explained, had been Morris T. Figman, the love of her life and Figman's father. She spoke of her late husband with a reverence that made Figman feel ashamed, for to him the man in the picture was nothing more than some stranger with a similar name. Figman's real sense of his father derived from his grief upon losing him. Like good health or happiness, his father was a thing defined more keenly by its absence, a warm complacency shattered in the course of a single day.

It had happened one morning in late October while Figman was in his backyard making mud patties and digging for potato bugs. Happily, he piled wet soil into mounds, first picking out the earthworms (which he discarded), then clawing deeper into the ground, rooting for the soft, fleshy bellies of the colorless insects. With dirt under his fingernails and his sneakers soaking wet, he felt that only a jelly sandwich on white bread could make his life complete. He called to his mother. When she appeared on the back patio, he saw at once she'd been crying.

His mother called Figman over to her and sat him on her knee. She rocked him and held him tightly so that his arms were pinned to his sides and his ribcage hurt. His father had had a terrible accident, she explained, choking on the word *terrible*. Figman—stunned, crushed, and morbidly curious—asked his mother to explain to him what had happened. But his mother refused. In fact, she never revealed a single detail of his father's passing, and Figman quickly learned not to ask.

For the duration of his childhood (and indeed beyond), Figman imagined all sorts of gruesome possibilities: His father, a kosher butcher, had sliced his arm off while band-sawing a side of beef, then had bled to death like some freshly slaughtered animal. Or the meat tenderizer (a terrible contraption with large, metal-spiked rollers) had swallowed his father whole when he'd stuck his hand inside to investigate its sudden malfunction. Or he'd slipped in the freezer and impaled himself on a meat hook, then all morning hung like a carcass until eventually he'd frozen to death. Or a customer, convinced that the butcher had tried to poison him by using a cheese knife to slice up his brisket, had grabbed the offending utensil and hacked Morris Figman into a nice hash.

These were just a few of the fantasies that sustained in Figman an image of his father. These scenes, morbid and fascinating, were the pictures he held on to; in many ways they seemed more real to him than the silver-framed portrait his mother set each spring at the head of their Passover table. As a result, Figman thought about death frequently—about loss and remembrance and their effect on a boy so young. Occasionally, people told him he was lucky—that it was actually a blessing not to have known his father well. "Less to mourn," as one well-meaning friend once put it. But Figman wondered if a father lost but not remembered were somehow the more painful. It was a question that troubled him, and one whose answer he would never fully comprehend.

Oma's father, he'd gathered from Dino's comment, had passed away also. He asked her about him on the drive home from Tinnie Mercantile.

"An accident," she replied.

Figman felt an all-too-familiar tightness grip the back of his neck.

"He was caught up in some farm equipment. It was pretty awful."

The Ochoa claim. It had been Litvak's case, but the whole office had heard about it. A twelve-year-old and a wind rower on a farm north of Fillmore.

Oma fixed her gaze on some distant point on the highway. "It was Dino who found him," she continued. "He was only nine, and on his way to the back pasture to look for his rabbit. Messed him up for a long time. Never found his rabbit, either."

Figman wondered how much more messed up a person could be than Dino was as a young man. "You've had a rough time of it, haven't you?" he asked.

Oma shrugged.

"Father. Husband." Figman was hoping (against better judgment) to lead her into a conversation about Jesse. At the same time, he wanted to hear nothing about Jesse. He imagined her story held considerable pain, and he'd just as soon talk about something uplifting after his day of depression. But he was curious as hell. Who was this guy? How had he died? How long had he and Oma been married? Was he anything like her psycho brother? Had it been Jesse who had knocked out her teeth—in a rage, perhaps, over some other man coming on to her? Perhaps he'd been so violent she'd had to murder Jesse in self-defense? Or maybe he'd just been offed in some warehouse by Dino.

But Oma was not talking about her late husband; she was too busy discoursing on more pressing issues: "Days of Our Lives"; some made-for-TV movie about babies switched at birth; the purple iris blouse she'd picked up at Something Different; her homecoming dance at Artesia High; Waylon Jennings, whom she'd once seen in concert in El Paso; her mother's sewing shop on Seventh Street; her girlfriend, Carla, who was dating some loser who traveled with a rock band; and how Lester's E-Z Mart compared to working at Abo Thriftway. What she didn't discuss were ideas, a failing Figman chalked up to first-date jitters. Still, Figman could not rule out the possibility that Oma O'Malley was merely superficial; for all he knew, the loss of their respective fathers might well be the only meaningful thing that he and this woman had in common.

But tonight, he didn't care. The wine had been good, and Oma looked magnificent. Away from fluorescent lighting, her skin took on a near-translucent quality. Her hair she'd pulled back in a tortoiseshell clip; a single strand had slipped from its teeth and fallen loosely across her shoulder. Occasionally it brushed the corner of her cupid's-bow mouth.

At nine-o-seven, Figman pulled up in front of Oma's house on Dallas Avenue. He walked her to her front door, then leaned forward to give her a kiss. All evening (indeed for weeks), he'd been anticipating this moment. He longed to experience the fullness of her lips, probe the inside of her mouth, run his tongue over her broken front teeth. Most of all, he wanted to taste her lipstick. It was bluish-red, an unusual color. Yet when he brought his lips close to hers, Oma turned her head and presented him her cheek. He kissed it dispassionately, as though he were greeting some East European uncle. "I'm not ready," she said apologetically.

For what? thought Figman. For Tantric massage on her front porch? He had only meant to give her a little kiss.

"It hasn't been that long," she continued. Her eyes filled with tears. She looked beautiful in moonlight.

"Shhh," said Figman, placing a finger over her lips. "I'm in no hurry." Oma smiled her broken smile.

"May I call you?" asked Figman.

She nodded. "I'm in the phone book under O. O'Malley."

"I'll call you tomorrow."

"Okay," she said. "Thanks for dinner. I really had a good time."

Figman stepped off her porch and headed down her walkway. "Oh," he said, turning back. "I forgot to tell you. You were right about that okra."

■

He had lied. Not about okra, but about not having been in a hurry. He was facing death, and it didn't get any more hurried than that. Though he'd hardly expected her to go to bed with him on the first date, Figman had hoped that a kiss would help them get a jump on their relationship. He wondered if Oma had been taught to be coy. Perhaps women in small towns were *all* taught to be coy, as a defense against becoming involved too quickly with the boys they had known since preschool. The same boys they would see every Sunday in church and later play checkers with in the nursing home.

Figman had lied about other things, too. There were, of course, no plant experiments; he was five years older than he'd admitted; and the only thing he'd ever done for ten hours a day was have a headache. His age, he figured, was the least significant of his deceptions; he'd be dead before it mattered. His headaches he'd best not reveal. As for his botanical research—that would require some immediate remedy. Tomorrow, he vowed, he'd visit Planter Box Nursery and buy a flat of daisies.

Figman saw Oma twice in the next week, once for lunch and once again for dinner. Both times, she seemed reluctant to talk about Jesse. Both times, they had to go to places where they were unlikely to run into Dino. Since that first night on her porch, Figman had refrained from any further attempt at kissing her. He would wait for some signal, some clear indication she was ready to meet his advances.

The wait was pure frustration. Oma was so beautiful it was hard not to touch her, hard not to want to kiss her on her exquisitely delicate mouth. Her teeth, he figured, could be easily fixed. He'd even pay for their repair, if necessary. He wondered whether they embarrassed her and made her hesitate in getting involved with men. Figman wondered, too, about the softness of her breasts and what her thighs looked like naked. His desire, plus the fact that he hadn't painted in nearly two weeks, was leaving him in a knot.

When he arrived home from their third date (having driven all the way to and from some barbecue pit in Cloudcroft), he stopped at the edge of his driveway to pick up his mail. His box held only one item, a letter addressed to William J. Forbes:

Dear Son,

I read your most disturbing letter just an hour before I received a call from Miriam Eisler, the attorney for the families of the men involved in your accident. As you predicted, she asked if I knew where you were. I had to lie and tell her I didn't have a clue. Louis, you have to know how hard that was for me. What on earth is going on with you?

Miss Eisler asked to meet with me in person, and I could hardly say no— she was so very pleasant over the phone. I invited her over for lunch tomorrow. As you wish, I will try to maintain your privacy, but I don't know how convincing I can be.

She did tell me about Mrs. Medina. The poor woman has had a complete nervous breakdown. It seems her oldest son was murdered in a drive-by shooting just four months before her husband was killed in your accident. I don't know how a person can live through so much pain. I'm tempted to call her myself to see if there isn't anything I can do.

Louis, I have always tried to respect your need for privacy, but I would hate to think that you were in trouble and keeping it from me. Won't you please let me know what all this is about? All this secrecy is making me worry. And this new name of yours—heavens.

Please write, or call me if you can. I have so many questions.

Love, Mother

The headache came upon him with unusual speed. It afforded no respite before the pain, no twenty-minute interval between warning and agony. His aura, consisting of the usual blob in the corner of his vision, evolved rapidly into flashing lights and a snake-like pattern of red, silver, and blue. The snake leaped and quivered. Figman took to bed immediately.

There, he tossed for hours, clutching his left temple, moaning into his pillow, hitting his headboard in sheer frustration as the snake ate away at his eyeballs and brain. For months he had sought a remedy. He'd tried everything his doctors had prescribed for him: Motrin, Ergomar, Vicodin, codeine, Darvocet, Percocet, and Toradol. He'd tried some new, self-administered injection whose name he could not remember. He'd even tried acupuncture, subjecting himself to multiple needles and downing all those bitter-tasting herbs. Was there nothing out there to relieve him of his misery? Figman pounded his pillow. Then he remembered.

Desperate and in terrible pain, Figman stumbled into his kitchen. The clock ticked loudly from its spot above the refrigerator; the light hurt his eyes. He reached for the bottle of Essence of Chicken that made its home on his windowsill. Figman opened it at arm's length, careful not to smell it or spill any of its volume. With each movement, the pain in his head intensified; he could actually feel his tumor growing. He took a deep breath, held his nose with his fingers, and swallowed the bottle's contents—then puked the bloody liquid into his white porcelain sink.

VALLEYS OF FIRE

Marilee woke up horny. For two consecutive nights, she had slept in the same room with Enoch, listened to his muffled snoring, felt his restless thrashing against the foot of her bed. Enoch's pheromones, she was convinced, were playing havoc with her body chemistry. It was not her time to be horny. Morning was her least sexual time of day; before her period, her least sexual time of the month. But horny she was. There was no denying it, and no appeasing it either, with Enoch in the room. Her pelvic region felt congested; her insides ached that pulling ache that by oneself one could mitigate but never fully satisfy. It would be five more days before she'd be alone with Larry.

She climbed out of bed and popped open the latches of her suitcase, awakening Enoch in the process. He yawned, stretched, and made gurgling noises in his throat as he transited into consciousness. "What time is it?" he asked.

"Ten thirty."

Enoch grumbled and wiped his puffy eyes.

They each showered, dressed, and returned to the Whispering Pines Restaurant for brunch. Enoch ordered grapefruit, coffee, and an English muffin with cream cheese. Marilee, who felt hungrier than she had the day before, chose the full buffet.

"Do you always eat like this?" he asked, as she polished off her second plate of pancakes and smoked sausage links. Sitting on his knees, he appeared taller than usual.

"PMS," she said. Marilee was shy about a lot of things, but menstruation was not one of them. "I'm always ravenous the week just before my period. Then once it comes, I can't even look at food. I guess I'm just a slave to biochemistry."

"Aren't we all?" said Enoch. He took a long drink of coffee. "Do you ever get cramps?"

"No, not usually."

"That's too bad," said Enoch. "I have a great cure for cramps."

Marilee considered asking him about it but changed her mind, recalling a magazine article she'd once read that suggested orgasm as a useful remedy. She was too stirred up to think about orgasms; too sober to consider one with Enoch.

"Well, I never get cramps," she said, as if this gave her an edge over women who did, probably the same women who never went back for second helpings from a buffet.

Enoch adjusted himself in his seat. "Most women get cramps at some point in their lives. Maybe you just haven't moved into cramp mode."

"I could use some more coffee."

"Leeches," said Enoch.

"What?"

"Old Indian remedy. Works like a charm."

Marilee glanced down at her smoky links floating in pools of syrup.

"You apply them to the abdomen," said Enoch. "It's quite pleasurable, I'm told."

"How many do you use?"

"Six or seven."

"For how long?"

"For as long it takes." He kicked his feet out from under him, losing four inches in the process.

"Where do you get them? I mean, don't leeches live in swamps?"

"You find them. Here and there," he said, flagging down their waitress. He was being coolly evasive. She hated it when men were coolly evasive. Larry was sometimes coolly evasive, which made her want to tweeze the flesh off his eyelids.

"Well, of course," said Marilee. "How silly of me. You just trot down to Bloodsuckers-Я-Us and order up a few."

Enoch tilted his chair back on two legs and gave her a bemused smile, a smile that made her wonder precisely whose cramps he had cured, and under what circumstances. Their waitress appeared, filled their coffee cups, and left them their bill.

"So, what do you want to do today?" asked Enoch, reaching into his sock for his wallet.

"Today?"

"Yeah. Today is the last day of your life up to now."

Marilee laughed.

"Wouldn't you love to see the poster that went with that?" he asked. "All in shades of gray. Maybe a casket or two."

She liked Enoch, despite his occasional weirdness. Or maybe because of it, she wasn't sure. This strange little man made her laugh. "Let's try the racetrack again," she said. "I think I'm going to need a bowl of that chili soon."

"My guess is the chili stand is closed for the season."

"Ah." She thought for a moment. "There's always Carlsbad. They might have good chili in Carlsbad."

"Nope," said Enoch. "I've scoured the whole town."

"Have you tried the caverns?"

"No chili in the caverns. Just ham and cheese sandwiches on wheat bread, and a barrel of pickles the night crew pisses in."

Marilee scrunched up her nose. "You're kidding."

"I have a friend who works there. Park ranger. Don't ever touch the pickles."

"How about Santa Fe? There's bound to be chili in Santa Fe."

"None that you'd want to eat," said Enoch. "Only place in New Mexico that has great chili is Malpaís. The Valley of Fires."

"Hot chili," said Marilee. "Just the way I like it."

■

The road to Carrizozo was mountainous and full of curves. Marilee missed the 37 turnoff to Nogal and had to continue on 48 to Capitan before picking up 380 West. They planned to visit Malpaís, spend the night in town, then continue on to the northern half of the state.

They drove mostly in silence. Enoch cracked his window and let the breeze fill the car with the wintry scent of creosote and pine. The road was full of curves. Eventually, Marilee drove up behind an old man at the wheel of a Rambler. The speed limit was forty-five, but most cars had been clipping along around sixty. She slowed to thirty-five.

Oncoming traffic was steady with vacationers heading up to Ruidoso for the weekend. Cars stacked up in the lane behind her. Occasionally, they pulled out across the center line looking for an opportunity to pass. One of them honked. The old man, a shrunken figure behind the wheel, seemed oblivious to the problem he was causing. He wore a fedora.

"Why is it some dildo pulls out in front of you doing about twenty, and he's always wearing a hat?" asked Marilee. She narrowed the gap between her Dart and the Rambler. "What really pushes my buttons," she said, "is when they get on the freeway doing twenty-five and you're right behind them, and some semi is bearing down on you going about seventy, and it's you who'll end up trash compacted, not the jerk-off in the hat who'll probably live to see ninety."

"Hundred and seven," said Enoch. "And he'll still be driving."

Marilee inched closer to the center line, looking for an opportunity to pass the Rambler, but each time she rounded a curve and headed into a straightaway, traffic in the oncoming lane inexplicably thickened.

"Bad timing," said Enoch.

"Story of my life." Marilee followed the old man for four or five more miles. At the bottom of a hill, he threw on his brakes for no apparent reason.

"A ten on the dildometer!" she said. "Will you look at this guy?"

"You're going to have to be gutsy. Make your move. Floor it."

Marilee checked for cops in her rearview mirror and waited for an appropriate break in traffic. At last, one presented itself. They were mounting an incline; although the center line was solid yellow, all other conditions seemed favorable. "Hold on," she said as she slammed her foot down hard on the accelerator and shot out around the Rambler.

"All right!" yelled Enoch. "Lose this mother!" The Dart shifted into low gear, its engine knocking hard. The climb was steep but the Dart held steady, sliding back into the right lane and enveloping the Rambler in a cloud of black smoke.

"Yo!" shouted Enoch.

"Yuck," said Marilee. Enoch pivoted and craned to see over the back of the seat.

"Good job," he said. "Blew out your carbon. The old girl must have really needed it."

■

Carrizozo lay in a small valley between the Jicarilla and Oscuro Mountains. The town looked surprisingly pleasant, not seedy like so many they had seen. Enoch suggested they check in at the Little Black Peak Inn, a leap in quality from the pink motel in Ruidoso.

A Chicana woman stood behind the reservations desk, punching figures into an adding machine. She had thick black hair with a streak of white at her temple. She was close to Enoch's age and beautiful, with full breasts and a large, sensuous mouth.

"¡Mi hombrecito!" she cried as soon as Enoch hobbled through the doorway. Her smile revealed teeth that protruded slightly. Two children, a boy and a girl, poked their heads out from behind the counter.

"Enoch!" yelled the boy. He ran out from behind the counter and jumped on him, Enoch managing to jettison his crutches before the boy landed on his chest. The girl, not far behind, flung herself on top of the boy, who, in chorus with his sister, giggled, squirmed, and vied for the best position in Enoch's arms. Marilee was surprised they hadn't toppled him.

"And you bring una amiga!" the woman said. Her English was accented and quick.

"Carmina," said Enoch, "meet Marilee; Marilee, Carmina."

"Hi," said Marilee, stepping around Enoch and waving. Enoch had failed to mention he had friends in Carrizozo.

The woman studied Marilee. "Así así," she said to Enoch, laughing. Así así was one of the few Spanish idioms Marilee knew. It meant so-so.

"No la echaría de la cama por comer galletas," said Enoch.

Carmina laughed. "And she is—¿Como se dice en inglés—se puso colorada?"

"Blushing," said Enoch.

"Sí, blushing," said Carmina.

"¡Mi sorpresa!" the young girl shouted to Enoch.

"¡Chocolate!" yelled the boy. He abandoned his perch and slid down Enoch's leg to the floor, where he stood expectantly while Enoch searched his pockets.

"Ay, soy un burro," said Enoch, patting each one down.

"¡No, no!" yelled the children.

"Sí," said Enoch. "Soy un zoquete."

"¡No!" the children persisted, laughing and jumping expectantly, as though this were some cherished ritual. Carmina stepped out from behind the counter.

"Wait," said Enoch. "¿Qué es esto?" The children drew silent as Enoch reached into his back pocket and pulled out two Tootsie Pops.

"I get the red one," shouted the boy, grabbing both of them. The girl squiggled out of Enoch's arms.

"Vámonos," said Carmina, clapping her hands. The children scampered back behind the desk and disappeared down a dark hallway. Carmina looked at Enoch. "So, my friend, where you been so long?"

"Here and there." He was being coolly evasive again, but Carmina seemed not to mind. She crouched down next to Enoch and gave him a hug, an action that seemed slightly patronizing. Enoch hugged her in return, his stubby arms reaching not quite around her waist. Marilee wondered if Carmina had a husband. She wondered if she ever got menstrual cramps.

"I wait for you, like you say. But you no tell me you be gone so long. Where you been all these months?"

"Arizona."

"Kingfield?"

"No," said Enoch. "Not Kingfield." Marilee stood off to the side, feeling as useless as wings on a wheelbarrow. Who was this woman to Enoch? A friend? His lover? She cased the small office. Red chiles dangled from hooks in the ceiling; a spindle of postcards stood behind the front door. Above the water cooler, a blue godseye hung like a crucifix. She assumed Carmina and her children lived in the quarters behind the office. Marilee peered down the hall into a modest living room where the boy and girl sat on the floor, sucking on their Tootsie Pops, watching "Wheel of Fortune." There was no presence of a man.

"Now you stay for a while," said Carmina. She returned to her spot behind the desk. "You and your señorita, you want one room or two?"

Enoch looked at Marilee for an answer. She shrugged, as if to say it didn't matter, but it did. She felt oddly territorial.

"One room, two beds," he said. "I'm tired of sleeping on the floor."

"The floor? ¡Ay, mi pobrecito! She make you sleep on the floor, like some animal?"

If she could have sunk through the vinyl beneath her feet, Marilee would have done so gladly. She wanted to dissolve, to drift through solid matter and reassimilate someplace else. Like Tibet. Or Alpha Centauri.

"Numero siete," said Carmina, handing Enoch two room keys. "Two big beds and a nice TV so you don't get too lonely." Carmina laughed, a wild laugh. Marilee wanted to punch her. "You come back tonight, okay?" she said to Enoch. "I have a surprise for you."

"A woman of mystery," said Marilee, once she and Enoch were out the door. She was happy to leave Carmina to her godseyes and chiles, and she was pissed at Enoch. Pissed that he had not told her ahead of time about Carmina. Pissed that he had spoken to her in a language she didn't understand. Pissed that he had mentioned his sleeping on the floor. She felt set up, as if Enoch had staged this little drama for his and Carmina's amusement. "You forgot to sign in," she said triumphantly.

"Not necessary," said Enoch.

Marilee didn't wait for an explanation. She drove across the parking lot to room number seven. She'd understood that much. Enoch hopped out and leaned his crutches up against the car's front fender. "Want me to get your suitcase?"

"Leave it," she said, unimpressed by his sudden interest in chivalry.

The room was clean and smelled of lemon. The bedspreads looked new, without rips, stains, or cigarette holes. On the wall hung pictures of sunsets; in the closet, more hangers than any traveler could use. Marilee liked the room. "I need to make a phone call," she said, once Enoch had opened the windows.

"Want me to leave?" he asked.

She did, but knew his option would be to return to the motel office. She was curious about Carmina's surprise. "No," she said, "I'll only be a minute." Marilee dialed nine, then her mother's number in Sherman Oaks. "Hi," she said cheerfully. "No, I'm in Carrizozo. It's in New Mexico. No, I didn't. I'll explain later. I can't talk right now. I just wanted you to know I'm okay. Things are fine. Look, I'll call you next week. Don't worry. Yeah, they were good. I promise. I will. I love you too," she said, and hung up the phone.

"Your mother?" said Enoch. He sat on the edge of his bed, swinging his legs against the side of the box spring.

"Um hmm."

"She asked if you ate the melons." He seemed pleased with himself.

"I told you she was a little out there."

"And you told her they were good, but you didn't tell her you shared them with a dwarf."

"She's not that out there."

Enoch laughed. "My turn," he said, reaching for the phone. Marilee didn't offer to leave the room. Enoch dialed a long-distance number. "Busy," he said, replacing the receiver in its cradle. He jumped off the bed and hobbled into the bathroom.

Marilee leaned back against her pillows and pressed her hand into the space between her legs. Her annoyance with Enoch had in no way diminished her libido. The region felt heavy; the pressure of her fingers, enjoyable. As soon as she heard the toilet flush, she brought her hands up behind her head.

Enoch tried his number again. This time he got an answer. "Hi, it's me. I'm fine. How's Barney? Good. Yeah, if you wouldn't mind. Send seven fifty to DonElla in Albuquerque and tell Dad to reinvest the rest. Just ask Dad to take care of it. Thanks. I'll call you on the fifteenth. You too. Bye." Enoch hung up the telephone.

"*Your* mother," said Marilee. She could be equally smug.

"No," he said. "My banker."

■

They headed off to Malpaís, which in Spanish, Enoch explained, meant badlands. Just five miles west of town, a lava flow stretched as far as the eye could see. It was black and jagged, a jarring intrusion upon the landscape. Huge boulders rose up in angry heaps, faces spiny and porous, an ossuary of charred bones. Smaller formations seemed to have tumbled like jacks from some giant hand held high above the desert floor. The Valley of Fires was aptly named; it looked like Hiroshima after the war. Marilee wished she'd brought along her watercolors.

They parked the car and walked down a steep incline to the nature trail, a path of red clay cut through the lava mantle. Small shrubs and bushes poked their way up through fissures in the rock. That anything could live in this harsh environment astonished Marilee, but the Valley of Fires was teeming with life. Trail markers spoke of birds, cats, deer, skunks, badgers, snakes, coyotes, and even tiny fish indigenous to pools. Enoch spotted a field mouse darting from one surface cavity to another.

The tour was slow going for Enoch, not only because he was on crutches but because he had a tendency to read every marker along the trail. He recited to Marilee the history of Malpaís: Fifteen hundred years ago, a volcanic fissure erupted at Little Black Peak at the northern end of the Tularosa Valley. Molten lava flowed forty-four miles southwestward, covering one hundred twenty-seven square miles of the desert floor. The flow itself was punctuated by at least three eruptions, accounting for many of the larger formations. As the lava cooled, escaping gases formed bubble holes and crevices in the rock's surface. Winds blew sand into the cracks, and with rain, fertile soil gave sustenance to plant life.

It was hot out on the black lava, the path littered with stones. When Marilee stumbled, Enoch let go of one of his crutches to steady her with his hand. He was stronger than she'd expected, and he held on to her arm for longer than she would have thought necessary.

It was only temporary with Enoch, she reminded herself. In five days, she'd be done with his evasiveness, his weird little outbursts, his subtle manipulations of her feelings. In less than a week, she would no longer have to tote him around and watch him romp naked in hotel rooms, a stunt whose sole purpose, she was certain, was geared toward her discomfiture.

Bored with the Valley of Fires, Marilee was anxious to return to Carrizozo and eat the chili Enoch had promised. She could feel her blood sugar falling, the nervous tingling that started in her extremities and worked its way inward toward her center. Low blood sugar was predictable the week before her period. Her heart raced and her hands felt clammy. She rummaged through her purse for the cinnamon candies she carried as an antidote.

She found none. Annoyed, she trudged onward, following Enoch's slow trek back to the beginning of the trail. Heat rose off the rocks like a sauna. She felt sticky and hungry and increasingly weak. When at last they came full circle, Marilee sat down on a sharp rock. "I don't feel so good," she admitted to Enoch. "I'm hypoglycemic." She wondered if Enoch would understand, or if he'd think she was being spacey and Californian.

"I've got a Baby Ruth in my backpack. I'll go get it."

Enoch's backpack was in the trunk of her car. In order for him to retrieve it, he would have to zig-zag his way up to the parking lot, then maneuver himself back down the steep path on crutches. It seemed a lot to ask, but she was angry with him still. "Fine," she said. "I'll wait right here."

Enoch started up the hill. "I'll need your keys," he yelled back down to her. Marilee dug through the mess at the bottom of her purse: pen caps, bobby pins, pennies, gum wrappers, paper clips, old receipts, web-like tangles of hair. She snagged her keys, then gave them a wild swing up to where Enoch was standing. He scrambled to intercept them, managing, somehow, to keep his balance in the process.

Lowering her head between her knees, Marilee waited for her dizziness to pass. She listened to the sounds of the desert: birds; insects; the wind blowing up the valley and over Malpaís, through spiracles and fractures, a mournful sound. She heard crunching noises coming up the trail, peered through her legs at passing Reeboks, Nikes, and cowboy boots; feet in white sandals, their pink toenails rimmed in dust. Little feet crunched by, then bigger feet, which came to a stop in front of Marilee.

"You okay, miss?" asked a male voice.

Marilee looked up into the slack faces of a man and woman in their six-ties. A boy, about six, scampered back to them. "I'll be fine," she an-swered. "Thanks."

"Can we get you anything?" asked the woman. She held her hand above her eyes to shield the sun.

"My friend's getting me something from the car. But thanks."

"You mean the midget?" asked the boy.

"Lyle-Ray!" said the woman.

"I'm sorry," the man said.

Marilee said nothing; she was trembling and breathing rapidly. The rock she sat upon dug into her right buttock, cutting off circulation to her leg.

"Would you like me to stay with you until your friend gets back?" the woman asked. Marilee shook her head no, hoping not to appear rude. Even talking was difficult.

The three went forward up the trail to the parking lot. Marilee shifted position and waited for Enoch to return. By now, she had broken into a cold sweat, the final stage of her attack. Where was he? If he didn't hurry, her siege would be over.

She waited another five minutes. When the worst of her dizziness had passed, Marilee stood up and searched the trail for Enoch. Seeing him nowhere, she sat back down on her rock. Ten more minutes passed and with them her cold sweats, but not her anger. It burned in her chest like a slow fire, smoldering, gaining righteous momentum with each passing minute during which there was still no sign of her rescuer.

Again she stood and scoured the length of the hairpin trail. Two young men in black pants, black ties, and white shirts made their way down the path, Jehovah's Witnesses come to convert the heathen rocks. Still, she saw no sign of Enoch. She would have to go looking for him, climb up to the top of the hill and hope, for his sake, he'd thought up some reason-able excuse for his delinquency.

Marilee started up the trail. She had little strength for the climb, the heat and sudden illness having sapped most of her energy. She rested at the halfway mark, then again at the next bend. Lightheaded and breath-ing hard, she placed her hands on her knees and leaned over. Sweat rolled off her forehead and trickled down her back. Where on earth was he?

When at last she reached the top of the hill, Marilee combed the parking lot, looking for a small figure on crutches. She rehearsed the tirade she would unleash upon Enoch; thirty minutes had elapsed since he'd abandoned her, thirty minutes in which she'd sat feeling lousy in the unrelenting sun.

Her car was parked in the center of the lot, beside a red Chevy Malibu. Both of the Dart's driver's-side doors were open. Enoch, she assumed, was in the backseat, enjoying the shade, licking Baby Ruth from his fingers. But the car was empty, and one of Enoch's crutches lay on the pavement beside the rear wheel. Her suitcase was missing, as was Enoch's backpack. Her keys were neither in the door nor in the ignition.

Panicked, Marilee scanned the parking lot but saw only normal-sized men and women walking without crutches. She slammed her doors shut and decided to go look for a park ranger. And then she heard it. A thump. Then another. Then an unintelligible sound: a moan, or deep wail, coming from inside her car. Coming from the trunk! She yelled to Enoch and pounded on the blue steel. He called to her from within.

"I'm here," she shouted, trying to steady her emotions. Think calmly. Be rational. "Hold on," she said. "I've got a spare key." Marilee dug into the bottom of her purse for the single key she had grasped a thousand times when it was not the thing she was looking for. She clawed and rooted, raked lint under her fingernails, but failed to locate its hard, serrated edge. She emptied her purse on the hot asphalt, spread its contents into a single layer, and combed it with her fingers. Where was it? Hadn't she just felt it yesterday, when she was rummaging for loose quarters? She stared desperately at the assortment of junk scattered on the pavement at her feet. She checked the pockets of her purse, which were empty. She started to feel faint, imagining Enoch suffocating or dying of heat stroke while she tried in vain to rescue him. What would she do then, with a dead dwarf in her trunk?

One by one, she replaced each item in her purse, and only through this process did she finally locate her key, wedged firmly into the stiff plastic teeth of her retractable hairbrush. She popped open the trunk, exposing a rumpled and sweaty Enoch sprawled on top of his missing crutch. His forehead revealed a nasty scrape; his hand, the squished remains of her Baby Ruth. He had not unwrapped it.

"What happened?" she gasped, grateful to discover him still breathing. Enoch squinted into the bright sunlight. "Bullies," he said.

■

They found their things scattered along the side of the highway—Enoch's backpack and Marilee's suitcase, forced open and disemboweled. Missing was her jewelry: a gold necklace, her diamond earrings, and the opal ring Larry had given her for her twenty-first birthday. Since he'd left her, she'd had a hard time wearing it. Enoch surveyed the ex-contents of her suitcase: shorts, shoes, tops, bathrobe, bras, underwear, and socks, all in a dusty heap. "Time to do more laundry," he said. His mood was upbeat; his suggestion, practical. The loss of her jewelry didn't bother her at all.

Together, they scraped Marilee's clothes up off the road's shoulder and stuffed them back in her suitcase. Enoch's backpack had been gutted in an apparent attempt to locate the wallet he kept rolled up in his sock. He spotted a few more of his belongings a couple miles down the highway. Somehow, through the scuffle Enoch had managed to hang on to Marilee's car keys. His rationale was understandable: The prospect of being locked, with keys, inside her trunk seemed infinitely preferable to abduction into the desert by two madmen perhaps intent on some serious dwarf bashing.

"What did they look like?" she asked.

"You know. Sort of big."

Marilee felt like crying. Why would anyone want to hurt a dwarf on crutches? She imagined the terror Enoch must have gone through, having been thrown into the trunk and locked inside. Hearing his assailants laugh and walk away. Wondering how long it would take someone to hear his thumps and shouts. Feeling the temperature rise, his air supply dwindling. Staring into the bleak darkness. Marilee had never understood this human capacity for cruelty.

She no longer felt angry at Enoch but ashamed of her own petulance and self-absorption. What right did she have to be upset with Enoch for having friends? For having relationships and a life of his own? She owed Enoch an apology, one she figured might be better received after something to eat.

By now it was five o'clock, seven hours after their last meal. She felt weak, drained by her sudden drop in blood sugar and its attendant sweating and shaking. And still, there was that dull yearning in her pelvis.

Back at the motel, she and Enoch showered successively, then walked to a nearby steakhouse. They ordered Caesar salads; T-bones; baked potatoes with butter, sour cream, and chives; and a bottle of Napa Valley Pinot Noir—a feast as much a cure for Marilee's low blood sugar as a celebration of Enoch's continued survival. Sequestered in a corner booth, Marilee felt nevertheless conspicuous, for the seat's thickly padded vinyl seemed to swallow Enoch whole.

"I'm sorry," he said, spreading butter on an end piece of warm sourdough.

"For what?"

"For getting you into all this." He looked pathetic with his bruised forehead.

"*You're* sorry? *I'm* the one who should be sorry. Making you climb all that way up to the parking lot. I feel terrible."

"But your jewelry?"

"Forget it. It's just stuff. Stuff doesn't matter. Anyway, I'm sorry for today."

"For what?"

"For being such a pain."

"I didn't notice."

"Bullshit."

Enoch laughed. "Okay, I noticed."

Their waiter, who had introduced himself as "your waitperson, Sean," arrived with two Caesar salads. He ground pepper first for Marilee, then Enoch. "Is that enough for you, sir?" he asked after what seemed like a full minute of wrist-twisting.

"That's fine, but could you leave it on the table?"

"Certainly, sir." Marilee could tell Sean was going to be one of those pretentious types who hover annoyingly between interminably long absences in the kitchen. She studied the scrape on Enoch's forehead.

"Doesn't it bother you," she asked, "what those creeps did to you?"

"The world's a dangerous place," he said.

"But they could have killed you."

"Not likely."

"Aren't you angry?"

"A little."

"You don't seem angry."

Enoch shrugged.

"I'd be livid," said Marilee.

Enoch swirled his wine in his glass and watched as its legs ran down the inside of the bowl. He gave her a little smile.

"Oh, my God," she said. "This happens to you, doesn't it? I mean more than it happens to most people. And that's why you're not angry—because you've gotten used to it, right?"

The look in his eyes confirmed her suspicions, and for one small moment Marilee forgot Enoch was a dwarf. Forgot he was deformed, or a man, or in any way different from herself.

Enoch went back to his salad. "It's a fact of nature," he said. "The strong conquer the weak. I'm not genetically programmed to survive. The way I see it, my being here at all is nothing short of a miracle."

"But people treating you like you're just here for sport—"

"Maybe I am," he interrupted.

"That's terrible."

"When I was in high school . . ."

"Go on," said Marilee.

"Oh, you know, the usual things. I'll tell you about it sometime."

Enoch was being evasive again, but this time Marilee chose not to let it bother her. She figured he had a right to keep his private life private. "You hear about these things," she said, "but you never think it's going to happen to somebody you know."

Enoch swirled his wine. "That's because you're not used to hanging out with freaks."

His words shocked her. She leaned across the table. "You're not a freak," she whispered, miffed that he would demean himself in this way.

"Of course I am. Who are we kidding?"

"It's just . . . that word."

"Yeah, yeah, I know," he said. "The Little People of America would be all over me for that. But it's just a word, and words don't alter realities. Not in any meaningful way."

"Is that how you think of yourself? As a freak?"

"Like it or not, that's what I am. As in 'not the norm.' As in genetic anomaly. An accident of nature. I don't want to pretend to be something I'm not, like 'special,' and 'exceptional,' and all those other politically correct euphemisms the media throws about. That semantic bullshit may help some people, but it doesn't help me."

She wanted Enoch, she couldn't deny it. There was something about him that turned her on, something appealing she could no longer deny. It had to do with the way he thought about things. The way he made connections and arrived at conclusions wholly his own. A shiver went through her as she considered, briefly, the things she would like to do to him in bed. The things she would like him to do to her. She felt heady from the wine, floating and free. Thinking of Enoch excited her, made her fingers tingle and drew blood to her lips. She poured herself another glass of wine and topped off his half-filled glass.

"Little people," said Enoch, shaking his head. "They make it sound as if we're gnomes."

"Actually," said Marilee, transferring a forkful of salad seductively to her mouth, "I was thinking more like trolls."

"No, definitely gnomes. With little red vests, and pointy hats, and bells on the tips of our shoes." He took his napkin, placed it on top of his head, and made a face she imagined he thought was gnome-like. He looked like a Pekingese. Together they broke into laughter, Marilee holding her napkin over her mouth so as not to spray Enoch with half-chewed anchovies. It felt good to laugh, good to let go. Enoch slumped onto his side, his head disappearing beneath the table's surface so that Marilee could no longer see him, just hear the sound of his laughter echoing off the booth's vinyl walls. Sean, their waitperson, appeared with a bottle of steak sauce.

"Would either of you care for a condiment this evening?" He seemed oblivious to the napkin-hatted dwarf convulsing on the seat in front of him.

"Chili," said Marilee. "My friend here promised to buy me chili in the Valley of Fires, but there wasn't a bowl to be found."

"Oh, *chili*," said Enoch, poking his head above the table. "I'm such a ninny," he said to Sean. "I could have sworn she said igneous rock."

■

They lingered over their steaks and another bottle of red wine. Marilee felt intoxicated, a warm sensation happily nourished by her awareness that tonight neither of them had to operate heavy machinery. The more wine she consumed, the more it fueled her passion for Enoch. She'd decided to seduce him once they returned to the motel.

She considered, briefly, how she would feel about Enoch in the morning. Would she feel ashamed (or worse, repulsed)? Would she feel guilty for having betrayed Larry, even though it had been he who had left her? Would she feel obligated to leave Larry and remain with Enoch? She weighed these concerns with the tiny part of her brain left unimpaired by alcohol and hormones. And then, just as effortlessly, she dismissed them.

She would start by taking off her clothes—no, half her clothes—then become too dizzy to maneuver herself out of the rest. She would lie seductively on her side and let Enoch take over, first removing her bra, then kissing and fondling her breasts as she felt him growing hard beside her. Slowly, his hand would make its way down into her underwear. He'd move cautiously at first, then with more confidence as she responded to his kisses. When she felt him growing harder still, she would move down on the bed (not far) and loosen his belt. Pull down his shorts. Take him in her hand and—

She stopped herself, astonished at the sleaze factor of her fantasy. It was not unlike the trash erotica in men's magazines, in which women spread their legs at the mere suggestion of anything longer than it is wide. Her daydream played like a porno film, with tongues flicking and hands groping and organs slapping in choreographed synchronization. All it lacked was canned music.

They left the restaurant laughing and weaving, Marilee brushing Enoch's shoulder as they crossed the street against the light. She realized she wanted this man more passionately than she'd ever wanted Larry, the primary object of her desire for years. She could already feel the touch of Enoch's fingers, his tongue against her skin, his full lips upon her open mouth.

The door to their room was locked and, for a moment, both of them fumbled for their keys. They jokingly considered having to spend the night in the Dart—it was so cramped, and the night was getting cold, and which one of them would have to sleep in the front?—Enoch did it the last time. When the door flew open, Marilee flopped down on the bed, giggling, head spinning, warm with wine and the thrill of illicit times upon her. Discreetly, she unbuttoned her blouse's top button. A start, she thought. A subtle sign of encouragement. She was drunk and aroused, a delightfully fluid state of being.

Enoch did not turn on the light but sat on the corner of the double bed she now occupied. He seemed not as tipsy as she, but he should have been, she thought; he was so small, and alcohol must do funny things to dwarfs. She contemplated his face in the light from the parking lot, an amber radiance, warm and diffused, which made him look as if he glowed through his skin, all beamy and yellow, he was so nice to look at, even handsome in a peculiar way. She nudged him with her foot, not an obvious nudge but one that could have been mistaken for a careless slip, the result of the room's general darkness and too many glasses of red wine. She waited for him to respond, say something, nudge her back, get up, close the door, lie next to her on the bed, it was so soft and flat, so soft and so warm, and she was lying upon it, blouse falling open, waiting for him, waiting for him to make his move and do something exceedingly naughty.

But he didn't move. Didn't budge from his corner. Said something to her she didn't want to hear. Said, "I'll be back in a couple of hours." Said, "Get some sleep." Patted her foot. Got up from the bed and hobbled out the door, shutting it behind him.

Tears welled up in Marilee's eyes as she fathomed the depth of her loss. There might never be so perfect a night, so ideal a moment to make love to a dwarf. He had broken the spell, awakened her from a sensual dream in which she'd wanted to remain just a short while longer.

She sat up. Focused her eyes. Swung her legs over the edge of the bed and pulled back the heavy curtains. She watched as Enoch made headway on his crutches, bounding across the parking lot like a ship cresting over waves at sea, a small but stable craft, steady on course, heading straight for Carmina's harbor. A light shone in the woman's apartment, her drapes drawn closed across the half-moon window of her living room. The room where her children had sat eating Tootsie Pops. The room where she would, undoubtedly, show Enoch her surprise.

Marilee let the curtains fall. She wept a while into the bedspread, then stumbled into the bathroom, locked the door, and switched on the light. Its fluorescence cast a greenish pall over the white tiled room; her eyes hurt from the glare. She turned on the tap and let the water run over her hands, cool water, as she leaned against the sink, dizzy, full, stung by the light, drunk on red wine, heavy with disappointment. She splashed her face with water, cool water, it made her cheeks tingle and her eyes feel gritty. She toweled off. Weaved. Avoided herself in the mirror.

She longed for Enoch to come back to her, to be naked and waiting when she emerged from the bathroom, the cool, clear water having washed away her tears. She longed for Enoch just to hold her, but she knew it was not to be. Enoch was with Carmina, her white-streaked hair falling loosely over her shoulders; her brown, happy children dreaming sweetly in their beds.

Marilee stood at the sink and took stock of her life, her safe, boring life, the last day of her life up to now. She thought about the eight years she'd known Larry, her four years in college; her three years teaching art therapy; her last four days, which she'd spent with a dwarf.

She exhaled deeply, reeled forward, steadied herself against the white porcelain. Several of her hairs fell into the basin, long and coiled as the earthworms she'd exhumed in her backyard as a child. She laughed, imagining her head a mass of squirming, red worms, like Medusa's head of vipers that lured men to their deaths. Only her mane would draw mockingbirds.

She lifted a red hair out of the sink, dropped it, watched it spiral to the floor, cascading slowly, dancing in the air in stop-frame slow motion. And in the rolling descent of that single hair from her fingers to the bathroom floor, Marilee lost all sense of place, of time, and of purpose. All experience seemed to coalesce in that solitary moment. All plans were abandoned, all worries forgotten, all desires forsaken. Except one.

In the green fluorescent glow of the room-number-seven bathroom of Carrizozo's Little Black Peak Inn, Marilee unzipped her jeans, locked her thumbs inside her underwear, thrust both garments to her ankles, and blew out her carbon.

POKER FACE

One day in late February, Figman received a visitor. The sky was semi-cloudy; Figman was busy trying to capture the light on Verdie's pink and green trailer before the next cumulonimbus threw shadows against its walls. Guilt had triggered his return to painting, an emotion that had surfaced shortly after his lie to Oma claiming he worked eight to ten hours a day. He was lucky if he managed to get in two.

His visitor drove up in a bronze Suzuki Samurai. When Figman heard the crunch of gravel in his driveway, he assumed it to be Verdie or Poe Titus. But when the car slowed instead of continuing on around to the rear of his house, Figman peeked out his living room window. The Samurai stopped and a man got out. He looked around, then stepped up onto Figman's front porch and knocked loudly.

Figman panicked. With his Aion in the driveway, he could hardly pretend not to be at home. Reluctantly, he opened his front door. "Yes?" he said. What could they do to him, really? Extradite him? They'd have to arrest him first, and this man, in his denim vest and turquoise jewelry, did not look like the arresting type.

"Benito Hooks," said the man at his door. He took a step toward Figman. "Mind if I come in?"

"Verdie doesn't live here," said Figman, neglecting to introduce himself. "She lives in the trailer out back."

"I know that," said the man. "I come to see you." This was trouble, for sure. "May I come in?" the man asked again.

"Look, I'm working," said Figman. "I'm on a tight schedule. This isn't a good time."

"I won't be long."

Figman could see the man had no intention of leaving; he opened his door wide enough for him to enter. Benito Hooks stepped into his living room. Though dark like Verdie, he looked nothing like her. His face was smooth and expressionless; his body, portly and tall. He combed his hair straight back off his forehead. Perhaps he was a relative by marriage.

"Benito Hooks," the man said again, this time extending his hand.

"William Forbes," said Figman. He shook the man's hand, which was cold and soft as ice cream.

"A pleasure," he said.

"Likewise," said Figman. "What can I do for you?"

"I come to check up on the place. Look around. Make sure everything's in good order."

"I don't understand."

"My mother can sometimes be, well . . . "

His mother? Verdie was this man's mother? She had never mentioned having children, but he supposed anything was possible.

The man walked around the small house, peering into Figman's rooms. Figman followed him, hoping he'd left nothing out that would reveal his true identity. Hooks peered into the bathroom, then his bedroom, then the spare bedroom Figman used for storage. He ran his hand above each doorframe, as if checking for dust. He ended his tour in the kitchen, where he studied Figman's painting. "What's it of?" he asked.

"Your mother's trailer."

Hooks stepped back and looked at the painting cockeyed.

"It's an abstract," said Figman.

"Ah," said the man, glancing first at the painting, then out the kitchen window.

"You work at home?"

"Yes," said Figman.

"Good. Good," said the man.

Who was this character? Was he really Verdie's son, or some private eye just pretending to be her son? What right did he have to be nosing around in Figman's kitchen?

The man picked up the new bottle of Essence of Chicken that Figman had set on his windowsill to replace the one he'd puked into the sink. "What's this?" he asked.

"Look," said Figman. "I don't mean to be rude, but I don't know you. And I don't know what you want here, or with me, but this is my house. I pay the rent. I mind my own business. And I don't appreciate people showing up out of the blue and poking through my belongings."

The man set the bottle of Essence of Chicken back on the windowsill. "Mind if I sit down?"

"Frankly, yes."

The man sat down at Figman's table. "I have some questions I'd like to ask you."

"Who are you?" asked Figman.

"Benito Hooks," said the man. He had eyes like Raul Julia.

"What do you want from me?"

"A favor," he said.

A favor? Perhaps Figman could bargain with the fellow. Make him a deal so he wouldn't return to L.A. and reveal his whereabouts.

"Care for a beer?" asked Figman, opening his refrigerator.

"Never touch the stuff."

Figman reached for an Anchor Steam and sat down opposite the man, his movements slow and deliberate so as not to convey fear. Sitting casually, he tried to open his beer bottle the way he'd seen Poe Titus open a beer bottle. Figman placed the cap between his front teeth and gave it a sudden twist. The cap rotated with the bottle and chipped out the inside corner of his right front incisor. "Shit," he said. He spat the shard of tooth into his palm and glared at the man across his table.

"Allow me," said Hooks. He reached for Figman's bottle and opened it with a turn of his wrist. Perhaps he'd been sent by Dino.

"Get on with it," said Figman.

"You live in my mother's house."

"And?"

"And someday it will be mine."

"So?"

"So, I need your help."

"With what?"

"With my inheritance."

"Get to the point," said Figman. He ran his tongue over his broken tooth.

"Well, Bill, the point is I want to make sure my inheritance stays my inheritance, if you know what I mean."

"I'm afraid I don't. And what does any of this have to do with me?"

"I live in Albuquerque."

"Yes?"

"And that's a ways from here."

"So?" The fellow's style was maddening.

"So it's hard to keep an eye on things."

"On your inheritance?"

The man shook his finger at Figman. "You're a sharp man, Bill. Very sharp."

Figman smiled wanly. The gap in his mouth felt cavernous; he found it impossible to stop feeling the missing part of his tooth with his tongue. Oma's gap, he imagined, must feel like an arroyo.

"Now, my daddy worked hard his whole life so that I could have something in this world. A small piece of himself. He even gave me his name."

"Hooks?" asked Figman.

"Of course Hooks. I was referring to Benito."

Benito. Benito Hooks. It conjured up images of one-armed dictators and gaffed tuna. It was positively the worst name Figman had ever encountered.

"So you're a second?" said Figman, trying to lighten the conversation.

"Third, actually. And there's a fourth. My son, Little Benito. We call him Beanie." The man pulled out a wallet and flipped it open to a picture of a scrawny kid in a cowboy hat. He had hooded eyes, an overbite, and looked remarkably like his grandmother.

Figman breathed a sigh of relief. "Fine-looking boy," he lied.

"Thank you," said Benito, returning the wallet to his back pocket.

"So what, exactly, can I do for you?" asked Figman, growing more impatient now that he'd nearly ruled out the possibility this man was on his trail.

"You like a mystery?"

"No. I like answers."

"When you were a kid, did you ever play spy?"

"I played baseball," said Figman. "And mah-jongg with my aunts and my mother."

"Well, I played spy," said the man. "Me and my buddy, Dicky-Lee. The two of us used to spy on the Rodriguezes across the way. You know that white house out across the highway? Used to look into their place with—what do you call them things? You know, them heavy things. For some reason I can't think of their name."

"Binoculars?"

"Yeah. That's it. Binoculars. From my bedroom window. Saw that Rodriguez woman half-naked once. Ooowee."

"You want me to spy on the Rodriguezes?"

Hooks smiled. His teeth were in need of a good cleaning. "No. No. Of course not. I want you to spy on my mother," he said, with an insouciance that made Figman shiver. Hooks pulled out a cigarette and lit it with a silver and turquoise lighter. Figman neither responded to his words nor rose to get him a dish to use as an ashtray. Hooks set his lighter on the table and leaned back in his chair, puffing. The lighter was shaped like the head of a steer. Figman wondered how the man kept from sticking himself on its horns when he reached for it in his pocket. "Now, it's important we keep this between you and me," said Hooks, finally. "Between men. You know, my mother's not right, and . . . well, I think you know what I mean."

"No, I don't," said Figman.

"Well, she has this, um . . . problem. It's fairly serious."

"Life threatening?"

"At times I think it could be." Hooks reached an arm backward and flicked an ash into Figman's sink. "Let's just say that it hasn't been easy." His face was expressionless, even as he smiled.

Figman smiled back. "I think I understand," he said.

"Good. Good. 'Cause I'm gonna need your help. Are you with me, Bill?" He took another puff of his cigarette. "I'll make it worth your while," he said. "If you know what I mean."

Figman hesitated just long enough to convey his thoughtful consideration of the matter. "I think I do know what you mean, Hooks. And I'm with you. All the way."

Hooks took another puff off his cigarette, then stubbed it out against the side of the sink. "I'm trying to cut down."

"Ah," said Figman.

The man set his chair upright, put his elbows on the table, and leaned in closer to Figman. "Now, where you come in, Bill, is this. See, it's rumored my mother has a gentleman friend. I don't know his name, and she flatly denies it, but I have it on good authority there's been somebody sniffing around the daffodils."

Sniffing around the daffodils? It was positively the most vulgar expression Figman had ever heard.

"Some yahoo who more than likely has an eye on my inheritance. Do we understand each other, Bill?"

"Not perfectly, Hooks. But well enough, I think."

"Good. Good. But call me Benito."

"Sure, Benito," said Figman.

"And this is where you come in, Bill. I want you to keep an eye on things. Look out the window occasionally. Jot down license plates and whatnot. Play spy with me."

"You got it, Benito. I know how a man feels about his inheritance."

"Good. Good," said Hooks, reaching across the table to clench Figman by the shoulder. "I had a good feel about you right from the start."

Figman was at a loss for a response.

"Damn good feeling," said Hooks, standing. "And now, I got to high-tail it out of here before my mother gets back and catches wind of me. Nice doing business with you, Bill." Hooks extended his hand, and Figman shook it. "You're keeping this place in fine order."

"Thank you," said Figman.

"Never looked better," he said. "You should have seen it with them Pontelle sisters. Jeez Louise. Used to have my eye on that younger one,

Esther, till she up and ran off with some Mexican. She taught English to them migrant kids. Wouldn't have worked, though. Couldn't keep house worth a damn."

Figman walked his guest to the front door. Hooks stepped off the porch and crunched his way through the gravel back to his Samurai. He climbed inside. "Getting warmer," he said. "Soon as you know, it'll be summer."

Figman looked up at the darkening sky. He was still waiting for spring.

"Be a good spy," said Hooks, winking. "Keep a sharp eye on things." The man backed his way out of the driveway and was gone.

Figman knew it would be Benito he'd be keeping an eye on. Never had he had so visceral a reaction to a man or his name. This fellow was worse than the daily contents of Verdie's mailbox. Figman had to find some way to protect her, he could see that. He returned to his kitchen and rinsed Hooks's cigarette and ashes down the drain. If only he could rid himself of the man so easily.

His workday was ruined. The clouds had thickened, changing the light on Verdie's trailer. It looked grotesque in shadow, a fallen behemoth preparing to die. Besides, his visitor had upset him. He could not imagine a son so callous as to ask some stranger to spy on his mother. Whatever would he tell Verdie? Your own flesh and blood asked me to keep an eye on you? He's afraid you're going to marry Poe Titus and he'll lose this pathetic patch of dust he refers to as his inheritance? He wants me to watch out for anybody sniffing around the daffodils? No, better to remain silent, thought Figman. Gather information from both sides and try to figure the whole thing out. He did not wish to become embroiled in Verdie's family problems. Indeed, he did not wish to be involved in her life in any way. He would keep to himself and think of something to tell Hooks the next time he came calling.

Through his living room doorway, Figman saw the mailman pull up in his Jeep. He knew there would not be much mail for him; most days he received nothing at all. Verdie always seemed to get something in the mail, and though it usually spelled disaster, it was indication that at least somebody, somewhere, knew she existed. Figman threw on a sweater and headed out to his mailbox, saddened at the thought of how little the world remembered him. Poe Titus's GMC truck turned into the driveway. The man waved to Figman on his way in to see Verdie. Figman nodded and waved back. His eyes fell instinctively on the man's license plate. It said WRANGLR.

Verdie's mailbox held the usual worries: a bill from a doctor in Roswell, another letter from the I.R.S. marked urgent, a third letter from that collection agency in Albuquerque, and a Notice of Hearing from the court clerk of Eddy County. Figman had received a package from his mother. As the day was blustery, he waited until he got back to his house before opening it. He knew its contents ahead of time: cash and a letter. He sat on his couch and began to read.

He'd written to his mother as soon as he'd recovered from his last headache, warning her not to make contact with Mrs. Medina. He'd insisted, also, that she not get too friendly with Eisler.

His mother's letter was maddeningly predictable:

Dear Son,

I had the nicest lunch with Miriam Eisler. What a lovely young woman! We chatted about all sorts of things and she had a thousand questions about you. They were not the kind of questions I would call at all intrusive, so I didn't hesitate in answering them. She asked about your friends, your hobbies, and where you like to go on vacation—that sort of thing. I even showed her your picture album. She loved that little picture of you in your cowboy hat straddling that fence with the missing rail. Do you remember that picture?

Maybe I'm just being a mother, but I think her interest in you may be more than just professional. She told me she found you quite handsome. And I was able to ascertain that she is both Jewish and single! She's quite attractive and obviously very bright to have gotten where she is while still in her thirties.

As you requested, I have not contacted Mrs. Medina, though it distresses me to know she is in such desperate need of help. Miriam told me she was recently laid off from her job at Thrifty Mart. It seems she'd taken too many sick days after the accident. Well, enough of other people's problems.

I do hope all is well with you, darling. I trust you are in good health and that your new job is sufficiently rewarding to justify the lies I've been forced to tell. As you requested, I have burned all your letters upon receipt, which pains me a bit as they are all I have of you right now.

Write soon. I do miss you. When might I come for a visit?

Love, Mother

Miriam. Just that one word, which seemed to leap off his mother's lavender-scented stationery, confirmed Figman's worst fears. His mother never referred to people by their given names without having developed an emotional attachment to them. Her neighbor for the past seventeen years was still Mrs. Helms. Her housekeeper, who also worked for Figman's aunt, Virginia, was still Mrs. Camacho. Even the paper boy was a Mr., especially when the paper landed on the roof. Eisler obviously had snowed his mother with the illusion of warmth. And now his mother was trying to use this woman—this opposing attorney, no less—as a lure to get Figman to return to L.A., as though the prospect of any single Jewish woman somewhere in the city were enough of an incentive for him to drop everything and come galloping home.

Figman returned his mother's letter to its envelope. He sat on his couch, staring out the window at the Rodriguez house where Bobo crouched under his clothesline, digging. Figman watched him for a long time. Eventually, Verdie's car turned into the driveway and headed back toward her trailer. Titus had obviously let himself in with his own key. Figman considered joining them but decided against it. He would wait an hour or two in hope that Titus would leave.

The thought of visiting Oma crossed his mind, but he also rejected that idea. After their first three dates, Figman had decided to take a break from her company. He'd seen her only once in the last week, when he'd gone to Lester's to buy groceries. This was his usual plan: Go out with a woman three times, then play it cool. It worked, usually. He would give Oma a call on the weekend.

Figman strolled into his kitchen and got himself another beer. There, on his shiny linoleum, were the same heavy, black scuff marks he'd spent hours removing upon moving in. He took out a scrub brush and went to work. An hour later, he'd removed all of them. It took him another hour to strip away the old coat of wax and repolish his kitchen floor. By the time he was done, he'd grown hungry.

Figman fixed himself a salami sandwich. He ate all of it and drank a third beer. Still hungry, he fished sliced dill pickles from their medium-sized jar. Titus's truck was still parked next to Verdie's green Impala.

Figman rinsed his dishes, gathered up his landlady's mail, and jogged the thirty feet to her trailer. He knocked briskly on the metal door; in a minute she answered it. Poe Titus sat at her table behind a stack of poker chips.

"Mr. Forbes," she said. "Good to see you." Titus looked up from his hand of cards. Verdie wore a bright pink bathing suit that accentuated her bony chest. Her skin, sun-weathered and dry, looked like cowhide.

"I brought you your mail," said Figman. "And came by to explain the new name."

"I thought you must have sublet the place till I seen you through the window."

"Oh, I would never do that," said Figman. "Not without talking to you first."

Verdie laughed. "It was a joke, Louis."

Titus chuckled, as if on cue.

"Come on in," said Verdie. Figman stepped up into her fetid trailer. "I can still call you Louis, can't I?"

"Whatever," said Figman. He handed over her stack of mail. Verdie's small, drooping breasts revealed silvery stretch marks, proof that Benito hadn't actually hatched from some egg.

"You know, you don't have to do this every day," she said. "My mail can just sit there and rot for all I care." She threw the stack onto the countertop; the top letter landed in her dish-filled sink.

"It's no trouble," said Figman. "Really."

"How about a drink?" she said.

"Sure," said Figman.

"Would you like another, Poe?"

Titus said, "No thanks. I've got to be driving soon."

Verdie rooted in her open cabinets for a glass. "Oh, hell," she said, fishing her letter from the brackish water.

"What game are you playing?" asked Figman.

"Five-card draw," said Titus. "Pull up a chair."

Figman did as he was instructed.

"So what's this Forbes business?" the man asked.

"My father's name. His real name, I mean. Figman was my stepfather's name, and when my father died and my mother remarried, she named me Figman. But it's never been my real name, even though it says Figman on my birth certificate. That was because my father died before I was born, and by then my mother had remarried. So I thought I'd go back to the name Forbes since that's the name I should have been given if it hadn't been for this other guy."

"Phew," said Poe Titus.

Verdie opened her freezer and took out an ice tray. "I like Forbes better than Figman," she said. Flesh sagged from the inside of her thighs like a turkey's wattle.

"So what's the W. J. stand for?" asked Titus.

Shit. He hadn't thought of that. Figman stretched casually. "That's my artist's name. That's how I sign all my canvases."

"Why?" asked Titus. He lit a cigarette.

"Just like the sound of it, I guess."

"What's it stand for?"

"William Justice."

Titus took a long pull from his cigarette and placed it in the ashtray next to his stack of poker chips. "Didn't you want to use the name of the man who'd raised you?"

What business was it of his? "Well, sure I did," said Figman. "For a while. Until I grew up and discovered who my real father was."

Titus eyed him suspiciously. "Forbes," he said. "That Jewish?"

Forbes Jewish? What planet did this guy hail from? "No it's not," said Figman.

"So your real father wasn't Jewish, but you are?"

How did Titus know he was Jewish? Figman hadn't told him that, even though he'd been asked. Why did the man care? "My mother is Jewish. Judaism is passed down through the mother's side of the family."

"No kidding? Hey, Verdie, did you hear that?"

"What?" she said.

"Jewishness is passed down through the mother's side of the family?"

"No shit?" said Verdie. She set Figman's drink in front of him on the table. "Want to play a hand?" she asked, taking the seat between them.

"I don't know how."

"It's simple, son," said Titus. He handed him a portion of Verdie's poker chips. "These are yours. You bet with them. I deal everybody five cards and then you ask me for more if you need to make a hand. A hand is like a straight, or a flush, or a full house. A pair. Two pair—that sort of thing. We go around the table. Best hand wins."

"I better not," said Figman.

"Suit yourself," said Titus. He looked at his silver and turquoise watch, not unlike the watch that Benito Hooks had been wearing. "Getting late," he said. "Looks like you won again, Verdeen." Titus stood up, stretched, then leaned over and kissed Verdie on the cheek. "I'll call you tomorrow," he said on his way out the door. He'd left his cigarette smoldering in the ashtray.

"Leave it open, hon," said Verdie. The screen door slapped shut behind Titus. "How about a tamale?" she asked Figman.

"Oh, no thanks," he said. "I just ate a sandwich."

"Well, don't mind, then, if I eat one in front of you." She rose from her seat and walked over to the hot plate on her counter, where she spooned something from a pan into a pink plastic bowl. It was brown and looked like mud.

"So, how are you feeling these days?" asked Figman. He was glad Poe Titus had left; his departure confirmed, more or less, a home elsewhere.

"I feel fine, Louis. How do you feel?"

"Fine," he said. "Never better." A breeze blew in through the open door. The sky had turned somber.

"Sure you don't want one?" asked Verdie. "I make a mean chipotle tamale."

"That's what Titus said."

"When was that? Oh, that's right. He told me you come by one day. That was sure sweet of you."

"No problem," said Figman.

Verdie sat down again at the kitchen table. Her breasts hung like two dead pheasants.

"So, how do you two know each other?" asked Figman.

"Poe and I—we go way back," said Verdie. "Grew up together. We was both delivered by the same doctor. Dr. Perdom. He's dead now." Sauce from her tamale dripped off her fork and onto her belly, round as a cantaloupe.

"Did Titus know your husband before he died?"

"Honey, everybody knows everybody in this town."

"Ah," he said. Verdie took another bite of tamale. Figman had to resist the urge to grab her napkin and wipe up the mess she had made on her bathing suit. "So, how long have you been a widow?"

Verdie laughed. "Not long enough."

Figman raised his eyebrows.

"Benny dying—best thing ever happened to me." She laughed again, wildly, then took a long drink of Scotch. It was not the response Figman had expected.

"How'd he die? I mean, if you don't mind my asking." He reached over and put out Titus's cigarette.

"Hell, I don't mind. Got no secrets around here." She took another bite of brown tamale. The glob of sauce on her belly jiggled. "It was an accident," she continued. "Working for Harley Stevens back in seventy-two—he's in concrete. Well, not literally, though some folks I know would sell their grandchild to see it." She laughed again, then took another bite. "Benny was fixing the bell tower out at Our Lady of Grace down on Roselawn. You been by that place?"

"I don't think so," said Figman.

"Real nice job he was doing. Real nice. Till he fell, that is, and busted his neck."

The Hornsinger claim. Truman Hornsinger, while changing sign lettering on the San Diego Freeway, fell off his scaffolding and crushed two cervical vertebrae. He lived but remained paralyzed from the neck down. "I'm sorry," said Figman.

"Pfft," said Verdie. She mopped up the sauce on her plate with her index finger, then licked it off. "My mother's recipe."

"I'll have to try one sometime. When I'm not so full."

"Had dessert yet?" she said, getting up from the table. The glob of sauce fell from her bathing suit to her linoleum floor, where Figman imagined it would live forever.

"Not yet," he said.

"Would you like some peach pie, then? I just got me some last night."

"What the hell," said Figman.

"Live dangerously," she said, opening the door to her refrigerator. Verdie lifted a pie tin out from the bottom shelf and placed it on top of the table. She took two salad plates down from a cabinet, then fished a knife and two forks from her sinkful of water. She rinsed them under the faucet and wiped them off on her bathing suit. When she sliced into the pie, her upper arms wiggled. She handed a plate to Figman. "Let's go out on the steps," she said. "Come on. Bring your drink."

Figman took his pie and drink and followed her outside. The air was warm and muggy. Bobo dug in Verdie's cactus bed at the side of her yard, a safe distance from the highway. Figman sat down next to Verdie on the top step of her trailer. He'd be glad when spring came. The snow had finally melted, but nothing green had pushed up through the earth. No grass. No wildflowers. No daffodils. "Strange evening," he said. "Good pie, though." Figman desperately wanted to ask her about Benito.

"Bulldog Superette had them on special. Two for one. I got another, if you want it."

"Let me buy it from you," he said.

"Pfft," said Verdie. "You do plenty for me just picking up my mail. One time, George—that's the mailman—well he couldn't fit no more mail in the box. Had to bring it out here himself."

"So, you and Benny, did you ever have—" Figman froze. On the bottom step, a huge black scorpion made its way toward their feet. It must have been three inches long. Figman tapped Verdie on the forearm and pointed to it. The thing had pincers.

Verdie eyed the scorpion. "Vinegaroon," she said. "Them things won't hurt you."

"It's horrible," said Figman.

Verdie laughed, then squashed it with her shoe.

Figman felt he might throw up. "Why'd you do that?" he asked. He could hardly bear to look at it.

"Smell," she said.

Reluctantly, Figman sniffed at the air. It smelled like vinegar.

"That's why they're called vinegaroons."

"Oh," he said.

Verdie took off her shoe and swept the black remains of the scorpion underneath the steps. "Wouldn't want to ruin your appetite," she said. Figman set his plate of pie beside him on the step. "Bobo!" Verdie hollered. "Get away from that prickly pear. You're gonna hurt yourself, child."

The small figure stopped his digging and looked up at them. He was no child. He had the features of a twenty-year-old. "Is he a dwarf?" Figman whispered to Verdie. The wind blew dust across the highway.

"Nah," she said. "He's just stunted. Some problem or other with his birth."

"Ah," said Figman. Bobo went back to his digging around Verdie's prickly pear.

"Bobo!" she yelled again. "Get yourself over here."

Bobo gathered up his metal spoon and bucket and strolled closer to the trailer. He looked down at the ground when he walked.

"What you doing, child, in my cactus bed?"

"Playing with my entrenching tool," said Bobo.

"Well, don't," said Verdie. "You'll grow hair on your backhoe."

Bobo took his spoon and yellow bucket and headed back across the highway.

"Is everything a joke to you?" asked Figman.

"I reckon," said Verdie, and he knew how bravely she was lying.

THE UGLIEST CHURCH
IN AMERICA

It wasn't quite a migraine. There had been no vision distur-
bance, no depression or euphoria the day before. Still, the pain she felt
upon waking was every bit as intense; the nausea, as equally debilitating.
Marilee opened her eyes. A crack of daylight shone like a sword through
the gap between the curtains. She squinted, rolled over, and raised her
head slowly off the pillow. The clock between the beds said two ten.
Enoch was still sleeping.

She had not heard him come in during the night. His clothes lay in a
pile on the floor, his backpack splayed open on the dresser. He snored
lightly, a low rumble to which Marilee had grown fondly accustomed. At
night, it eased her into sleep like white noise; in the morning, it gently
roused her from her dreams.

Though she needed to go to the bathroom, she blenched at the
thought of getting out of bed. So unremitting was the pounding in her
forehead, so constant the rolling in her stomach that Marilee lay motionless for a good twenty minutes before finally waking Enoch. "Yo,"
she whispered. It hurt to talk, hurt even to lie still.

Enoch didn't budge.

"Yo," she said again.

Nothing. He must have gotten in very late to be still sleeping at this
hour. She called his name. Enoch turned over, rubbed his eyes, and
scratched at his shoulder blade.

"I feel terrible," she said.

"Hangover."

Marilee winced, embarrassed to admit it.

Enoch swung his legs out from under the sheets and sat on the edge of his bed.

"Got a cure for headaches? Some leeches or something?"

"Leeches are for cramps. For headaches you need fly amanita."

"Fly what?"

"Wild mushroom. Toxic if you don't know what you're doing."

"There's Percocet in my purse. Could you bring me a couple?"

"Heavy duty," he said, slipping out from under his sheets.

Marilee shut her eyes, in no frame of mind to look at Enoch naked.

"Jesus, this thing must weigh ten pounds," he said, lugging her purse off the chair and into the bathroom. "What do you have in here, pluto-nium?" In a moment, she heard water running. Enoch returned to her bedside, Percocet in one hand, glass of water in the other. Marilee raised her head off the pillow so as not to dribble. Taking a swig, she rocked her head back slowly, inserted the pills between her lips, then swallowed. "In-teresting technique," said Enoch.

Marilee lowered herself onto her pillow and lay flat on her back with her eyes closed.

"Is there anything else I can do?" asked Enoch.

Last night she would have welcomed the question. "Could you pee for me?"

"I haven't mastered that one yet, but I could bring you the ice bucket."

Marilee opened her eyes. The bruise on Enoch's forehead, now a nasty purple-green, lent an aura of seriousness to his offer.

"I'll pass," she said. "Wouldn't want to scare the horses."

Enoch laughed.

"Not so loud," she whispered.

"Sorry."

Enoch showered, then put on a clean pair of jeans and his red shirt. She listened to him puttering about the room, scraping his change off the dresser, zipping up his backpack. "Would you like some breakfast?" he asked her. "Some eggs or some toast?"

The thought of food was nauseating. "I just want to sleep," she said.

"Okay. I'll go do the laundry and be back in a few hours. What do you want washed?"

Marilee tried to think about laundry but couldn't get beyond the throbbing in her temples. "Could you stay with me?" she asked. "Just until the pills kick in?"

"Sure," said Enoch, his voice suddenly tender. He took her hand. She didn't want him to.

"Could you rub the back of my neck?" she asked. "That sometimes helps."

"Of course," he said.

Carefully, Marilee rolled to her side with her back to Enoch. He massaged her neck and shoulders, his hands small but surprisingly strong. They felt good, his hands; they lessened her pain. When she expected him to stop, he kept on rubbing.

"Thanks," she said, after twenty minutes. The Percocet had finally made her drowsy.

"Anytime," said Enoch.

She listened to him walking about the room, gathering her clothes for the laundry, she imagined. His noises sounded amplified as she drifted in and out of consciousness, a pleasant crossing. Soon, she felt his presence near her. "Should I just wash everything?" he whispered. "It all looks pretty road-worn."

"I guess so," she said. Enoch closed up her suitcase. She heard him open the front door. A sudden rose-tinged brightness shone through her eyelids.

"Get some sleep," he said.

"Thanks," she said, then added, "I'm sorry."

"For what?"

"For being sick."

"Don't be a twit," said Enoch.

■

When Marilee awoke, Enoch was sitting in the chair by the window reading a paperback upon whose title her eyes would not focus. Beside him was a stack of clean clothes, folded in neat piles on the dresser. He was munching on something that smelled like peanut brittle.

"Hi," she said, waving her fingers. She was still too dopey to assess her level of pain.

"Well, hello," said Enoch. "How you feeling?"

"Woozy."

He put down his book. "What's wooze?"

"Huh?"

"If you're boozy, you're full of booze. So what's wooze?"

"Don't talk about booze."

"Sorry," he said. "You do look better."

Hearing this was anything but comforting. "At least I feel better. Worst is over, I think."

"Terrific," said Enoch.

"But I'm spacey as hell. And I've really got to pee." She sat up slowly, swung her bare legs out from under the sheets, braced herself with her hands, and stood upright. Her head throbbed when she moved it. Cautiously, she made her way to the bathroom. She peed, brushed her teeth, and splashed water on her face. When she returned to her bed, she discovered Enoch had straightened it for her. Her pillows had been fluffed and stacked against the headboard. He had even turned down the bedcovers.

"Thanks," she said. "I'll leave your tip on the dresser."

"Now, what can I get you? Cold washcloth? Water? Something to eat?"

She climbed into bed and thought for a moment. It was good to lie back against the pillows and wallow in the Percocet afterglow. She felt mellow—the way Californians were supposed to feel, a rare state of mind for Marilee. "I guess food would be good."

"Great," said Enoch, jumping off the chair and grabbing his crutches. "Carmina spent all afternoon in the kitchen."

Carmina again. He had obviously spent the day with her while Marilee slept.

"I'll be back," he said, and was out the door.

Marilee reached for the phone on the table next to the bed. She dialed nine for an outside line, then Larry's number. She was glad she hadn't slept with Enoch, relieved that the night before had not worked out the way she'd intended. It would have been awkward to be with him again once she was sober and back in control.

On the fourth ring, Larry's answering machine switched on. She hung up without leaving a message. Where was he? She struggled to remember what day it was.

When she first planned her trip to Alamogordo, she'd scheduled her departure so as not to arrive on a weekend, for though Larry's letters implied a hermetic lifestyle, it was not inconceivable he had resumed dating. How embarrassing it would be to show up at his apartment and have a woman answer the door. That had happened once to Marilee, when she and Larry were in high school. Late one night, she'd dropped by his house unexpectedly to pick up a forgotten Government book. Rachel Zimmovich greeted her in a towel.

"Yeah?" said Rachel in her thick New Yorkese. Marilee recognized her as the woman who ran the poetry series at the coffeehouse. Rachel was pretty in an Old World sort of way. She had Byzantine eyes, olive skin, and hair like an unwatered fern. Usually, she wore clothing.

"I'm sorry," said Marilee, feeling as if a bomb had fallen on her head. "I just came by for my Government book. Tell Larry I'll get it in the morning."

"Here or at school?" Rachel went to USC. Her legs were wet.

"When he picks me up."

"And you are . . . ?"

"Marilee."

"Mary?" Rachel shifted her balance from one foot to the other and hoisted up her towel, thus enhancing her ample cleavage. Where were Larry's parents?

"Marilee," she said distinctly. She had assumed Rachel knew who she was. Was she doing this to be mean?

"One word or two?"

"One." Did it matter?

"Oh, like the song? 'Merrily We Roll Along'?"

"That's right," said Marilee. "Just like the song."

■

Enoch returned to their motel room looking like a court jester bearing gifts for a queen. He carried a bed tray on top of which were two plates of chile rellenos, silverware, napkins, chamomile tea brewing in a mug, a Dos Equis, a basket of sopaipillas, a jar of honey, and a vase full of pink daisies.

"My God," said Marilee. "Somebody went to a lot of trouble."

"Carmina. Wait till you taste these babies." Enoch deposited the tray in front of Marilee, shut the door behind him, and climbed up onto the bed. He sat cross-legged with his napkin in his lap.

"Where are your crutches?" she asked, wondering how he'd managed to carry the tray across the parking lot without spilling anything.

"I left them in the office. Dig in."

Marilee took a bite of her relleno. "Oh, this is good," she said, savoring the flavors. "Really good. The chiles are great. Nice and smoky." There were few things better than good Mexican food after a bad headache. She took another bite. "They're so light. And the cheese—what kind of cheese is this?"

"Jack," said Enoch.

"And the sauce—it's fabulous!"

"Carmina can cook."

"No kidding," said Marilee. "She should be doing this for a living, not schlepping behind the desk of some crummy motel."

Enoch gave her a funny look.

"So, how do you two know each other?" She tried to sound casual.

"We're old friends." A bite of chile relleno slid off his fork and landed on the bedspread. "Shit!" he said, wiping it up with his napkin.

"From Kingfield?"

"No, from Juárez." He hopped down off the bed and hobbled into the bathroom. She heard water running. In an instant, he returned with a wet washcloth, which he applied to the greasy spot.

"Just leave it," said Marilee. "They have maids." Enoch kept scrubbing. "So, how did you meet, then?"

"Working."

"Doing what?"

Enoch stopped scrubbing. "Look, I know this sounds weird, but I really don't want to talk about it."

"All right," said Marilee. She took a sip of tea, grateful he hadn't brought her a beer.

"Now, don't get that way," said Enoch, depositing the washcloth on the tray.

"What way?" She knew exactly what way.

"Like you're pissed at me again."

"I am pissed."

"Why? Because I don't want to talk about Carmina?"

"Because you're acting like an asshole."

"An asshole?"

"Yeah. What makes you think you have to act so fucking mysterious all the time?"

"Fucking mysterious?"

"Yeah. You think it's cool? You think it gives you some sort of tragic persona?"

"I don't need a tragic persona."

"That's just what I mean."

"What is?"

"Shit like that. And all the secrets. I mean, what kind of game is this, anyway? Here I am bumming around the state with you, sharing motel rooms, watching you traipse around naked night and day—and I don't have a clue who you really are."

Enoch took another bite, then wiped his mouth with the part of his napkin he hadn't used to clean up his spill. "I'm Enoch Swann. And you can ask me anything you want. Just nothing about Carmina."

"That's exactly what I mean! Right there!" She was yelling.

Enoch steadied his Dos Equis and gave her a stern look. The vein in his forehead bulged. "Look," he said, "you want to know something about Carmina, then walk across that parking lot and ask Carmina. You want to know something about me, then ask me."

She had never before seen Enoch angry. Not after the cop had given him a hard time. Not after she had dropped him off in Alamogordo. Not even after being thrown in the trunk of her car by a couple of punk Nazis. "All right," she said. "How come you hitchhike around the desert?"

"Because I like to," he said flatly.

"Why don't you have a job?"

"Don't need one."

"What are you, independently wealthy or something?"

"Or something."

"Is that so?" Marilee bit the corner off a sopaipilla and drizzled honey into its center, exactly as she'd seen Alcie Britton do it in Rocket City. It was a small gesture of regional sophistication she hoped Enoch would notice. "And where does all this independent wealth come from? Our taxes?"

"I resent that."

"Well, where then? How are you able to afford all these meals and hotel rooms? Why don't you need to have a job?"

Enoch smiled out one side of his mouth; she felt her anger mount.

"Is it because you're a dwarf? Is that it? Dwarfs don't have to work like the rest of us? Does the government give out dwarf benefits or something? Or maybe you just don't want to work. That's easier, I suppose. It helps compensate for having been dealt such a lousy hand. And it makes you all the more tragic, doesn't it? No past. No future. Being blown where the wind blows. Drifting around the Southwest like some character in a bad novel."

She stopped short, sensing she had gone too far. Enoch locked eyes with her as he had with the scorpion, staring her down, daring her to strike. Marilee stared back. Hot. Righteous. Waiting for an answer to a question she had already forgotten. She stared at him for a long time. "Shit," she said finally. She tossed her sopaipilla down on the tray. "What the fuck are we doing?"

"What are *you* doing?" asked Enoch.

"I don't know. Shit."

"Then let's drop it," he said.

"How'd we get off on this, anyway?"

"You called me an asshole."

"I said you were *acting like* an asshole."

"Oh. That's okay, then."

"No it's not," said Marilee. The cheese oozing out of her rellenos had congealed.

"Let's forget it," said Enoch.

"It's fine if you want to have secrets."

"Everybody has secrets."

"Yeah, but most of us don't lord them over the people we know."

"I think most people do just that," said Enoch.

"What do you mean?"

"Use secrets as power." He tore off a hunk of sopaipilla and popped it into his mouth. "As weapons, even. It builds their mystique and makes others think they have a past more interesting than their own. Some event or circumstance more special than anything they themselves have experienced."

Marilee shrugged.

"And there are people who do legitimately have things like that in their history," he continued. "Something dark and painful that gives their lives hidden meaning. Some of them use it on other people. But that's not what's going on with Carmina."

Motivated by hunger and a weariness that transcended her residuum of pain, Marilee felt willing to extend Enoch a tiny benefit of the doubt. "I'm sorry," she said. "I don't know why I said all those things. I guess I'm just going through a lot of changes."

"I understand," he said.

"Do you?" At once, she regretted having asked him that. She wished she could take it back, swallow her words like bitter medicine. Enoch sat motionless across from her on the bed. She hoped he would say something to end the silence, but he said nothing. Instead, he did something that caught her by surprise: He balanced on his knees, leaned over her bed tray, took her face in his hands, and kissed her.

■

"Welcome to earth," said Enoch.

Marilee looked at the clock. It said six thirty-seven. Night? Morning? She had no idea. Enoch was sitting in a chair by the window. "What day is it?" she asked.

"Saturday. How do you feel?"

"Groggy." She thought about it. "What's grog?"

"It's a rum drink," said Enoch.

"Oh. Well. Then that's how I feel. Like I've had too much rum."

"Too much rum to drive to Albuquerque?"

"Definitely too much rum."

They showered and dressed, then walked to breakfast at the Four Winds Restaurant, where the waitress knew Enoch. Marilee felt terrible, having just gotten her period. She ordered fruit and an English muffin. Enoch ordered the large stack of pancakes, two eggs over easy, link sausage, and a side of toast.

"These headaches of yours," he said. "You get them often?"

"About once a month. Migraines run on my mother's side of the family, but this wasn't a migraine. Or maybe it was. I woke up with it, so it's hard to tell."

He looked nonplussed.

"I didn't get an aura. But since I was sleeping, I may have not noticed it if I did get one. Then again, since I'd been drinking, maybe it was just part of my hangover. Or the hangover triggered the migraine. I don't know."

"So what does an aura look like?"

"Patterns. Shimmering lights. Like a snake sometimes, that starts as a pinpoint and grows larger."

"Cool," said Enoch.

Marilee shot him a dangerous look.

"I mean, it's like acid without the expense."

"There's plenty of expense."

"You're right," he said. He drank down his coffee, then held his empty cup up to the waitress. She arrived with a fresh pot. "Still in pain?" he asked Marilee, as soon as the woman had departed.

"A little. But only if I shake my head."

"There's balloons."

"What?"

"Hot air balloons. We could go up in one."

"What are you talking about?"

"The Balloon Fiesta in Albuquerque. If we leave today, we can catch the best part of it."

"How far is it to Albuquerque?"

"A few hours. I know a place we can stay."

"I bet you do."

"We could get up early and watch the ascent at sunrise. It's magnificent. Hundreds of balloons of every conceivable pattern and color, all taking off at once as the sun comes up over the mountains. You'll never see anything more beautiful. We could hang out a few days. Go up in a balloon. Take the tram to the top of Sandia Peak. Check out the ugliest church in America."

"The what?"

"Little church on the edge of the city. Baptist, I think. It looks like a drive-through chicken place."

Marilee laughed, which hurt her head.

"Then we could go up to Santa Fe and Taos," he continued. "Los Alamos, even. There's a giant caldera up in the Jemez and Indian cave dwellings at Frijoles Canyon that are really something to see."

She had three more days with Enoch, then her week was over. But did the number of days really matter, or even her commitment? Could she not return to Rocket City immediately, if she chose? On the other hand, if she were having fun, could she not spend another month with Enoch? Or a lifetime? He looked handsome this morning in his weirdly appealing way, despite the crumb of toast sticking to his bottom lip. Marilee reached across the table and brushed it off, a gesture he appeared not to notice. "Up for driving yet?" he asked her.

"I don't think so," she said. "But I could use some exercise."

They walked down into the heart of Carrizozo. It felt good to be out in the morning air, even though it did look as if at any minute it might rain. Gusts of wind blew dark clouds from the south, kicked up dust from the desert floor, bowled tumbleweeds down Central Avenue at the split pins of tree trunks. After two blocks, Marilee's fingers went numb. She clutched at her sweater.

"Did you bring a jacket?" asked Enoch.

"Nope. My mom was going to ship me my clothes as soon as I got settled."

"Was?"

"Is. I should call Larry as soon as we get back to the room. Let him know that I'll be there on Tuesday."

"I thought you wanted to be a surprise?"

Enoch never missed a beat. She found his doggedness in calling her on things irritating; at the same time she respected him for it. Until Enoch, she had never met a man who would (or could) stand up to her, an irony she enjoyed privately as his arms worked his crutches somewhere down around her waist.

As they approached the county courthouse, three men and a woman, all in business suits, stood huddled in a tight cluster on the walkway. When they caught sight of Enoch, they collectively paused, stared, then resumed their conversation with exaggerated vigor. Enoch whispered to Marilee out the side of his mouth. "I'm not looking at the freak. Not me. I'm just standing here, talking torts, and playing with the dial lock on my briefcase."

"Freak?" said Marilee. "What freak? I don't see any freaks. Do you see any freaks?"

"I see four," said Enoch.

Marilee wondered what people were doing in front of the courthouse on a Saturday morning. "I hate lawyers," she said. "But not nearly as much as I hate doctors." She expected Enoch to concur, imagining he'd suffered more than his fair share of the medical profession, but he said nothing, just kept working his crutches like scissors as they walked.

Marilee was fascinated by the various ways in which Enoch seemed to adapt to his environment. In a headwind, he used his crutches as canes, leaning forward into the gusts, alternately casting one in front of the other. Out at Malpaís, he had walked down the steep footpath to the trail sideways, using both crutches together as a brace against the incline. And in Ruidoso, she'd seen him carry them both under one arm when he descended a set of stairs. She wondered why Enoch relied on crutches at all; walking without them, he looked awkward but always managed to maintain his balance.

At the next intersection, they crossed the street and headed back toward the Little Black Peak Inn. The wind blew at their backs, cold and angry; Enoch shifted back to his usual gait, swinging both crutches in unison as though missing a leg. They passed shops that looked warm inside, but neither of them stopped. Heads down, they strode back toward the junction of Highways 54 and 380.

Marilee, in a pensive mood, reflected upon Enoch's kiss. How he had risen up on his knees so that he seemed taller than she. And how that had made it all seem more natural—not awkward, as she might have imagined, but comfortable and easy. His advance had surprised but not embarrassed her, and that in itself had been a surprise; his kiss, mercifully uncomplicated, had made her feel cared for and forgiven, coming, as it had, on the heels of her insensitivity.

Enoch's voice intruded on her reminiscence. "Why do lawyers always wear neckties?"

Marilee thought for a minute. "I'm game."

"To keep their foreskins from rolling up over their heads."

The sudden blast of air brakes startled them as a caravan of southbound charter buses came to a halt at the intersection.

"Trinity Site tours," said Enoch. "Check it out."

"You're kidding."

"First Saturday in October. They do tours every six months. That's the only time they let you in. Watch. Bet they head west to Stallion Gate."

Marilee studied the faces through the window. They looked ordinary—adults and children, some wearing hats, shoulders crossed with camera straps. She wondered why anyone would want to tour a fifty-year-old bomb site. "What's out there?" she asked.

"A crater. A monument."

"Have you seen it?"

"Nope."

"Do you want to?"

"Sure. At Ground Zero the sand fused into green glass. Now that's something."

"Well, I'd have a hard time with it," said Marilee, starting across the intersection.

"Why?"

"Because it's all so horrible. Nuclear attack. People being burned. Blinded. Slow death from radiation."

Enoch shrugged.

"That doesn't bother you?"

"Of course it does." He was loping along briskly. All three buses turned right onto 380.

"But you'd take a tour of the place where it all started?"

"Why not?"

"Because they're billing it like Disneyland. Bus tours, for God's sake."

"At Auschwitz there's a souvenir shop."

"No!"

"I think so," said Enoch.

"And *that* doesn't bother you?"

"Not really. It gets people in the door. And it doesn't change the fact that people were murdered there."

"But it cheapens it."

"Does it?" Enoch resumed walking. "I've never been to Auschwitz," he said, "but I'd check it out if I had the chance."

Marilee frowned and shook her head.

"It's important we face these things," he said. "So we don't repeat our mistakes."

"*Their* mistakes," she reminded him. She hadn't even been born yet.

"A useful distinction," said Enoch. "And bullshit."

■

As soon as they'd returned to the sanctuary of their motel room, Marilee kicked off her shoes and stretched out on top of the bedspread. Still heady—sleeplogged, as she called it—she knew it would be a day in which she would never completely awaken. On the opposite wall, a picture hung crookedly, a nature scene of an Indian woman gathering water from a river. Would her own life ever be that simple?

Enoch sat on the floor with his back against the dresser, looking as small and unfathomable as a child's dream. She had to admit she felt sorry for him, despite his being the one person she knew most likely to reject pity. Was it pity that kept her in his spell, or something less obvious? Enoch licked his fingers and thumbed a page of his paperback.

Marilee's eyes were now able to focus upon its title, *Pride and Prejudice*, a book she'd been assigned in high school but had never finished reading.

The next thing she knew, she was waking out of sleep. The first day of her period she was usually so fatigued she spent the entire day dozing. Enoch, who had finished his book, sat in the chair by the window, thumbing through a magazine. "I'd like Thai food this evening," said Marilee.

Enoch looked up at her and smiled. "No can do in Carrizozo."

"Cajun, then."

He laughed.

"I'm sick of American and Mexican food."

"You'd better get used to it," he said. "This is New Mexico, emphasis on the Mex."

"Italian, then."

"I'll see what Carmina can do."

"Or not Italian. I'm sick of Italian. It's all Larry ever wanted."

Enoch eyed her curiously. "Have you thought about the balloons? I need to be in Albuquerque by three AM."

"Need?"

"That's right," he said.

"Are you being mysterious again?"

"*Fucking* mysterious. You have to put the fucking in or it doesn't sound as accusatory."

Marilee laughed.

"And the answer is yes," he said.

"And you're not going to tell me?"

"Nope."

"By three AM?"

"Trust me," said Enoch. The light fell on his face at just that certain angle.

■

They loaded up the Dart around seven thirty, Enoch seemingly unconcerned that he would be paying for their motel room for a night they would not be using it. The plan was to drive to Socorro, eat dinner, and reach Albuquerque just past midnight.

Enoch left their room keys and the copy of *Pride and Prejudice* on the round table by the door. Then he picked up the phone and dialed zero. Carmina was not in the office. Someone named Gussie was working the front desk, a person with whom Enoch also seemed familiar. He chatted with Gussie for a while, then asked to talk to Chico and Marita. In a minute, he was rattling away in Spanish.

They drove west through the Valley of Fires. In twilight, the lava flow resembled a dark ocean: deep, churning, ready to engulf them in one angry swallow. The night was cold, the sky filled with black clouds. Gusts of wind blew sand across the highway; it crackled against the Dart's windshield.

Beyond Malpaís, the harsh landscape gave way to gently rolling hills. Clumps of trees dotted grassy hollows where roots were able to reach water. Bats flew in pursuit of insects. Shadows lengthened. They came upon an abandoned Santa Fe boxcar by the side of the road, a rusty Ford Galaxy with its hood up, a rock formation that looked like an eagle, the tiny town of Bingham. They sped west through White Sands Missile Range until they reached Stallion Gate, the northernmost entrance to Trinity Site. Marilee slowed as they passed the marked turnoff, forsaken now for another half year.

In Socorro, they ate dinner at Frank and Lupe's El Sombrero. The food tasted better than what you'd expect from a restaurant featuring paintings on black velvet and lacquered bagels hanging from the walls. They ordered chalupas, tostadas, and Mexican beer. They ate leisurely, splurged on ice cream for dessert, lingered over cups of hot black coffee. Not until their check arrived did Marilee realize they had never paid for their room at the Little Black Peak Inn. "Shouldn't we call?" she asked Enoch. This sort of thing made her nervous.

"Nah," he said, picking a mint up off the tray and removing its cellophane wrapper. He popped it into his mouth and sucked hard.

"Why not?" She could hardly believe he would stiff Carmina.

Enoch smiled. "Because I own the place," he said.

Back on the road, they headed north along the Rio Grande. "How's your head?" asked Enoch. "Pain gone?"

"Pretty much," said Marilee.

"Excellent." He patted her hand on the steering wheel.

"What's drowse?" she asked.

"Good one. Feeling full of drowse?"

"A little." The Dart's heater pumped warm air in their faces. "Seems like all I've done since I got here is eat and sleep, sleep and eat."

"Two of my three favorite things," he said.

She didn't ask.

Enoch stared out the windshield at the markers along the highway. "It's the altitude. Takes getting used to. Couple of weeks."

Marilee turned the heater down to low. "So, you own the place?" She tried hard to sound indifferent.

"Yup."

"And Carmina works for you?"

Enoch nodded. He kicked his boots up on the dashboard and stretched in his seat.

"You own other motels?"

"A few."

"Motels must be a good investment."

"They can be." He was falling into one of his cryptic moods.

"Is that what you did with your inheritance? Invest in motels?"

Enoch was silent for a moment; she worried he might be mad at her for leaping to conclusions, trying to make the pieces fit. "No," he said, finally. "I got a settlement. From that fire I told you about."

"Were you burned or something?" She hadn't noticed any scars.

"No."

"What, then?"

"Like I told you," he said, tapping his foot on the dashboard. "Rumors started. I got hurt."

"Hurt?"

"Worked over."

"Where?"

"At the high school."

"No, I mean *where* did they hurt you?" Marilee glanced occasionally at the road, but mostly she stared at Enoch.

"All over. Head mostly."

"Who did this?" She was trying to remember the name of that guy—not Lucid Moments, but the other one.

"Twelve guys."

"Twelve? Twelve guys beat up on you?"

Enoch squinted into the oncoming headlights. "I survived."

"But were you all right? Did you have to go to the hospital?"

"No. And yes."

"For how long?"

"Four months. But most of that time I was in a coma."

"Oh, God," said Marilee. She felt sick.

Enoch turned to face her. "Look, I'm fine now. See." He pounded his chest with his open hand and grinned. "That was years ago. It's history."

"What kind of macho assholes would gang up twelve to one against a . . ." She hit her palm against the steering wheel; the Dart shimmied from the blow.

"Normal people," said Enoch.

"Normal? They're not normal. They're not even people. They're monsters. Freaks."

Enoch stared out his window as rain began to fall. "We're all of us freaks, Marilee."

■

At Belen, she pulled off the interstate to stop for gas. Enoch filled the tank while Marilee headed off to the restroom at the far end of the parking lot. On her way back, she found a pay phone recessed into an alcove. She charged the call to her mother's number and waited for the connection.

The rain fell harder now. From the darkness of the parking lot, Marilee watched as Enoch paid for their gasoline, shoving money through a slotted window into which he could not see. She was *not* a freak. Enoch could call himself one if he chose to, but he could not lump her into the same category. She wouldn't let him.

The number she had dialed started ringing. "Hello?" said a voice on the other end of the line. "Hello? Who's there?" Marilee heard a click, then an unfamiliar dial tone.

Smiling, she placed the receiver in its cradle. It was Saturday night, and Larry was home.

SGRAFFITO

Spring was late in coming to Artesia. By the end of the second week in March, Figman had seen no flowers, no butterflies, not a single hummingbird. Where were the tiny blades of grass he'd anticipated all winter? Where was the sunshine?

Again, the day was cloudy. Unable to paint Verdie's trailer or the Rodriguez house or his feral cat in so muted a light, Figman decided to try his hand at sgraffito, a technique he had read about in his painting book. Sgraffito was the process of scratching through the surface of a painting to reveal its underlying layers of color. Figman liked the sound of the word, so much so that despite his book having suggested the process worked best with acrylics, he opted to abandon his painting of Verdie's trailer and attempt sgraffito with his oils.

The imprimatura he'd applied to his canvas the night before had dried. Over this, he painted a thick coat of rose madder. It took him a while, but it covered his canvas nicely. Next, he added chromium oxide green; the corner of canvas he applied it to turned the color of Verdie's tamales. Was he supposed to let the first layer dry before layering on a second? Where on earth had he left his book?

Figman walked into his kitchen to scrub the paint off his hands; turpentine made his skin crack, and he had taken to using just plain soap and water in washing. It took him ten minutes to remove all the pigment from the creases of his knuckles and beneath his cuticles.

He was scheduled to meet Oma at five thirty. He'd seen her three more times in the last week and a half, and each time he'd taken her to

Carlsbad. They'd seen a bad play at the community theater and two so-so movies. Before each event, he'd taken her out to dinner.

More and more, Figman found himself enjoying Oma's company. Her life was uncomplicated. She had no neuroses that he could discover, no lingering traumas that made her difficult at times. She was simple, and he liked that. He still hadn't kissed her anywhere but on the cheek.

Figman dried his hands and looked out the window. Poe Titus's truck was parked next to Verdie's green Impala. Figman headed for his bedroom. His book on painting lay on the table beside his bed, opened to the section on sgraffito. He sat on his bed and read the paragraph over again in hope of discovering whether or not he was supposed to let his paint dry between applications. The book didn't say. Through his window, he saw the mailman headed north on the highway.

Verdie's mailbox held the usual horrors: a letter from some mortuary in El Paso, another from an attorney in Mayhill, a propane bill marked overdue, and a manila envelope from the Eddy Abstract Company. He weighed the envelope in his hands. It was postmarked Artesia.

Was Verdie buying property? Some cozy little cottage for herself and Poe? Where would she get the money? Why wasn't Titus buying it on his own? Or was she selling her place because she was desperate and running out of money?

Figman stacked Verdie's mail on the counter next to his kitchen door. He would take it to her later, after her boyfriend had left. He sat down at his table and opened the letter he'd received from his mother:

Dear Son,

I haven't heard from you in over a week, so I thought I'd say hello. Much has happened since I last wrote. Mrs. Helms had her house broken into! They took her television, her silver, and all her jewelry. The poor woman is beside herself with fear every night. I see her lights on at all hours. I'm thinking about having one of those alarm companies come and give me an estimate. What do you think?

Dee called again to ask if I knew where you could be reached. As you've requested, I told her I didn't know. You can't imagine how hard it was for me to say that—to tell her I didn't know my only son's whereabouts. What must she think?

Last week I had a cold. Nothing serious—just a stuffy nose and a temperature. I'm afraid I gave it to Virginia. She's really feeling poorly. I may have to take her to the doctor tomorrow if her fever hasn't broken.

I'm still waiting for you to tell me when I can come visit. I know how important your work is, so I'll only stay a day or two. I'd just like to see you. Things aren't the same since you've been gone.

Here's the registration for your car—I've been meaning to send it to you. I paid it out of your account. Do you still want me to keep your car in my name?

I guess I'll just have to be patient to learn what's going on with you. I do hope you'll tell me before too long. I don't like all this secrecy.

Well, that's all for now. Write soon. I miss you.

Love, Mother

P.S. On Thursday I'm having lunch with Miriam. Don't worry—it's strictly social.

Figman removed the car registration his mother had included in her envelope. Folded into it, he found a new California sticker for his Aion. He'd been driving with an expired sticker for six weeks and hadn't even known it.

Figman put on water for tea. When his chamomile had steeped, he sat down at his kitchen table and began writing.

Dear Mom,

I hope this letter finds both you and Virginia healthy. Colds can be such an annoyance. I've been lucky and haven't had one this winter.

So sorry to hear about Mrs. Helms. By all means, call an alarm company. I'll help you out with the expense.

Thanks for sending me my car registration. While I appreciate your forwarding it to me, I cannot stress enough how important it is that these things be handled on time. Were I to have been picked up for an expired registration, it would have been disastrous to the company. And yes, I still need you to carry my car in your name. Don't worry. I'll drive safely.

Also, I have to ask you please not to see or talk to Ms. Eisler. I know you are fond of her, and that she is showing an interest in you, but she is not without her motives. Please try to remember that she is the attorney for several of the parties suing me.

As for Dee (or anyone else who wants to know my whereabouts), please continue to be discreet. No doubt Ms. Eisler has been in touch with all my ex-girlfriends, and is using them to try to locate me.

Again, I apologize for the secrecy. Someday you will understand. In the meantime, please know you are doing the right thing for your son.

Love, F.

Figman folded his letter and sealed it in an envelope. He thought about Dee—poor, fragile Dee—who'd been molested as a child and had never gotten over it. He remembered how she'd wept when Figman told her he was moving, and how secretly relieved he'd been to have had so timely an excuse to say goodbye.

He finished his tea and rinsed his cup in the sink. Titus's truck was still parked alongside Verdie's trailer. Figman had decided not to tell Benito that it was Poe Titus sniffing around the daffodils. He didn't like Titus, but not so much as to sic Benito on him. Besides, Verdie's business was her own, not her son's—if Benito were her son, a conclusion of which Figman wasn't entirely convinced.

Figman did his exercises for an hour, showered and dressed, then put his new registration sticker on his Aion. Afterward, he drove into town to buy stamps. On his way out of the post office parking lot, a metallic green Firebird changed lanes just as Figman pulled out onto Fourth Street. Figman slammed on his brakes to avoid being hit. The driver of the Firebird honked and gave Figman the finger. "Asshole," the man yelled out his window. He was big and blond and had a scraggly moustache. Figman glanced at the Firebird's license plate. YPU 002. It rhymed.

It was five forty-five and he was late meeting Oma. As Dino was in bed with the flu, she and Figman had decided to take their chances on meeting at a local restaurant. He hated having to sneak around with Oma, as if by dining together and catching an occasional movie they were engaging in something illicit. He hated having to answer to a little asswipe like Dino.

Standing outside the restaurant, Oma waited with her denim jacket slung over one shoulder. She wore jeans and a purple sweater that picked up on her eye that was violet. She was not wearing a bra. Figman took it as a sign of encouragement. Putting his arm around her waist, he kissed her lightly on the lips. She didn't turn away. He kept his arm around her as he held open the restaurant door. She was tall, but Figman was taller, and her body felt good alongside his own.

"How's Dino?" he asked, as soon as they were seated.

"Better. He's stopped throwing up and says he feels well enough to go back to work tomorrow."

"Good," Figman said with all the sincerity he could muster. "Did he ever tell you I tried to apologize to him?"

"When?"

"About a month ago."

"He never said a thing."

"Well, I guess he wouldn't have," said Figman.

"How come you didn't mention it to me?"

"Oh, I don't know. It didn't go very well."

"What do you mean?"

"He told me to stay away from you." Figman lowered his voice. "He threatened me."

Oma looked off into the distance. "I'm sorry," she said. "He's just . . . like, overprotective or something."

"Why?" asked Figman.

"After Dad died . . . well, things got pretty bad. Mom got sick and couldn't work for a while. Dino had to—"

"Look, maybe we shouldn't go into this," Figman interrupted. "Maybe we should talk about something lighter."

"Sure," she said. "What do you want to talk about?"

"Anything," he said. "Just not people dying, or your brother." Despite his contempt for the little asshole, Figman understood Dino. He knew what it was like to lose a father. Still, one couldn't go through life blaming the world for accidents of chance. Fate happens. He knew that. He'd seen the bumper sticker.

Their waitress appeared at the table, and they had to scramble to order. "What happened to your tooth?" Oma asked, as soon as the woman left.

He'd forgotten all about his chipped tooth; his tongue must have gotten used to the space between his front teeth. "I was trying to open a bottle of beer."

"Eeeuw," said Oma. She was achingly beautiful.

"I'll have to get it bonded," he said.

"Whatever," said Oma. She dipped a chip into salsa.

"Ever heard of bonding?"

"Sure," she said. "My uncle's a dentist."

Her uncle's a dentist? And he lets her walk around like that, with horribly broken front teeth? "So why don't you ask him to fix yours?"

Oma shrugged. "I guess they never bothered me. I'm sure he'd do it for free. We're real close, me and Uncle Eddie."

"Ah," said Figman. He felt desire stir.

"I've lived with them so long. And Jesse—well, he kind of liked them this way."

"Really?" said Figman. It was unimaginable.

"He told me not to even think of getting them fixed."

"If you don't mind my asking," said Figman, "I was wondering how it happened."

"Playing softball. Junior high." She dipped another chip into their salsa. "I was the catcher that day, and I wasn't wearing a mask."

"A softball did that?"

"No, the bat."

Figman shivered. Their waitress brought two large margaritas to their table. Oma smiled at the woman. Figman was baffled. How could she hate her eyes, which were so beautiful, and not care at all about her teeth?

"It was stupid, really," said Oma, once the woman had left. "I shouldn't have been standing that close to the batter."

"It wasn't your fault," said Figman.

"Sure it was."

"No, it wasn't. Really."

"Well, it wasn't the batter's fault. She didn't know I was right on top of her."

"It was the school's fault."

"The school's?"

"It was their liability. The teacher in charge should have made you wear a mask. It was *her* responsibility. You could have sued them and won."

Oma laughed. "I'd never do that."

"Why not? Your teeth got broken. They were negligent. There was pain and suffering, not to mention the cost of getting them reconstructed some day."

"Are you a lawyer?" asked Oma. She ran her finger over the rim of her glass, removing most of the salt.

"A lawyer?" Figman laughed.

"Well, then, how do you know so much about this stuff?"

"Just common sense." Behind Oma, Figman saw Poe Titus and Verdie walk into the dining room. Figman pushed his napkin from his lap (a trick he'd learned from Flechteau) and dove under the table to retrieve it. He lingered for a moment. When he resurfaced, Verdie and Titus had disappeared. Oma smiled at him from across the table. Her mouth looked like a hunter's trap.

■

After dinner, Figman invited Oma back to his house. When she didn't say no, Figman suspected that after six long weeks, he was about to get lucky. She followed him south on the highway in her white Corvair, a car he'd been meaning to caution her about.

"Who's Forbes?" she asked, as soon as she stepped outside her car.

"Ah, Forbes," said Figman. He searched in the dark for his house key.

"It says Forbes on the mailbox, next to Hooks. I know Hooks is Verdie."

"You know Verdie?" He was surprised the topic of his landlady had never before come up.

"I know everybody," she said, laughing. "Except that waitress tonight. She must be new. But I've never heard of any Forbeses in town."

"Well, that's me," said Figman, inserting the key in his front door and opening it. He switched on the light in the living room and held the door open for Oma. She stepped inside. "I had two fathers," he said. "One who died before I was born. That was Forbes. Figman was the man who raised me. I use both names."

"Isn't that confusing?"

"Not too," he said.

"Which name do you like better?"

"Figman. Can I get you something to drink?"

"Do you have any Coke?"

"I've got mineral water and beer."

"Nothing sweet?"

"Sorry."

"I'll have a beer, then," she said, looking around. "Just don't open it with your teeth."

Figman retrieved two Anchor Steams from his refrigerator. When he returned to his living room, Oma was studying the painting on his easel. Just this morning, he'd moved it back to its spot beside his front window. "What is it?" she asked.

"Just technique," he said. "Sgraffito. It's where you scratch through the surface so that what's underneath can come through."

"Where's the scratched part?"

"I haven't gotten to that yet."

"Oh," said Oma. She sat down on his couch.

Figman sat down next to her and felt himself getting hard. "You know the Rodriguezes across the way?" he asked.

"I told you, I know everybody."

"What's with it with that son of theirs?"

"Bobo?"

"All he does all day is dig in the dirt."

"He's . . . not right," she said.

"Sort of spooky," said Figman. "He gives me the creeps."

"Oh, Bobo wouldn't hurt a soul," said Oma.

Figman looked at their reflection in the window. The moment was growing awkward. "Want the grand tour?" he asked.

"Sure," she said, rising up off the couch with her beer. Figman led Oma from room to room, showing her his bedrooms and bath, ending up in the kitchen. "So, where are your experiments?" she asked.

"Experiments?"

"The ones with aloe?"

"Right," he said. "In that trailer, out back."

Oma looked out the window. "There's a light on," she said.

"Yes," said Figman. "It's a grow light on a timer. It goes on and off at certain times."

"So, then, where does Verdie live?"

Figman coughed. "Out there. In the trailer."

"With the plants?"

"They don't take up much room."

"Doesn't the light going on and off bother her?"

Figman felt his erection diminishing. "Well, you know Verdie," he said. "Not much ever bothers her."

Oma gave him a funny look.

"Why don't we go back into the living room?"

"What's this stuff?" she asked, reaching for his bottle of Essence of Chicken.

"That's nothing. Just a reminder, of sorts."

"Of what?"

"Lots of things."

"Like what?"

"Like California."

Oma shook the bottle and watched the chicken parts settle. "It looks gross."

"It's just a curiosity," he said, taking the bottle from her hand and returning it to his windowsill. "Let's listen to some music." Figman steered Oma back to his living room.

"Got any Billy Ray Cyrus?" she asked, flopping back down on the couch.

"Nope. How about Charles Mingus?"

"Is he country?"

"In a way," said Figman. He loaded the tape into his tape player and switched it on. Then he walked over to the window and shut the curtains.

Oma scrunched her nose. "This is jazz," she said.

"It's all I have," said Figman. "Sorry."

Oma tucked her feet up under her and ran her fingers through her hair. She looked directly at Figman with her blue and violet eyes. "You'll just have to find some way to make it up to me," she said.

Was this it? The sign he'd been waiting for? Oma stretched and took a long swallow of beer. She leaned back on the couch, adjusted her hair, and smiled at Figman with her lips closed. Figman dimmed the light and sat down next to her, sliding his arm across the back of her shoulders as he settled into the cushions. Oma hiccupped, then giggled. Figman leaned over and kissed her on the mouth. Her lipstick was sort of a cinnamon peach. It reminded him of Sandy, the woman who used to give him head while he drove the streets of L.A., something he could hardly imagine anyone doing in Artesia.

With his tongue, Figman gently explored the inside of Oma's mouth. He tasted the warm, beery lining of her cheeks and felt the jagged hole between her two front teeth. Their edges weren't as sharp as he'd expected. They felt more like his own chipped tooth, rough but strangely touchable. Oma kissed him back warmly. And then she did something that took him by surprise.

With her right hand, she reached down and unbuckled Figman's belt. In no time, she had unzipped his zipper and pulled his cock out of his underwear. He'd grown hard again, much to his relief. Then, without even the slightest warning, Oma leaned over and put the whole of him into her mouth. She cupped his balls in her hand and worked him like a pro. Zero to sixty in four-point-nine seconds. Unsafe at any speed.

Figman's eyes rested on his latest attempt at art, a pinkish field with a single brown splotch. The splotch looked a little like the blob he'd been seeing before his headaches came on. Oma moaned as she moved her lips up and down on him, the broken rim of her incisors providing just enough pain to make his pleasure nearly unbearable. He understood, suddenly, why Jesse hadn't wanted her to get her teeth fixed.

When he felt himself on the verge of coming, Oma stopped what she was doing and looked up at him. "I like Forbes better," she said. "Why don't you use that name instead of Figman?"

"Sentimental reasons," he said, brushing her hair out of her face so he could better see her features. "Figman's more my real name."

Oma scrunched her nose.

"Would you rather call me Forbes?"

"Would it bother you?"

"Not at all," he lied.

She went back down on him, tonguing his cock, stroking his balls with her fingers. Her other hand crawled up under his shirt and found his left nipple. She pinched it sharply, and again Figman felt himself on the edge.

"Wait," said Oma. Abruptly, she pulled her sweater off over her head so that she sat half-naked before him. Her breasts were beautiful. Full. Creamy. Pink-nippled. Around her neck, she wore a cross studded with opals. Oma straddled him on the couch, facing him, pinning his arms over his head with her hands so that her left breast dangled seductively over his mouth. He flicked at her nipple with his tongue, and she arched backward. He wanted the whole of her breast, but Oma wouldn't give it to him and he couldn't reach for it with both his arms pinned. She tantalized him with her nipple, drove him crazy, moved it just within his tongue's reach and then back again, exciting him more than he felt any man had a right to be excited.

When his arms started tingling, Figman squirmed and Oma released him. Once again, she moved her head down below his beltline and took him into her mouth. For a third time, Figman felt himself about to come.

"Forbes?" she said, looking up at him. The name sounded alien. "I just wondered something."

"What?" he said. He wanted her to stop talking and keep doing that thing she was doing with her tongue.

"If you—say by accident—pricked your finger on an AIDS needle, and there just happened to be this meat cleaver on the table next to you, do you think you'd have the guts to chop off your own hand?"

The Muncy claim. Figman felt a tightening at the base of his neck and the blood draining away from his penis. "What do you say we talk about it later?" he said. "Let's just concentrate on the here and now."

"You devil," said Oma, running her fingers up and down his cock. The blood returned, Oma's breasts jiggled, and Figman came, most spectacularly.

∎

At six twenty the next morning, Figman was awakened by a knock at his front door. His first thought was of Dino; his second, how to conceal the naked woman lying next to him in bed. Oma stirred as Figman slid out from between the sheets and threw on his bathrobe. "Who is it?" he called.

"Benito," said a voice on the other side of the door.

Figman opened it. Benito Hooks stood on his front porch wearing a cotton shirt, plaid shorts, and knee socks. "Good morning, Bill," he said. "I hope I didn't wake you."

"Of course you did," said Figman.

"I was just in the neighborhood. May I come in?"

"Actually, no," said Figman. "This isn't a good time."

"I'll only be a minute," said Hooks.

"I'm sorry," said Figman. "You'll have to talk to me outside." Figman stepped out onto the porch and shut the door behind him.

Hooks glanced at Oma's Corvair in the driveway. "Ooowee," he said. "Oma O'Malley." His teeth were still in need of a cleaning.

"What can I do for you, Benito, at this early hour?"

"I was wondering if you'd had an opportunity to check up on things. You know, look around and whatnot."

"As a matter of fact, I have," said Figman. "I've seen lots of cars come and go, but the one that comes by most often is a metallic green Firebird. It's probably out there right now."

Benito jumped off the porch and peeked around the corner hydrangeas. "I don't see it," he said.

"Really?" said Figman. "It's there all the time."

"What's it look like?"

"It's a Firebird. It's green."

"Who's it belong to?"

"Well, that I don't know," said Figman. "I've just seen him drive in here a lot. Kind of a young kid. Blond."

"I knew it," said Benito. He took out a cigarette and flipped it into his mouth. He lit it agitatedly. "You didn't happen to catch the fellow's license plate?"

"YPU 002."

Hooks's face lit up. He fished around in his breast pocket for a pen. "YPU 002," he repeated as he wrote it on his palm. "Much obliged," he said.

"Don't come by here this early," said Figman.

"By the way, how's my mother doing?"

"Kind of ailing, I'd say."

"Hmm," said Hooks. His brow knit into a solid black line.

"Of course, I don't see much of her. Unless I bring her the mail."

Hooks climbed into his bronze Samurai. "You're a good man, Bill," he said. "There's plenty in this for you."

"Oh, I know there is," said Figman.

■

Oma was awake when Figman returned to his bedroom. "Who was that?" she asked sleepily.

"Paper boy," said Figman. "I asked him not to come by this early."

"What time is it?"

"Six thirty."

"Ugh," she said. She looked great in the morning.

Figman made her a breakfast of poached eggs on English muffins, then sent her on her way. She had the day off but needed to be home before eight lest Dino drive by on his way to work and find her car not parked in the driveway.

At nine thirty, Figman crawled back into bed, exhausted from having made love all night. When he awoke at two, the day had turned windy. Figman did his exercises, showered, then drove into town to buy groceries. He hated the idea of squandering a shopping trip on a day when Oma would not be at Lester's. But he'd run out of aloe. In the last two weeks he'd had three headaches; he didn't want to risk their coming more frequently.

Dino snirked at him as he entered the E-Z Mart. Figman smiled at the boxboy. He bought milk, toothpaste, and four bottles of aloe. He went through Gert's line, where Dino was bagging groceries.

"Dust storm coming," said Gert. She wore heavy perfume that smelled like bug spray.

"Dust storm?" said Figman.

"Gonna be a doozie," she said.

"Can I leave this stuff here a moment?" asked Figman.

"Sure as shootin'," said Gert. Dino moved to the other line and started bagging for Lester. Figman seized an empty hand basket and headed down aisle three. There, he loaded up on masking tape, duct tape, and clear silicone caulk. He grabbed all of it he could find; when he plopped it down on Gert's counter, the woman broke into laughter. "Oh, lordy, honey," she said. "You ain't lived here long." But it was simple. You plug up the holes, nothing gets in.

Figman paid in cash and carted his stockpile to his Aion. He put on a tape of Branford Marsalis and headed south on the highway. A mile down the road, he passed Benito's bronze Samurai, heading north, toward Albuquerque. The wind blew in gusts; the sky grew darker.

FLIGHT

The morning after Rachel Zimmovich greeted Marilee in a towel, Larry arrived at Marilee's house at a quarter to eight. He acted as though nothing were wrong. Marilee, who'd had all night to think about his transgression, was prepared to break up with him if his explanation warranted. Tossing her books in his backseat, she wondered how she would launch into what she'd encountered the previous night. But Larry preempted her. "Look," he said, handing her a sheet of notebook paper. "Rachel wrote you a poem."

BEECHNUT BIAFRA REV 2
for merrily

a baby wails
eats fingers
splinters into shards
glass teeth gnaw rubber flesh
as the world
an empty stomach
belches up another bone

rachel zimmovich

"It sucks," said Marilee. "And she spelled my name wrong, but that's beside the point."

"You don't like it?" He sounded wounded.

"I think it's shit," she said. "Look at this." She pointed to a section with a newly manicured nail. "Is the baby eating the fingers that splinter into shards, or does the baby splinter into shards? It's not clear. And this, down here. How can the world, an empty stomach, belch up bones? How can an empty stomach belch up anything? If it was empty, it wouldn't have bones in it, now would it?" Marilee handed Rachel's poem back to him. "Even the title sucks. 'Beechnut Biafra.' Wasn't that back in the sixties? It's passé. If she wants to exploit a starving third world country, she should read the front page of the newspaper."

"What's eating you?" asked Larry.

"You know exactly what's eating me." She looked away from him; her eyes were red.

"No, I *don't* know. Rachel wrote you a poem. You should be thankful."

"Does she always write in a towel?"

Larry laughed. "Is that it?"

"Well, what was she doing at your house in a towel?"

"Taking a shower."

"Obviously."

Larry turned off the ignition; his Pinto had never left her driveway. He rolled down his window, rubbed his forehead, and turned to face her. "I can't believe you're jealous of Rachel."

"You didn't answer my question."

"This is really sweet."

"Go to hell," said Marilee. She threw open the car door.

Larry reached over and grabbed her sweater. "I'm sorry," he said. "Don't go. Please. I can explain."

"Talk fast. I have a test first period."

"I will. But you have to promise not to tell anyone. Rachel would be embarrassed."

"She *should* be embarrassed."

"She lost her apartment. She lives out of her car, mostly, although sometimes she stays with this friend of hers who's married. She doesn't have many friends, Marilee."

"Why doesn't that come as a surprise?"

"She has nothing at all. Not even a suitcase to put her clothes in. About a month ago, I asked my parents if she could use our shower."

"And where were they last night while you were doling out charity?"

"In the family room, where they always are. Watching TV."

"And you?"

"I was at my typewriter." Larry laughed again. "You think I'm going to be screwing Rachel Zimmovich with my parents in the next room?"

The question was not as reassuring as she knew Larry had intended it to be. Still, she wanted desperately to believe him. "Why's Rachel writing me poetry, anyway?"

"She said you inspired it."

Marilee did not find this entirely complimentary.

"And she felt bad about last night. Oh, here's your Government book." He reached for it under her feet. His arm brushed her leg, sending a tiny chill through her body.

"Thanks."

"Can we go now?"

Marilee nodded.

Larry restarted his Pinto and backed out of her driveway. "It's a fine poem," he said, once they had merged into traffic on Fulton. "Not her best work, but quite good, really. I think you're being too literal."

Too literal. It was what Larry accused her of whenever they disagreed. He saw the world loosely; she longed for it to be precise. Larry embraced disorder, finding beauty in disconnectedness, art in chaos, possibility in the breaking apart of things. Marilee wanted all things to come together, for pieces to fit in logical ways. In art (as in life), order was indispensable. Though her medium was watercolor, she painted tightly and with great attention to detail. Each leaf had its own pattern; each blade of grass its separate texture and hue. She found beauty in exactitude, whereas uncertainty made her nervous. Indeed, she was happiest when things were in their rightful place. Her rightful place, she knew, was with Larry.

■

Larry and Marilee spent the next four years at UCLA, living in the same dorm. They broke up during their senior year but got back together within months. Upon graduation, they leased an apartment on Barrington Avenue in West L.A.

They set up an orderly house (at Marilee's insistence) in which Larry was careful to pull his own weight. He did the cooking (because he knew she hated it) and cleaned house with her every Saturday. She washed the dishes and ironed his shirts. The grocery shopping they split between them. He told her he never wanted to make her feel like the domestic help or, worse, a wife.

With a degree in philosophy, Larry took to working full-time at Mojo's Books and Coffee Beans, making double espressos and warming carrot-pineapple-poppyseed muffins in the microwave. When business was slow, the owner allowed him to work on his poetry. At night, he read at the open mike. The job didn't pay much, but he seemed to enjoy it. Rachel had long since moved back to New York City.

Marilee found a job teaching art therapy for a chain of nursing homes. Life Care Management Systems owned fifteen residential care facilities, all with names like Shady Oaks, Brook Haven, Idyll Acres, and Sunnyhill Woods. Often she confused one name with another, or mixed them up entirely, scribbling Sunnyhill Acres or Oak Haven into her calendar. Her work took her all over the city. But she was painting (which not many art graduates were paid to do), and that alone made her happy.

Marilee liked working with the old people, some of whom were surprisingly competent artists. What she didn't like was the smell of these places, a mix of medicine, urine, blood, and feces that after work hours clung to her hair and clothing. It was the smell of death, a heavy mephitis to which, after years of daily visits, she never grew fully accustomed.

Gradually, the apartment on Barrington became a refuge for Marilee and Larry from the escalating craziness of the city. They gave parties occasionally, made love regularly, and argued infrequently. When they did argue, it was always Marilee who, after they'd gone to bed stonily clinging to their separate edges of the mattress, would then nudge Larry's leg in a gesture of reconciliation. She'd run her toes up and down his calf, sometimes for as long as a full minute, before he'd roll over and take her into his arms. They had never once gone to sleep angry.

The few disputes they did have almost always came down to issues of control. Larry wished Marilee would lose ten pounds because, as he put it, she was not living up to her potential. She wanted him to quit smoking dope. He'd argue that his was a victimless crime. She'd tell him she was happy with her body just the way it was. They'd go round and round. He'd say he had a right to smoke whatever he wanted; that it was a matter of personal freedom. She'd say that, by logical extension, she had a right to eat whatever she wanted. But then Larry would shake his head and inform her that she was only deluding herself. That she really wanted to be thinner, but she was just too stubborn to admit it.

Sometimes, after these quarrels, Marilee would study her body in their bedroom mirror. It wasn't perfect; that she knew. She was shaped like her mother, with small breasts and full hips. But unlike her mother, her waist was delicately small. In the right clothes, Marilee thought she looked respectable. Attractive, even.

Still, on those nights when Larry would send her running to the mirror, she'd worry that he didn't find her appealing. She'd vow, then, to go on a diet. To cut out sugar and fat and live off nothing but vegetables for a month. She'd vow to do it for Larry, in those private moments before drifting off to sleep. The next morning, she'd rise early and fix herself a cheese and mushroom omelette with bacon, potatoes, and toast with marmalade.

After their first two years on Barrington, the neighborhood began to change. Gangs moved in, their jagged scrawl appearing on fences, trashcans, and carport walls. Strangers in red jackets met each other on the sidewalk, coming together briefly, like goldfish kissing. Money changed hands. Marilee watched it from their living room window.

It was after the apartment next to theirs was burglarized that Larry first brought up the idea of moving out of state. They were in a rut, he said, being forced out of one neighborhood, not making enough money to afford another. To move to a better one, he'd have to get a better job, one that afforded him little time to write poetry.

"Wyoming is nice," he said one night over spinach lasagne. "And Kent says it's cheaper to live there. He says that in Laramie, he's now able to afford a house and two cars on half of what he made here." Marilee had her doubts; Kent Bagely was the ex–stockroom clerk at Mojo's.

For several weeks, Larry talked about an out-of-state move, but he dropped the subject once Marilee informed him she was tired of discussing it. Around Christmastime, a drug dealer was knifed in the alley behind their apartment. It was weeks before the rains washed away all remaining traces of his blood.

On January nineteenth, Marilee's twenty-fifth birthday, she came home to find dinner waiting: tortellini al pesto, artichokes with drawn butter, Caesar salad, and a bottle of chardonnay. It was her favorite Italian meal. Larry lit candles and pulled out the chair for her when she sat down. They talked about the usual things: who'd come into Mojo's that day, which nursing homes she'd been to, what to do about her car's slipping clutch. And then Larry asked her to marry him.

Marilee pricked her finger on the spine of an artichoke leaf. Could this be the same Larry Johnston who maintained that marriage was an instrument of the ruling class to keep the lower classes in line? The same Larry Johnston who refused to attend weddings because he didn't want to make that kind of political statement? Who had once written a poem called "Wedding Bell Hell"? She laughed, incredulous, and asked him what had changed his mind.

Everything, explained Larry, is made up of a component and its opposite. Thus, to experience the Zen of one's being, one needed to apprehend the antithesis of what one believed in and held true. To understand fullness, one had to know hunger. To appreciate wealth, one needed to know poverty. To apply oneself to vegetarianism, one needed to savor the essence of eating meat. And to understand personal freedom . . .

Marilee considered flipping her plate of tortellini into his lap.

Similarly, he continued, in order to understand pacifism, one had to embrace militarism. Thus, he was leaving in four weeks to work for the Air Force in New Mexico. He wanted her to go with him.

Marilee was stunned. "But you hated ROTC," she reminded him, too bewildered to think of anything else to say. "You dropped out your sophomore year."

"That was just kids playing," he said. "I need to get inside the real system. See how it feels to be a cog in the wheel of the war machine."

"So you're joining the Air Force?"

"Not joining. Just working for them. As a civilian."

"Doing what?" Her finger throbbed where she had pricked it.

"I can't tell you. It's classified."

Marilee was speechless. She was sure this was some kind of cruel birthday joke, but Larry assured her it wasn't. From his back pocket, he produced a paper instructing him to report to Holloman Air Force Base on the fifteenth of February. It was then she realized he'd most likely had this plan in the works for months.

"I've rented us an apartment," he continued. "In Alamogordo—that's the nearest town. I have no idea what it looks like, but if you don't like it, we can look for someplace else. As for getting married, I think we should do it here. Nothing fancy, just a few friends and family. I thought January 30th would be a good day. What do you think, Mar?"

"I think you're making some rather large assumptions."

Larry gazed openly at her from across the table. She glared back at him, squinting into the candlelight. "Come on, Mar, be reasonable. I thought you'd be happy. You're the one that's always so mushy about these things."

Didn't he see that he had just planned her whole life without consulting her? Didn't he see how arrogant that was? How impossible he had made it for her to say yes to his proposal? Didn't he see a thing? "I'm confused," she said. "I need time to think about it. To sort things out."

"Well, it seems pretty clear-cut to me. You can either go with me or stay in L.A. It's your choice, Mar. No one can make it for you. But I'll tell you one thing," he said, stabbing a round of tortellini and shoving it into his mouth. "I have to go. I love you and want to be with you. But I can't stay where I'm not happy just because you're resistant to change. It's a matter of personal freedom."

Marilee thought if she heard the term "personal freedom" one more time she was going to take her fork and ram it into his neck. "Let's just move to another apartment," she suggested. "We can move down the coast. It's cheaper in places like Redondo and Huntington Beach."

"You're missing the point," he said. "It's about more than just moving south. It's about getting out of this pit. Feeling less anonymous. Not feeling like you're just some speck of dirt among all the other specks of dirt in this city. I need to get back to nature."

"You want nature and you pick New Mexico?" She wondered if he were back on his Rousseau kick.

"I think the desert's beautiful."

"But the Air Force? Why?"

"Because it's the last thing anybody would expect me to do."

Marilee failed to see the logic. Tears welled up in her eyes.

"Look," he continued, "I'm sorry that my doing this forces you to make a decision about your own life, but maybe that's not such a bad idea. You seem kind of in a rut yourself, when you stop to think about it. How long have you been working for Life Care? Two years? Three? You want to work in nursing homes all your life? Teach old people how to mix colors and hold a brush without shaking? Make friends with them only to have them get sick and die? You think that's a good life, Marilee? Think about it. And consider this: You're seventy-five years old. You've done this one thing your entire life. You've never seen the world. You've never lived in another country. You're not even a real artist. In fact, you've never done anything really important at all. Is that what you want to see when you look back on your life? Is that all you want?"

Marilee thought about it. He was right about some things. Her experiences were limited, but she was happy. At least she thought she was. Still, Larry had a lot of nerve pulling a stunt like this. He hadn't even given her a ring. "I'm not going," she said, rising from the table.

"Then I'll have to leave without you," he said without missing a beat. It was her birthday, and he had ruined it.

"Fine." Marilee stomped off into the bedroom, threw herself on the bed, and cried. It was all too unbelievable. The Air Force. New Mexico. When Larry came into the room quietly around eleven, Marilee rolled over to face the window. She did not rub her toes up and down his leg, as she thought he might have expected her to do.

The next morning she called in to work sick. Holed up in the bedroom, she spent hours on the telephone, pumping her friends for advice. Most of them agreed she shouldn't go to New Mexico. Most thought she shouldn't even get married, given the insulting nature of Larry's proposal. Suzette Kellerman, her college roommate, suggested she dump Larry and move someplace else without him. Suzette was an ethnomusicologist, always heading off to parts unknown. She had just returned from a year in Bali, studying gamelan music and the festival of the Wayong Night. Suzette liked things exotic. She had never liked Larry.

Marilee resisted calling her mother for advice. She wished she had known her father. The son of a Russian immigrant, Anton Levitay had left her mother before Marilee was born. As far as she knew, her mother was still married to the man, although no one had seen or heard from him in a quarter century.

Marilee, however, was rarely devoid of male influence while growing up. Indeed, the house was always full of the men her mother brought home from the Savoy Lounge. Marilee would find them sitting at the breakfast table in the morning, smoking a cigarette, their saxophones and dinner jackets on the table by the front door.

Most often, Ramona's men would stay for only a night or two. Sometimes, they stayed longer. Freddie de Castro, a Latin percussionist with a pencil-thin mustache and thinning black hair, stayed for a couple of years. He'd take Marilee out for burgers on his nights off if Ramona had to work. He'd buy her a milk shake and onion rings, then take her bowling, or to a Disney movie, or to Van Nuys to play miniature golf. Freddie had a belt he wore with his favorite blue jeans. Its buckle featured a hairy tarantula frozen in amber. Marilee never liked the belt, but she liked Freddy; he was the closest thing to a father she had ever known.

One afternoon, Marilee came home from school to discover Freddie's conga drums missing and the hall closet devoid of his clothes. Ramona had locked herself in her bedroom and refused to come out. "Don't ask questions that are none of your business," was all she said to Marilee. The next morning, Marilee took a pair of scissors to her mother's scrapbook. The scrapbook held pictures and articles from when Ramona was a singer and played clubs all over L.A. Marilee cut up every picture in it. She went to bed hungry for a week.

In her kitchen on Barrington, Marilee made a tuna sandwich and thought hard about becoming Mrs. Larry Johnston. They would have security and a retirement fund if Larry stayed with the Air Force. They could have children, which she wanted; perhaps a house. It might work out in the long run. It might even be fun.

But New Mexico? The state was one big dust bowl, with icy winters and blistering summers and insects the likes of which defied imagination. For this she was supposed to give up her job? Her friends? The city she was born in? Was she really expected to ship everything she owned a thousand miles east to spend the rest of her life with a man who'd proposed marriage as a socio-religious experiment?

Later that day, Marilee broke down and called her mother. Ramona was of little help. "I'd move to Mississippi if I were you," she cooed into the telephone. "I adore the South. I could spend all day just looking at kudzu."

Their last three weeks together were not pleasant. Larry's moving out meant Marilee had to find another situation, for she could not afford their apartment on her salary alone. She considered taking a roommate, but as their place had only one bedroom, she'd be forced to relinquish much of her privacy. She considered, also, linking up with a friend, but most of her friends were married or living with boyfriends of their own. The ones who weren't were a bit crazy. In the end, she had no choice but to move back in with her mother.

"Goody!" said Ramona when told the news. Marilee moved what she could into her old bedroom and stored the rest of her belongings in the loft in the garage. When her Audi gave out in the middle of her move, Ramona took her to buy the Dart. Marilee let her. She figured it was what any mother would do.

She lived with Ramona for seven months. Her mother worked her coat-check job at night; Marilee, her nursing-home job by day. She was lonely and consoled herself with Larry's letters. Love letters. Dozens of them mailed from the post office on Holloman Air Force Base. Letters proclaiming his love. Letters begging her to join him. To move to Alamogordo where the sky was vast; the air, clean; and the people, unaffected. Letters begging her to settle down, asking her to become his wife.

In the end (and of necessity, for she feared she might commit matricide if reminded one more time to wear her slippers or eat five servings of fruit a day), Marilee came to the conclusion that she knew Larry wanted. She quit her job at Life Care, packed all of her belongings, and loaded up the Dart. She took clothes for a week; a road map; her mother's knife, two honeydews, and a casaba. She said goodbye to her friends (who'd tried to dissuade her) and to her mother (who had not). She drove halfway across the country—all night and all day and into the night again—across mountains and desert to the southwestern town of Alamogordo.

And along the way, she met a dwarf.

■

"Tip failure," said Enoch, once they had pulled out of the gas station in Belen.

"What?"

"Tip failure. Check it out." He shoved the base of his wooden crutch between Marilee and the steering wheel. "Worn clear through. That's why I almost fell back there."

Marilee hadn't noticed. "What'll you do?"

"Get a new one in Albuquerque."

Enoch tore open a bag of something. "Want one? I bought two." He held up a fried chocolate pudding pie.

"No way."

"Great," said Enoch. "More for me."

"How can you eat that stuff?"

"Easy." He bit off a large hunk of it; pudding dripped onto the seat of her car.

Marilee bristled.

Enoch scooped up the glob with a couple of fingers; it left a brown streak where the melons had been. "I'll clean it up at the next stop."

"Ever think about what all that packaged stuff does to your insides?"

"Nope."

"All those cheese balls and pork rinds. Twinkies and Ding Dongs and Drumsticks and pudding pies?" She scrunched up her nose for emphasis.

Enoch shrugged and licked glaze from his fingers. "I don't worry about it. Keeps me sane."

"Right," she said.

Enoch laughed.

Marilee looked at the smear on her upholstery. "Do they have crutch tips in Carrizozo?" she asked. They were headed north.

"Why?" Enoch drew the top of his crutch down into his footwell.

"Because I can't go with you to Albuquerque," she said matter-of-factly. "What I mean is, I can't stay with you once we get there. I've got to get back to Alamogordo. Tonight. But I'll drop you off first in Albuquerque. Or take you back to Carrizozo, if you like. I just—"

"Whatever," interrupted Enoch.

"I'm happy to take you wherever you'd like to go. You just need to tell me." She was trying to sound upbeat.

Enoch was silent.

"Look, I'm sorry about the balloons. I'm sure they're wonderful. Maybe next year we can do it. Just the three of us. I'd love to fly in a balloon."

Enoch picked at the remaining rubber on the base of his crutch. She continued north. Rain beat steadily against the windshield.

"Come on. Don't be that way," she said.

"What way?"

"You know exactly what way. This isn't easy for me."

"It sounds easy."

"Well, it's not. Come on, let me take you to Albuquerque. Didn't you say you had to be there by three?"

Enoch shrugged.

"Besides, you just paid for a full tank of gas. It's the least I can do."

Enoch stood on his seat and reached for his backpack.

"What are you doing?"

"Getting out," said Enoch.

"Here?"

"Bingo."

"But it's dark out. It's raining."

"I can see that," said Enoch.

"Can't we talk about this?"

"About what?"

Marilee hit her brakes and pulled sharply to the side of the road. There was no green bench. There was no anything. "You got it," she said, suddenly glad to be rid of him.

"This is great," said Enoch.

"Yes, I thought it would be."

Enoch opened his door and swung his crutches out in front of him. "Dull as dust," he said, slipping his arms through the straps of his backpack.

"Excuse me?" said Marilee. His words sounded disturbingly familiar.

"Duller than dust."

She did not so much as glance at him in her rearview mirror.

■

She continued north, just to spite Enoch. In Albuquerque, Marilee pulled over on Gibson Boulevard to consult her road map. Plotting her way back to Rocket City proved easy. She'd head east on Interstate 40, then south at Moriarty through the towns of Estancia, Willard, Corona, and Carrizozo. From there, she'd pick up Highway 54 and drop down into Alamogordo. They were small arteries, perhaps even dangerous at night, but they would take her to where she was headed, and she'd encounter no dwarfs along the way.

Marilee drove all night through the back roads of central New Mexico. Around three, it stopped raining. She thought about Larry. She thought about Enoch, too. He infuriated her. She would miss him, she knew. He made her laugh and think about things in interesting ways, but she would not miss his insults or his daily assault of nudity.

In Carrizozo, Marilee passed the Little Black Peak Inn. She saw a light on in Carmina's apartment. She wondered how long it would take for Enoch to find his way back to her. Hours? Months? Years? He probably had hotels and women all over the Southwest; Marilee was determined not to become one of them.

Instead, she would become the wife of Larry H. Johnston. Mrs. Larry H. Johnston. And it would not be dull. How could it be, with a man who had first flirted with her in German? Who wrote poetry? Who worked for the Air Force in order to learn about peace?

■

She arrived in Rocket City with her gas tank nearly empty. Tomahawk Trail was easy to locate from memory. It was almost sunrise, and Larry's place was dark; she knew he would be sleeping. Marilee parked her Dart and stepped out into the night. An owl hooted. A train rumbled in the distance. Timbales kept beat from the apartment above. Perhaps he would not be sleeping.

But awake or asleep, she knew Larry would be thrilled to see her. Surprised, of course, but truly happy to find her standing there. He would take one look at her, realize she'd driven all night just to be with him, and take her into his arms. His fine, strong, masculine arms. He would not say a word, so special would the moment be. He'd just smile his bashful smile and surround her with his embrace. And she would meld into him like breath into warm air. Like a stream into a slow-flowing river.

Marilee headed straight up Larry's walkway and knocked on his front door. There was no answer. She knocked again, a bit more aggressively. The timbales quieted. Soon a light came on in Larry's living room, and Marilee felt her pulse quicken. "Who is it?" she heard him call through the heavy oak door.

"It's me," she answered, hoping he wouldn't have forgotten her voice.

The door opened, and Larry H. Johnston stood before her in his underwear. "Jesus fuck," he said.

He was taller than she remembered.

DUST

As soon as Figman returned home from his shopping expedition, he began to wage his one-man war against dust. He caulked the corners of each single-hung window, then ran duct tape along the juncture between each bottom rail and sill. Next, he taped between the meeting rails so that all potential cracks were sealed. Once his windows were airtight, he turned his attention to his two external doors. He completely sealed their openings, taping between the doorjambs and the stiles and then between the thresholds and rails. He even taped the keyholes. When at last he felt his house was secure, Figman fixed himself dinner and went to bed.

All night, the wind grew stronger. At times he awoke to the pings of sand-like dust beating against his windowpanes. Drawing the blankets up around him, he returned to his slumber, content in the knowledge that no dust was entering his domicile.

By morning, Figman's house was a disaster. Dust was everywhere. In his bed, on his counters, in his soon-to-have-been sgraffito painting. Sand crunched under his feet when he walked into his kitchen. Outside, the sky was a murky brown. "Shit," he said, taking stock of the hours of work ahead of him. "Fuckingcocksuckerassholedamn."

He'd have to start his cleaning again from scratch, but not until the storm had passed; until then, he'd have no choice but to live with the dust. But how had it gotten in? Figman examined his taped kitchen window. A fine layer of grit covered the sill and his bottle of Essence of Chicken. Was it possible the dust had somehow made it past his barricade? Or had it blown in from somewhere else and dispersed throughout his interior? He'd plugged up all the holes he could think of. Which opening could have eluded him?

Throughout the morning, the dust storm worsened. Figman exercised, showered, then sat before the canvas in his living room. Through the window, he could barely discern the Rodriguez house. It looked eerie, like a ghost ship in mist. Sheets billowed like sails from its sagging clothesline. Verdie's comment about Bobo having the smarts in the family was beginning to make sense.

Figman's thoughts turned to Oma. Their night together had held all the romance of an hour at a massage parlor; still, there was something about her impelling him to see her again. Figman was torn. He'd vowed to spend his remaining time painting. But he was not painting. Since he'd moved to Artesia, he had failed to complete a single canvas. His headaches had worsened, and he suspected he was beginning to lose weight. The thought of dying and not leaving behind a single work of art depressed him as no thought had ever before.

And here he sat, another painting day shot. Figman stared out his window at the Rodriguez laundry turning brown in the wind. Dust had settled on the windowsill. It was anathema to him, this dirt in his living space. In his sheets. In his paints. In his food. Figman took out a rag and began to clean. It took him forty minutes to wipe down his living room. He dusted every surface with Windex, vacuumed his floor, then ran an extra layer of duct tape over the seams of his doors and windows. He moved on to his bedroom and repeated the process. Half an hour later, when Figman returned to his living room, a new layer of grit had settled. Like water in a flood, the dust kept invading, seeping in through tiny chinks, blowing in through openings he did not know his house contained.

Figman got himself a beer and leaned over his sink, studying the sky through his back window. Across the highway, a small figure squatted by the Rodriguez well pump. Dust blew all around him, but Bobo seemed not to care. He was in his element. The wind gusted, rattling Figman's windowpanes. It seemed to distort the glass like a lens, reeling in the corners of his vision like the aura of an impending headache. Below, on his windowsill, his bottle of Essence of Chicken stared up at him like the bloodshot eye of God. An idea came.

He would paint Bobo. Right then, right there, in the swirling tempest of dust. It would be a dark piece, an abstract that he'd paint over his aborted sgraffito. Figman hurried to the canvas in his living room. Were he to move it to the north side of his window, he would have an oblique view of Bobo digging. Figman studied the light on the rusty well pump. The light was mutable and dim; it would not matter that there was dirt in his oils. Perhaps that, in itself, would be something artistic. Paint dust with dust. He liked the idea. So unique a take on form and function might land him in art history books.

With grand strokes, Figman sketched in the east-facing Rodriguez house upon his dust-encrusted canvas. The colors were not right, but now it hardly mattered. The house took on a life of its own he'd previously been unable to capture. At last Figman felt he was getting somewhere.

But how to go about painting Bobo? The trouble was one of scale. Bobo Rodriguez was small and lumplike. He was not a dwarf, but he looked like a dwarf, especially from a distance. A dwarf in one's picture could definitely screw up one's perspective. Tentatively, Figman dipped his brush into raw umber and applied it to his rose-colored canvas. He painted a triangular shape, then added streaks of cerulean blue for definition. He added chrome yellow for the bucket, then watched, astounded, as tiny grains of black settled into his wet paint. Where on earth was it coming from? Figman stepped back to examine his ceiling. It was made of plaster and, like the walls, was solid.

Out of the corner of his eye, he saw George, the mailman, pulling up in his Jeep. Figman had forgotten all about his mail, so intent had he been on fortifying his house against the storm. He ripped the tape off his front door. Outside, the wind blew in flurries.

Drawing his collar up over his mouth, Figman darted out to the highway. He felt he could hardly breathe, the air was so thick with particles of dirt. Without examining any of it, he grabbed the entire contents of his mailbox and sprinted back to his house, slamming the door shut behind him. Grit fell from his hair and clothing, small bits of blackish sand. He would have to take another shower.

Verdie's mail was refreshingly benign, mostly bills and store fliers. He added it to the pile on his counter. Figman had received the same store fliers and a letter from Litvak, forwarded by his mother. Reluctantly, he opened it.

Dear Figman,

I just received a call from Miriam Eisler, one of the lawyers for the opposing litigants. She said she'd been in contact with your mother, who let it slip
that you are somewhere in Mexico. She asked me if I knew where, exactly.

I don't know what you are doing there, other than hiding out. You have to
know it's only a matter of time before she or the district attorney finds you.

Your preliminary hearing is scheduled for the middle of June. I beg you
to give yourself up. I'm sure a good attorney could arrange a plea bargain,
and time served would be reduced to a minimum. They're not talking about
state prison. They're talking country club—assuming you've had no priors.

So do the right thing, Figman. You know as well as anybody you can't run
from fate. It really is only a matter of time.

Your friend, Aaron

Litvak was right about one thing: It *was* only a matter of time. Before he
died. Before he perished forever, lost and forgotten, another speck of dust
blown hither in the wind. Figman took out paper and pen and wrote to
his mother:

Dear Mom,

Got a letter from Litvak. Very disturbing. Perhaps it would be better not
to forward any more of his mail.

He mentioned that you told Ms. Eisler that I was living in New Mexico.
It appears she misheard you, and thinks I am in Mexico. That's fine, but
still, this is just the sort of thing I was worried about. I don't want to alarm
you, but there is more than just company security at stake here. There is my
own safety to think about. When you consider that, I'm sure you'll see how
imperative it is you cease talking to her immediately.

Sorry to be so abrupt. I'm writing you at the end of my lunch hour and
have to go.

Love, F.

Figman sealed his letter in an envelope, then stamped and addressed it. He heard a knock at his kitchen door and, when he looked out his window, saw Verdie. She wore an orange sweater and her awful pink-purple lipstick.

"Just a second," he yelled. He ripped tape from the inside of his threshold and doorjamb, hoping she would not hear its tearing. "Come in," he said as he swung the door open.

"Louis," she said, stepping into the room. "Sorry to bother you, but I was fixin' to—What's that?"

He'd forgotten he was holding the wadded-up duct tape in his hand. "I was taking this off the door." Figman tossed the wad into the trash under his sink. "Keeps the dust out," he said feebly.

Verdie broke into raucous laughter, her gums showing large and pink. "Lordy!" she said. "That's a good one."

"Want a beer?" asked Figman.

"Sure," she said, sitting down at his table. Figman handed her his last Anchor Steam. She opened it with her teeth. "Sure looks clean around here," she said.

Figman brushed the dust off his chair and sat down opposite her. "So what's up?" he asked. He was relieved to have company.

"Oh, I was just wondering if you was okay, with the storm and all." She drank from her bottle.

"Really?"

"Why sure," she said. "Sometimes the furnace blows out, or the lights go. Once, the wind blew the shingles and tarpaper clear off the roof. Left a hole the size of a football in the attic."

The attic. He'd forgotten to seal the kitchen access panel.

"At any rate," continued Verdie, "I just come by to see you're okay."

"I'm fine," he said. "How about you?"

"Just ducky," she said.

"How's your trailer holding up?"

"Like a bra on a battle ax."

Figman smiled. He was genuinely touched she'd thought to check in on him. "So how long do these storms usually last?"

"Day or two, mostly. But this is a bad one." She took another swallow. "Real bad," she said.

"So it might last longer?"

"I reckon," said Verdie. She looked through the doorway into the living room. "Is that Bobo?" she asked, pointing at his painting.

Figman felt the blood rush to his cheeks. He didn't blush easily, and he failed to understand why he was blushing now. "Well, I sort of tried . . ."

Verdie got up and walked into the living room. "It's good," she said. "Damn good. I could tell who it was right away."

Figman followed her to his canvas.

"I've been fixin' to do this myself, one of these days."

"Paint?" asked Figman.

"Nah. Dig up them weeds around the well pump."

"Is that what Bobo's doing?" Figman glanced out his window. Bobo was still out there, crouching in the same spot as before.

"Honey, only the Lord in heaven knows what Bobo's doing." Verdie laughed. Figman smiled. She polished off the rest of her beer. "Well, I'd best be going. Let you get back to your work, here."

Figman was sorry to see her go but could think of no reason to detain her. "It was nice of you to drop in," he said.

"Pfft," said Verdie, walking back into his kitchen. Her hair looked thinner, and she appeared to have dropped some weight.

"Look, it's none of my business," he said. "But are you sure you're okay? I mean if you needed any help with anything, or if you just needed to talk, I'd be there, you know. Just hypothetically. Well, I'd be there for real, I mean, if you were to need me, hypothetically."

"What the Sam Hell are you talking about?" said Verdie.

"I just want you to know I'm here for you, that's all. If you were to ever need anything. Like if you were to, say, get sick or something—not that you look sick, but—"

Verdie reached up and cradled his cheek in her palm. "Well, aren't you just the sweetest thing."

For a moment, Figman was afraid she might kiss him. "I mean it," he said.

"I'd best be going," said Verdie, removing her hand. She exited out the back door.

Figman watched as she trotted the short distance to her trailer. And then he remembered. "Your mail," he yelled to her.

"What?" she yelled back. She was shouting into the wind. Figman held up the stack of letters he'd been collecting on his counter. "I'll get it later," she hollered. "I have to go meet Poe."

Figman sat down at his kitchen table, feeling instantly lonely. In a moment, he heard Verdie's car start up, and then her tires crunching their way out of the driveway. It was ironic, both he and Verdie dying and neither able to admit it to the other. He wondered which one of them would be the first to go. Probably her, he thought. She wasn't looking too well, and she was older by twelve years. Still, there were no guarantees. He could drop dead tomorrow and she wouldn't have had a clue. He knew one thing, though: As long as he was alive, he'd do all he could to protect her. As far as he could tell, Verdie's only family was one no-good son checking in every couple of weeks just to make sure her cancer had spread.

Figman rinsed out Verdie's beer bottle and tossed it into the trash. Bobo, visible from his kitchen window, had moved to a spot closer to the clothesline. It would be hard, now, to paint him at the well pump. Figman eyed his bottle of Essence of Chicken. Oma had been right: It did look gross. He wondered why he continued to keep it on his windowsill.

Figman walked back into his living room. Small grains of sand had accumulated on his palette, coming in through the attic or his newly unsealed doors, spreading to his floors and furniture, making his life miserable. He hunted for his car keys.

In a minute, he was headed north on the highway, toward Dallas Avenue. Visibility was low, making the trip difficult; what few cars had ventured out into the storm proceeded cautiously. It took Figman twenty minutes to travel five miles. He worried about Verdie driving to meet Poe Titus.

When he turned down Oma's street, Figman switched off his headlights. Parked in her driveway was a car he didn't recognize, a red '59 Cadillac convertible. It had been restored with lots of gold ornamentation. Gold wheels. Gold trim. Gold doohickey on the hood. The car looked like a whorehouse on wheels. Though he knew Oma would not be working that day, Figman had not expected her to have company. He parked in front of a neighbor's house and waited. There was dust on his dashboard.

Seventeen minutes later, Dino bounded from his sister's front door. The wind had let up a bit, and Figman could make him out clearly. Dino swaggered over to the Cadillac and climbed inside. When he backed out of the drive-way, Figman noted his license plate.

As soon as Dino turned the corner, Figman hopped out of his Aion. He sprinted to Oma's front porch, shielding his face against the onslaught of dust. He knocked urgently. In a moment she opened her door.

"You shouldn't open your door without asking who's there," he said.

Oma smiled at him. "Don't be paranoid," she said, standing aside for him to enter. "This isn't California."

"Things can happen anywhere." Figman stepped up into her living room. It was a shrine to Jesse: pictures of him on the walls, the shelves, the stereo cabinet. Their wedding picture hung above the fireplace; on the mantle stood a large porcelain urn. Figman didn't ask.

"What brings you here?" asked Oma. She wore jeans and a rumpled blue sweater.

"My Aion," said Figman. Oma looked at him blankly. "It's a joke," he said.

"It's not very funny."

"I guess not," said Figman. "At any rate, I've come to relieve you of your misery."

"Cool," she said. "Let me get my purse."

■

Oma's purse was enormous, a small duffel bag she'd stuffed into her footwell. "Where are you taking me?" she asked, twenty minutes out of Artesia.

"The only place I know where there's likely to be no dust," said Figman. He could see Oma was thinking hard. "The caverns," he said.

Oma groaned. "It's not like I haven't been there on every field trip since the first grade."

"But you've never been there with me," he said.

"So?" They'd been talking about breasts and whether or not a man can tell if a woman has implants. He'd been trying to recall the feel of Oma's breasts, if they felt at all funny. Oma pulled down her visor mirror and applied lipstick, a sort of violet shade that matched her eye.

"Well, then," said Figman, "I'll have to show you things you've never before seen."

"Like what?"

"Like . . . a cave snake." Figman smiled roguishly.

Oma looked at him as if he might at any moment return to his home planet, a notion that seemed not at all unappealing as he peered beyond his windshield. The sky was a black-brown swirl. Cars drove in caravan like a train of ants, nearly touching one another for bearings. Occasionally, the wind gusted and they'd all slow to a maddening crawl. Figman flashed to the morning of his accident.

"So, Forbes," said Oma, "do you think we're going to make it?"

Figman smiled. They'd already made it, and it had been most exciting. "Of course," he said, but secretly he was worried. Directly ahead of them was a Winnebago, a vehicle so enormous Figman could not see beyond it. It would brake suddenly, he knew, and he'd be distracted by Oma's talk of breasts and go plowing into the rear of it like a train into a cow. There'd be blood and glass everywhere, and broken teeth. And when the dust finally cleared, a rescue team would come with the Jaws of Life to cut them free. But it would be too late. They'd both be history.

Yes, this was his fate; he could see that now. He was not going to die of a brain tumor. He was going to die with Oma O'Malley right here on the Carlsbad Highway. In an impact so sudden, neither of them would see it coming. In an accident so terrible, their bodies would not be recognized. In a crash so fiery, his ashes would mix with hers and blow forever over the plains of New Mexico.

MESCALERO ARMS

Larry didn't take Marilee into his arms. He didn't invite her inside, even. He just stood on his doorstep, looking troubled, repeating the words *Jesus* and *fuck* and *forchrist'ssakemarilee*. A military hat sat atop the counter in the kitchen. Marilee spotted it and knew immediately what he was hiding. "So, I guess you went all the way with it?" she said.

"All the way with what?"

"Joined up. What is it, two years or four in the Air Force?" She wondered if he would want them to live on the base once they'd gotten married.

Larry glanced at the hat on the yellow-orange tile. "Fuck," he said. He ran his hand through his hair and placed his arm up against the doorframe.

"That's okay," she said. "I kind of suspected you'd enlist. Can I come in? It's cold out here."

"I didn't join up, Mar."

A man stumbled out from Larry's bedroom. He covered himself when he saw Marilee.

■

Due to evidence to the contrary, it took Larry a good two weeks to convince Marilee he was not gay.

"I can handle it," she said, once the shock had subsided. "We can still be friends. People are what they are; that can't be changed."

226

"But I'm not gay," he persisted. "I want to marry you."

Marilee was tired of discussing it; she thought about how she was going to tell her mother.

"Why would I want to convince you I'm straight if I were gay?"

"You were in bed with this guy."

"It happened twice."

"You were jacking each other off under the covers. How is that not gay?"

"It's just not," he said. "I know how it looks. But I also know what I feel inside."

Marilee fingered the tasseled corner of the bedspread. She and Larry were sleeping together, all too literally. "But if you're capable of it—capable of going through the motions—there must be some part of you that enjoyed it on some level."

"None."

"Not some tiny part of you that was turned on?"

"Nope."

"Just a little?"

"Not at all."

"You said you got hard."

"That's involuntary. I could get hard rubbing up against a tree."

Marilee didn't doubt it.

"Listen to me when I tell you this. It didn't repulse me. I'll admit that. But I didn't enjoy it, either."

"Then why do it more than once, if you didn't enjoy it?" It was the question she'd asked him a hundred times since her arrival.

Larry rubbed his eyes. The clock on the bedside table said two seventeen. "It was an exercise," he said wearily.

"An exercise?"

"To better understand my heterosexuality."

Marilee broke into laughter. Had she caught Larry with a woman, she would have walked out on him immediately. The fact that he was with a man made all the difference. A man was not direct competition; surprisingly, she found herself not the slightest bit jealous. Major Blackwell, who'd flown in from some air base in Maryland, had disappeared into the

night, military hat in hand, fear etched into his brow. Marilee figured he
was worried about his career.

"It's not funny," said Larry.

"I'm sorry," she said, shaking her head. It wasn't funny. It was lunatic.
And it made sense in a weird, Larry sort of way. Marilee's relief was pal-
pable. At the same time, she was pissed that he'd screwed up their sex life
in so crucial a manner. She propped herself up on one elbow and studied
his features in moonlight. "Here's an exercise for you," she said seductively. "I'm not making love to you for a full six months. Not until you
test negative at least three times in a row. I want total abstinence. No
touching, no kissing, no physical contact whatsoever. You can think of it
as an exercise to better understand desire."

By the first of March, Larry's AIDS tests were still coming back negative. Though he swore no bodily fluids had ever been exchanged, Marilee
had insisted he get himself tested at eight-week intervals for up to six
months post–Major Blackwell. "The earlier you find out," she told him,
"the greater your chances for long-term survival." He had one month to
go before she'd consider him out of the woods.

It had been a strange five months in Rocket City. The place was truly
odd, with its decorative show of rockets and omnipresence of blue-cam-
ouflaged fighter jets. The jets performed cryptic maneuvers high above
the Tularosa Basin, weaving in and out of formation, inaudible at times,
nearly invisible to the naked eye. Occasionally, Marilee thought she
heard low rumblings from far off in the desert—explosions, perhaps,
from a remote location miles beyond the horizon. Afterward, she'd scour
the *Daily News* for some logical explanation. The paper never offered
one, and that worried Marilee. She'd learned that the atomic test at Trinity Site, which had blown out windows one hundred twenty miles away,
had been explained to the public as the accidental explosion of a muni-
tions storage facility.

The paper did offer plenty of news about Alcie Britton, the gynecologist mayor of Alamogordo. One day, he'd be on page one, shaking hands

with Hillary Clinton. The next week, he'd be signing some ordinance, boarding an airplane, breaking ground for the new medical building at the corner of Scenic Drive and Soltero. Marilee wondered if he'd been able to quit smoking and, if so, whether he'd employed her technique with rubber bands.

Her days had become depressingly routine. Up at seven to fix Larry breakfast. Magazines and soap operas till three. Then cleaning, shopping, chores, and dinner. Sometimes, she and Larry went out to eat; other times Larry cooked Italian. On the weekends, they'd go bowling at the Apollo Lanes or to a movie at the Camelot Twin with friends from the air base. The men wore crewcuts and talked about fighter jets. The women wore ponytails and talked about babies. It had been months since Marilee had felt like painting.

Occasionally, she'd check the want ads for a job teaching art. Month after month, she found no such job advertised. Larry suggested she not look for work until after the wedding, which they'd tentatively scheduled for the month of May. It was to be a simple affair at the Otero County courthouse before a few friends and a justice of the peace. Until then, she was free to do as she pleased. Larry said he wanted to give her plenty of time to acclimate to her new environment. To relax, make friends, and, above all, be artistic. Instead, she watched "Another World" and read *People* magazine. Larry never questioned her use of time; Marilee figured he still felt guilty.

In the evenings, Larry worked on his poetry. He was doggedly persistent, never missing a day despite his understandable fatigue. For an hour each night, he'd sit at his desk at the living room window, hunched over his old Royal, banging out his free verse. Often, his clacking irritated Marilee. She wished *she* had a muse, some friendly spirit to fly in through the window and carry her off the sofa to her box of watercolors.

Sharing Larry's bed, but not making love to him, proved an exercise in frustration. He was in top shape, having spent the last six months working out during his lunch hour. Marilee admired his body all the more, it seemed, now that she was unable to avail herself of its pleasures. Her abstinence, seven months in the making, had unexpectedly been prolonged another six. Resentment festered. She took to dressing more provocatively, donning see-through bras, silk teddies, and black, lacy underwear cut high above her hips. She had to drive to Las Cruces even to find such lingerie. She wore it around the house while reading and watching TV. She slept in it. It was her way of punishing Larry—not for Major Blackwell, per se, but for having complicated their lives in so reckless a manner.

She got little sleep at the Mescalero Arms. Señor Escamilla kept her up all night with his clogs and timbales; Larry kept her awake with his snoring. Unlike Enoch's, his snoring was arhythmic and raspy, a dissonant counterpoint to the incessant drumbeats from the apartment above. Marilee knew she would never adjust to such a racket.

Larry, evidently, had grown accustomed to the cacophony from above, for he routinely slept right through it. No longer did he throw on his bathrobe, ascend the stairs in the middle of the night, and try to make his needs comprehensible. That was left for Marilee to do. The good news, however, was that Señor Escamilla had taken a wife, a Spanish teacher from Artesia. Marilee could now throw on a bathrobe, tromp upstairs in the middle of the night, and talk to Esther.

"Excuse me," Marilee would say in her tiniest voice, peeking in at the mess that was their apartment. Trash was strewn everywhere; the place smelled terrible. "I know it's not that late, but Larry and I have to get up early in the morning. Do you think you could turn down your music?"

"Oh, I'm *sorry*," Esther would say, as though it were the first time this particular problem had ever been called to her attention. "I'll have Rico turn it off."

"That would be great. Thanks."

Rico would wave from his beanbag chair in front of the speakers, his feet tucked into his clogs. He'd be smiling, which made it harder for Marilee to feel angry. Esther never smiled at all.

The Escamillas turned off their music whenever Marilee asked them to. The problem was that she had to ask them to night after night, week after week, month after month until she thought she might go crazy. In bad weather, Marilee took a broom handle and banged it up against the ceiling, eliciting silence from above and anger from Larry; if it hadn't routinely awakened him, she would have utilized this method more regularly.

"Jesus!" he yelled the first night she banged the broomstick up against the ceiling. Rocket City had been dusted by an unseasonably early October snow. The apartment above grew noticeably quiet.

"I'm sorry," said Marilee. "I didn't think you could sleep through all that noise."

"I get up at six thirty," he said. "It's easy." That night, they had lain awake past midnight, Larry trying hard to convince her he wasn't gay.

"Doesn't he have a job?" she asked, leaning the broom up against the doorframe.

"Who?"

"Tito Puente upstairs."

"He fixes cars," said Larry. "Haven't you seen all his crap out behind the building?"

"No." She felt cold, suddenly, and pulled the covers up around her shoulders. "What happened to your Pinto?" In the turmoil of their first few weeks together, she'd forgotten to ask.

Larry rolled over and studied the clock. It said three eleven. "I sold it. To this guy in L.A.—Luis somebody. It was getting old. What happened to your Audi?"

"Clutch gave out. I thought you knew that."

"I knew it was having problems."

"Well, it died. The same weekend I moved in with my mother."

"You like that old Dodge?"

"I love it," said Marilee.

"It's kind of ugly."

"But it runs. It got me all the way here."

"Yes, it did," said Larry. He took her hand and kissed it.

"I told you no kissing."

"You can't give someone AIDS by kissing their fingers."

"That's not the point."

"What is, then?"

She heard the toilet flush upstairs, then clogs clopping over the linoleum. Larry caressed her long, thin fingers.

"What happened to your ring?" he asked.

Marilee flashed on the contents of her suitcase scattered along the highway. "I lost it."

"You never lose anything."

"Well, I lost this."

"Where?"

"I don't know."

"You don't know?"

"If I knew, I might have found it."

"That's not like you."

"I know," she said, pulling her hand away from his. "Sometimes I surprise myself."

■

The following morning, after fixing Larry a breakfast of pancakes and link sausage, she asked him if she could put away his painting. By this time, Marilee had decided to stay with him for at least six months to wait out the results of his AIDS tests. Were he to test positive, she had no idea what they would do; her solution was not to think about it. In the meantime, she preferred not having to look at that mournful old Indian. "Let's put him in the closet," she suggested. "Like we did in L.A."

"I like him there," said Larry. "He looks great over the couch."

"I'll let you keep your message on the answering machine."

"That's big of you."

"Oh, come on," she said. "I have to live here too." Larry put on his overcoat and closed his briefcase. "It's so . . . tacky," she persisted.

"Mar," he said, "unpack your suitcase. Send for the rest of your stuff and put it anywhere you like. Fill up the drawers and closets. Rearrange all the furniture. Hang your watercolors all over the house. I love you, and I want you to be happy. I'll even let you change my message on the answering machine. But don't touch my painting."

"Okay," she said.

Larry blew her a kiss from the doorway. He shut the door behind him, then opened it and stuck his head back inside. "Oh, God," he said. "Did I just give you AIDS?"

Marilee laughed, then flipped him the bird.

■

By her twenty-sixth birthday in January, Marilee had gained twelve and a half pounds. She was bored in Rocket City. She had no job, and the miserable weather prevented her from getting any meaningful exercise. Larry, dismayed by the change in her appearance, stopped cooking Italian and started mixing up various green salads for dinner. He lost seven pounds. Marilee gained another three. She ate while he was at the Air Force base, during "One Life to Live" and "Days of Our Lives" and "General Hospital." In the mornings, she drove to Furr's and loaded up on Ding Dongs and Ho Hos and sour cream potato chips. She'd burrow into the couch, under the watchful gaze of Larry's old Indian, and stuff it all down, feeling as young and restless as any character on TV.

Larry, who had quit smoking marijuana once he'd moved to New Mexico, condemned her hips and thighs with newfound self-righteousness. He'd gone clean, he said, not because he was working for the Air Force but as an exercise to learn about dependency. Marilee, who'd grown weary of his Zen experiments, almost wished he'd resume the loathed habit so she'd have some viable counterattack. "I'm sublimating," she'd yell back at him from her berth on the couch whenever he'd find Ho Ho wrappers in the trash under the sink. She'd long since abandoned her sexy lingerie.

Further aggravating Marilee these days was Larry's insistence on maintaining secrecy about his job at Holloman Air Force Base. She'd discovered nothing about the work he was doing there, something classified, he'd told her. Holloman, she had learned, was largely geared toward aeronautical research and training. A technical position seemed highly unlikely without a background in technology. So what kinds of jobs were left that would need to be classified? Larry was mum. He would reveal neither the department in which he worked nor the name of his supervisor, and Marilee learned not to ask.

Occasionally, he let drop bits and pieces about ongoing military projects at the base. Over dinner, he'd mention the G-force gondola, or meteorological balloons, or the base's high-velocity accelerator. In the car, he'd talk about primates and AIDS research (which Marilee found ironic). But Larry refused to be more specific. It had taken him six months to get his security clearance before moving from L.A., and he was determined not to jeopardize it. Marilee was left no choice but to assemble a hazy scenario of his life at work: Obviously, he sent AIDS-infected monkeys up in balloons after subjecting them to high velocities and too many Gs.

Once a month, around the time of her period, Marilee came down with a migraine. Larry rarely took care of her when she was in pain. By helping her in any way, he explained, he was indulging the psychosomatic nature of her illness. He refused to accept that her headaches were biochemical, triggered by the sudden fluctuation in hormones before menstruation. Nor would he acknowledge that they followed a pattern, the same pattern that had been her mother's and her grandmother's before her. Marilee worked at forgiving him. How could he know what it was like to be a woman and at the mercy of fluctuating hormones?

Instead, when she awakened with a migraine, she downed two Percocet and zoned out for the day. She did not bemoan the loss of her time, drugs proving not all that different from daytime television. And with the Percocet in her system, she slept soundly, in spite of Señor Escamilla's clogs and timbales. When she stumbled back into the living room, usually around eight, Larry would abandon his old Royal and begin his doting: fetching her a blanket, the newspaper, her *People* magazine; pouring her a diet soda; serving her dry toast and salad on a tray. It was, she knew, his Zen-Pavlovian reinforcement of her conscious decision to get well. Marilee accepted his favors, albeit reluctantly.

One blustery day in mid-February, red roses arrived. The deliveryman handed her the vase with an envelope taped to its rim. At once, she knew the flowers were from Enoch. She had no real reason to suspect him of having sent them to her; indeed, she'd not heard from him at all since she'd deposited him so unceremoniously on that dark, rainy highway. In all of five months, Enoch had elicited barely a thought, having been relegated to some pocket of her memory he shared with Major Blackwell. But Marilee thought of him now, so delightful and unexpected was the arrival of his roses.

But the flowers were not from Enoch. They were from Larry, along with a Valentine's Day poem he had written for her.

LOVE IN THE DEAD OF WINTER
For Marilee

The twilight of a dying moon
Cast its eerie shadow on your lips
And from the barren lust of ghostly dreams
The teeming ocean of my soul cries
  My love
  My lady
  Born of a thousand dreams and more
  To know but once your warm embrace
  is to kiss the mannequin of death.

Lawrence Hurd Johnston

 The mannequin of death? She read it again. And once more. It made
no sense. Perhaps she didn't get it. She folded the paper and slipped it
into the side compartment of her purse.
 Larry's flowers she placed in a vase on the coffee table in the living
room, where they picked up on the reds in the old Indian's serape. How
sweet, she thought, for Larry to have gone to so much trouble; not once
in their entire relationship had he ever sent her flowers. That night, she
almost slept with him.

  ■

 After Larry's flowers arrived, Marilee thought about Enoch more often
than she wished. She'd had a spell of difficulty back at Christmastime,
when she'd seen elves everywhere. In store windows. In street decora-
tions. In holiday specials on TV. But once New Year's had passed, the
memory of Enoch had receded. Now, after the arrival of Larry's flowers,
she thought about Enoch constantly. She wondered where he'd gone
after she'd left him out on the highway. Where he was now. If he were
angry with her. If she'd ever see him again.

The day after she'd returned to Alamogordo, she'd unpacked her suitcase. A Tootsie Pop lay buried beneath her underwear. It was grape, and she had no idea how it had gotten there. She'd placed it in the jar in the kitchen where Larry stored pens and pencils. It was an odd thing to do. All winter long, the Tootsie Pop lived in the pencil jar by the telephone. No one had eaten it, or even asked what it was doing there.

On March 15th, the night before Larry was to leave on a business trip, he and Marilee ate dinner at the home of Dwayne and Nancy Sonnleitner. The Sonnleitners lived out at Holloman, in the barracks-style apartments behind the security gate. Marilee had never met them but recognized them both as having been at Larry's party the previous fall. Dwayne was the owner of the orange Camaro; Nancy, the skinny-assed woman with the long chestnut hair.

The couple had a two-year-old, Dwayne Jr., whom they affectionately called Dwaynie. Dwaynie fussed all through dinner. His nose ran into his plate of fish sticks. He ate his peas with his fingers and ground french fries into the cracked vinyl of his highchair. His hair smelled like sour milk. Marilee was certain she had never seen a child more awful.

"What a doll," said Larry, on their way back to Alamogordo. Marilee thought, for a moment, he was referring to Nancy. "I'd like to have one, someday. Larry Jr. What do you think, Mar?" Larry was in a fine mood. He sang along with the radio.

"Oh, I don't know," she said.

"I'd like to have two," he said wistfully. "Say, how about we start trying? Sometimes these things can take a while."

"The month's not up yet." Marilee was not ready to start having babies. She was not even ready to *think* about having babies. She wondered if Larry's sudden interest in having children were not some Zen experiment to teach him about sanity.

"Well, when it's up, then."

Marilee shrugged. If she ignored him, he might drop the subject.

"*Love can lift us higher than a mountain,*" he crooned. The wind blew sand across the highway. "We'd have to move, of course, to a larger apartment. And you'd have to get a job."

Marilee wondered if that were not the real issue.

"Oh, Mar, it's going to be so good. Just you, and me, and Larry Jr. I'll work at the base, and you'll find a job teaching watercolor. We could be just like Dwayne and Nancy."

"What about your poetry?"

"What about it?"

"There are no coffeehouses in Alamogordo."

"I'll send my poems out. To magazines. It takes time, but it'll happen. In the meantime, one has to go on living. Do normal stuff. Hold down a job. Get married. Raise a family."

"Does that mean you want to stay here?" She had never considered it a possibility.

"Of course," said Larry, throwing his Mustang into fifth. "I love New Mexico. I love my job, too. I wish I could tell you more about it."

"I wish you could tell me anything about it." A gust of wind kicked up dust along the roadside and spun it into a small tornado.

"*Love can sail us far across the sea . . .*" sang the voice on the radio. It sounded suspiciously like John Denver.

"It's weird not knowing what you do."

"It doesn't matter," he said, placing his hand upon her knee. For the last three weeks, she'd let him touch her through her clothing. "All that matters is that it's happening for us now. Dreams. Plans. It's all coming true." The Mustang roared down the interstate. Larry turned up the volume on the radio. "We're the lucky ones, Mar," he said. "We're definitely the lucky ones."

The voice warbled over the airwaves. "*Love can see us clear of any danger. Yeah, only love can set us free.*"

Larry squeezed her leg above the knee. A moth lost its wings against the speeding windshield. Marilee stared beyond its fuzzy smear at the distant lights of Rocket City.

■

When they got home, they spent an hour in their living room, Larry at his typewriter and Marilee on the couch beneath the gaze of his old Indian. Soon he would need to begin packing, as he was leaving at six the next morning for Bethesda. He'd be there a week, on the same base as Major Blackwell. As a concession to his personal freedom, Marilee had refrained from asking Larry any details about their relationship.

"It's getting windy," she said, thumbing the pages of the *Alamogordo Daily News*.

"Hmm," said Larry, typing.

"Can planes take off in high winds?"

"Yes."

"In a hurricane?"

"I don't think so. But maybe," he said.

Marilee turned the page of her newspaper and folded the section in two. She sipped at her tea, then laughed abruptly. "Listen to this," she said.

Larry stopped typing and turned to face her, annoyed. Marilee proceeded to read him an article on page seven:

"GIMP" ON LIST OF BAD WORDS
Washington

An organization called the International Exceptional People's Task Force seeking more rights for people with disabilities is vowing to get people to watch their language.

The group warns that words can lead to wrong images.

It advises against referring to people as midgets or dwarfs except when describing a medical condition. Instead, say "person, man, woman, child of short stature."

"Gimp" is a no-no. Say "walks with a limp" instead.

"Deaf and dumb" is banned by the task force, which suggests "hearing impairment" or "unable to hear or speak."

"Cripple" can convey the image of "a twisted, deformed, useless, unattractive body" and "disabled" is considered better.

"Monster, freak, vegetable, neo-morts, beating heart cadavers, lost souls, cognitive dead, decaying individual are obviously extremely dehumanizing," says the group, which suggests specific descriptions—such as "born without arms."

"'Born without arms.' How ridiculous," said Marilee.

"Oh, I don't know," said Larry, turning back to his typewriter.

"I hate all that politically correct bullshit. Born without arms. Jesus."

"It seems to me we should be sensitive to these people."

"Mr. Ambassador," said Marilee. "I'd like you to meet my husband, Larry Johnston. He was born without arms."

Larry ignored her.

"He's really a neo-mort. His mother was a beating heart cadaver and his father, a lost soul. We don't like to use those words, but you can see where he gets his special tendencies."

Laughing, she spilled tea on her jeans. Larry rolled a fresh sheet of paper into his Royal. He clacked away for a minute or two, typing furiously, like a rooster pecking out the eyes of a rival. Then he got up and walked down the hall to the bedroom. Marilee heard the locks on his suitcase pop open.

She rose and strolled over to his desk by the window, in search of a pair of scissors to clip out the article on the language police. Larry's poem was still in the carriage:

BORN WITHOUT ARMS

born without arms
blinded without nails
burned without fire
kissed without germs
hung without rope
spun without gold
bitten without teeth

stabbed without steel
born without arms
born without arms

Lawrence Hurd Johnston

A new style. Marilee switched off Larry's desk light and headed off to the bathroom. She'd seen the pinpoint-sized hole in her vision, then the snake-like pattern growing. Half blinded, she searched the medicine chest for her bottle of Percocet. The snake danced upward and grew larger. She downed two pills. Then another. The wind overturned a chair on the patio. She was weeks away from her period.

AD&D

It took Figman and Oma two hours to drive the thirty-six miles to Carlsbad. At the southern end of town, they realized they could travel no farther. The storm had become impossible; Figman doubted the caverns would even be open on a day like this.

They rented a room at the La Caverna Motel. The place was cozy but lacked the sense of deliberate cheer that it had, undoubtedly, striven to attain. Perhaps it was the Mexican-jail-cell windows, or the mattress whose dip in the center spoke of countless others who had lain there before them.

When they checked in, it was only midafternoon; Figman wondered what they might do to pass the rest of the day. Oma obviously had it all figured out. She pulled off her sweater and unfastened her bra. It was lacy and had an underwire.

Two and a half hours later, Figman lay on top of her, exhausted. Beads of sweat ran off his forehead. Dust speckled the pillow. He wondered if Oma had always been this insatiable, or if she were making up for lost time since Jesse. He recalled the wedding photo hanging above her fireplace. The groom in the picture was short, light-haired, and wiry. He didn't look like the sort of man who could satisfy a woman like Oma.

"I'm starved," she said.

Figman didn't doubt it. "I need a shower," he said.

An hour later, the two of them were seated at a back table of the Cortez Cafe. Their waitress brought them enchiladas swimming in cheese, rice and beans, and hot corn tortillas. Figman ate hungrily.

"Don't you love it when you're having sex and you just keep on coming and coming?" asked Oma.

Figman didn't want to think about sex. "It must be a female thing," he said.

"Really?" Oma piled beans and rice on a buttered tortilla.

"Men have to wait a while. Between, I mean."

"Jesse didn't have to wait."

Figman took a long swallow of his Dos Equis. *And he's dead now,* he wanted to say.

"Jesse could just keep going all night long, till I was nearly drained."

"Well, Jesse was twenty, not forty. There's a bit of a difference."

Oma put down her tortilla and looked up him. "You're *forty?* I thought you said you were thirty-four?"

He was sunk and he knew it. "I lied. To get you to go out with me. I thought it would be the only way. Can you blame me?"

"You're *forty?*"

"Not yet. But soon."

"I've never even gone out with a man in his thirties. Until you, that is."

"And you survived," said Figman, thinking his best tactic might be to humor her. Oma's face didn't move.

"How soon?" she asked, after an uncomfortable few moments.

"How soon what?"

"Until you turn forty?"

"Two weeks."

Oma looked stricken, or repulsed—he couldn't tell. "What day?" she asked.

"April 1st."

"No, I mean what day? Monday? Tuesday?" There was impatience in her tone.

"It's a Wednesday, I think," said Figman. "Why?"

"I was just wondering if I'll have the night off." She went back to her tortilla.

"So you're not too mad at me?"

"I'm furious," she said.

■

Oma refused to acknowledge him for the rest of the meal. Figman tried apologizing and even ordered her a flan, which she left uneaten, undoubtedly just to spite him. It would be a quiet night at La Caverna (which, once he thought about it, seemed like a fine idea).

No sooner had Figman switched on the light of their motel room than Oma switched it off again. She made a growling sound from low in her throat and then laughed wildly, grabbing his crotch through his jeans and pushing him onto the bed. She climbed on top of him and arched her back like an angry cat. Clearly, he had a decision to make. He could go along and assuage his guilt, or decline and risk seeming forty. He kissed her on the mouth. Oma bit his lip.

"Jesus!" he yelled. Her lipstick tasted like some hybrid melon.

Oma growled again, then laughed, throwing her hair about wildly. "You're mine," she purred, nipping Figman on his earlobe. She unzipped his fly and pulled off her rumpled blue sweater. Then she reached into her purse on the bed. For what? he wondered. A gun? A knife? Just how had Jesse died?

From her bag, Oma produced something long and stringy. A cord, he thought, or maybe several. The room was dim, and Figman's eyes had not yet fully adjusted to the darkness. Still straddling him, Oma tied his wrists to the two bedside tables. He felt splayed, like a gaffed tuna.

Oma next turned her attention to each of Figman's legs, securing his feet to the bottom of the bedframe. She worked diligently, like a dock worker tying a yacht to a cleat. Like a cowboy roping a steer. She laughed as she cinched the cord tightly around his ankles. "You're mine," she repeated.

Oma stood to remove her jeans and underwear but left on her bra. Then she reached into her bag and slipped something onto her feet. Socks, perhaps, for the room was chilly. "You're mine," she said again, just before going down on him. "Completely, absolutely, positively mine." She was an animal—almost feral in her desire. Her eyes flashed; her teeth looked like fangs. Figman wondered whether he'd be found like this in the morning, drained of blood from her bite marks.

Oma stopped, suddenly, and fished something else from her huge canvas purse. She looked beautiful in the shadowy light; despite his exhaustion, Figman grew harder. This time, Oma straddled him backward, with her feet beside his ears, the mysterious something from her purse in her hands. She wore not socks but stiletto heels, like he'd seen in porno films, and when she bent over, she afforded Figman a most spectacular view.

"Oma, what's that you've got?" he asked. She worked him harder. He was raw from their earlier session; the broken edges of her teeth felt like razor blades. "Oma," he asked again, "what's that in your hand?"

"A surprise," she said, surfacing for air. Figman strained against his wrist ropes. He imagined no end of possibilities, the least grievous of which was her slathering his cock with a handful of leftover flan.

Between fatigue and imagination, it took Figman a long time before he felt even close to coming. Oma coaxed him on, whispering "yes, yes," and "do me, do me," between tickles with her tongue. When he finally did come, she let out a moan and slapped something shocking on his testicles. Figman screamed. Oma laughed. Then he blacked out as if he had died.

■

On the hike down into the caverns, Oma confessed to Figman that the ice had come from the Cortez Cafe. While Figman was at the register getting change for a tip, she'd spooned it out of their water glasses and wrapped it in her napkin; surprisingly little had melted into her purse.

Figman was less than impressed by her resourcefulness. He wanted only to take a quick tour of the caverns (since they'd driven all this way), then return home as quickly as possible. Overnight, the dust storm had broken. All Figman could think about was his long-neglected painting and the mess inside his house waiting to be cleaned.

It took them an hour to descend the trail down into the cave. The air grew cool, and Figman wished he had thought to bring a jacket. They passed the Whale's Mouth, the Devil's Den, the Iceberg, and the Boneyard. To Figman, it was all just one big hole in the earth. Stalactites. Stalagmites. Bat guano. He wanted out of there, but Oma had grown hungry.

They made their way to the lunchroom, where they feasted on ham and cheese sandwiches, coleslaw, and dill pickles. "Let's leave after this," said Figman.

"But we'll miss the Big Room. That's the coolest part."

"It's not like you haven't come here on every field trip since the first grade," said Figman. Oma laughed. He wished she would have her teeth fixed. "These are great pickles," he said.

"Want mine?"

"Sure," he said. "I haven't had a really decent pickle since Canter's."

"What's that?"

"Jewish deli in the Fairfax district of L.A."

"I wish I had a nickel for every ham and cheese sandwich I've eaten down here. They're awful, but I'm going to miss them."

"What do you mean?"

"They're talking about closing down the lunchroom."

"Why?"

"With all the elevators, they don't need it. You can be up and out of here in minutes."

"There's elevators?" He felt the walls of the cave beginning to close in on him.

"Just around that corner," she said, pointing to an aperture in the rockface. They'd walked right by there. How could he not have seen them? "Well, let's go," he said.

"You sure you don't want to see the Big Room? The Bottomless Pit is really cool."

Figman shuddered. "I'm out of here," he said.

■

On the drive back to Artesia, Oma explained to Figman in great detail the politics of Lester's E-Z Mart. How Gert kept getting raises while her own raise was long overdue. How the woman maneuvered this by sleeping with Lester Meany, although both of them were married. How Santos refused to believe it, but she and Dino knew it was true because Dino had walked in on Lester kissing Gert in the meat locker.

"That's a strange place to be kissing," said Figman.

"Oh, I don't know," said Oma. "All that body heat could keep you warm."

"Yeah, but meat hanging from hooks . . ." A chill ran through him.

"There's no hooks," said Oma. "Just hunks of beef and stuff on shelves."

"Still, it's hardly what you'd call romantic." Figman shifted in his seat; his testicles ached.

"Me and Jesse made it in there once," said Oma, giggling.

"Why doesn't that surprise me?"

"What do you mean?"

"Seems like you and Jesse had quite a time of it." Oma looked out her side window and grew ominously silent. Figman could have kicked himself. The last thing he wanted was to get her all moody and depressed this far from home. "So what happened after Dino walked in on Gert and Lester?"

Oma faced forward. "Dino demanded a raise and more time off, and Lester gave it to him. But only if he promised not to tell anyone what he'd seen."

"He told you."

"Yeah, but he swore me to secrecy."

Figman did not pursue the obvious. "Say," he said, looking across the seat at her, "do you know a guy named Poe Titus?"

"Yeah, why?"

"Well, he's a friend of Verdie's, and he seems to know you."

"Oh my God!" yelled Oma. Figman's eyes darted back to the road. Directly ahead of them, an oncoming blue sedan had drifted across the center line and into their lane. The driver, a woman, appeared not to have noticed, so busy was she talking to the child in the seat next to her. Oma screamed. Figman clenched. He sounded his horn, and the child waved his arms excitedly. The woman looked up, startled. Inexplicably, she stayed on course. Oma screamed again. Figman cut sharply left, into the oncoming lane. A truck barreled toward them, headlights flashing. Oma screamed louder.

"Shut up!" yelled Figman. He wanted to strangle her. He'd seen the truck and knew he had plenty of time to pass the woman's car and cut back into his own lane. Without warning, Oma grabbed his steering wheel and jerked his Aion back into the path of the blue sedan, all the while screaming like some wild animal. The woman looked terrified; the child looked like Bobo.

Figman yanked the steering wheel back in his direction, but his Aion would not respond. Something had gone wrong! He struggled to regain control of his automobile as it stayed on course, headed straight into the blue sedan. Oma screamed again and yanked harder on the wheel. Figman wanted to kill her. He wanted to rip the steering wheel right out of her hand and shove it down her shrieking throat. Again, he jerked the steering wheel in his direction. But his Aion would not obey him. It was obeying her. Her caterwaul was drowning out his orders, his thought-commands telling his car what he wanted it to do.

"Shut up!" he yelled, prying her fingers off the steering wheel. "Shut up! Shut up! Shut up!" He spun the wheel madly, but his car stayed on course, ignoring him, barreling toward the road's shoulder as the blue sedan swerved suddenly into its rightful lane and passed them on the left, shimmying.

Figman's Aion rolled off onto the gravel. For a moment he thought they were destined to crash through a barbed-wire fence, but just as mysteriously as it had failed him, his car's steering mechanism reengaged, and Figman found himself once again in control of his vehicle. Heart pounding, he pulled back into the northbound lane. He slowed, instinctively, then continued toward home. In his rearview mirror, he saw the blue sedan pull over to the side of the highway.

Oma huddled in her seat, whimpering; Figman didn't care. He was freaked. He could have been killed. Dismembered. He could have needed the Jaws of Life to extricate his body from the wreckage. If he'd lived, which seemed unlikely, he'd have been taken to a hospital where he'd have been required to produce health insurance and his name. He could have been located this way, through his insurance company, which was Goetschke Life and Casualty.

Figman had no clue as to what had gone wrong with his Aion. Its malfunction was completely inexplicable, as though the hand of God had reached down and taken control of its steering. Had it reengaged just a moment sooner, Figman might have veered to the left just as the blue sedan veered right. Surely, they would have all been killed. But his Aion had saved him. Again. It was another miracle. Fate *does* happen, thought Figman.

Oma sulked all the way back to Artesia. By midafternoon, when Figman pulled into her driveway, he'd relaxed some from their near catastrophe. He was anxious to drop her off quickly and get home to his dirty house. He set the emergency brake. "Would you like me to walk you to the door?" he asked.

"I can manage," she said coolly. Oma grabbed her purse from the backseat, threw open her door, and stomped up her porch steps. He watched as she fiddled with her keys. The door opened. She slammed it closed behind her.

He should apologize, he knew, but what to say? He sat in his car with his windows down, breathing in the clean air whose early return he celebrated. He was sure his lungs were black with dust. Figman wondered how long they would take to clear and whether this gave him the same mortality odds as a smoker.

Oma's curtains parted, then closed abruptly once she saw Figman's Aion still parked in her driveway. It hadn't been fair of him to have yelled at her. She'd only been frightened out there on the highway. He was being too harsh. She hadn't meant to endanger them that way.

Figman stepped out of his car and climbed the steps to her entry porch. He knocked, then heard her moving about inside. He knocked again and called her name. Still nothing. "I'm sorry," he shouted. The door opened. Figman stepped into her shrine to her dead husband.

"Are you?" she said coyly.

"Yes," said Figman. "Truly sorry."

"Prove it to me," said Oma. Her eyes were red, a condition that made her blue eye seem larger than the other.

"Prove it to you? How?"

"Come on, you know," she said, moving close to him. She put her arms around his waist and pressed her hips into his. Would she never tire of this activity? Oma took him by the hand and led him into her bedroom. It was baby blue and ruffly. Her window shades were drawn. Above the bed hung an eight-by-ten picture of Jesse.

Within minutes, they were naked and going at it under the covers. Her sheets smelled like lilac. Figman's cock was sore. He hoped to get her off quickly and go home and take a nap.

"Forbes?" she said.

"Yeah?"

"What shampoo do you use?"

"Suave."

"That doesn't smell like Suave." She looked troubled and had stopped rocking her hips beneath him.

"They were out of Suave, so I picked up a bottle of Pert Plus. Why?"

"We don't carry Pert Plus."

"I got it at Batie's."

Oma started crying.

Figman stopped his thrusting. "Don't take it personally," he said. "I run in there sometimes because it's quicker."

"Your hair smells like Jesse's hair," she sobbed, tears streaming onto her lacy pillow.

Figman arched his back and pulled himself out of her.

"No, don't stop," she said. With her hand, she reached down and maneuvered him back into position. Perfunctorily, he continued.

"So tell me about Jesse," he said, glancing up at the picture above her bed.

"You really want to know?" she asked.

"Sure," he lied. Why was he doing this? Why was he here at all?

"Jesse died in a potash mine. He was only twenty-three. A mine train ran over him."

The McQuiddy claim. It had been horrible, what with the loss of limbs.

"Jesse lived for a week before he died. He was in a coma, but he kept calling for me."

Figman wanted to tell her this wasn't possible, but he resisted, afraid of losing his erection.

"His arms were crushed and his head was dented in. When he died, the doctors told me it was a blessing."

Out of the blue, and for no apparent reason, Figman suddenly remembered he had yet to insure his house. He would have to devise a plan to convince Verdie to carry the insurance in her name even if he paid for it.

". . . and that's when things really got bad," said Oma, voice breaking. Figman hadn't been listening. "When what?"

"When I lost the twins."

Twins? Had she been talking about twins?

"I just couldn't deal with them, with the grief and all." Figman scrambled to make sense of what she was saying. He thrust harder.

"They were my babies."

"So how did they die?"

"Die? They didn't die. Did I say they died?"

"I guess not. So, then, what did happen?" Figman felt himself going limp.

"I dropped them off with Jesse's parents one weekend when it seemed like the day would never end. Drove all the way to Sweetwater."

"And?"

"And?" She looked up at the picture of her dead husband. "And I never went back."

Figman felt a stab at the base of his neck; the blob took form in the upper left corner of his vision. Why did so many women insist upon talking during sex? He thrust deeper into Oma, trying to regain his erection, but it was no use. His clutch had slipped. "I'm sorry," he muttered. "I guess I'm just not into this."

"That's okay," she said.

"No, it's not okay." Figman rolled off her. He felt hot and kicked the blankets aside.

"Look, it happens," said Oma. "It even happened once to Jesse."

"Will you shut the fuck up about Jesse?"

"Fuck you," said Oma. She rolled onto her side, opened the drawer to her bedside table, and took out a pack of cigarettes. She lit one. Figman had never seen her smoke. He could tell she was doing it to keep from crying again, like plugging up a hole. The smoke made his head throb.

"I'm sorry," he said. "I didn't mean that. Go on."

Oma shifted to her back and stared up at the ceiling. In a moment, she continued. "His people never called me or nothing. It was so hard. I wanted to go back for them, but I just couldn't. Or didn't—I don't know. One day led to the next, and then the next. You know how it can be."

Figman didn't. Oma's body was beautiful; when she drew on her cigarette, the glow of its ember brought the roundness of her breasts into op-
ulent relief. Still, Figman felt nothing.

"Someone told me they moved away last April, but I've been too
scared to go see for myself."

"How long has it been since you've seen them?" His headache was
coming on quickly. He would have to leave immediately if he wanted to
make it home.

"Couple of years."

Figman clutched at his temples. "My head hurts."

"Want some Tylenol?"

"I mean it really hurts. I get these headaches. They can be pretty bad."

"I could put ice on your neck."

Figman thought better of it. "I think I should go."

Oma burst into tears. "I knew it," she sobbed. "I knew it, I knew it, I
knew it!"

Figman was at a complete loss.

"Every time I tell a man about what happened after Jesse, he just ups
and leaves."

"Then I'll stay," he said. Oma rolled into his arms. His head pounded.
The snake danced with a vengeance.

■

Figman awoke the next morning in a room he didn't recognize. Blue.
Frilly. Smelling of lilac. And then he remembered. How all night long he
had moaned into Oma's pillow. How she had rubbed the back of his neck
and called him her baby. How he had felt himself completely lost in her,
as though he'd fallen from the sky into some dark cave.

The clock on her table said 11:30. She'd be at work now. Figman rose,
dressed, and left her a note. It said: "Thank you for taking such good
care of me." He signed it "F," which, when he thought about it, could
stand for either Figman or Forbes.

On his way into his driveway, Figman stopped to retrieve his and
Verdie's mail. A bronze Samurai stood parked in front of his house. Benito
sat on his front steps.

Figman took his time getting back into his Aion. He considered back-
ing out the driveway and hurrying away, perhaps to K-Mart or Colorado.
But that was not the answer, he knew. Figman parked alongside Hooks's
Samurai. "Benito," he said, stepping out of his car.

"Bill," said Hooks. He wore a cowboy hat.

Figman grabbed his mail and bounded up his front steps. His head
ached with every movement. "What brings you here?"

"My Samurai," said Hooks. He burst into laughter.

Oma was right; it wasn't funny. "Look, Benito, I'm not feeling well.
You'll have to come back another time."

"What you got?" asked Hooks.

"Stomach flu. Highly contagious. I wouldn't get too close."

Hooks took a step backward. "I done checked out that license plate
number you gave me. The guy's a pipe fitter from White's City."

"Well, he's not your man," said Figman, opening his door. "The guy
you want drives a red and gold Caddy."

Figman gave Hooks Dino's license number and sent him on his way.
He strolled into his kitchen. Verdie's mail was a disaster: a letter from
that lawyer up in Roswell, another from a lawyer in Hobbs, a mailing
from some hospice center in Hagerman, and a large manila envelope
from a mortuary in Santa Fe. Her end must be getting near; he would
miss her when she was gone.

Figman added her letters to the pile on his counter, relieved he'd received no mail of his own. He looked around at his filthy abode. Virtually
everything he owned needed to be washed or vacuumed. Cleaning would
take him most of the day. He would have to devise some way to keep the
dust out in the future, perhaps by sealing up that access to his attic.

It was dark when he finally finished vacuuming. The lights were off in
Verdie's trailer; her car had been gone all day. Figman fixed himself a
light dinner and went to bed. He planned to rise early and resume his
painting.

An hour later, Figman heard a crash out on his back porch. He'd been
sound asleep, and the noise had startled him. It was probably Bobo's cat,
he thought, scavenging for more chunks of hamburger. Figman had almost drifted back to sleep when he heard it again—a crash, and then an

eerie scraping. No cat ever made a sound like that. He threw on his bathrobe and padded into his kitchen, careful not to turn on the light. He peeked outside his window, across his backyard. Verdie's trailer was still dark.

Again, he heard a scraping—perhaps a branch against a window, he thought, failing to consider that his yard had no trees. Opening his back door, he stepped out onto his porch. The punch caught him blindsided, a sharp blow to his right cheek. Then a kick in the balls, then laughter.

"What the fuck?" rasped Figman, doubled over in pain.

"That's for dicking my sister, Lou."

Had Oma gone straight to her brother and reported details? Had Hooks caught up with him? Figman's head reeled from the blow, revitalizing his headache. He pressed his fingers to his cheek.

"I saw your car, asshole. Parked all night at my sister's house."

Figman had forgotten about his car parked in Oma's driveway.

"If I see it there again, you won't have a dick left to fuck her with." Dino swaggered off down the driveway.

"I could have you arrested," yelled Figman.

Dino stopped and placed one hand on his hip. "Yeah, and who are you going to get to arrest me, shit-for-brains? My uncle, the police chief?" Dino snirked and climbed into his Cadillac. He threw his car into reverse and squealed out of the driveway.

Figman stumbled inside and studied his face in the bathroom mirror. His cheek had begun to swell, and the skin beneath his eye was torn. He took ice cubes out of his freezer and wrapped them in a towel, knowing exactly where he would like to apply them to Dino. His crotch throbbed; his cheek ached. They would both look nasty in the morning.

He held his ice pack to his eye and sat in his unlit kitchen. It was well past eleven, and Verdie was not yet home. Was she out with Titus? Visiting her son? Languishing in some hospital? Finally, a little before midnight, Figman heard the crunch of tires roll past his open window. A car door slammed. He got up to investigate. Verdie was alone. He'd give her five minutes to get settled, then head over to her place with her stack of mail. Figman hoped to receive some sympathy, or at the very least a drink.

Five minutes later, Figman crossed his backyard to Verdie's trailer, one hand clutching her mail, the other pressing his makeshift ice pack to his cheek. Halfway to her door, he tripped on something and fell. Verdie's mail went flying; Figman's towel and ice cubes landed at his feet. Pain like a dog bite shot through his right ankle. Figman grabbed at it and winced.

He looked around for what he had tripped on. The yard was dark; he saw nothing unusual. He tried to stand, but his ankle would not support him, so he sat cross-legged on the ground. The night was clear; stars shone brightly in the heavens. The light went off in Verdie's trailer.

With his bare hands, Figman rooted in the dirt, determined to discover the instrument of his undoing. Had Dino left some booby trap for him to stumble into? Had he strung tripwire to fell him? Figman patted the soil, probing the earth around him, combing it with his fingertips. Dirt got under his fingernails. A meteor blazed across the sky.

Figman dug into the cool, sandy dirt. Something glinted in the flash of headlights from a passing semi. It was shiny and off to his left. He reached for it and felt something cold. He examined it with his fingers. It was a large metal spoon, the kind a housewife uses. It stuck straight up out of a freshly dug hole.

PIQUE EXPERIENCES

Despite having taken three Percocet, Marilee was unable to get to sleep until an hour after Larry had departed for his week in Maryland. It was neither his snoring that had kept her awake nor the Escamillas' timbale music, but some small anxiety she could not pinpoint. Around eleven AM, she was roused by a knock at the door. She wondered if it were Esther Escamilla asking her to turn down her quiet. Percocet caused neurons to synapse in strange, unexpected ways.

Throwing on her bathrobe, Marilee checked herself in the mirror. She had sleep in her eyes and dark circles beneath them. Her mouth was a petri dish; her hair, a bird's nest. The knock came again. Perhaps Larry had sent her more flowers.

Marilee stumbled to the front door, the left side of her head throbbing. She opened it. It was Enoch, balancing on his crutches, eating Cheese Nips out of a box. "What's up?" he asked.

Enoch's appearance on Marilee's doorstep did not surprise her; in fact, she'd secretly been expecting it for some time. "Migraine," she said. "What took you so long?"

"Had to wait for lover-boy to leave."

Had Enoch been watching them?

"Come in," she said, opening the door wider. Outside, the sky was dark. Pods blew from the mesquite trees.

Enoch tucked his box of Cheese Nips under one arm and bounded over her threshold. "Nice art," he said, glancing at the wall above the couch.

"It's Larry's."

"I'm certain," he said.

"Have a seat," she instructed.

Enoch tossed his backpack on a chair, rested his crutches against the wall, and climbed up on a barstool. His head seemed to grow out of the top of the counter. Marilee put on water for tea. "Where've you been?" she asked.

"Here and there. Zaragoza, mainly."

"Where's that?"

"Mexico." He located the Tootsie Pop in the pencil jar on the counter, unwrapped it, and shoved it into his mouth. "Cheese Nip?" He tilted the box in her direction.

Marilee took a handful. She was glad to see Enoch despite the pounding in her left temple.

"Where's the band?" he asked.

"Upstairs. All day. All night. Drives me crazy."

"Retaliate," said Enoch.

"How?"

"Put on Whitney Houston."

Marilee laughed. The teapot whistled. Her head ached violently. "So how'd you know Larry was gone?"

"Sources," said Enoch. "Friends in high places."

"Sounds pretty low to me."

"Depends on your vantage point."

Marilee sneezed into her assortment of tea bags.

"Gesundheit."

"Thank you," she said. Enoch sucked on his Tootsie Pop.

"A week in Bethesda. Nice weather there, this time of year."

"How'd you know that?" she demanded.

"Did my homework."

His smug attitude annoyed her. Wind howled down through the stove vent. She sneezed again and blew her nose into a napkin. "What's going on?" she asked him.

"Dust storm," he said. "Gonna be a doozie. Maybe once every ten years we get one this bad."

"Swell," she said, plopping a bag of Grandma's Tummy Mint into the cup of hot water and sliding it toward him.

"I thought that was for you?"

"You're on your own," she said. "I'm going back to bed. There's Hershey bars behind the silver tray and Ding Dongs in the back of the hall closet."

"What's in the refrigerator?"

"Lettuce," said Marilee.

■

Two Percocet later, she crawled back under her bedcovers. Upstairs, Rico put on Eddie Palmieri loud enough to be heard through his open window while he tinkered with somebody's Chevy in the backyard. Marilee listened to Enoch typing on Larry's old Royal. It was then she remembered "Born Without Arms" still rolled in its carriage. She pulled the covers up over her ears. At least Enoch had said nothing about her weight gain.

She awoke around eight to the smell of chile rellenos. She never doubted Enoch would still be there, eating her chocolate and watching TV. "How you feeling?" he asked from the couch beneath the old Indian.

"Hungry."

"Excellent," he said, jumping up and hobbling, sans crutches, into the kitchen. "I took the liberty."

"I didn't know you could cook."

"I'm a genius in the kitchen." Outside, the wind howled; the windowsills looked dusty.

Marilee sat at the counter while Enoch dished up rellenos, refried beans, and something that looked like corn pudding. "What's that?" she asked.

"Corn pudding," said Enoch.

"Where'd you get the ingredients?"

"Big 8 Food Plaza." It was not far from the apartment. "Want a beer?"

"God, no," she said. She took a bite of relleno. His were every bit as good as Carmina's.

"You got a call," said Enoch, dishing up a large helping for himself. "I let the machine get it."

Marilee reached over and pushed the message button. "Hello," said a male voice. "I guess I'll go ahead and embarrass myself. This is Gil at Trinity Auto. We were scheduled to work on your Mustang today . . ."

"Shit," said Marilee, hitting the stop button.

"What's the matter?"

"I was supposed to take Larry's car in. I forgot all about it."

"You were sick."

"He'll be pissed at me."

"So we'll take it in tomorrow."

"It won't be done on time."

"What's wrong with it?"

"What isn't?" said Marilee. "Clutch, solenoid, starter. It may also need a new transmission." Marilee sneezed.

"That's major," he said, joining her at the counter. "We'll drop it off on our way to Carlsbad."

Marilee shot him an evil look.

"The caverns," said Enoch. "Great ham and cheese sandwiches."

■

When Marilee rose the next morning, Enoch had breakfast waiting. He'd slept on her couch with a pillow and blanket he'd found while searching for Ding Dongs. Marilee called Trinity Auto before jumping into the shower. Gil was out buying parts. She tried him again before she and Enoch departed for Carlsbad. This time she got an answering machine. She left a message for Gil to call her, then loaded up the Dart.

The sky was cloudy, but the wind had subsided. Dust was everywhere: on store windows, rooftops, sidewalks, the street. Her car was covered in a thick layer of it; she debated washing it before they left.

"Don't bother," said Enoch. "It'll look the same once we get there. We can wash the windows when we stop for gas."

Marilee reset the answering machine and turned off the lights in the kitchen. When she went to close the curtains, she saw Enoch's typing from the night before. "Written without talent," it said at the bottom of Larry's poem. Marilee would have to retype it as soon as she got home.

"That wasn't very nice," she said, once they were headed east on Highway 82.

Enoch seemed to know what she was talking about. "The truth can be cruel," he said dramatically.

"Oh, please," she said. "What do you know about poetry?"

"Nothing," said Enoch. "But I know about people. What they have and haven't got."

"That's right. I forgot. You're a dwarf and you see the world more profoundly than the rest of us."

Enoch laughed.

"I was being serious," she said.

"I know."

"Look, what is it with you, anyway? We know each other for a week—not even a week. I drop you off on some highway and six months later you come knocking on my door like nothing happened."

"Nothing did," he said.

The Dart struggled up the mountain.

"I'm tired of all your cryptic nonsense, too. Like having to be in Albuquerque by three AM."

"I was kidding about that. Anyway, how can you be tired of something you haven't been subjected to in six months? That's like that joke about the nuns."

"What joke?"

"You know, the one where the whole cloister has taken a vow of silence, but once a year one of them is allowed to speak. So the first year, Sister Theresa, for lack of anything better to say, says, 'I don't like the soup.' And the next year, Sister Josephine says, 'I like the soup just fine.' And the third year, Sister Beatrice says, 'I'm sick and tired of all this bickering.'" Enoch looked across the seat at Marilee. "You're not laughing," he said.

"Look, can we just cut the bullshit?"

"What bullshit?"

"We're going to spend the day together. A trip to the caverns, you said. I've had a migraine, and I'm not in the best mood. The caverns sound like a nice diversion. So let's not argue or play games with each other. Let's just go and try to have a good time."

"I'm not playing games."

"You're always playing games. Everything's a riddle with you. A mystery." Marilee sneezed. "Damn this dust."

"There's no dust in the caverns."

"Good," she said.

"There. That wasn't a game," said Enoch.

"And *that* was." Enoch chuckled and rolled down his window. Marilee worried about dust getting inside her car. "I just never feel like I'm connecting with you. Maybe once," she said. "Up in Ruidoso, when you told me what it's like to be a dwarf. But the rest of the time it's always something else."

"Like what?"

"I don't know," she said. The Dart downshifted into second. "Like everything's a secret."

"We all have secrets," said Enoch.

"But yours seem to be more . . . monumental. The fire. Carmina. What happened to you in high school."

"What happened to me in high school?"

"With that guy. What was his name?"

"Chester?"

"Yeah. And that cop, the drug case."

Enoch was silent.

"Why all the suspense? Why not just tell me about it?"

"Why not tell me something about you?" said Enoch. "A secret of your own."

"This is what I mean," she said. "This is playing games."

"Perhaps," said Enoch. His look was resolute.

She drove for a moment in silence. "Okay," she said, "but then it's your turn." The Dart barreled up the mountain. "I'll tell you something," she said, "but it's embarrassing. You've got to promise not to tell anyone."

"Who would I tell?"

"Carmina."

"Carmina wouldn't care."

"*I* care."

"Sounds good," he said, kicking his feet up on the dashboard.

"Larry would kill me if he knew I was telling you this. A couple of years ago, he and I were folding laundry, and he holds up a pair of his Jockey shorts and says, 'Do you ever wonder what the slits in these things are for?' He was dead serious. He didn't have a clue."

Enoch looked at her blankly.

"He'd been pulling it out over the elastic his entire life."

"That's it?" said Enoch. "The slits in Larry's Jockey shorts?"

"Yeah."

"Your big secret?"

"You didn't say it had to be a *big* secret." She stepped harder on the accelerator.

"That was about Larry. Tell me something about you."

She thought for a moment. "When I was a kid, my mother brought home men every night."

"That's not about you."

"I had to live with her."

"I don't care about your mother. I care about you, Marilee." He said it tenderly. When she glanced at him and saw the look on his face, her heart leaped into her throat.

"Well, what do you want to know?"

"Just something about you. Something personal. Something real."

They passed their first pine tree. "All right," she said. She thought about the things she wished she could tell Enoch. How she liked the way he looked when the light hit his face at just that certain angle. How she liked his voice, his smile, and the way his eyes lit up when his thoughts were flying. How he infuriated her at times but never bored her, or made her feel stupid, or made her feel ugly. She wished she could tell Enoch how she'd wanted to make love to him that night.

Marilee leaned back into her seat and stretched her left leg out into the footwell. "Okay, here goes. Once, I was at this party in Beverly Hills where everything was very chichi. Lots of silver and crystal and a butler named Jonathan. There were about ten of us, sitting around the table after dinner, telling stories. Well, this one woman there was just crazy.

This big blond with ratty hair—you know the type. And she told this hysterical story about some biscuit company in England that had spent a hundred thousand pounds on market research to come up with the perfect name for their new chocolate cookie. And all of us got to laughing really hard, you know, because it was one of those stories that just builds and builds. And by the end of it, we all had tears rolling down our faces and one man spilled his wine, and . . . well, I didn't mean to, but I sort of peed through my underwear."

Enoch was silent.

"On a satin chair."

Enoch just looked at her. "Everybody's peed through their underwear," he said. "Tell me something I don't already know."

"Well, Jesus, I've already told you three things."

"Tell me a fourth," he said.

Marilee took a deep breath. She stared at the scenery and tried to think of something safe but personal she could tell Enoch. She didn't have many dark secrets—just one, really, and she wasn't sure she wanted to share it. But she was at a loss, otherwise. "All right," she said. "I hope you'll still like me after this."

"We'll see," said Enoch, which didn't make it any easier.

Marilee tried to think of a graceful way to segue into her story. There wasn't one. "When I was in college, Larry and I broke up for a couple of months. During that time, I had an affair with a married man."

Enoch didn't blink.

"I told myself it was okay because I didn't know the guy's wife—which was a cop-out, I know, because it didn't matter whether I knew her or not." She paused, hoping Enoch would respond, but he didn't. "At the time, I guess I rationalized a lot of things. We both did. It was a real number we did on ourselves, like telling ourselves we were above sneaking around behind her back. As if being open about it somehow exonerated us. Daniel just came out one night and told her we were in love. That he was moving out. That we were going to get married, and that she could keep the kids and he'd pay her child support and alimony. I think he thought that anything said in the name of truth was okay. But it wasn't okay. I think a lot of what he said was intended to hurt her."

"Like what?"

"Like when he told her that he'd never loved her."

"Heavy duty," said Enoch. "What did she do?"

"Freaked out. Bleached her hair—it looked terrible. She used to call me on the phone and scream at me and quote passages from the Bible. Most of the time she just called and hung up. Over and over. Day and night. Hundreds of calls."

"Did you do anything about it?"

"I called the police. They had the phone company put a tracer on my line. They wanted me to press charges against her, but I couldn't do it."

"Then what?"

"The usual script. He got cold feet. Realized he was going through some sort of midlife crisis. That he didn't know what he wanted, whether it was her, or me, or anybody. He'd break it off with me, then call a day or two later and beg me to take him back. Drove me crazy. I finally broke up with him. Eventually he went back to his wife."

"Did Larry know about this guy?"

"Not at the time."

"Did you love him?"

"I thought I did. We were planning to get married. It would have been a big mistake."

"Do you think he loved you?"

"I don't know. What's love?" She laughed.

"Don't you know?"

"Does anybody?"

Enoch didn't answer, just sat with his feet up on the dashboard, staring out the window.

"I was stupid," said Marilee. "I acted like a jerk."

"How so?"

"I went along with him. Assumed that honesty was some sort of vindication for the choices we made. Very convenient. But stupid. We all went through a lot of pain."

"Do you regret the experience?"

Marilee thought about it. "Yes and no," she said. "No, because I learned a lot. Yes, because we hurt somebody. She didn't deserve that. I mean, she was a first-class bitch—spread a lot of lies about me—but I don't think she deserved what we put her through. We were reckless. Very full of ourselves."

"Cruel?"

Marilee thought about it. "I'd say Daniel was cruel."

"And you?"

"Just . . . naive."

"Hmm," said Enoch. He seemed not entirely satisfied.

"Your turn," she said. "Tell me about the fire."

Enoch shifted in his seat and rolled up his window. "I'll tell you about Chester Chittibaugh. And Lucid and Cherry and what they did to me in high school."

"Shoot," she said. It was better than nothing.

"As soon as we get to Artesia and I've had something to eat."

■

Artesia was a pit of a cow town. Or maybe it was a pit of an oil town, Marilee couldn't tell. Either way, it was barren and ugly and looked particularly depressing covered in dust. She wondered why anyone would choose to live in such a place.

At Enoch's suggestion, she pulled into Lester's E-Z Mart on Main Street to buy snacks. Their checker was named Gert, an older woman who looked incomplete without a cigarette dangling from her lips. Her orange hair was piled on top of her head, which was egg shaped and welded to her shoulders. When she saw Enoch, her eyes turned to asterisks.

"I wouldn't play poker with that one," she said to Marilee. "Take your clothes or your money and make you thank him for the privilege."

Was there anyone in New Mexico Enoch didn't know? Marilee strolled over to the magazine rack. The bagboy's staring had been making her nervous.

"Strip poker?" she said, as soon as she and Enoch had gotten back into the car. "Who even plays that past fourteen?"

"She's a pro," said Enoch.

"I think she's weird."

Enoch shrugged. "And she thinks you're too tall for me."

■

They drove to the United New Mexico Bank on Main Street, where Enoch withdrew cash from the automatic teller. Afterward, they continued down the street to a Mexican restaurant, La Fonda. *"The Man Who Fell to Earth* was filmed in this town," Enoch informed her, once they'd ordered chimichangas with sour cream and guacamole. "David Bowie has probably eaten at this very restaurant."

"They should make it a shrine," said Marilee.

"Don't you like David Bowie?"

"I *love* David Bowie." She noticed two men staring at them from across the room. She stared back at them until they turned away. "Come on, out with it," she said to Enoch.

Enoch loaded up a tortilla chip with salsa. "Chester and Cherry were brother and sister."

"I remember."

"I had this thing for Cherry. Cherry had this thing for Lucid. Chester arranged for me to discover them getting it on in my bed."

"That's it?"

"What were you expecting?"

"I thought they beat you up or something."

"That was later."

"You make it sound like no big deal."

"I've had years to get over it," he said, smiling. "But at the time it was very traumatic. There are few things more depressing than sleeping in someone else's wet spot."

Their waitress arrived with Enoch's Coke, plus coffee, milk, and a glass of ice for Marilee. She poured coffee into the ice, then added milk and and lo-cal sweetener. Enoch watched, intrigued. "The coffee keeps you awake and the milk, which has this natural sedative in it, takes the edge off so you don't get the jitters," she explained.

"So you're neutral?"

"Yeah."

"I like that." The light caught Enoch's face at just that certain angle; for the first time, Marilee noticed his scars. He had four of them on his face: a fine white line that traversed his forehead at an angle, one that stretched from his right ear to his eyebrow, another on his cheek, and another near the cleft in his chin. She wondered why she had previously failed to notice them.

"So tell me about the fire," she said, as casually as she could.

"Let me tell you about the bat flight at the caverns. In the summer, there's thousands of them. They all come screaming out of the cave at dusk like this giant black cloud, making this buzzing sound you've never heard." Enoch went on describing the bats, but Marilee caught only half of what he said. She was lost in thought, imagining the fire that had killed twelve people, including his best friend, and for which Enoch had been wrongfully blamed. A fire so horrible, he avoided ever talking about it. She would broach the subject again later, perhaps after night had fallen. Darkness made all things possible.

■

After lunch, they continued past Carlsbad toward the Texas border. The sky had begun to clear, and the temperature grew warmer the farther south they drove. The landscape looked barren. A roadrunner darted across the highway and hit Marilee's right front fender with a thud. She jumped.

Enoch stood on the seat and looked out the rear window. He shook his head. "Deader than Elvis."

"I hate it when that happens," said Marilee. "I hit a cocker spaniel once. I could feel it rolling under the car."

"It happens," said Enoch. He sat back down. "Fewer stupid genes to pass on to future roadrunners."

In her rearview mirror, Marilee checked out the black and red splotch on the highway. Her heart was pounding. "I hope it didn't suffer," she said.

"I think it's beautiful," said Enoch.

"What?"

"Well, not road kill. But the system. It's remarkable. Those who don't adapt get eaten. Or left on a rock to die. Or run over by a big steel box on wheels."

"What makes that beautiful?"

"The fact that it works," said Enoch. "The fact that it allows the rest of us to evolve."

"In earlier times," said Marilee, "*you* would have been left on a rock to die."

"In earlier times, that would have been called mercy. It still is in certain parts of the world."

"How so?"

"It beats being ostracized by your village. Or made the court jester."

"Why does the village have to ostracize anyone?"

"Because people are cruel."

"Not all people."

"Sure they are. They're as much a part of the system as a roadrunner or a cocker spaniel. Or a pit bull. 'All life is a cruelty.' Artaud said that."

"Are you sure it wasn't Woody Allen?"

Enoch laughed. "Yes. But I'm sure he'd agree."

They drove the next few miles in silence. At White's City, Marilee noticed a sign touting the Carlsbad Caverns. "Is this where we turn?"

"No, that's just a tourist trap."

She continued south. With each passing mile, the countryside grew drier and less hospitable. It seemed they'd been driving forever, toward some parched, forsaken land that would crack wide open and swallow them whole. "Where are we?" she asked.

"The road to Thebes."

Marilee laughed out loud. "What's that supposed to mean?"

Enoch smiled, inscrutably.

"Like in *Oedipus Rex*? The guy who slept with his mother?"

"And killed his father," said Enoch.

She looked over at the dwarf in her front seat. "It's a fairy tale," she said.

"Myth. Fairy tale. It's all the same."

"I don't get it."

"It's what we all have to do. Marry the mother and slay the father."

"What?"

"Not literally," said Enoch. "Metaphorically. It's unavoidable."

"You act as if we don't have free will."

Enoch stretched and put his feet up on the dashboard. "The engineer just thinks he's driving the train. In reality, he can only go where the tracks are laid."

"To Thebes?"

"Grand Central."

She laughed again, looking beyond him at the scenery outside his window. She loved Enoch's wacky sensibility, his weird but intelligent humor. He made her laugh. He made her think about things.

"Look out!" he yelled suddenly, taking his feet off the dashboard and waving his arms. She had drifted across the center lane, directly into the path of a white Aion traveling north. The driver looked startled; his female companion appeared to be screaming. A horn sounded, and Marilee hit her brakes. She stayed on course until she could assess which path the white car's driver was going to take. The Aion cut sharply across the center line, and Marilee knew they would pass each other on the wrong sides of the highway. She would wave at him as they passed, in a gesture of apology.

But suddenly, the man's female passenger grabbed the steering wheel. The Aion swung back into the path of the Dart. Marilee checked her rearview mirror. A semi approached from behind, flashing its lights.

"Holy shit!" said Enoch. The Aion was headed directly toward them, the man struggling for control of his vehicle, the woman fighting for same; the man pushing her off the wheel, the woman cowering, eyes shielded by latticed fingers. The truck behind Marilee had backed off a bit. She cut sharply to her right, back into her own lane, where she passed the Aion with mere inches to spare. In her rearview mirror she saw the Aion roll onto the shoulder, then back onto the pavement. It slowed, then continued north on the highway.

"Jesus Christ," said Enoch.

"Fucking asshole," said Marilee.

"Assholette," he said. "The driver wasn't the problem."

Marilee pulled to the side of the road and stopped the car. The truck honked as it passed them. Marilee rolled down her window and pulled her keys out of the ignition. She threw them down into the footwell, hard. She was shaking and began to cry.

Enoch slid into the space next to her and put his arms around her middle. They didn't reach far, and for some reason that made Marilee cry even harder. She sobbed into his shoulder, making a mess of his yellow shirt. He seemed not to mind. Cars passed them on the highway. Enoch held her tighter. It felt good to make contact. Good to feel him touching her. Good to be held by another human being in so godforsaken a place.

And as Enoch held her, Marilee felt herself falling: the lump in her throat, the flip-flop in her stomach, the sudden gasp of air, as though she were tumbling through miles of space, the way she had fallen for Larry, the way she had fallen for Daniel, who was married and didn't really want her love. Only now she was falling for a dwarf. She felt terrified, as she did whenever she fell, only this time her terror seemed more real. She felt as if she could hold it in her palm, feel its texture and weight, finger it in her moments of disbelief. How in heaven's name could she be falling in love with a dwarf? He was half her size and twisted at the knees. He had humps and concavities and walked with little wooden crutches.

Enoch brushed her hair away from her forehead. Was he falling too? Had he fallen long before, perhaps months earlier when he'd kissed her? Or days before that, in Rocket City, when he'd told her he was her prize? She remembered that clearly: He was her prize. But what, exactly, had he meant?

"I have an idea," he said, wiping the tears from her cheek. "Let's spend the night in the caverns."

Marilee sniffed and wiped her nose with the back of her hand. "Will they let you?"

"Of course not. But I know a way. I have friends—"

"In low places," she said, suddenly laughing.

"You're quick," said Enoch. He was smiling, and he looked beautiful.

■

They drove all the way back to Carlsbad. At K-Mart, she and Enoch bought lightweight blankets and two flashlights. They filled the Dart with gas, then drove back to the Carlsbad Caverns. In the parking lot, Enoch emptied the clothes out of his backpack, then filled it with both flashlights, a blanket, and the snacks they had purchased in Artesia. They each put on extra layers of Enoch's clothing; Marilee wore his turtleneck and stuffed the remaining blanket up under her sweater. She looked big enough for anyone to wonder if Enoch hadn't impregnated her with twins.

At a time when most visitors were ascending from the caverns, Marilee and Enoch took the last elevator down. Enoch led her to the lunchroom, where they dumped their things onto one of the many picnic tables. He walked over to the counter, then returned with three sandwiches wrapped in wax paper, two cartons of orange juice, a container of coleslaw, and two Milky Ways. "Snack time," he said, unwrapping a sandwich. "Caves make me hungry. Want one?"

"Sure," she said.

"Just don't eat the pickles," he reminded her.

"Is that what I smell?"

"No, that's bat guano. When the caves were first discovered, they found the floors covered in bat shit. They carted out one hundred thousand tons of the stuff. Shipped it to California to grow oranges."

Marilee shivered. "Do the bats live down this far?"

"Oh, sure," said Enoch. "But only in the summer. They winter in Mexico."

"Like you do," she said.

Enoch chuckled and took another bite of his sandwich. "There's raccoons in the caves, too. At night they try to tip over the trashcans."

"Raccoons?" She felt sweaty with the blanket under her sweater.

"And mice, but they're harmless. It's the hodags you have to worry about."

"Hodags?"

"Cave creatures. They're invisible, and they have one eye, which they exchange while mating. They're sneaky little devils. They prey on spelunkers. They'll blow your lantern out, or coil your ropes when you've left them down, or make little noises when there's nobody else around."

"Let's not do this," she said.

Enoch laughed.

"This is creepy. I don't know if I can stay down here all night."

"Don't worry, I'll protect you," he said, then he laughed even louder.

"Right."

"There's really nothing to it. Lots of people have spent the night down here."

"But what if it's scary?"

"It's not. It's magic."

"What if we get caught?"

"Six months or five hundred dollars. Come on," he said, stuffing his candy and remaining sandwich into a side compartment of his backpack. "Let's go look for Fred."

They started off down the trail to the Big Room. She wanted to take the whole tour, but Enoch told her they had only about an hour before the caverns closed down and the clean-up crew arrived. "We can see the rest of it tomorrow," he explained. "If the hodags haven't gotten us."

The beauty of the Big Room was beyond comprehension. Marilee was sure she had never seen anything more captivating, any natural wonder more enchanting than this. It was fairyland, eight hundred feet beneath the earth's surface. The stalactites and stalagmites she'd expected, but not the worm-like helictites or bubbly cave pearls. Nor the draperies that hung in translucent folds. Nor epsomite needles, and hydromagnesite balloons, and cave popcorn, and pools with glass surfaces reflective as mirrors. "This was all once an ocean," said Enoch. It didn't surprise her. The water was still at work, dripping ceaselessly, leaving its limy deposits as soda straws, crystals, columns, and rocks. Dripping endlessly into dark pools that rippled rhythmically with each heavy drop. For an hour or more, Marilee basked in this mythical world, certain that her memory would never do justice to this secret wonderland. Enoch walked ahead of her, keeping an eye out for his friend.

When they returned to the lunchroom, the counter had closed, and the lights had been turned off in some back sections of the cavern. "Are you sure Fred still works here?" she asked.

"I'm sure. I just hope he's working today."

They took a seat in the lunchroom and ate their Milky Ways. The place was nearly deserted. A woman behind the food counter eyed them suspiciously.

"He was the *king* of Thebes," said Enoch.

"What?"

"That's important."

"I'm sure it is," said Marilee.

"Yo!" he shouted, his voice echoing off the cavern walls. In an instant he was up, bounding between the benches toward a park ranger who had just entered from the path. The man looked happy to see him. They talked for a few minutes, then Enoch returned to their table.

"What's the plan?" asked Marilee.

"He's going to clear the way to the Green Lake Room. Make sure no people are left in that area. Then he'll give us the high five, and we're out of here. We'll have to use our flashlights and be careful not to be seen."

"And nobody comes by at night to check on things?"

"Nope. They've got electronic sensors that go off if anyone steps off the trail. Fred's going to disarm the system in that area."

She and Enoch split the last ham and cheese sandwich, watching for Fred's return. More lights went off. Park rangers came and went, some of whom waved to Enoch. The woman working the lunch counter headed past them toward the elevators. Now they were the only visitors still left in the lunchroom. "Better pee now," he said. "Your last chance till morning, unless you want to brave the hodags."

They both used the restrooms, then met at the trail entrance to a section of cave called the Boneyard. Lights went out ahead of them, and soon Fred appeared at the trailhead. "Be cool, Swann," he cautioned. "Don't step off the footpath until after five thirty." Marilee had forgotten Enoch even had a last name.

The ranger was gone as quickly as he'd emerged from the darkness. Marilee and Enoch walked slowly into the cavern's black interior. She was glad it was March and the bats were safely in Mexico. Slowly, they felt their way along the footpath with Enoch's crutches, she with one, he with the other. They were useful now, as blind-man walking sticks. Still, she wondered why Enoch bothered at all with his clumsy wooden appendages.

Marilee followed a short distance behind Enoch, listening for the irregular crunch of dirt beneath his feet. She carried her purse and his
backpack while he scouted the trail ahead of her. Once they were safely
around the second bend, Marilee switched on her flashlight. The caves
took on an eerie glow, like a campsite lit by a fire. Enoch pressed forward, using her light as a guide and his single crutch to steady himself
along the way.

He led her downward and downward, past the Boneyard, past the tow-
ering Iceberg, past the trail that led up out of the caves, into the hollow
chasm of the Green Lake Room. Marilee shone her flashlight into the
chamber's interior. She saw a flat clearing in front of a pool. Water
dripped onto the cavern floor, and cave popcorn bubbled from the rocks
overhead. The scene took her breath away.

"This is one of the lowest rooms," whispered Enoch.

"Is this where we're going to sleep?" The ground looked rocky.

"Further down," he said. He continued along the footpath, leading
Marilee downward until they came to a flat area next to a frozen water-
fall. "Here," he said. "This is the deepest section we mortals have access
to." Enoch checked his watch in the glow of Marilee's flashlight. "It's
time," he said, then gingerly stepped off the trail. No alarms sounded.
"Watch yourself," he said. Marilee stepped over the rocks that lined the
footpath. The ground felt soft as moondust beneath her feet.

One blanket they spread out on a dry section of ground next to a rockface; the other they wrapped around themselves. They sat Indian style,
sharing the warmth beneath the blanket. Enoch switched off the flashlight. Marilee had never seen such blackness, and at first it frightened
her. She strained to make her eyes adjust, but they would not find so
much as a pinpoint of light to assure her she had not indeed gone blind.
It was a darkness that had form and dimension. A darkness one could
feel. Quiet now, she and Enoch listened to the nocturne of the caves: the
empty drone of the still, cool air; the tinkling voices of water kissing
rockbeds and pools. Cold seeped up through the blanket beneath her.
She leaned closer to Enoch, grateful for what warmth she could garner
from his small body. "What now?" she whispered.

"Let me tell you about Carmina."

She was not at all surprised by his offer; she'd sensed Enoch had brought her to this place to tell her everything.

"When I got out of the hospital," he began, "I realized I had to leave Kingfield. I'd have been killed if I stayed there. So I headed to Juárez, where I knew I could find work. That's where I met Carmina."

"How?" asked Marilee.

"In a freak show. They have these roadhouses there that specialize in oddities. Bearded ladies. Contortionists. Hermaphrodites. Fat women that do striptease."

"Carmina's not fat."

"They also have sex shows. Women on stage with men. Women on stage with dogs and donkeys."

Marilee felt her heart stand still. She said nothing and let Enoch continue.

"Carmina was one of those women. She was fourteen when she was first brought to the Gomez brothers. They owned the place. I'd been working for them for about a year, doing the freak show with this midget named DonElla."

"The name sounds familiar."

"You heard me mention her once. She lives in Albuquerque now, and I help her out now and then." Enoch paused. The dripping seemed to get louder.

"I spent two years working for the Gomez brothers. When I signed on, I thought I'd be able to leave whenever I wanted to. But I became their prisoner. We all did. They locked us up after each show. Made us work fifteen, sixteen hours a day. Fed us rice and beans and made us sleep on the floor with the German shepherds."

Marilee felt the blood rise to her face. "Did they pay you?"

"They did, but it was just a technicality. All your wages went for room and board. And health care, if you needed it. No one ever actually saw any money." Enoch shifted under the blanket. She listened for his voice in the darkness. "The women were always needing abortions. The Gomez brothers charged you for everything. They kept you indebted to them this way. So they had to lock you up until you could work off your debt, which nobody ever did."

"Weren't you furious?" she asked.

"At the time, yes."

"You're not still?"

"I've had years to get over it."

"Jesus," said Marilee. "Why'd you go to work for them in the first place?"

"I was stupid. I thought it would be an adventure."

"Sounds like it was an adventure, all right."

"And then some. In my second year, when Kingfield had started to look like Disneyland on a summer Sunday, they brought this new girl on board. Carmina. She'd been drugged by her father and sold to them for five hundred pesos. When she came to among the dogs and the pinheads and me, she was terrified. Had no idea where she was. She kept crying for her mother."

"This is horrible."

"Do you want me to stop?"

"No," she said. "Go on."

"Carmina was a hard one to tame. That's what drew me to her, that she didn't roll over and die like the other girls. It took them weeks to break her. The two brothers beat her and raped her and withheld her food. It damn near killed her. The other girls despised her for what she was doing."

"For resisting? Like they hadn't?"

"Exactly. They called her La Orgullosa, the proud one. Carmina wouldn't speak to them. The brothers kept on raping her and starving her and holding her down to be taken by the dogs, but she still refused to do anything on stage. Once, she spit in their faces and told them she'd rather die. They beat her unconscious for that."

"Why didn't they just kill her?" She could hardly believe she could ask such a question.

"Because she'd cost them five hundred pesos."

"Ah," she said, as if the logic of it made sense.

"One afternoon, when Carmina was very close to dying, she rose up off the floor and got in line with the other girls to go out on stage. I asked her why she was doing this after all she'd gone through. She said, 'Hay veces que haces lo que tienes que hacer.' Sometimes you do what you have to do. It was a matter of survival. In the face of dying, none of us is immune. Not even the strong ones, like Carmina."

"So she went on stage?"

"All day and all night. It was horrible the things they made her do."

"How'd the two of you get out of there?"

"That's another story. When Carmina was fifteen, this man came to the show. Some sheik or something, in robes and a turban. He bought us to take back to his country."

"He *bought* you?"

"Me, Carmina, and this other girl."

"DonElla?"

"No. Her name was Bernarda. She had this act with a python. She was huge—must have been four hundred fifty pounds. She got fed all day long, and the other girls were jealous. The sheik paid good money for us, but he wasn't very smart. He was drunk when he took us to his hotel room. He locked the door, then went into the bathroom and hid the key. While he was raping Bernarda, Carmina stabbed him with a ball-point pen."

"Did she kill him?"

"Oh, yes."

"My God," said Marilee. She felt hideous, sick. The cold from the ground was penetrating. Enoch felt for her hand. He held it in his, his pudgy dwarf fingers entwined with her own.

"It took an hour to find the guy's room key. He'd hidden it in his rectum. It was Bernarda who thought of looking for it there, after his corpse had farted. She fished it out, ran to the door, unlocked it, and was gone. We never saw her again."

"What did you guys do?"

"Carmina took the man's cash, his rings, and his car keys. I grabbed as much food and beer from the refrigerator as we could carry. We headed west. Drove straight off into the desert in the middle of the night. We didn't dare take any roads. We knew that come morning, they'd be looking for a woman and a dwarf. When the car ran out of gas, we started walking, but we didn't get very far because I tripped in a snake hole and twisted my ankle. So we sat in the desert and waited for the sun to rise.

When it did, we discovered we weren't very far from some foothills. Carmina helped me to make it to them. We hid out in this cave for three days, until we ran out of peanuts and beer. My ankle had swollen badly. I told Carmina just to leave me there, but she refused. On the third night, she carried me over the border."

"Carried you?"

"On her back. It took her fourteen hours. I've never seen a woman so brave."

Marilee drew her knees to her chest; her tailbone hurt from sitting. "Then what?" she asked.

"Then . . . I went to Flagstaff for a while. Got a lawyer and sued the guys who'd put me in the hospital. I got some money from the settlement and bought the motel. I let Carmina run the place. She'd learned to speak a little English. The next year, she married this guy from Carrizozo, but it didn't work out once he learned what she had been through. He left her four or five years ago."

That explained Carmina's children, but there were so many questions left unanswered. "How'd DonElla get away?"

"I bought her. Hired a man to go down there and bring her back. Cost me three thousand dollars."

"What was Carmina's surprise?"

"What surprise?"

"That night we were there. She told you to come back to the office because she wanted to show you a surprise."

"Oh," he said. "She'd had her tattoo removed. Some laser procedure that doesn't leave a scar."

"Her tattoo?"

"The word *Gomez* on the inside of her thigh. I've got one too."

Marilee had never noticed it. "Why don't you get it taken off?"

"Don't want to. It's a reminder."

"Of Carmina?"

"Of freedom. Or the lack of it, and what it can do."

"Ah," she said. Some of the pieces were beginning to fall into place.

"And of Carmina, too, I guess. That night she carried me on her back, I fell in love with her."

Marilee felt her chest cinch. She was afraid of her next question but couldn't stop herself from asking it. "Are you still in love with her?"

"Hopelessly," said Enoch.

"Does she love you back?" Her voice sounded tight and small.

"Nope," said Enoch, matter-of-factly. He cleared his throat. "I think somewhere along the way, she must have lost the ability."

"But she married."

"She never loved him."

"And she had children."

"That's not the same thing."

Marilee knew that it wasn't. "Did you ever make love, the two of you?"

"Every night," he said. "In between the acts with the dog and the donkey."

Her body shook, and soon Marilee could not stop herself from crying. She felt suddenly dizzy and weak. She leaned against Enoch, and he held her as he had earlier that day, steadying her against his shoulders, his arm halfway around her waist. She let him stroke her hair and tell her not to cry, that it was over, that it had all happened a long time ago. It didn't matter. What mattered was that it had happened at all. Marilee had heard of such things, but they'd always seemed safely distant and unreal. Now, however, there was no denying it: The world was a terrible place.

Marilee stretched her legs out beneath the blanket, leaned back on one arm, and kicked her feet out from under their cocoon. With her free hand, she wiped the tears from her eyes. She listened to the walls dripping, the cave darker than night, darker than a universe without stars. She listened for a long time, and as she did a peace came over her. She and Enoch beneath the blanket, their breath mingling in the cool, damp air. The darkness all around them, the unremitting dripping. Dripping onto the path. Dripping onto the formations. Dripping into the still, black, bottomless pools. Slowly, Enoch let go of her hand. She felt the loss of his warmth, sensed him lying down beside her. She laid her body next to his and smiled up into the cave blackness.

Within sadness lives a happiness deeper than any pain. Her fingers, cold from the chill dampness, found Enoch's mouth. She ran her fingers over his lips, then explored their soft interior. When her lips found his, his response was without hesitancy. He kissed her deeply and with great tenderness. When she felt his hand move down to her breast, his breath on her neck constant as a tide, Marilee knew she could resist no longer.

Enoch removed her clothing as though it were her first time making love. Tenderly. Tentatively. As though she were fourteen, beaten, hungry, and abandoned. In the darkness, she could feel his sad deformity: the twist of his knees, the calluses in his armpits, the chasm in his chest, the cleft between his shoulder blades. His body did not repulse her. She felt delicate beneath the weight of it. Soft, fragile, unexpectedly small.

When he placed his tongue into the space between her legs, her gasp echoed off the cavern walls. Its toll seemed to return to her forever, ringing distantly off the ageless formations, resounding against the pinnacles and columns until it mingled, imperceptibly, with the low, eternal chorus of water turning to stone. She clutched at the rockface, knocked the back of her hand against the jagged limestone and felt its sting. A lump rose up under her skin, but its pain was such that it made the pleasure of Enoch's loving her all the more discernible.

She came twice in this manner, then Enoch rose up on top of her. He kissed her neck, her breasts, the flesh of her naked belly. She felt him hard against the inside of her thigh, large and strong as any giant. Upward he moved, into the dark, moist recess where his mouth had given her such pleasure. And when he entered her, assuredly as a king enters his own lost kingdom, it felt crueler and more wicked than any fairy tale.

THE JAWS OF LIFE

It took Figman five days after his mishap to get back to his life's work. His cheekbone ached. His ankle hurt. He tried elevating it on a footstool and pillow while he painted, but then his leg would go to sleep. Figman found himself lifting it up and down, up and down while he struggled to concentrate on his work at hand. He was sure it was just a sprain, but a nasty one. Verdie brought him a pair of Titus's old crutches.

He couldn't go to the market. He couldn't go anywhere. Oma, who by virtue of her kinship with Dino felt in part responsible for Figman's injuries, brought him meals twice a day; less regularly, Verdie brought him his mail. He told neither of them he had tripped over a spoon.

Again, he attempted to paint Bobo, the engineer of his current distress. He would paint him in close-up this time, from memory; though he'd seen his face only once, he had not forgotten it.

His painting's composition was triangular, not unlike Leonardo's *Virgin of the Rocks*, a color plate of which filled page twenty-two of Figman's art book. He hoped to employ the Renaissance technique of chiaroscuro, in which areas of light are bordered by the darkest of shadows. It seemed an appropriate treatment for his subject.

Figman wondered about Bobo. Had he deliberately left his spoon sticking up out of the hole? Had he intended to trip him? Had Bobo known all along that he occasionally walked to Verdie's trailer after dark? Figman dipped his brush in cadmium yellow and mixed it with a dab of Roman ochre. Propping his leg up on his pillow, he started in on Bobo's bucket.

Ten minutes later, he heard a knock at his kitchen door. Figman glanced at his watch. It was dinnertime. Oma opened the door with the key Figman had given her, thus saving him a trip through his house on crutches.

"Forbes, you're never going to believe what happened!" she hollered, arms loaded with paper bags.

"What?" said Figman. He went back to his painting.

Oma made a beeline for the easel in his living room. "Dino's car—you know, the '59 Cadillac he spent a year and a half restoring? Well somebody totaled it last night."

"He had an accident?" Figman tried not to sound enthusiastic.

"No, I mean somebody took a tire iron and banged the hell out of it. It's all dented up."

Figman added a dot of cerulean blue to his spoon's handle and suppressed a smile. "That's terrible," he said. "Who would do a thing like that?"

"I have no idea," said Oma. She returned to his kitchen. He heard her rustling about in there, opening and closing the refrigerator, removing food from bags. He smelled cheeseburgers and french fries. "But Dino thinks he knows who did it," she continued. "Boy, I sure feel sorry for that guy."

Figman set down his paintbrush and lifted his foot off his pillow. His calf had fallen asleep. Oma walked back into the living room with a Coke in one hand and a Heineken in the other. She handed the beer to Figman, then leaned over and gave him a kiss. "I sure do miss you," she said.

Figman laughed. "You see me twice a day."

"You know what I mean."

Figman did. In some ways, Bobo's spoon had been a godsend.

"I'll get dinner," she said, ducking back into the kitchen. Figman dropped his brush into his jar of turpentine and took a sip of his beer. Bobo's bucket was coming along nicely.

In a moment, Oma returned with two dinner plates. "I'm sorry it's cheeseburgers again. I just don't have time to cook anything." She handed Figman a plate and sat down on the floor at his coffee table.

As best he could, Figman turned to face her. "I'll need a napkin," he said. His leg tingled.

Oma looked at him as though he were a beggar child in India. "I feel so sorry for you," she said. She jumped up and hurried into his kitchen, returning with a handful of paper towels. "I mean, you can't do anything. How do you even manage when I'm not here?"

"It's hard," said Figman.

"And look at your poor face. I hope it doesn't leave a scar. I could just kill that brother of mine."

The bruise on Figman's cheek had turned a ghastly purple-green. It reminded him of the lipstick he'd once seen on a punk down on Melrose. "I'll live," he said, then laughed at the irony.

"What's so funny?" asked Oma. Her mouth was full of french fries.

"Nothing."

"You laughed."

"Did I?"

Oma shrugged and took a bite of her cheeseburger. "Mmm, this is good."

"Yeah," said Figman. It was his fourth cheeseburger that week. "Say, there's something I've been meaning to ask you."

Oma looked up from her french fries.

"Do you have an uncle on the police force?"

"Yeah, Uncle Dil. That's short for Dilbert. He hates it when people call him that."

"What's his job?"

"He's the chief. Why?"

"Oh, Dino said something. About not going to the police." Figman had never had any intention of going to the police.

"Yeah, that wouldn't be cool," said Oma. "Dino's, like, his favorite of all his nephews. He's trying to get him to enroll at the academy."

"What a scary thought," said Figman.

Oma shrugged. "Dino's not that bad. He's just got this temper, that's all."

Figman was in no mood to argue with her. He wondered whether her brother had ever worked in the potash mines. "Do you think maybe tomorrow we could have chicken or something?"

"Sure," she said. "Colonel Sanders okay?"

A car rolled into Figman's driveway. He glanced out the window and saw what was left of a red and gold '59 Cadillac. "Company," he said.

Oma started to get up. "Damn, I just spilled mustard all over my jeans."

A car door slammed, and the next minute Dino was standing in Figman's living room. He hadn't bothered knocking. "You're going to pay for this, asshole!" he yelled at Figman. His face was cadmium red.

"Pay for what?"

"You know what. Don't fuck with me." It was then that Dino noticed Oma sitting on the floor across from Figman. His face grew redder. "What are *you* doing here?" Figman wondered whether Dino would attack him with his sister in the room.

Oma looked disgusted. She wetted her napkin with her Coke and scrubbed at her jeans.

"What does it look like she's doing?" said Figman.

"You stay out of this, dickhead. I'll deal with you in a minute." Dino took a step closer to his sister. "Where's your car?"

"In the back."

"Well, get it. You're going home."

"The hell I am," she said.

"What?"

"I'm not going anywhere. And who are you to come barging in here like this?"

"I'm your brother, that's who. And I say you're out of here."

"Fuck you," said Oma.

"No, fuck you," said Dino.

"No, fuck you," she said, louder.

"No, fuck you!" shouted Dino. "And fuck you, too, Lou!"

Figman didn't know if he'd become a piece of the furniture or a member of the family.

"Leave him out of this," said Oma. "He hasn't done anything."

"Oh yeah? You want to come take another look at my car?"

Figman lifted his swollen foot up onto his footstool. It was twice the size of normal and matched the color of his right cheek. He winced a little when he lowered it onto his pillow.

"What happened to you?" asked Dino.

"You should know," said Oma.

"Honeybun?" said Figman. Oma's face brightened upon hearing a word that Figman, otherwise, never would have used. "Would you mind helping me with my crutches?"

"I'd be happy to, sweetheart," said Oma. She shot her brother an evil look. "How could you even think such a thing? This is the first day he can even walk to the bathroom." Dino looked confused, as if trying to assemble the pieces of a jigsaw puzzle whose straight-edge pieces were all missing. "And if you ever lay another hand on him," she continued, "I'll marry him just to spite you."

Figman's heart jumped. Had he heard her correctly?

"I mean it," she said. "Don't tempt me."

Dino's slits-for-eyes narrowed. "Then fuck you," he said. He spun around to face Figman. "And fuck you, too. Fuck everybody." Dino pounded his keys on the doorframe on his way out, leaving a gash in the painted wood. He climbed into his beat-up Caddy and screeched out of the driveway.

And his uncle the police chief, thought Figman. Life sure wasn't fair.

■

By the following weekend, much of the swelling in Figman's ankle had subsided. It still hurt him at times, and he had to be careful not to put any weight on it, but it had definitely improved. He figured he'd be able to walk in another week or two. Titus's crutches had come in handy.

Figman spent most of his days working at his canvas. He'd had trouble capturing the metallic sheen on Bobo's digging spoon. Oma brought him both breakfast and dinner and left him a sack lunch each morning in his refrigerator. Usually it was a bologna sandwich; always there was a pickle.

As much as he could, Figman tried to keep an eye on Verdie's trailer. She'd been gone lately during the day. It was obvious she was receiving more frequent treatments.

Sometimes Titus came by when she was there in the evenings. Figman still had trouble getting an angle on the guy. Was he Verdie's lover? Just a friend? Or was he some opportunistic creep sniffing around her daffodils? Figman kept meaning to ask Oma about the man but forgot as soon as she came by with cheeseburgers.

Since his accident, Figman had received two visits from Benito Hooks. He'd seemed agitated both times, wanting to know if Figman had seen any more of that red and gold Caddy. The first time he'd visited, Figman had said no, not wanting to waste his precious painting hours on the likes of Benito. The second time, Hooks was lucky to have caught him after he'd finished for the day.

Figman sat down with Verdie's son at his kitchen table. Hooks pulled out a pack of cigarettes. "Do you mind if I smoke, Bill?"

"Let me get you an ashtray."

"No, no," said Hooks. "I'll just use the sink. Seeing as you're still all crippled. I've been meaning to talk to my mother about that broken step. Dicky-Lee—he's that friend of mine I was telling you about. Him and me used to spy on them Rodriguezes across the way. Ooowee! That woman was really something. Now, what was I saying?"

"I don't know," said Figman.

"That's the funniest thing. I don't remember."

"Are you sure you wouldn't like a beer?"

"And watch you break another tooth?" Hooks laughed. "You know, your luck ain't so good."

If only he could tell him.

Hooks puffed on his cigarette. "No, no," he said. "I'll just sit here and enjoy my smoke. I reckon my mother will be getting back pretty soon, so I'd best be on my way."

"Where does she go during the day?" There were scuff marks on Figman's linoleum.

"Damned if I know," said Hooks. A troubled look came over his face. He seemed restless.

"You know, she's gone a lot."

"Probably out with that no-good sonofabitch in the red Cadillac. You seen any more of him?"

"Oh, yes," said Figman. "He was parked here just last night."

Hooks's eyes widened. "He was back?"

"Same guy, same Cadillac. But now it's all dented. Poor fellow must have had one hell of an accident."

■

Exactly two weeks after his fall, on the first of April (which was also Figman's birthday), Verdie brought him a week's worth of his mail. "I'm sorry, Louis," she said. "I know you can't get out there. But I've just been so darned busy lately." She handed him two envelopes. One was a coupon packet from Lester's E-Z Mart; the other, a letter from his mother. He tossed them both on his kitchen counter.

"How about a drink?" said Figman. He was thrilled to have some company. He'd taken the morning off from painting, then had wasted it by staring out the window. Bobo had been digging around the edge of his hydrangeas.

"I'd love a drink," said Verdie. "But I can't, hon. Got to get me up to Roswell. I'll be back tonight if you want to swing by for a nightcap."

"I'll watch for your car," he said.

"Tootles," said Verdie. She hurried back to her trailer. He wondered how she still had so much energy.

The only good to come of his fall was that for the last two weeks, Figman had not had to encounter any of Verdie's mail. No coming face to face with her overdue bills and chemotherapy. No wondering which mortuary would finally get hold of her remains. Figman got himself a beer, then picked up the envelope from his mother and opened it. It was a birthday card. Its cover featured a bunny holding a birthday cake. Inside the card was a three-page letter:

Dear Son,

Happy birthday, darling. I haven't written because I don't know what to make of your last letter. When you spoke of your own safety being in danger—well, I just didn't know what to do. So I did nothing. I haven't spoken to Miriam or anybody else. A letter came from Aaron, but I threw it away. I know you've never been in any kind of trouble, but I do so worry about you.

I have something to tell you—something I would have preferred to tell you face to face. But I guess there isn't much chance of that these days. So forgive me, please, for disclosing this in a letter.

I didn't want to burden you with this on your birthday, either. I know what a happy day it's always been for you. But since you were little, I promised myself I would tell you the truth about something before you turned forty. The years have just flown by.

Darling, I want to tell you about your father. Your real father. I know these words must come as a shock to you, and I hope when you hear the truth you will forgive me. Please understand how difficult this is for me.

Your real father was a man named Emory Worthington. (That's right, he was not Jewish.) That was one of the problems when we fell in love—his parents and mine were both against the union. We begged them to let us marry, but they refused. We were so young, and so in love. We could have run off, I suppose, but that would have just killed Nana. And Emory's father said he'd disown him—things were very different in those days.

Eventually, Emory's parents sent him to stay with his cousins in Boston. I guess they thought it would be better that way. Our last night together was sheer torture. I knew I was pregnant with you, but I couldn't tell him. I think I was afraid of what he might do.

The first week Emory was in Boston, there was a terrible storm. He and his cousin Francis were putting up storm windows. The wind gusted, and they were struck by a downed power line. It killed them both. His family never knew about you.

When the news of his death came, I cried for a solid month. I thought I was going to lose you, but then one day my pains stopped and life went on. And I realized I would have to do something soon about my growing pregnancy. So I married Morris Figman. He'd been in love with me since the first grade. He used to call me Pretzel. That was his little name for me—Pretzel. He never knew you were not his own. Thank God you were small when you arrived in April.

I did grow to love Morris—I want you to know that. But not the way I had loved your real father. I think Morris must have known this, and that's why he eventually left me. A man can tell these things. I'm sure you know.

I'm telling you this now not to hurt you in any way, but because I feel you have a right to know who you really are. All these years I've felt so guilty about telling you your father had died. But it wasn't such a lie. Your father *had* died, he just wasn't the man you thought was your father.

So forgive me, please, for having kept this from you all these years. I feel so much better having unburdened myself. I hope you feel better now, too.

Please don't let this news spoil your fortieth birthday. More than you know, I wish I could spend it with you.

Love always, Mother

P.S. I bought an alarm system. I keep setting it off by accident, but I do like knowing it's there.

Figman sat at his kitchen table. He looked out his window at the vast New Mexico sky. Death. Lies. Abandonment—it all felt the same. What did it matter who his real father was?

And yet it did matter. Who *was* this Emory Worthington? Should he carry on his name? What *was* his name? Figman? Worthington? Forbes? He leaned back in his chair and put his injured foot up on the table. He sipped at his beer. The sun hid behind a puffy white cloud. It was his birthday, but instead of feeling happy, Figman felt lost. He was forty. He was dying. He hadn't completed a single painting. He had a sprained ankle, a chipped tooth, and he'd never even known his real father.

Oma used her key to let herself in his front door. Figman had not heard her car pull into the driveway. "So, Forbes," she yelled excitedly. "Are you ready?"

"Ready as I'll ever be for another cheeseburger," said Figman.

Oma burst into his kitchen. "No cheeseburger for you today, birthday boy. I'm dragging your butt out of here."

She'd remembered. In an odd way, Figman felt relieved.

"It's steak and champagne and then all-night dancing—which, of course, you can't do." She wore high heels and a short yellow dress. Figman imagined the sort of men who might ask her to dance. "Or, I know this other place, if you think watching people dance might be too depressing."

"It might," said Figman.

"Then let's go there. It's kind of far, but it's really cool. I'm not going to tell you a thing about it. It'll be a surprise. But first, I've got to tell you this. Oh, this is so awful!"

"What?"

Oma took a deep breath. "It's Dino. He's in the hospital. Those guys came after him—the same guys that totaled his car. At least he figures they're the same guys."

"What happened?"

"Dino got off work last night and was on his way home when he noticed he was being followed. So he headed out to the fairgrounds—which was pretty stupid if you ask me, but I guess he thought there'd be somebody out there. But there wasn't, and when he tried to turn around, the other car blocked him. So he locked his doors, but then these two guys jump out of their car with baseball bats and smashed in all his windows. The ones he'd just gotten fixed. Then they dragged him out of his car and beat the shit out of him."

"Jesus," said Figman.

"They just pulled him out of his car and attacked him, like animals. He has two broken arms and a broken wrist and three broken ribs and a fractured pelvis and a broken nose and a shattered jaw and all sorts of cuts and bruises."

The Putterman claim.

"They had to wire his mouth shut. And his teeth are all broken. You should see him, he's a mess."

Figman shook his head and looked troubled.

"It happened just last night, while I was here with you. Poor Dino lay bleeding out there for hours until the 4–H Club found him."

"The world's a dangerous place," said Figman. He sipped at his Anchor Steam. The sun broke through the clouds.

Oma sat down at the table. "I can't say as I feel all that sorry for him, given the way he's been acting lately. But he is my brother and all, and I hate to see anybody get hurt. He's in a lot of pain. I mean a *lot* of pain. And he can't hardly talk with all that hardware in his mouth."

Figman shook his head. "You just never know," he said.

"But he did mention something interesting. He said the big guy kept kicking him in the ribs and telling him to stay away from his mother—which is super weird because Dino isn't seeing anybody right now, and even if he was, he wouldn't be going out with somebody's mother, for God's sake. And you want to hear the weirdest thing of all?"

"What?" asked Figman.

"Dino said the big guy kept repeating the name, Forbes. He thinks maybe that was the other guy there, but he's not sure. Anyway, Dino said it all had to do with this Forbes person and the big guy's mother. Or something like that. It was real confusing. Still, don't you think that's the strangest thing? That the guy's name was Forbes?"

"Very strange," said Figman.

"Now, I know it couldn't be you, because I was with you all night—anyway, your name's Figman. I mean, your real name. By the way, did I tell you you were wonderful last night?"

"I think you mentioned something to that effect."

"And I know it couldn't be you because you're still on crutches. You couldn't beat up Dino, anyway."

Figman didn't quite know how to take that.

Oma took a swallow of his beer. "There must be some other Forbes in town that nobody knows about. Some guy, maybe, who's with the Mafia."

"Could be," said Figman. "I hear the Mafia's everywhere these days."

Oma gulped down the last of Figman's Anchor Steam and stood up from the table. She pulled her skirt down over her hips. "So come on, birthday boy, grab ahold of your crutches. I'm driving you out of here."

Figman thought about her Corvair. He thought about the Jaws of Life. He thought about Dino with his mouth wired shut.

He had more than she knew to celebrate.

APRIL FOOLS

They made love most of the night, she and Enoch under the blanket. It helped keep them warm; it helped keep Marilee from going crazy. At some point, exhaustion and the sound of water dripping carried her off to sleep. She awoke with a cramp in her shoulder.

Marilee tapped Enoch on the forearm and asked him to check the time. He fumbled in the dark for a flashlight. When he switched it on, the sudden brightness hurt her eyes. "Eight seventeen," he said.

The back of her hand throbbed where she'd hit it against the rockface. She studied its purple bruise.

"Let me see," he said. He cradled her hand in his and ran his fingers over its hard lump. "We'll have to stop for some aloe," he told her. "That'll help it heal."

"No fly amanita? No leeches?"

"Leeches might work."

If he'd had some with him, she might have let him try. "Now what?" she asked, stretching. She felt chilled and had to pee.

"Breakfast," said Enoch, producing the box of Ho Hos they had bought in Artesia. He opened the box and offered it to her. She ate two of them. Enoch ate three. He was naked and sat Indian style. High up on the inside of his thigh she saw a dark, inky blotch that might have been the word *Gomez*.

As soon as he'd finished eating, Enoch licked his fingers. The cavern lights switched on. "Yo," he said. "We've got exactly sixty seconds to get back on the trail."

Quickly, they gathered up their belongings and carried them over the rock border of the footpath. "Oops," said Enoch, checking his watch. He took his sweater, hopped back over the rocks, and beat the ground where they'd been sleeping. Dust rose in clouds. "Can't leave any evidence," he said, returning to where Marilee was standing.

Marilee buttoned her jeans and took another look at the place where they had spent the night together. The spot was hauntingly beautiful, an appropriate setting, she thought, to have made love to a dwarf. Had Enoch known all along the caves would have this effect on her? Had he planned for it to happen this way? She eyed him as he pulled on his turtleneck. Sometimes she wondered if he understood her better than she understood herself.

"Want to do the rest of the tour?" Enoch asked, lacing up his walking shoes.

"No, I'm freezing," she said. "Let's just go."

"Reality ho!" said Enoch.

"Hmm," said Marilee.

■

The drive back to Artesia was uneventful. Quiet for most of the way, Marilee thought about what had happened the night before. It had been good with Enoch, deep inside the earth, in the safe, watery darkness of the caves. It would be good with him still, she told herself, above ground, in the light of day. She glanced over at him as they drove north, his small figure sitting upright on her car seat like a shopping bag. He smiled. She smiled back at him. "I haven't been sleeping with Larry," she said.

Enoch shrugged.

"Not interested?" she asked.

"Not particularly," he said. "It's none of my business."

"It is now." The day was bright, the storm clouds having moved off to somewhere in the Midwest. "Larry and I haven't so much as touched each other in over a year."

"No foreplay?"

"No one-and-a-half play, even."

Enoch chuckled. Ahead of her, she saw the town of Carlsbad.

"When I arrived last fall, I found Larry in bed with another man."

Enoch whistled. "Heavy duty," he said.

"He's getting himself tested for AIDS. We had to wait six months. It's almost up, but I'm not sure—"

"You weren't concerned about catching AIDS from me," Enoch interrupted.

She hadn't even given it a thought.

"Not that you have anything to be concerned about," he added. "I'm safe."

"I guess I knew you would be."

"You're lucky," he said. "Next time you may not be."

"I guess I am," she said. "I guess you are, too, huh?"

Enoch unwrapped a jawbreaker and popped it in his mouth. "So when's your period due?"

Marilee's heart sank. She counted the days. "Oh God," she said.

"Not pretty?"

She shook her head. A thousand possibilities raced through her mind as she steered her Dart through the streets of Carlsbad. Could dwarfs really have children? Obviously, if Enoch was asking about her period. What were the odds of a dwarf fathering a dwarf? Twenty-five percent? Fifty? Would he want to marry her? Would they live in a house like a real family, or hitchhike up and down the highway, she and Enoch and their little dwarf baby whom they'd have to name Elwyn?

"So Larry's bi?" said Enoch. The jawbreaker bulged between his teeth and cheek.

"He swears he isn't, not that it would matter. He claims he was just experimenting. He does stuff like that."

"Why wouldn't it matter?"

"I have nothing against bisexuals."

"Neither do I, but I wouldn't want to be married to one."

"True," she said. "When on earth is this light going to turn green?"

■

In Artesia, they stopped at Lester's to buy aloe. Enoch had grown hungry again. He selected orange juice and freshly baked oat bran muffins for the drive to Alamogordo. To Marilee's relief, neither Gert nor that creepy bagboy were working that day. She picked the shorter of the two checkout lines. The woman behind the counter was beautiful. She wore a cross studded with opals. "You from California?" she asked Marilee. Her fingers danced over her keypad.

"Yes," said Marilee. She felt ugly under the fluorescent lights.

"That comes to ten twenty-nine," said the checker.

Enoch rooted in his pockets for the appropriate combination of bills and change while the woman bagged their purchase. "Have a nice day," she said, handing the bag to Marilee.

"Did you see that woman's teeth?" she asked Enoch once they reached the car.

"Grisly," he said.

"How'd she know I was from California?"

"Beats me. Why didn't you ask her?"

Marilee's shoe accidentally hit a small black beetle, tearing off one of its wings. "Oh, yuck!" she cried. The beetle ran in circles, then pressed its head to the ground and shoved its butt straight up in the air. Its flesh was pearly beneath its missing appendage. "Oh, it gives me the creeps."

Enoch eyed the insect behind the Dart's front tire. A red, tail-like protuberance extended from its rear.

"Why do they do that?" she asked.

"It's waiting for the danger to pass. The Indians thought that in times of trouble, the beetle would listen to the spirits of the earth."

"Let's move him," said Marilee. She stepped back to kick the beetle away from her tire.

"Let's not," said Enoch.

"He'll be crushed when I back out of here."

"As he should be. He's doomed anyway with only one wing." The beetle continued to moon the sky.

"You're sure big on Darwin," she said, once she had backed out of her parking space. She could have sworn she'd heard the insect crunch beneath her tire.

"It's so perfect," said Enoch. "Everything's adaptation."

"Not everything," she said, shifting her transmission into drive.

"Name something that isn't."

Marilee thought about it. "Wearing glasses instead of struggling to improve your eyesight."

"The glasses *are* the adaptation. It took a certain intelligence to come up with the lens."

Marilee merged into traffic heading west on Main Street. "Women who paint their toenails. Not exactly a matter of survival."

"Body painting. It's as old as we are. Attracts a mate," he said, with a smile.

"Okay, then," she said. "Not getting your teeth fixed when the result would make you look beautiful."

"Self-preservation—the first instinct. Protection against the unwanted advances of overly aggressive males."

Marilee thought about the checker. If she, herself, were that beautiful, she'd have her teeth fixed in a heartbeat. "How about a dwarf who can walk quite well but insists on using crutches?"

Enoch glanced at her out of the corner of his eye. "It helps me get by in the world. It helps me look more normal."

"That helps you get by?"

"More than you'll ever know," he said.

■

They were quiet for most of the drive back to Rocket City. Marilee thought about Carmina, about what she'd been through, about how she'd managed to survive. Enoch dozed on the seat next to her. He stirred during the descent from Cloudcroft to Alamogordo. The town stretched before them like a mirage. In the distance, Marilee could see Holloman Air Force Base. "So what does Larry do for a living?" she asked. "I'm sure you know."

Enoch stretched. "He hasn't told you yet?"

"Not a word. He says it's classified."

Enoch laughed, then choked and started coughing. He took a large swallow of orange juice. "Larry's an assistant administrative assistant to the chief of media relations."

"What does that mean?"

"He's a secretary."

Marilee felt the blood rise to her face.

"Quite frankly, it didn't surprise me," said Enoch.

"You don't even know him."

"I know his type."

She remembered, then, that she had to retype Larry's poem before he returned from Bethesda. She despised typing. Her fingers would never work the way she wanted them to. She wondered how she would feel about Larry when he got back. How she would feel about Enoch. What on earth she was going to do about the two of them. Marilee gave it serious thought for the next half hour, but reached no conclusions. By the time she pulled into her driveway, she felt more confused than ever. "Want to come in?" she asked.

"Nah," said Enoch. "Got to head up to Santa Fe."

She felt the loss of him like a limb being ripped from her body; it had never occurred to her he wouldn't stay. "So, when will I see you?" she asked.

Enoch kissed her on the forehead. "Soon," he said.

■

A week after the dust storm, Larry returned from Maryland. "Where's my car?" he asked, dumping his suitcase in the entryway.

"Is that how you say hello after being gone a week?" Marilee sat on the couch eating Fritos and California dip. Maury Povich asked some woman why she had suffocated her baby.

"It's not in the driveway. Is Gil still fixing it?"

"I forgot to take it in."

"What?"

"I had a migraine. You wouldn't have wanted me driving it, anyway."

"Then where is it?"

"I'm taking care of it," she snapped. She was not in the best of moods. Typing a clean draft of "Born Without Arms" had taken her over an hour.

"How are you taking care of it?" Larry demanded. "And why are you eating that crap?"

Marilee pointed to the upstairs apartment. Larry bolted out the front door, toward the rear of the apartment building.

■

By Friday, Señor Escamilla still had not fixed Larry's Mustang. Its transmission lay strewn on the lawn next to its dismantled engine. Larry had had to take Marilee's Dart to work. When he returned, he found his car still in pieces.

"What on earth were you thinking?" By this time, Marilee had grown tired of discussing it. The music of Airto and Flora Purim wafted in through the back window. "How do you even know this guy's good?"

"He works on cars. It's what he does all day."

"It's no wonder. It takes him six weeks to fix a transmission."

Marilee went back to reading *People* magazine.

"I'll have to take your car tomorrow," said Larry.

Marilee knew what he was referring to. It was time for his final AIDS test, the results of which would be ready in a week. She wished Enoch would return. Two days later, Enoch did.

"Some little person came to the door looking for you," Larry announced as soon as Marilee came in from her hour-long walk. She'd been exercising daily and in a week had lost four pounds.

"He's a dwarf," she said, peeling off her sweater. Her heart danced.

"Okay, then. Some dwarf came looking for you. Who is he?"

"A friend," she said.

"Obviously. From where?"

"I picked him up hitchhiking."

"My God, Marilee. Haven't I told you to never—"

She was out the door, car keys in hand. She drove the length of White Sands Boulevard, looking for Enoch. All over town she searched for him, up and down Tenth Street, out to the college, down Indian Wells Road, and then out to the fairgrounds. She checked the green bench on New York Avenue where she had once abandoned him. She scoured Alameda Park, where she had found him again. For hours she combed the streets of Rocket City, looking for a small figure on crutches. He was nowhere to be found. That night, Larry barely spoke to her.

"Where's the spicy mustard?" she asked while broiling herself a chicken breast.

"In the side compartment of the door."

"Where are the paper towels?"

"We're out."

All evening, Larry held her hostage to his silence. He went to bed early. Around midnight, Marilee turned off the TV, brushed her teeth, and climbed into bed next to him. The music from upstairs was merciless: lots of hoots and hollers and clacking castanets. Marilee wondered what drugs the Escamillas took to keep them awake twenty-two hours a day.

Though it was not snowing, she got out the broom. She rammed the handle hard against the bedroom ceiling. It made a loud bang. Larry pulled his pillow over his ears. Bang, bang, bang. Still no quiet. Suddenly, she understood. It was some weird Zen exercise to teach her about the need for sleep. She hit the ceiling with the broom handle another five times. On the sixth, the stick broke clear through the sheetrock. Texture dust fell into her eyes. "Shit!" she yelled. Larry snored through all of it. Born without ears, she thought, brushing the dust off her nightgown. She had worn one every night since Larry had returned.

■

She and Larry were out on the lava flow when the rocks started to grow. She glanced up at him, and he too was huge—a giant in a prehistoric landscape. Then she realized that the rocks hadn't grown at all, but that she had gotten smaller. Larry was laughing and holding something in his hands, a box-like device with a joy stick. With this box, he was controlling her size. But then the box started to smoke, and suddenly there was a blinding flash. For a split second, the world was in negative: the rocks of Malpaís, white; the pale sky, black as a moonless night. And in that one awful moment, Marilee realized that Larry had detonated an atomic bomb.

She awoke with a loud cry.

"Who's there?" Larry yelled, bolting straight up beside her. "What is it? What?" The room was pitch black, silent.

"Nightmare," gasped Marilee. Her heart pounded.

"Jesus fuck," he said, then got up to use the bathroom. The next morning, he demanded an explanation.

"They were making too much noise," said Marilee. She'd assumed he was referring to her yelling, or to the hole in their bedroom ceiling.

"I'm talking about the little person."

She pulled a bag of English muffins from the refrigerator. "He's a dwarf," she said.

"And?"

"And what? He's a friend of mine."

"I thought you said you picked him up hitchhiking."

"I did. And then we got to be friends."

Larry's eyebrows arched; he drank meaningfully from his cup of coffee.

"What's that supposed to mean?" she asked.

"What?"

"That look."

"What look?"

"You know what look."

"No, I don't."

"Okay, then, end of discussion."

"Are you interested in him?"

"What kind of question is that?" She ripped apart her English muffin and shoved the halves of it into the toaster.

"Just a question. Why won't you answer it?"

"My God, Larry, he's a dwarf!"

"Little person."

"Don't call him that."

Larry laughed. "What's he going to do, beat me up?"

"Now you're being mean."

"Okay, dwarf. See, I said it. Dwarf. Dwarf. Dwarf."

Marilee took her half-toasted English muffin into the living room and switched on the TV. Willard Scott wished some centenarian a happy birthday.

Larry left his dishes in the sink and took Marilee's car keys from her purse on the counter. "I may be late tonight," he said. "I have a meeting."

"Take good notes," she said.

"Excuse me?"

"Take good notes. Type them up nice and pretty."

"What the hell are you talking about?"

"I know what you do. You're an assistant to some assistant to some media somebody."

"You don't know squat."

"Oh, yes I do. I know that you're a secretary. And that you've been playing it up, pretending to be something you're not so I'll think you're some big shot or something."

"What's with you these days?" he asked. "What's gotten into you?"

He would not have believed her if she had told him.

■

On the first of April, Larry called the clinic for his test results. Not surprisingly, they were negative. "Time to celebrate," he announced to Marilee over the phone. "I'll make fettucini al pesto. We'll have wine and I'll even pick up some rocky road ice cream. It's okay if you eat fattening for just one day." He seemed to have forgotten he'd been mad at her all week.

Marilee said, "Sure," and hung up the phone. She'd grown tired of his dinners of fruit and lettuce. She'd grown tired of a lot of things. A change might do her some good. She knew Larry would want to make love to her tonight. But so many months had passed since they'd been intimate, it seemed strange even to think about it, as if a wall had risen between them. Perhaps wine would help.

Larry got home from work at four forty. When the doorbell rang, it was he who answered it. Señor Escamilla stood on the front walkway. "Very sorry," he said. "I have your car tomorrow." He smiled largely; Marilee waved.

"Tomorrow?" said Larry. "Jesus, Rico, it's always tomorrow. I need my wheels. We can't go on sharing a car like this."

"No habla inglés, señor. Very sorry. Mañana," said Señor Escamilla. He seemed proud of the little English he had mastered.

Larry left the door open and returned to his typewriter. He was working on a new poem; Marilee perused the newspaper. The front page carried a picture of Alcie Britton shaking hands with the state's budget secretary. He looked better, as if his Bell's Palsy had resolved.

Around six thirty, Larry left to go grocery shopping. Marilee spent the time alone in the bathtub, finishing *Pride and Prejudice*. She'd picked up a copy from Books Galore; at the time, Larry had congratulated her on her improved taste in reading.

Dressing carefully, she selected jeans and the green silk blouse she saved for special occasions. She put on new pearl earrings and her sexy lingerie. She sprayed perfume behind her ears and applied a little too much makeup. Tonight, she would need to feel pretty.

When she walked out into the kitchen, she saw Enoch sitting on the living room couch, eating pretzels from a bag. Pesto sauce bubbled in a saucepan. Larry stood over it, stirring diligently. "We have company," he said, with a look that screamed: *Get rid of him!*

"You've met?" she asked Enoch.

"Oh, yes," he said. "I've come by looking for you several times."

"Really?" Marilee walked up behind Larry and put her hand on his shoulder. "We have pasta enough for three, don't we, darling?"

"Of course," he said. He looked up at Enoch. "Would you care to join us for dinner?"

"Cool," said Enoch.

What's smarm? thought Marilee.

■

"Great fettucini," Enoch said, once he'd finished the tidy serving of it Larry had placed in front of him. Outside, crickets tuned up for their evening reverie.

"There's tons more," said Marilee.

"I'll get it," said Larry, grabbing Enoch's plate and taking it into the kitchen.

Marilee smiled at Enoch across the card table Larry had set up in the living room. He returned her smile conspiratorially. In an instant, Larry returned with another plateful of fettucini.

"The salad's orgasmic," said Enoch. "What's in it?"

"Lettuce, walnuts, gorgonzola, sundried tomatoes, olive oil, and balsamic vinegar," said Larry.

Enoch dug into his fettucini.

"You sure eat a lot," said Larry.

Marilee shot him a disapproving look.

"Just an observation," he said, throwing up his hands. "He's not fat or anything."

"High metabolism," said Enoch, with his mouth full.

"I should be so lucky," said Marilee.

"You're not fat," said Enoch. "You're just right. Don't change one bit."

Marilee helped herself to another bowl of salad. Larry, who'd hardly touched his dinner, sat back in his chair and watched them eat.

Once the table had been cleared and the dishes rinsed and stacked, Enoch suggested they go dancing. "I know just the place," he explained. "Little roadhouse on the edge of town. Got some friends who work there."

"What's it called?" asked Larry.

"The Launch Pad. Heard of it?"

"No. Are you able to dance? I mean, with crutches and all?"

"No can do," said Enoch. "I like to people-watch."

"Sounds like fun," said Marilee.

"Great fun," said Larry.

"Then we're on," said Enoch.

■

They locked up the apartment and climbed into the Dart, Larry driving and Enoch taking the back seat behind Marilee. Halfway down White Sands Boulevard, she began to feel the familiar twinges low in her abdomen that signaled the advent of her period. She was right on schedule. She checked her purse but had forgotten to bring anything. "I need to stop for Tampax," she said to Larry.

"Yo!" said Enoch.

Larry shot her a disapproving look.

"Well, what am I supposed to do?"

Larry pulled into the J & J Mini Market.

"Allow me," said Enoch, swinging open his door. He winked at Marilee, then hobbled into the convenience store.

"I don't believe this," said Larry.

"Believe it," said Marilee.

She and Larry watched from their vantage point in the parking lot as Enoch strolled up and down the aisles, looking for the appropriate feminine hygiene display. He stood in the center aisle for a minute, then walked back out to the car. The store clerk eyed him suspiciously.

"Super or regular?" he asked through Marilee's open window.

"Super," she said. Larry cringed. Enoch returned to the store, walked down the aisle, and reached for a blue box on the top shelf. It was too high up for him. He took one crutch and knocked a box from the top of the display, and the whole lot of them came tumbling down. The store clerk ran over and started helping Enoch pick up boxes. "Jesus," said Larry.

Marilee knew Larry hated these moments. In markets, he would wander over to the magazine section whenever she was checking out with tampons in their basket. Once, when she had a yeast infection while down with a migraine, he'd refused to pick up her Monistat 7. Marilee had to pay to have it delivered. And here was Enoch buying her Tampax. She liked that in a man.

He was grinning when he came back out to the car, holding the top of the bag between his palm and the handgrip of his right crutch. "Priceless," he said, dumping his load into the back and resuming his seat behind Marilee. "Can I do that again sometime?"

"In a month," said Marilee. Larry rolled his eyes and started the engine.

They drove south on Highway 54 toward El Paso, Enoch chatting about the joys of interstate travel, Larry stonily silent. A mile or so past the Trinity Motel, they came upon a roadhouse across from the Southern Pacific Railroad tracks. The building was as nondescript as a building could be: square, flat-roofed, windowless, and brown. Pickups and motorcycles ringed its perimeter like a metal fringe. Guitar music screamed from the open doorway.

"There's Rocket All Night," said Larry. "Back on Highway 70. I hear they have a really good band."

"Trust me," said Enoch, patting Larry on the back. "You're both gonna love it." Larry bristled. Marilee hopped out of the car. Enoch followed, leaving his crutches behind.

Inside the Launch Pad, the noise was deafening. People of all ages crowded into its single square room. The bar stood against the right wall; along the southernmost end, a makeshift stage and dance floor had been erected. The Crawdaddies played their country swing. At the center of the far wall lay an array of heavy floor mats. "Swell," shouted Larry into Marilee's hair. "Mud wrestling."

They pressed through the crush of bodies and found an empty table near the far side of the stage, close to the floor mats. For once, Marilee loved the feeling of being among a crowd. It felt raw and dangerous and elementally human. People laughing, dancing, having a good time. The smell of sweat from their bodies mingling with the stench of cigarettes and beer. A scuffle broke out at one corner of the bar. Enoch had been right.

The Crawdaddies finished their set just as the waitress came by to take Larry's order: three gin and tonics, with a twist of lemon in Marilee's. As the music died, the crowd groaned ritualistically. "We'll be back," said the head Crawdaddy. Cheers erupted from the people exiting the dance floor.

The room grew quieter. Larry seemed agitated. "So, who are your friends here?" he asked Enoch.

"Some guys I know from Juárez."

Marilee's heart beat faster. A man in a white suit jumped up onto the makeshift stage. "I want to thank y'all for coming here tonight," he said into the microphone. "Now, I know the Crawdaddies are the real reason you drove all the way out here . . ." The crowd roared with laughter and seemed to rearrange itself, separating down the middle of the room along an imaginary line drawn from the floor mats to the building's entrance.

"What's going on?" asked Marilee.

"You'll see," said Enoch.

Two men carrying a mattress emerged from a door in the back wall. They propped it up against the wall on top of the floor mats. ". . . and if it wasn't for the beer, you'd all be down at the Firing Range," said the man on stage. The crowd shouted in unison, "Five, four, three, two, one, blastoff!" The two men disappeared, then returned with a red carpet, which they rolled out like a runway. It must have stretched thirty feet, from the edge of the floor mats clear to the front door. "But it's time to bring on the sideshow," said the announcer. The bar patrons clapped loudly, yelling and hooting and stomping their feet. Nearby, a man with a scorpion tattoo on his biceps whistled between his teeth. Larry looked miserable. Soon, the clapping fell into a steady rhythm, with people shouting on the downbeat: "Sneezy, Dopey, Bashful! Sneezy, Dopey, Bashful!" Now, this was interesting. Marilee decided to postpone a visit to the bathroom.

The lighting shifted away from the stage and onto the floor mats. The chanting grew to a near frenzy. "Sneezy, Dopey, Bashful! Sneezy, Dopey, Bashful!" Soon, a door in the back wall opened, and out walked three male dwarfs in Dallas Cowboys helmets and black leather harnesses. The crowd went crazy. Enoch climbed up on top of the table.

"Dwarf tossing?" shouted Marilee. It had been years since the fad had swept the country.

"They're the best," said Enoch. She stood beside him to get a better view.

"This is sick," said Larry. Their waitress arrived with their gin and tonics; Larry handed her a ten-dollar bill.

"Now, y'all get in line," said the announcer. "There's no betting on the premises. But if y'all were to, say, step outside . . ." Once again, the crowd went wild with applause and laughter. "We'll be getting under way in about ten minutes. Give you plenty of time to come size up these little fellows."

The dwarfs strutted in circles on the floor mats, bowing dramatically and flexing their muscles. "Achy Breaky Heart" poured from the speakers in each of the room's four corners. When Enoch climbed down from the table, Marilee sat down on the seat next to him.

"Where's the bathroom?" she asked.

Enoch pointed to a door at the far side of the bar.

"This is disgusting," said Larry.

"Why?" said Enoch.

Marilee reached for the table's bowl of peanuts.

"It's blood-sport entertainment. These people ought to be ashamed."

"Lighten up," said Marilee. "Nobody's holding a gun to their head."

"That's cavalier," said Larry.

"That's business," said Enoch.

"Would you do that? Strap on a helmet and let some two-hundred-pound redneck throw you clear across a room?"

"If I could," said Enoch. "But I have brittle bones. I could be paralyzed."

"Well, I think it's despicable," he said. "They're exploiting these little people."

Enoch laughed. "You should see how much these guys get paid. Then you'd see who's exploiting whom."

Marilee reached for more peanuts. Billy Ray Cyrus sang about heartbreak.

Larry patted the back of her hand. "Don't be eating those," he said.

"Why not?" asked Enoch.

Larry didn't answer him. Marilee reached for another handful.

Enoch shifted in his seat to look at her. "By the way, what was the name of that cookie?" he asked.

"What cookie?"

"The one that made you pee through your pants. You never told me."

She shot Enoch a dangerous look. "Poodle Doos."

Enoch burst into laughter, banging hard on the table with his fat little hands. Larry took a long swallow of his drink. The dwarfs paraded up and down the runway while the crowd chanted, "Sneezy, Dopey, Bashful! Sneezy, Dopey, Bashful!"

"This is obscene," said Larry. "When I get home I'm going to write a poem about it."

Enoch buried his head in his hands. Marilee rose to seek out the bathroom. "Larry," she said, placing her hands on his shoulders. "The world's a harsh place. Why not use this as an exercise to learn about compassion."

It took Marilee a full two minutes to wend her way through the throng of people milling about the bar. She had to wait in line another five for the solitary toilet. She was happy to discover she'd indeed gotten her period. But her relief was forgotten as soon as she emerged from the small cubicle. The dwarf toss had already begun.

Marilee charted her way back to her table. She would have to navigate all the way up the bar side of the room, then cross behind the four or five men waiting in line for the dwarf toss. She inched along the barstools, where fewer people were assembled; most everyone's attention was now focused on the runway. When she reached the bar's far corner, a man on a single crutch pivoted unexpectedly, spilling his drink all over her. "Shit," she said, brushing the mess from her green silk blouse.

"I'm sorry," said the man. The fabric was soaked through; she stank of rum and strawberries. "I'm so sorry," he said. "Let me get you a towel." Before she could refuse, he had removed his sweater and handed it to her.

"Damn it," she said, dabbing at the wet spot.

"I'm really sorry," said the man. "Can I buy you a drink or something?" He had a nasty bruise beneath his right eye.

"Or something?" she asked. "What's that supposed to mean?"

"Nothing. I just thought—"

She gave the man a disgusted look and continued on toward her table. "Some asshole just spilled his drink all over me," she said flopping into her seat. Marilee reached for the napkin under her drink, but it was wet from the glass's condensation. "Shit," she said. "It's ruined."

"Lighten up," said Larry. He was smiling.

"Then he propositioned me."

Larry stood up from the table. "Where is he?"

"Oh, sit down," she said.

"Dopey!" yelled the crowd. "Three, two, one!" A dwarf came flying down the runway and landed on the floor mats in front of their table. The crowd cheered. The dwarf got up and ran back to the holding pen that had been set up by the front door. It looked like a giant playpen.

"Where is he? What does he look like?" asked Larry. He stared across the room toward the bar, holding a new drink in his hand.

"Survival of the fittest," said Enoch to Marilee.

"What's that supposed to mean?" asked Larry.

Marilee stood up. "He's on crutches. And he has a bruise or something under his eye. There he is," she said pointing. "Talking to that woman in yellow. At the table in the corner. She has dark hair. You can't see her face. He's leaning over her now."

"Got him," said Larry. He headed off in pursuit of Marilee's transgressor.

"Get your period?" asked Enoch.

She gave him a thumbs up.

"¡Que bueno!" he said.

Marilee watched as Larry tried to push his way through the tight clot of people crowding around the dwarf pen. Across the room, the man on crutches disappeared in the direction of the bar. In a moment, Marilee caught a glimpse of Larry arriving at the man's table. The woman in yellow glanced up at him. Marilee still couldn't see her face. Larry smiled and said something to her. Then he sat down.

"'Tossed Without Remorse,'" said Enoch.

"What?"

"Larry's poem. The one he's going to write when he gets home."

Marilee hit him playfully on the arm.

"Sneezy," yelled the crowd as another dwarf was selected from the holding pen.

Marilee finished her drink, then exchanged her empty glass for Larry's half-full one. "This is fun," she shouted across the table. "Three, two, one!" yelled the crowd. Another dwarf came flying down the runway and bounced along the floor mats. Then another. In a while, Larry returned to their table.

"Couldn't find him," he said. "Probably saw me coming and made a run for it. What happened to my drink?"

"Must have finished it," said Enoch. Larry waved for the cocktail waitress. Marilee watched as the man on crutches left through the front door, the woman in yellow in pursuit. Good, she thought. One less asshole to deal with.

"Dopey!" shouted the crowd. A short man built like a Harley-Davidson lifted a dwarf from the holding pen. The crowd shouted, "Three, two, one!" as he swung him like a bowling ball and flung him down the length of carpet. The dwarf hit the floor hard and rolled up onto the floor mats. The spectators hissed. "Now, you folks know the rules," said the announcer. "No dwarf bowling. These little fellows aren't equipped." But Dopey was up in a flash, posturing like a heavyweight. The crowd roared. "Let's go," said Larry. "I can't deal with this level of inhumanity."

"Oh, chill out," said Marilee. "Life doesn't always have to be so serious."

"Any ladies out there who'd like to give it a try?" asked the man with the microphone.

Enoch looked at her devilishly.

"What did he say?" said Larry. "I couldn't hear him."

Could she do it? Were she able to lift him, could she pick up a dwarf and toss him clear across a room? What were her limits? Was there any part of her that wanted to do this?

"No takers?" said the announcer. The crowd booed. "No little woman out there dying to get her hands on some helpless man? Now, I know there are times y'all would like to toss us straight out the window."

The crowd erupted into laughter. Marilee rose up out of her seat.

"Yo!" shouted Enoch.

Larry looked stricken.

She pushed her way through the crush of people toward the line of men behind the red carpet. "Looks like we got ourselves a live one," said the man in white. "Let the little lady through." The crowd hooted and whistled, then parted to make way for Marilee. She got in line behind a man in a cowboy hat.

"Now, y'all be gentlemen and let the lady go first," said the announcer.

Marilee moved to the front of the line and sized up the dwarfs in the holding pen. "I'll take that one," she said, selecting the lightest looking of the three.

The man in the cowboy hat lifted the dwarf out of the pen and handed him to Marilee. "Bashful!" yelled the crowd. She wrapped both her hands around the handle of his harness. She lifted him carefully; he was lighter than she had imagined. Marilee carried him a ways down the carpet runway and came to a stop. "Have a nice ride," she said, and swung him back with both hands like a scythe.

"One!" yelled the crowd.

CATHRYN ALPERT

310

She swung him forward, then back again. Bashful put his arms together, as if diving.

"Two!" yelled the roomful of people.

Forward, like a child on a swing, then back again. Her own strength surprised her.

"Three!" the crowd shouted, and Marilee let him sail. She watched as the dwarf flew headfirst down the runway, airborne, seemingly in slow motion. The room grew still. And in that small moment between releasing the dwarf and his hitting the ground, Marilee saw all the pain that Enoch had ever suffered. Everything that had happened and would ever happen to him and all the other little people of the world. Not just dwarfs and midgets, but every weakling ever bullied by someone larger and more powerful. Every mouse ever eaten by a hawk. Every toad ever swallowed by a snake. Every baby ever left out on a rock to die. She had tossed the dwarf. She was part of the system. She had proof right before her eyes, as Bashful sailed headfirst down the length of the red carpet. She had tossed him with all her might—as hard as she could heave a human body—with a force so brutal and unforeseen that when he hit the floor mats, the dwarf tumbled clear to the back wall and slammed hard against the mattress. The mattress fell over on top of him; the Launch Pad crowd went crazy.

"Let's give the little lady a big hand," shouted the man in the white suit. "Free drinks for the lady's table."

Time accelerated, and sound returned to full volume. Marilee looked up and saw Enoch standing on their table, cheering loudly. Larry was nowhere to be seen. Enoch hobbled down from the table and made his way through the crowd. The man in the cowboy hat grabbed Marilee and swung her round and round in a circle. "You might just be the big winner," he said, standing her upright in front of the dwarf pen. She fought to regain her balance.

"That was great!" said Enoch, catching up to her. "Let's get out of here."

"Where's Larry?" she shouted.

"He left," he said. "When you picked up Bashful."

Left? She hadn't noticed him leaving. Had he taken her car?

"Sneezy!" the crowd shouted, as the man in the cowboy hat pulled a fresh dwarf from the holding pen. Marilee and Enoch bolted out the door into the cool desert air. Larry sat behind the wheel of the Dart, looking angry.

"I'm driving," she said, opening the door next to him. She felt exhilarated.

"I'll drive," he said.

"You've had too much to drink. Scoot over."

He did as she asked; Enoch hopped in behind Larry. Marilee started the Dart's engine and pulled out onto the highway. She headed north, back to Rocket City.

"'This thing of darkness . . .' Yo!" said Enoch. He beat his hands against Larry's headrest and stomped his feet.

"Excuse me?" said Larry, turning all the way around to face him.

"'This thing of darkness I acknowledge mine.'"

"That ain't Woody," said Marilee.

"Shakespeare," Enoch said.

"You're weird," said Larry.

Marilee slammed on her brakes and steered sharply to the shoulder of the highway.

"Jesus!" said Larry, bracing himself against the dashboard.

"Get out," she said, as soon as the car had come to a stop.

Larry laughed at her, then his mouth fell open.

"I said get out."

"Don't make a fool of yourself," he said.

Marilee took a deep breath and tried to speak calmly. "This is my car, Larry. I'm asking you to leave it. Right here. Right now."

"And do what?" he said. He laughed nervously.

"Hitchhike."

"Hitchhike? You can get killed doing something stupid like that. I'm not going to hitchhike. I'll get picked up by some yahoo from that idiot bar. I'll be killed."

"No you won't," said Enoch.

Larry spun in his seat. "You stay out of this."

"I said get out!" shouted Marilee. "GET OUT! GET OUT! GET OUT!"

Larry threw open his car door and stumbled out onto the highway. He looked more bewildered than angry. A truck flashed its brights as it rumbled past them, kicking up gravel that spattered the car like buckshot. "I can't believe you're doing this," he said to Marilee.

"Believe it," said Enoch.

"I told you to stay out of this, you little . . ."

"Little what?" said Marilee.

Larry looked flustered.

"Come on," said Enoch. "It's not as difficult as it seems. Few things are. I'll teach you."

"Go to hell," said Larry. "Both of you."

"Larry, my man," said Enoch, opening his door and tossing his backpack and crutches out onto the pavement. "'You gotta have faith in people.'"

Enoch slammed both doors shut, and Marilee sped off into the desert, laughing wildly. In her rearview mirror she saw two dim figures standing on the edge of the roadway. The smaller of the two stuck out his thumb.

Marilee drove for most of the night, to nowhere in particular. The farther from the lights of the city she traveled, the clearer the stars shone in the sky. She was not at all tired. She drove west, into Arizona, then back east into southern New Mexico. "Land of Enchantment," said the border sign.

For hours, she drove through the desert night. When she passed White Sands Missile Range, the sky had turned to fire.

APRIL FOOLS REDUX:
THE ROAD TO THEBES

"You know what I'd really like for my birthday?" said Figman. He and Oma had just descended the mountains from Cloudcroft, where they'd eaten a steak dinner at Rebecca's. The Tularosa Basin stretched before them like a lunar landscape.

"A roll in the hay?" said Oma.

"I'd like for you to stop calling me Forbes."

Oma looked troubled. "That's all?"

"That's enough," said Figman.

"Okay. But I did get you something." Her Corvair barreled down the mountain; Oma drove it like a bumper car. "I just can't believe you're forty. I mean, that I'm going out with a guy who's actually forty years old."

"Believe it," said Figman. "Watch out!" The car had drifted precariously close to the edge of the highway. Figman stared down a steep gorge.

Oma overcorrected, then steered her Corvair into the center of her lane. She'd had three wine coolers at the restaurant. Figman wished his ankle were healed so he could take control of her vehicle.

By the time they reached Alamogordo, the sky had turned a deep purple. Figman was sure he had never seen a place more alien. The town was studded with rockets—on billboards, on roofs, in the courtyards of buildings— idols to a recondite technology. He saw it as no different from ancient man erecting great shrines to a god he feared but could not understand.

313

On his initial drive through New Mexico, Figman had avoided Alamogordo, having taken the southern route through El Paso. Surely there was radiation lingering in the soil and air, radioactive ions that would mutate the cells of his already failing body. Figman shut the air vents of Oma's Corvair. He wished she had told him she was bringing him here.

The Launch Pad lay on the outskirts of town, a mile or so past some rickety motel. Pickup trucks and motorcycles littered the parking lot; music poured from the doorway. Oma tore into the driveway, leaving a wake of dust and gravel. "We're here," she said. "Just wait till you hear the band."

Inside, the air was stifling. The room was jammed with people, so many that Figman worried about being able to navigate the place on crutches. There was a bar, a dance floor, some mats on the floor, and a makeshift stage. A band called the Crawdaddies played something country.

It took them a while, but eventually they found a table in the corner, not far from the bar. Figman hated the place; the crush of humanity was not his scene. He wondered why Oma had brought him here.

When the music stopped, the crowd groaned. At least now they'd be able to make conversation. "Can I get you a drink?" he asked her.

"Strawberry daiquiri," she said.

Figman made his way to the bar, wondering how he was going to carry two drinks back to their table. He had to wait in line to order. A man in a white suit came out on stage. "I want to thank y'all for coming here tonight," he said into a microphone. "Now, I know the Crawdaddies are the real reason you drove all the way out here . . ." The crowd exploded with laughter. At the far end of the room, two men set up a mattress against the wall. ". . . and if it wasn't for the beer, you'd all be down at the Firing Range," said the man in the white suit. The crowd chimed in: "Five, four, three, two, one, blastoff!" Figman wondered what was going on.

The bartender lingered at the opposite end of the bar, talking to a woman in a black see-through blouse. Directly behind Figman, a man jockeyed for position, shoving him into the bar. To Figman's left, a Mexican woman smoked Marlboros; to his right, a leather type stared forlornly into his beer.

"But it's time to bring on the sideshow," said the man in the white suit. The place went crazy, with people stomping and yelling and whistling through their teeth. As the clapping coalesced into a unified rhythm, Figman tried in vain to catch the bartender's eye. Soon, the crowd was shouting, "Sneezy, Dopey, Bashful! Sneezy, Dopey, Bashful!" Figman waited and kept his eyes on the bartender.

At last, Figman won the man's attention. He ordered a Miller on tap and a strawberry daiquiri. With his order in, Figman turned around to check things out. A long red carpet had been rolled from one end of the room to the other; light fell on the floor mats. The crowd kept yelling over and over, "Sneezy, Dopey, Bashful!" Then three male dwarfs emerged from a door and started prancing around on the floor mats. They wore football helmets and black leather harnesses.

Dwarf tossing? Had Oma brought him to see dwarf tossing?

"Now, y'all get in line," said the man in white. "There's no betting on the premises. But if y'all were to, say, step outside . . ." The crowd cheered; the woman next to Figman relinquished her stool. Figman seized the opportunity to get off his feet. "We'll be getting under way in about ten minutes," said the announcer. "Give you plenty of time to come size up these little fellows." And Oma had worried that dancing might depress him.

Figman waited for the bartender to return with his order. A song poured from the speakers in the corners of the room—a bouncy tune about some poor guy's heart aching and breaking. Breaking hearts were all country artists ever sang about, which was one of the reasons Figman didn't like country. The dwarfs continued to parade in circles around the floor mats. The crowd grew more subdued.

Then, as if on cue, the three dwarfs ran toward the front of the building. The man in white stepped up to the microphone. "Y'all ready?" he said. More yelling and whistling and stomping of feet. Figman hoped the noise and smoke wouldn't bring on one of his headaches. "Here we go," said the man, and people started clapping. "Bashful!" they hollered. "Three, two, one!" A dwarf went flying down the length of carpet. He landed on the floor mats with a thud.

Now, this bothered Figman. It seemed a stupid thing to do, what with the liability and all. If one of those little guys got hurt, the Launch Pad could have quite a lawsuit on its hands.

Figman paid for his drinks and even tipped the bartender. But how to get himself and his two full glasses back to the table? He would have to transport them one at a time, using a single crutch in the process. "Excuse me," he said to the motorcycle man.

The guy looked up at him. He had a hoop through his nose.

"Would you watch this beer and my crutch while I take this drink to my table?"

"No problem," said the man.

Figman secured one crutch under his right armpit; in his left hand he carried Oma's daiquiri. He started out toward their table, hanging close to the bar. "Sneezy," yelled the crowd. People were clapping and jostling and standing up on barstools to get a better view of the dwarf toss. Figman held the daiquiri up high while using his crutch to forge a path in front of him. When he saw an opening, he darted for it. A woman crashed into him. Oma's daiquiri spilled all down the front of her blouse.

"Shit," said the woman, brushing the mess onto Figman's sweater. Her red hair shone beautifully.

"I'm sorry," said Figman, though he realized the accident had not been his fault. The woman glared at him; her blouse was soaked clear through. "I'm so sorry," he said again. "Let me get you a towel." Figman looked for a towel at the end of the bar but didn't see one. He took off his sweater and handed it to her.

"Damn it," she said. She patted the wet spot with his cardigan. Her breasts were lovely.

"I'm really sorry," said Figman. "Can I buy you a drink or something?"

"Or something?" she asked sharply. "What's that supposed to mean?"

"Nothing. I just thought—"

The woman gave Figman a disgusted look and disappeared into the crowd. "Jesus," said Figman. When he returned to the bar, the leather man was gone, as was his Miller. His crutch leaned against the counter, next to the man's empty stool. Figman sat down and ordered another round of drinks.

It disturbed Figman that the red-haired woman had not accepted his apology. Obviously, he hadn't meant to spill his drink all over her. It hadn't even been his fault. So why had she been so hostile?

This time, Figman asked a waitress to carry his drinks to the table. He tipped her when she got there. "What took you so long?" asked Oma. She had emptied the table's peanut bowl.

"Some woman crashed into me and spilled your drink. I had to go back for another one."

"Oh," she shouted. "Isn't this fun?"

"I can't believe they're still doing this anywhere."

"What do you mean?" yelled Oma. It was hard to hear above the din.

"Dwarf tossing. It's passé."

"It's what?" She sipped her daiquiri through its straw.

"Dopey," yelled the crowd. "Three, two, one!"

"Never mind," shouted Figman. He looked down the runway toward the floor mats at the far end of the room. Dopey landed hard. The crowd cheered. Oma drank down her daiquiri.

At a table near the mats, Figman noticed the red-haired woman. She was laughing and cheering. With her were a man and a boy. Were children actually allowed in here?

Suddenly, the woman stood up with the man and pointed in the direction of Figman. He leaned over the table to talk to Oma. Oma seemed annoyed that he was shouting in her ear. The man standing next to the redhead fixed his eyes on Figman, nodded, and headed in his direction. "I said I'm going to the bathroom," Figman shouted.

"Okay," yelled Oma.

"Do you want another daiquiri?"

"Margarita," she yelled.

"Salt?" he yelled back at her.

"No salt," she hollered.

"Sneezy," shouted the crowd.

Figman grabbed his crutches and headed off as fast as he could in the direction of the bar. He grabbed an empty barstool in the corner, behind a cluster of men with their girlfriends on their shoulders. The man made his way to Figman's table. He was tall, blond, and looked angry.

Figman ordered a margarita without salt and kept an eye on his table. The blond man sat down in the chair next to Oma. He was talking, and she was smiling. Figman nursed Oma's cocktail. The tall guy lingered. If he were waiting for Figman, he'd have a long wait. The man wrote something down on a piece of paper and handed it to Oma. She smiled and tucked it into her purse. "Dopey," yelled the crowd. Figman finished her margarita.

As soon as the fellow left, Figman maneuvered his way back to his table. "Where's my drink?" asked Oma.

"Too crowded," he said. "Let's try to find a waitress."

"Okay," she said, sounding slightly annoyed.

"On second thought," said Figman, "let's get out of here."

"But it's just started."

He rose and adjusted his crutches for battle. Oma stayed seated while Figman started for the door. She would follow, he knew, whether she wanted to or not. He looked back and saw her coming.

"Now, you folks know the rules. No dwarf bowling," said the emcee.

"Excuse me," shouted Figman. "Excuse me." Slowly, the throng parted, and he reached the exit door. Beside it stood a holding pen for the dwarfs. Two of them jogged in circles; a third came running down the runway and climbed in. The smallest of the dwarfs stopped his strutting and stared up at Figman, perhaps expecting him to lift him out of the pen. Jesus, thought Figman: as if there weren't already enough injury in the world. He shook his head.

"Get a life," said the dwarf. He had a voice like a Munchkin.

"What?" said Figman. Was he talking to him?

The dwarf stuck his tongue out and thumbed his nose.

Figman hurried through the doorway.

■

"What's the matter?" asked Oma, trailing Figman to her car. She sounded more hurt than angry.

"I don't know," said Figman. "I just had to get out of there. Claustrophobia, or something."

"It *was* kind of crowded," she admitted. "Want to go somewhere else?" she asked. "Rocket All Night's got a good band."

"I'm tired," said Figman.

"But it's your birthday."

"Guess us old guys poop out pretty early."

Oma laughed and unlocked her passenger door. "Well, don't get too pooped," she said. "I've got plans for you."

Oma headed north on Highway 54, toward Alamogordo. When she reached the edge of the city, she rolled her window down. "Smell it," she said to Figman.

"Smell what?"

"Perfect air," she said. "No stock yards. No oil wells."

"Ah," said Figman. He could practically see the ions settling onto his skin.

Oma merged onto White Sands Boulevard and floored her accelerator. "I really like this place," she said. "I mean, if I was to ever move, this would be the place I'd move to."

"Jesus, will you look at all these rockets," said Figman.

"Don't you love 'em?"

"I think they're ludicrous. All these silly monuments. Look at these things."

"Mmm," said Oma. She put her hand on his knee. "I think they're exciting."

Figman stared out his window and pretended not to have understood. He was in no mood to get physical. He felt disturbed, as if something prickly had worked its way under his skin. It wasn't just that redheaded woman being rude to him—people were rude every day. It was that dwarf in the holding pen. Get a life? What was that supposed to mean? And why had he stuck his tongue out at him?

Without warning, Oma braked and pulled over to the side of the road.

"What are you doing?" asked Figman.

She parked in front of a school for the blind. "I forgot," she said. "Your present." Oma reached into her back seat and brought forward a package. "Open it," she said, presenting it to him.

Figman tore apart its wrapping paper. Inside, he found a framed certificate from the International Star Registry. He saw the name Forbes printed in the center. "What is it?" he asked.

"It's a star. Named after you. Your very own star. Only I blew it, I guess, when I had them name it Forbes."

"A star?"

"Yeah. Neat, huh? It's in the constellation Scorpio 'cause I'm a Scorpio. It's not visible or anything."

"They name stars after people who aren't astronomers?"

"Well, you have to pay for it. Kim Basinger had one named for Alec Baldwin. Or was it Prince? Anyway, I think it's pretty cool. To know that something that cosmic will live on forever in your name."

"Thanks," said Figman. It was, perhaps, the most depressing gift he had ever been given.

"Do you like it?"

"It's . . . unbelievable."

"I'll call them tomorrow and see if I can get its name changed to Figman."

"Great," he said. Oma started the car and headed out of Alamogordo. Figman felt as small and insignificant as a star could make a man feel.

■

When Oma pulled into Figman's driveway, the lights were off in Verdie's trailer. Her Impala was gone, as it had been for most of the day.

Figman was relieved to have made it home at all. On the road to Cloudcroft, they'd passed a horrible accident on the highway. A Volvo appeared to have missed a turn, rolled over an embankment, and wrapped itself around a tree. Traffic had backed up a quarter mile while rescue teams used the Jaws of Life to set the driver free. Once past the wreckage, Oma had decided to make up for lost time. As a birthday joke, she'd killed the headlights just as they'd sped up over the summit, going seventy.

Figman hobbled into his bedroom and collapsed onto his bed. He felt exhausted and disturbed, still bothered by what that dwarf had said to him. Oma followed him in and started to undress.

"You know what?" he said. "I'm awfully tired."

"But it's your birthday. You can't not make love on your birthday."

"Is that some kind of rule?"

"It'll be your real present, since I messed up on your star."

"You didn't mess up," he said. He rotated his sprained ankle. It hurt to move it. Oma unhooked her bra and ran her fingers over her nipples. Figman felt himself stir.

They made love, it seemed, more out of duty than desire, as if both Oma and Figman were just going through the motions (though her motions were a bit more exotic than his). When he felt himself near climax, Oma put her hands up behind her head and stared at the ceiling. "Let's take pictures?" she said. "Spice things up."

"Pictures?"

"Polaroids. Of you and me. You know, doing it."

Figman felt himself getting softer. "I don't do pictures."

"Come on, it's fun," said Oma. "Jesse and me, we took lots of pictures. I'll show them to you some day."

"You'd show me pictures of you and Jesse?"

"Sure."

He felt a tension at the base of his neck. "Don't you think that's kind of a betrayal?"

"Oh, no." Oma giggled. "Jesse was proud of them. He once even showed them to his brother."

Figman rolled off her and sat on the edge of his bed. The snake started dancing.

"What's wrong?" Oma asked.

Figman found himself at a loss for words. He took his bathrobe and his crutches and stumbled into his kitchen. He grabbed a Dos Equis from his refrigerator and carried it over to the sink. Resting his elbows on the counter, he stared out the kitchen window, remembering his long-forgotten vow to buy curtains. He'd actually come to enjoy the view of Verdie's trailer; it was comforting, somehow, in its wretched ugliness. Figman opened his beer with a bottle opener and took a long, deep swallow. He knew drinking would exacerbate his headache, but he didn't care. It felt deserved.

A light had come on in Verdie's trailer, a singular glow from the Christmassy fixture above her bed. He hadn't heard her car drive in, but there it was, parked right next to the steps to her trailer. Figman looked up at the stars in the sky and wondered which of them was named

Forbes. To his left, across the highway, the Rodriguez house stood
bathed in moonlight. Sagging from its clothesline hung a week's worth
of laundry: work shirts and denim overalls; old sheets and women's underwear. And there was Bobo at his well pump, digging. Why on earth
was he digging? Digging, digging, forever digging in that horrible dirt.
The dirt that made the dust that crept into his house's pores and cavi-
ties. He'd never seen a stranger creature, nor one seemingly more
at peace.

Figman stood at his window for a long time, sipping his beer, thinking
about the people in his life—Dino, Hooks, Oma, Verdie—each with his
own secrets; each with his own pain. Figman rubbed his eyes. He'd had
enough of the world's misery.

When Oma called his name, Figman pretended not to have heard her.
He wanted her out of his bed. His house. His life. He grabbed his
crutches and hobbled out into his backyard. He was careful crossing it in
the darkness.

Though her light was on, Verdie had been dozing; his knock had most
certainly awakened her. "Come in," she called drowsily. For once, he
didn't hesitate. She was in bed, under purple blankets piled high with un-
sorted laundry. Her eyes looked swollen.

"I need to talk to you," said Figman. "Right now. I'm sorry."

Verdie sat up and pushed an armful of laundry off the mattress onto
the floor. Figman moved a pair of sweatpants and sat on the bed's far corner. "What is it, Louis?" she asked him. Her pink-purple lipstick was
smeared around her mouth, like clown makeup.

"For some reason," said Figman, "I felt this need to come talk to you.
To tell you something."

"All right," said Verdie. She looked bewildered.

"It's a true story."

"Is there any other kind?"

Figman smiled. "When I was living in L.A., I had this gardener named
Velasquez. He was a good gardener. Very hardworking and dependable.
Velasquez worked for several people in the neighborhood. One of them
was this guy named Tildeman. He was a television producer. You've
probably seen some of his shows."

Verdie looked intent, as though she were trying hard to make sense of this story. Her hair was wild.

"Tildeman had this wife named Sugar. One day he and Sugar got into a fight, and the next thing he knew, his wife was fucking the gardener. I'm sorry," said Figman. "My language."

"Pfft," said Verdie.

Figman smiled again, briefly. "So Tildeman did this incredibly mean thing. He told everyone in the neighborhood to fire Velasquez. Well, this was as unfair as life gets. I mean, homeowners were dropping the poor guy right and left. Bernie Tildeman was a powerful man, and I guess people were anxious to please him. But not me. I kept Velasquez on. Gave him a raise and even referred him to my friends."

"That was decent of you, Louis." She looked satisfied that his story had come to its conclusion.

"I'm not done yet." Figman shifted on the bed; the mattress surely lacked adequate back support. "The other thing I did was screw Sugar Tildeman. Just to get back at that sonofabitch. I made sure it happened at my house on a day when Velasquez was due to arrive. I left the curtains wide open so he would see."

"Why'd you do that?" asked Verdie. Her breath smelled like Scotch whisky.

"So Velasquez would see us. So he'd know I was doing this for him." Verdie's face folded into a net of lines. "Now, I know that sounds strange, but I thought he'd perceive it as a kind of victory."

"I'd put money on it he didn't."

"No. He didn't," said Figman. "I'd called him at home the night before and asked him to prune the rose bushes, which were right outside my bedroom window. Sugar and I were heavily into it when I heard his truck drive up, and then his music. He played Mexican music from his truck's stereo—left the windows open so he could listen to it while he worked. I never could figure out why he didn't wear down his battery."

"Maybe he had a tape player in there. A portable."

"Could be," said Figman. He was silent for a moment. "So when Velasquez started his pruning, he saw us going at it through the window, just like I'd planned. I looked up at him. And the man was crying."

"Crying?"

"Sobbing. It was the strangest thing—not at all what I'd imagined. The next thing I knew, he was gathering up his tools and running off toward his truck in the driveway. I threw on my bathrobe and ran after him. By the time I caught up with him, he looked like something the cat had spit up. He was really a mess. Tears streaming down his hairy cheeks. Eyes all puffy. And when I asked him what was wrong, he said that *I* was what was wrong."

"Hmm," said Verdie. She pushed the hair from her face.

"So I told him I'd only done it for him. That the whole thing had been staged just for his benefit so together we could get back at Tildeman. And Velasquez looked at me and said something I've never been able to forget. He said, 'You don't know nothing, man. You don't know nothing. I feel sorry for you.' And then he drove away."

"Jeez," said Verdie.

"I thought about it for days—weeks probably. Finally, I figured I better get the hell out of Dodge. Go somewhere and learn something to make up for the nothing that this Mexican gardener was all too certain I knew. So here I am." Figman snorted a little and glanced up at Verdie. He felt small and slightly foolish.

"Did you?" she asked. She looked wide awake now, and vaguely appealing.

"Did I what?"

"Learn anything?"

"I'm not sure," said Figman. "I don't know why I'm even telling you this. But I do feel better having told you."

"That makes sense," she said. "Would you like a drink?"

Figman realized, then, that the snake had stopped dancing and his headache had never come. "Better not," he said. "But thanks anyway. I should let you get some sleep. Thanks for listening."

"Anytime," said Verdie.

Figman rose from her bed and made his way to her entry. His crutches squeaked over her linoleum. When he opened the door, the stars shone down on him. "It's my birthday today," he said. "I'm forty."

"A young 'un," said Verdie.

Figman laughed. "It's all relative."

"Most everything is," she said. "Happy birthday, Louis."

"Thank you," said Figman. "Good night."

When he returned to his house, his bed was empty. Figman was not sure when Oma had left, or which door she had used as an exit.

■

Two days after Figman's fortieth birthday, Verdie received the death knell he'd been anticipating: a letter from Woodbine, the local cemetery. This could only mean her end was near. She'd lived her entire life in the town of Artesia; she had no reason to be buried anyplace else.

Though tempted to open it, Figman tossed her letter on his kitchen counter and returned to his easel. He was working on a still life he'd begun that morning: two oranges, a rose in a vase, and his bottle of Essence of Chicken. He felt agitated but also wobbly, it being his first day off crutches; he knew it would still be a matter of weeks before his ankle completely healed. Also, for three days now, he'd felt a tension at the base of his neck which he'd come to recognize as a precursor to one of his headaches. But the headache had not materialized.

Figman glanced out his window at the Rodriguez house across the highway. He had not seen Bobo all day. Benito's bronze Samurai cruised up the road, toward Carlsbad. Hooks would not stop to visit him, Figman knew, as long as Verdie's green Impala was clearly visible.

Figman put down his paintbrush and got himself a beer. Verdie's mail stared up at him from the counter. It taunted him. It dared him to open it. Figman had never in his life not responded to a dare. The letter said:

Dear Mrs. Hooks,

On behalf of the staff at Woodbine Cemetery, I'd like to thank you for your regard for our organization. We are only too pleased to have received your check.

Mr. Carpenter, with whom you spoke on the telephone, informs me that there are still some documents to sign, which he is happy to send to you.

However, we would be delighted to have you sign them in person so that you might tour our facilities.

Please call me or Mr. Carpenter at your earliest convenience to discuss these final arrangements.

Yours,
Mary-Louise Spoonamore
Director of Internal Affairs

Figman limped to Verdie's trailer, letter in hand. He knocked loudly on her metal door. She opened it, wearing a pink two-piece bathing suit. The day was warm. Her stomach was tan. Poe Titus was nowhere to be seen.

"I brought you your mail," said Figman. "I opened it."

"You what?" said Verdie. She took the envelope from his hand and glanced at the front of it.

"I could have told you it was an accident, but it wasn't," he said. "I opened it on purpose. Please forgive me."

Verdie's look was troubled. "Come in, Louis," she said. She held the door open for him. Figman stepped up into her hideous trailer. It smelled like fried fish and tamales.

"I apologize for what I did," he said. "I take full responsibility. It's just that I'm worried sick about you."

"About me? Mercy Maude, whatever for?"

Figman looked down at his feet. "I know you're dying."

"Dying?"

"I know you have cancer and not much longer to live."

Verdie broke into violent laughter, her gums showing large and pink. The flesh of her belly jiggled when she laughed, like aspic in an earthquake. Figman wished he could sink through her dirty linoleum.

"Louis," she said, as soon as she'd regained her composure. "What in Sam Hell led you to that conclusion?"

"Your mail, mostly. All those letters from doctors and hospitals and cancer agencies. And hospice centers. And mortuaries. It seemed fairly obvious."

Verdie laughed again. "Oh, Louis, bless your sweet soul."

"Plus I've heard things."

"What things?"

"Nothing specific. Just that . . . well, you know . . . that you weren't all that well."

Verdie took a glass down from her doorless cabinet. "Have a drink," she said. It was not a question.

"That would be good," said Figman.

"Scotch?"

"What the hell."

She poured it straight up and handed him the glass. It had lipstick along its rim.

Figman sat down at her table and crossed his legs. Verdie seated herself next to him. She pointed to the window above her sink. "See that land out there?" she asked.

"Which land?"

"All that land. As far as the eye can see."

"Yes?" said Figman.

"It's mine."

"Yours?" said Figman. "All of it?"

"Sixty-two thousand acres."

"Holy Jesus," he said. He could hardly imagine a real estate holding so vast. "It must be worth a fortune."

"Not nearly as much as the oil underneath it."

None of this was making sense.

"Now, I got me an idea who's been talking to you, putting crazy ideas in your head. That good-for-nothing son of mine. Am I right?"

Figman shifted in his seat. "He has dropped by on one or two occasions."

"Well, don't I know it," she said. "You want another shot?"

"Please," said Figman.

Verdie rose quickly and brought the bottle of Scotch back to the table. "He don't know it yet, but he's got some pretty mean surprises coming his way."

Figman wondered if his delight were visible. "Benito did tell me Poe Titus was just after you for your money. I think he was afraid you were going to marry Poe."

"Poe? Poe Titus?" Verdie laughed her wild laugh; tears ran down her cheeks. "Me marry Poe Titus?"

Figman sipped at his drink.

"Honey, Poe Titus has a wife of thirty years, eleven grandbabies, and two years ago, he lost his balls to seminoma."

Benito was a dead man.

"Lordy," said Verdie. "Poe Titus has got no more use for my money than I do. That man owns this whole town and everybody in it."

"Oh," said Figman.

"Poe Titus?" she said, still laughing. "Let me get you a tamale." Verdie spooned a brown glob from the pan on top of her hot plate into a plastic bowl. She set it and a soup spoon in front of Figman. "All my forks are dirty."

Figman ate his tamale; it was lukewarm but good, surprisingly.

"My mother's recipe," she said.

"I remember," said Figman. "So, what did you mean when you said you had no use for your money?"

"Just that," said Verdie. "I'm giving it all away. Well, not all of it, but most of it, anyway. I like to live simple."

That much was obvious.

"I'm selling off my land in fifty-acre parcels and giving the proceeds to charity."

Figman was floored. "That's awfully benevolent of you."

"Pfft," said Verdie.

Figman tried hard to make sense of all of this. "So how'd you come by all this property?"

"It was my mother's, and her mother's before her. I was her only child. We got along real good, her and me. I sure do miss that woman."

Figman spooned the last of his sauce from his bowl.

"Have another," said Verdie.

"All right," he said. "I'll think I'll have two."

Verdie smiled and brought the pan of tamales over to the table. It looked as though it had been sitting out for a while. "Just help yourself," she said.

Figman spooned two more tamales into his bowl. It had been months since he'd felt this hungry. "So you're giving it all away?" he said. For some reason, the thought of it made him happy.

"As much as I can. I give it to the churches. The hospitals. The mortuaries to bury the indigent. Any of those places that sends me letters. My lawyer over in Hobbs keeps track of the books for me—I'm not real good with numbers."

"What about all those doctors? From Carlsbad and Las Cruces, and that one in—" Figman put down his spoon. "Jeez, will you listen to me? Here I am, eating your food, drinking your liquor, and giving you the third degree. None of this is any of my business. I don't know why you don't just kick me out of here."

Verdie smiled. "I'd never do that, Louis. I've grown fond of you."

Figman felt himself blush. "But what *about* those doctors? You do get mail from an awful lot of them."

Verdie laughed. "Honey, the only doctor I've seen in the last twenty-five years is Ferrell Jarboe up in Roswell. I've been having me some trouble with the change. Those other doctors—well, they just write to me with their patients' hard luck stories, and I send them a check."

"You just send them money?"

"Sure."

"No questions asked?"

"I reckon I don't have time to be suspicious. Life's too short. There's golf to be played."

"I'll have to learn it some day."

"I'll get Poe to teach you. He's the one who taught me."

Figman's mind raced, trying to discover some hole in Verdie's story. He had difficulty recalling all her mail. "What about that collection agency in Albuquerque?" Now, there was one she'd have trouble explaining.

"That's Benito. He works for them, in car repossessions. I keep telling him he'll get caught one of these days using company stationery."

Figman drank his Scotch whisky. It tasted good, all of a sudden, as if his brain had forgotten his having gotten sick on it as a teen. He looked around Verdie's decrepit trailer. "So why'd you rent your house out? Don't get me wrong, I'm glad you did. But it seems kind of strange, considering."

"Too big to clean. You'd think that's all I ever did. Clean. Clean. Clean. Damn near wore me out, all that scrubbing."

Figman took another bite of tamale to keep from smiling, then washed it down with the last of his Scotch. Verdie refilled his glass on cue. "So there's one last thing I don't understand—if you don't mind my asking."

"Shoot," she said.

"Exactly why are you giving away all your money?" Figman could not imagine a thing less comprehensible.

Verdie leaned over the table. "So Benito don't get his grubby little hands on it. Not one red cent. Not while I'm living and not while I'm dead—which will be some time from now, I reckon."

Figman felt the tension at the base of his neck subside. "I reckon it will," he said.

Verdie reached over and stroked his cheek with the back of her hand. "But how sweet of you to worry about me, Louis. I swear, in my whole life I never had any man ever worry about me."

At that moment, Figman was certain he had never seen a woman more beautiful. Was this lust, he wondered. Or was it love? As if guided by some hand from above, he leaned across the table to kiss her. But Verdie kissed him first. Passionately. Over her pan of hardened tamales. Her mouth tasted of Scotch whisky and her pink-purple lipstick. Its flavor was rhubarb (though not quite rhubarb) and disturbingly familiar. Figman grew hard and knew loving her would be easy.

When he touched her breast, she smiled her great smile. Her weathered chest rose up to meet his fingers. He pulled the top of her bathing suit up and felt the cool skin underneath, smooth, white, wholly unexpected. He'd found it, he thought, her soft, undamaged center. Figman kissed Verdie's cheek, her mouth, her leathery neck. Her hair smelled like a warm kitchen. When he slid his mouth down to her breast, his lips left a streak of pinkish purple.

He remembered, then, where he'd first encountered her terrible lipstick. It had been *her* lipstick, the woman who'd told him to go to Idaho. Figman's hand found the space between Verdie's skinny legs. He kissed her on the mouth and whispered, "Idaho."

"Wyoming," she whispered back to him. "South Dakota. Colorado."

She was good, this woman. Sexy, too. They groped and kissed and tugged at one another's clothing until they both lost their balance and fell painfully to the linoleum. By some miracle, Figman did not reinjure his ankle. They were laughing now, flopping about the floor of her tiny trailer like fish dying. Like gaffed bonita. "Utah," he whispered. "The State of New Mexico." A chair fell over. Next, the table. Verdie howled like no tomorrow.

Dust flew everywhere.

WHITE DWARFS

Marilee was forty miles west of Alamogordo when she first noticed the flashing red and blue lights in her rearview mirror. She'd been speeding most of the night, tearing through the desert like a blue meteor. She deserved the ticket she was about to be given; still, it made her angry.

She pulled over onto the shoulder of the highway. "Driver's license," said the cop through her open window. He was the same state trooper who had stopped her before, roughly in the same spot. Marilee handed it to him. "Your license is expired," he said.

"Let me see," said Marilee. The cop showed it to her. It had expired on her birthday, almost three months earlier. "Shit," she mumbled. The cop walked back to his patrol car to use his radio. The sky grew lighter. Birds and insects began their morning ritual.

In a few minutes, the cop returned to her window. "You have an outstanding warrant," he said. "For an unpaid speeding ticket issued last September."

Unpaid ticket? She'd forgotten all about that. It was probably still in her glove compartment. Flustered, she reached over and opened it. Her knife fell out onto the floor.

The cop pushed his sunglasses up the bridge of his nose. "Step out of the car, please," he said. "Stand over there where I can see you."

Marilee did as he asked, walking to a place about ten feet in front of her car. She wondered if he remembered her.

The cop sat on the front seat and rifled through Marilee's glove compartment. When he emerged from her car, he had her knife in his belt. "I'm going to drive to Alamogordo," he said. "You're going to follow me."

"To where?" she asked.

"To the state police station." He was tall and lean; his lips were pursed.

The cop drove forty-five the whole way; it took them almost an hour to reach Rocket City. With each passing mile, Marilee grew more angry. At herself for not having paid her previous ticket; at the cop for being such an asshole; at Larry for having turned out to be so fucking average.

Larry and everything about him had begun to feel wrong, like a coat that no longer fit, or perhaps never had. For years, she'd clung to the notion that he was someone special. She'd had dreams for him. Hope for his future. But now she realized she'd confused differentness for uniqueness; weirdness for artistic flair. Larry was a dilettante, just another Joe whose dreams exceeded his talent.

When they reached the turnoff to Holloman Air Force Base, the cop switched on his blue and red emergency lights. She was sure people in other cars were craning their heads to look at her. Marilee felt like a criminal. She switched on her radio and spun the dial, hunting for a rock station. A man's voice poured from her tinny speaker: "Adapt or survive. It's the law of the desert." She spun the dial again. At last she found a station playing something she could listen to, Julie Brown singing "I Like 'Em Big and Stupid."

At the police station, the cop asked Marilee to follow him into the building. He walked briskly, several steps ahead of her. "I remember you," he said, leading her down a hallway. "You had some midget in your car."

"A dwarf," she said.

The cop smiled. "What's the difference?"

"There's a big difference," she said. "It would take me too long to explain it to you."

"You'll have plenty of time," he said. His sunglasses looked huge; when he smiled, his mouth became a small, dark oval. He reminded Marilee of pictures she'd seen in *People* magazine, drawings made from memory by ordinary citizens who claimed they'd been abducted by aliens.

He led her through a doorway, then down another long corridor to take her to his leader. Holding a door open, the cop pointed to a metal desk in the center of a room. He told her to sit down at it. Marilee did as he commanded. The place was dismal: cracked linoleum, torn window shades, the smell of burnt coffee. The clock on the wall said seven ten. In a moment, a second officer materialized.

The leader cop sat across from Marilee at the desk and thumbed through a stack of papers. He was fifty pounds overweight and smelled like a cigar. "What's she in for?" he asked the cop who had brought her here.

"Speeding violation, expired license, outstanding warrant, concealed weapon, out-of-state plates."

Concealed weapon? Hadn't he seen her knife the first time, half a year ago, when he searched her car and tasted her makeup?

"You have the right to remain silent . . ." said the second cop.

"What's happening?" said Marilee. "Am I being arrested?"

"That's correct," he said. "You have the right to remain silent . . ." The officer finished reading Marilee her rights, then asked her if she wished to make a phone call.

"I most certainly do," she said.

He pushed the desk phone over to her. "Five minutes," he said.

"I'll need a phone book," said Marilee. The cop opened his bottom desk drawer and produced one. He sat in his chair, watching her. The tall cop stood at his side. "Do you mind?" she asked. The two men looked at one another. The fat one stood, and they both walked over to the coffee machine. She heard them talking in muted tones, then laughter. She wondered at what point they were planning to harvest the eggs from her ovaries.

His home number was not listed in the directory, but his ex-wife's number was, under Lucie with an ie. Marilee dialed the woman's number and waited for it to ring. A voice came on the line.

"My name's Marilee Levitay. I'm sorry to call you so early. I'm trying to reach Alcie Britton."

"Alcie?" said the woman. "Who did you say you were?" The voice sounded sleepy.

"Marilee Levitay. I'm at the state police station. There's been a mistake. I need him to come down here."

"I'm not supposed to give out his phone number," said the woman.

"I know you can't. But could you call him for me? Please? Could you ask him to come down here? I'm at the state police station. I don't know what else to do."

The woman was silent for a moment. "*What* was your name?"

"Marilee Levitay. Tell him UCLA. Tell him I'm the woman with the dwarf."

Forty minutes later, Alcie Britton walked into the booking room. Marilee had never felt so relieved to see anyone. The fat, alien-leader cop had spent the entire time asking her questions and typing her information onto a form. The tall one had sat in a chair alongside hers, smoking Camel Lights and sipping burnt coffee.

When the mayor of Alamogordo called Marilee by name, the fat cop yanked the form from his typewriter and tore it in two. "Thank you, Glenn," said Alcie Britton, placing a hand on his shoulder. "Will there be anything else?"

"Nothing, sir," he said. The tall cop stood; he looked nervous.

"Were you treated well?" Alcie asked Marilee. His Bell's Palsy was completely gone, but he looked tired.

"More or less," she said. "I'll tell you about it in the car."

The two cops glanced at one another.

"Do you have all your things?" asked Alcie.

"My driver's license."

The fat cop handed it to her.

"And my knife," she said.

The tall cop removed it from his belt and set it on the desktop.

"Obliged," she said, dropping it into her purse.

■

"I'll never be able to thank you," said Marilee, as soon as she and Alcie were outside the building. A parking lot had never looked so good.

"You already have," he said. Alcie held up his arm and pulled down his sleeve. He wore a rubber band around his wrist. "It's been five months. I still wear it, just in case."

"All right!" said Marilee. "I'm proud of you." He smiled up at her. She'd forgotten how short he was. "I hope you don't mind that I called your ex."

"I don't mind. But she wasn't too happy about it."

"Well, thank her for me."

"I will." He unlocked the door to his Lincoln. "Breakfast?" he said. "I know a little place that has great huevos rancheros."

El Ratón opened its doors at eight AM. The hostess led them to a table by the window and offered them coffee. Marilee took the seat facing the green bench on New York Avenue. "So, did you ever find your dwarf?" Alcie asked, once the woman had left the table.

"Oh, yes," she said. "He found me."

"And?"

"And . . . we took a trip together. For five days. Then I came back here to be with Larry."

"Larry?"

"My boyfriend. The one I came out here to marry."

"Oh, that's right," he said. Their waitress brought chips and salsa. Dr. Britton ordered huevos rancheros for both of them, and a side of guacamole. "So how was it?"

"What?"

"The wedding?"

"Oh. It wasn't."

"I'm sorry."

"Don't be," she said. Marilee ate a chip and sipped at her coffee. It was strong, hot, and just what she needed. "Larry and I . . . well, I don't think we're right for each other."

"Better you find that out now," said Alcie. "Before you get hitched."

"Eight years. Eight and a half, really." She felt tears welling up in her eyes.

"That's a long time."

"A third of my life."

"Pretty soon it will be a fourth, then a fifth, and sixth, and then you'll have forgotten him."

"And then I'll be old," she said, laughing.

"There's worse things that could happen to a person."

Marilee was all too aware of that. She looked out the window at the lime-green bench. A pigeon sat on its slatted back.

"So what happened this morning?" asked Dr. Britton.

"I got picked up for speeding. I had a ticket from last fall I'd completely forgotten about. So Ranger Rick brought me in."

"*Were* you speeding?"

"Oh, yes. Out by White Sands Missile Range."

"What were you doing way out there?"

"Just driving. Thinking. About what I'm going to do."

"About Larry?" The glare from the window lit up his bald spot.

"About the dwarf."

"Ah," said Alcie. Their waitress brought their huevos rancheros and refilled their cups of coffee. "Do you mind my asking you a personal question?"

"Ask away. If it weren't for you, I'd be rotting in jail."

"Are you in love with this dwarf?"

She looked up at him. "Yes."

"Is he in love with you?"

Marilee gazed out the window. "He's in love with the woman who saved his life twenty years ago."

"But does he love you, too?" Dr. Britton spooned guacamole on top of his fried eggs. "You know, it *is* possible to love more than one person at a time."

Marilee thought about it. "He might be in love with me."

Alcie's face brightened. "Then there's hope," he said.

Hope for what? thought Marilee. Hope that she and Enoch would ride off into the sunset? That he'd teach her how to hitchhike and they'd grow old together on the road, a couple of directionless hobos? Or that maybe he'd buy them a little house in town and settle down? Get a job in some office? Have two-point-three children and invest in real estate? Either future seemed about as likely as being abducted by aliens.

"So how are your migraines?" asked Dr. Britton.

"They might be getting better," she said. "I didn't get one this cycle."

"Terrific," he said, taking a tortilla and mopping up his egg.

"There's something I want to ask you," she said. "How are you able to be both the mayor and a gynecologist?"

Alcie laughed. "The mayor's job . . . well, that's just a hat you wear for a couple of years. The city council does most of the work. I'm really just a figurehead."

"You were more than that back there at the police station."

Alcie shrugged. "Power's a strange thing. It changes the way people think about you. Kind of like fame, I imagine. I wouldn't want to have too much of it."

"I agree," said Marilee.

"Glenn Whitsett, back there? He's the stocky one. I went to high school with him. There wasn't a day he didn't make my life more miserable than a polar bear in a rain forest. But now that I'm the mayor, it's 'Yes, sir,' and 'No, sir,' and 'Is there anything I can get for you, sir?' It's kind of sickening."

"Hmm," she said, loading beans and salsa onto her fork.

"Truth was, I liked him better before I became mayor. At least then I knew what he was thinking."

"Do you think it's important to know what people are thinking about you?"

"You're the one in love with a dwarf. You tell me."

Marilee thought about it. "It's not," she said. "Not to me, it isn't. Not anymore."

The corners of his mouth turned upward. "But sometimes it helps." He pushed his empty plate to the side of the table and sat back in his chair. "This is when I want a cigarette the most. After a good meal."

"Not after making love?" she said.

"Nope," said Alcie. "After fried eggs and coffee."

Marilee folded her napkin in her lap. "I want to thank you again for coming down to the station. You really did save me."

"You saved yourself," said Alcie. "By being the kind of person I'd get out of bed and go down there for."

Their waitress brought their check to the table and refilled their cups with coffee. "My turn," said Marilee, snapping the bill from his fingers. "That's another thing I have to thank you for. Lunch."

Alcie looked at her and smiled warmly. "Good luck with your dwarf," he said.

■

Alcie dropped Marilee off at her car at the police station. When she returned to the Mescalero Arms, she parked in the rear. Señor Escamilla was in the backyard working on a Jeep Cherokee; Larry's Mustang was nowhere to be seen. "Término," he said, grinning largely. Congas sounded from the upstairs window.

Taped to her front door, Marilee found a note addressed to her. It was not in Larry's handwriting. The note inside said, "Pool tonight. 9:30."

Marilee turned her key in the lock and stepped inside the apartment. She felt exhausted and headed straight for the bedroom. Larry had left the bed unmade. On her pillow, she found a poem:

DESTINY'S INQUEST
For Marilee

The twilight of a dying love
Made fresh by the sweet sorrow of your song
I long for slumber's wrenching grasp
To tear me from the icy silence of tomorrow

To taste the longing passion as it lingers
To kiss the arms of Fate as she surrounds me
To soar a thousand times higher
        than the eagle of the gods

All this, and more, lies inches from my
        screaming fingers

And still, my blood-stained passion slumbers in the pocket
Of your old, gray winter coat

Will the pain of poverty arouse you
to retrieve it from
the sticky attic of your soul?

Lawrence Hurd Johnston

Gads. Marilee set her alarm clock for four thirty, pulled the covers over her head, and slept as though she'd been standing for a week. When she awoke, the alarm had been buzzing for half an hour. She hit the off button and jumped into her jeans. She was out the door by five eleven.

■

At nine thirty, Marilee arrived at the Trinity Motel, where she found Enoch floating naked in the pool. The place looked otherwise deserted. She took off her clothes and stepped into the water.

"Yo," he said, as soon as he saw her.

"Does anyone actually stay here?" she asked, treading water next to him.

"I do. Tonight. Room eleven."

"What's it like inside?"

"Seedy," said Enoch. "But I like it."

"So what happened after I left the two of you out there on the highway?"

"We got a ride. Larry lived."

Marilee laughed. The night was dark and the moon had not yet risen.

"Where'd you stay the night?"

"At the Satellite Inn."

"He wouldn't let you sleep on our couch?"

"He offered. I said no."

"Don't you ever get tired of just bumming around?"

"Nope," he said. "Don't you ever get tired of living in one place?"

"No." She dove down to the bottom of the pool and touched her fingers to the drain. It felt good immersing herself in the cool water; she hadn't been swimming since their night in Ruidoso. "So tell me about the fire," she said, once she'd broken through the surface.

Enoch looked over at her and smiled. "After high school, I got this job out at the butane fields."

"Doing what?"

"Payroll," he said. "I'm good with numbers. One day, the place just exploded."

"How?"

"Just blew up. Storage tank overheated."

"Were you hurt?"

"Nobody was initially. I was in a building. But a lot of guys were burned trying to put out the fire. Took three days just to get it under control. Twelve of them died."

"Firemen?"

"Yeah."

"Your friend? What was his name?"

"Norm," said Enoch. "Norm Feinberg. That was the worst thing, really. He had just passed his training. I saw his face when they pulled him out. All you could see were bones and teeth."

"Jesus," said Marilee.

"This was a guy I'd known since I was three. His mother and my mother were like sisters. He lived two doors down from me."

"I'm sorry."

"I remember his eye sockets. They were huge. But mostly, I remember his teeth. All in a row. Straight. Real pretty. Not a chip in them. They weren't always like that. He used to have real crooked teeth. Wore braces and headgear all through high school. But here he was now, staring up at me with those huge eye sockets and those perfectly straight teeth. And all I could think of was Norm's father, and how he'd worked a double shift for four years so he could pay for his son's teeth to look that way."

Marilee floated on her back next to Enoch. A light came on in a corner room.

"Too much heat," said Enoch. "Way too much heat. At the funeral, Mr. and Mrs. Feinberg wouldn't even look at me."

"Why?"

Enoch turned his head toward Marilee. "Because her son was dead. Because I wasn't."

"Oh," she said. "What happened after the funeral?"

Enoch looked back up at the sky. "That's where Chester steps in. One night, about two weeks after the fire, Chester told his wife he'd seen me running from the explosion with a can of gasoline. His nephews were over that night, eating dinner. They were eight, twelve, and fourteen. Half the town had heard about it by morning."

"Why would Chester say such a thing?"

"Because he's evil. Some people just are. There's no explaining."

"You think some people are just born that way?"

"I do."

Marilee looked up at the stars. The night was clear. She could see the whole length of the Milky Way. "So then what?"

"Next thing I knew, people were looking at me funny on the street. Not that they hadn't always done that. But I mean funny, funny. Like I'd never been looked at before. Friends I'd known for years stopped talking to me. Mothers put their arms around their children when I walked into a store. Even my father looked at me differently."

"Your own father?"

"It took me years to forgive him."

"Is he a dwarf too?"

Enoch shook his head. "Five-eleven. My mother was five-foot-seven. Double recessive genes."

"Do you have any brothers or sisters?"

"Nope," he said, smiling. "Guess my parents thought they'd quit while they were ahead."

"They did," she said.

Enoch smiled.

Marilee's fingertips were beginning to wrinkle. "So when did they beat you up?"

"Not long after Norm was buried. Lucid put together a small contingent of his buddies. Chester, and this guy—"

"I thought you said Chester was the one who started the rumors?"

"He was."

"And then he beat you up, knowing it was a lie?"

"Yup."

"That *is* evil."

Enoch bared his teeth like an animal. "See these? They're all caps. Chester broke every one of them."

"With his fist?"

"With a baseball bat."

"Whoa," said Marilee. She was beginning to feel cold. A breeze blew the leaves of a yucca.

"I don't actually remember much of the beating. I remember them kidnapping me, and taking me out to the high school. I remember a bunch of guys on the football field. Some of them I knew. Some I'd never seen before. I think they must have come in from Seligman or something. They were big, like Lucid. Probably buddies of his from cop school. Chester was the first to hit me. Next thing I remember, I was in the hospital and fourteen weeks had gone by."

"Maybe it's better you don't remember."

"Maybe," said Enoch. "Maybe not." He had floated over to the edge of the pool. Kicking off from the side, he propelled himself back into its center, next to Marilee.

"Then what happened?"

"Then I got the hell out of Dodge. Went down to Juárez. You know the rest of it from there."

"Not all of it. When did you get your settlement?"

"After Juárez. I went up to Flagstaff and hired a lawyer. Sued Chester and Lucid and the four other guys I could identify. By that time, the arson investigator's report had cleared me. I sued the town of Kingfield, too. Turned out when the beating took place, Lucid was on duty."

"You said he wasn't very bright."

"I won two-point-six million. The lawyer took his third and left the rest to me."

"Whoa," said Marilee. "That's a whole lot of Ding Dongs."

Enoch laughed softly. "At the time, I thought it was everything. But it doesn't give you back four months of your life. It doesn't give you back your teeth."

"Did they put away the guys who beat you?"

"Nope. Lucid's father was the sheriff. I think I told you that. Not one of them went to jail."

"Weren't you angry?"

"Furious. They all got probation, which was as good as getting off scot-free."

"It happens," said Marilee.

"It does," said Enoch.

She was silent for a moment. The stars flickered in the sky. From one of the rooms, she heard a couple arguing.

"So what was it like, being in a coma?"

"Like sleeping without dreaming."

"Do you remember anything?"

"I remember my mother's voice," said Enoch. "I remember her talking to me."

"What did she say?"

"Not to die. To go back. To go on living."

"Go back?"

"My mother had been dead three months by that time. Heart attack. I think the stress of the whole thing killed her."

"Because you were in a coma?"

"Because of what people in town were saying about me. About her family."

"But it was all a lie. Didn't she believe you?"

"She did. I know she did. But people were saying her son had done this terrible thing. Set fire to the butane fields. Killed his own best friend and eleven other men. Sons and husbands and fathers. People she'd grown up with. You don't understand small towns. The grocer closed her account. Judith Feinberg wouldn't speak to her. People she'd sung with in the Methodist choir crossed the street when they saw her coming. That town was her entire world. It turned on her overnight."

"What happened to your father?"

"He's still alive."

"Do you ever see him?"

"Every now and then."

"How's he doing?"

"Not too well. He's got emphysema."

"Do you miss him?"

"No."

Marilee waved her arms in the water to keep herself warm. The couple's arguing had quieted. "You've had a rough life," she said.

"Show me someone who hasn't," said Enoch.

"Larry hasn't. His life's been relatively easy."

Enoch laughed. "His life's been relatively unconscious. Talk about living in a coma. You know what he said to me?"

"What?"

"This is great. The two of us are out on the highway. Five or six cars have passed us by, but none have pulled over, and he's getting freaked out because nobody's stopping. We've been out there maybe ten minutes. So he asks me if I think we should call the police. I say, 'With what, Larry? Our G.I. Joe walkie talkies?' And he says, 'No, Enoch. With our minds.' I say, 'What the fuck are you talking about, Larry?' And he says, 'Let's just put out that good energy. We'll focus on the police coming. They'll pick up on our vibes and come rescue us.'"

"That's Larry," said Marilee.

"Another ten minutes goes by. It's not that cold out there, but Larry's beginning to freak. Starts talking about freezing to death or getting eaten by coyotes. It's all I can do to keep from busting up laughing. So I say, 'Larry, you're not putting out the right energy. See this car coming?' He says, 'Yes.' And I say, 'Will it to stop, Larry. Do like G. Gordon Liddy. Send it your vibes.' So Larry shuts his eyes real tight, and I can almost feel him concentrating. And damned if the car doesn't pull right over."

"That's great."

"It gets better. Larry's beside himself by now. He's sure he's performed some kind of new age miracle. But when the guy opens the door, he says, 'Not you, big guy. I'll take the little fellow.'"

"You're kidding?"

"I'm not."

"So what happened?"

"So I tell the guy to go fuck himself. He slams his car door and takes off down the highway. But now Larry thinks I've saved him, see, by not going with the guy and leaving him out in the desert to be eaten by wild animals. So he starts thanking me and apologizing and shaking my hand. Falls all over himself trying to make it up to me."

"What a cluck," said Marilee. She felt the water gliding through her fingers, smooth as New Mexico sand. "Take good care of him for me."

Enoch turned his head to look at her.

"I'm leaving tomorrow. Before he gets home from the base. Going back to Los Angeles."

"Ah," said Enoch. He dove under the water. He swam to the shallow end, then back to Marilee, holding his breath the entire time. When he surfaced, he swept the hair from his eyes and resumed his place next to her. "I'll miss you," was all he said.

She reached over and took Enoch's hand. "I'll miss you, too," she said. He didn't pull away. She felt his stubby fingers in her own, his handclasp gentle but determined, like the grasp of a child. They floated, and they gazed up into the endless sky, holding on to one another as the moon rose up over the mountains and shone down on them like a benediction.

"Do you ever wonder where they landed?" asked Marilee.

"Who?"

"The astronauts. Back in '69."

Enoch didn't answer, just stared up into the clear, black night. The stars shone like distant headlights. The howl of a coyote. The low, steady rumble of a train.

■

She was packed and on the road by two thirty, headed home to California. Her last night in New Mexico she'd spent with Enoch in room eleven of the Trinity Motel. They'd made love until half past two; when she awoke that morning, Enoch was gone.

Before noon, Marilee returned to Larry's apartment. His poem was still on her pillow. She made herself a sandwich, packed her suitcase, and called Alcie Britton at the hospital to say goodbye. After loading up her car, she sat down and penned a four-page letter to Larry. Then she tore it up and flushed the pieces down the toilet. In bold letters across his poem she wrote, "NO CAN DO." It was cruel, yes; he'd get over it.

Was her leaving Enoch just as cruel? Marilee didn't think so, but time would tell. She loved Enoch but knew it would never work with him. He would always be traipsing off into the desert, backpack slung over his shoulder, wallet in his sock, showing up on her doorstep weeks or months later as if no time had passed. And he would always be in love with Carmina.

In her rearview mirror, Marilee watched the town of Alamogordo meld into the horizon. Two fighter jets from Holloman streaked across the sky. They wove in and out as she had often seen them do, leaving their crisscrossed trails high above the desert. The sun beat in through her dusty windshield. She was glad to be leaving New Mexico. Too much heat, she thought, rolling down her window. Way too much heat.

■

In Casa Grande, Marilee stopped for dinner at the Hobo restaurant. She'd been driving for hours, and her neck and shoulders felt cramped. Her waitress, Doreen, was the same waitress she'd had when she'd eaten there with Enoch. The woman looked silly in her red ruffled skirt and name-embroidered hat. Perhaps Marilee, bleary-eyed in her T-shirt and faded jeans, looked just as silly to Doreen. Marilee chuckled. Enoch had been right: We are all of us freaks. And what does one freak owe another in this world? Compassion. Forgiveness. Nothing more. Nothing less.

Back on the road, the sky had turned to coral. Clouds floated by like leaves in a pool. A hawk flew in circles. Marilee drove onward into the setting sun, toward the once-fertile valley of her beginning. Five miles west of Sentinel, she came upon a one-armed man hitchhiking on the side of the highway. "Yo!" she said as she drove on by.

ACKNOWLEDGMENTS

My deepest gratitude to those friends and family who supported and encouraged my efforts in writing *Rocket City*. Additionally, I would like to thank several people whose valuable insights helped shape this novel: Yvonne Elder, Felicia Eth, Candida Lawrence, Anne Marie Mackler, Dana Massie, Kevin McIlvoy, Greg Michalson, Carl R. Mueller, Fred Ramey, Carol Houck Smith, and Carol Staudacher.

Cathryn Alpert

VINTAGE
CONTEMPORARIES

___	**Rocket City** by Cathryn Alpert	$12.00	0-679-77016-X
___	**The Fermata** by Nicholson Baker	$11.00	0-679-75933-6
___	**The Mezzanine** by Nicholson Baker	$ 9.00	0-679-72576-8
___	**Room Temperature** by Nicholson Baker	$ 9.00	0-679-73440-6
___	**Vox** by Nicholson Baker	$10.00	0-679-74211-5
___	**Gorilla, My Love** by Toni Cade Bambara	$10.00	0-679-73898-3
___	**The Salt Eaters** by Toni Cade Bambara	$11.00	0-679-74076-7
___	**The Last Good Time** by Richard Bausch	$11.00	0-679-75556-X
___	**Rare & Endangered Species** by Richard Bausch	$12.00	0-679-76310-4
___	**Rebel Powers** by Richard Bausch	$12.00	0-679-75253-6
___	**Violence** by Richard Bausch	$13.00	0-679-74379-0
___	**The Burning House** by Ann Beattie	$11.00	0-679-76500-X
___	**Chilly Scenes of Winter** by Ann Beattie	$12.00	0-679-73234-9
___	**Distortions** by Ann Beattie	$12.00	0-679-73235-7
___	**Falling in Place** by Ann Beattie	$12.00	0-679-73192-X
___	**Love Always** by Ann Beattie	$11.00	0-394-74418-7
___	**Picturing Will** by Ann Beattie	$11.00	0-679-73194-6
___	**Secrets and Surprises** by Ann Beattie	$11.00	0-679-73193-8
___	**What Was Mine** by Ann Beattie	$12.00	0-679-73903-3
___	**The Revolution of Little Girls** by Blanche McCrary Boyd	$11.00	0-679-73812-6
___	**A Closed Eye** by Anita Brookner	$11.00	0-679-74340-5
___	**Brief Lives** by Anita Brookner	$11.00	0-679-73733-2
___	**The Debut** by Anita Brookner	$10.00	0-679-72712-4
___	**Dolly** by Anita Brookner	$11.00	0-679-74578-5
___	**Fraud** by Anita Brookner	$11.00	0-679-74308-1
___	**Hotel du Lac** by Anita Brookner	$11.00	0-679-75932-8
___	**Latecomers** by Anita Brookner	$11.00	0-679-72668-3
___	**Lewis Percy** by Anita Brookner	$12.00	0-679-72944-5
___	**A Private View** by Anita Brookner	$12.00	0-679-75443-1
___	**Providence** by Anita Brookner	$11.00	0-679-73814-2
___	**Big Bad Love** by Larry Brown	$12.00	0-679-73491-0
___	**Dirty Work** by Larry Brown	$11.00	0-679-73049-4
___	**A Stranger in This World** by Kevin Canty	$10.00	0-679-76394-5
___	**Sleeping in Flame** by Jonathan Carroll	$12.00	0-679-72777-9
___	**Cathedral** by Raymond Carver	$11.00	0-679-72369-2
___	**Fires** by Raymond Carver	$10.00	0-679-72239-4
___	**No Heroics, Please** by Raymond Carver	$11.00	0-679-74007-4
___	**Short Cuts** by Raymond Carver	$10.00	0-679-74864-4
___	**What We Talk About When We Talk About Love** by Raymond Carver	$ 9.00	0-679-72305-6
___	**Where I'm Calling From** by Raymond Carver	$13.00	0-679-72231-9
___	**Will You Please Be Quiet, Please?** by Raymond Carver	$10.00	0-679-73569-0
___	**The House on Mango Street** by Sandra Cisneros	$ 9.00	0-679-73477-5
___	**Loose Woman** by Sandra Cisneros	$10.00	0-679-75527-6

VINTAGE
CONTEMPORARIES

___ **Woman Hollering Creek** by Sandra Cisneros	$10.00	0-679-73856-8
___ **Dancing Bear** by James Crumley	$11.00	0-394-72576-X
___ **The Last Good Kiss** by James Crumley	$11.00	0-394-75989-3
___ **One to Count Cadence** by James Crumley	$13.00	0-394-73559-5
___ **The Wrong Case** by James Crumley	$11.00	0-394-73558-7
___ **Breath, Eyes, Memory** by Edwidge Danticat	$11.00	0-679-75661-2
___ **Kirk? Krak!** by Edwidge Danticat	$11.00	0-679-76657-X
___ **Great Jones Street** by Don DeLillo	$13.00	0-679-72303-X
___ **The Names** by Don DeLillo	$12.00	0-679-72295-5
___ **Players** by Don DeLillo	$12.00	0-679-72293-9
___ **Ratner's Star** by Don DeLillo	$14.00	0-679-72292-0
___ **Running Dog** by Don DeLillo	$13.00	0-679-72294-7
___ **Through the Ivory Gate** by Rita Dove	$11.00	0-679-74240-9
___ **The Commitments** by Roddy Doyle	$ 9.00	0-679-72174-6
___ **Selected Stories** by Andre Dubus	$13.00	0-679-76730-4
___ **The Coast of Chicago** by Stuart Dybek	$10.00	0-679-73334-5
___ **American Psycho** by Bret Easton Ellis	$14.00	0-679-73577-1
___ **The Informers** by Bret Easton Ellis	$11.00	0-679-74324-3
___ **Platitudes** by Trey Ellis	$ 9.00	0-394-75439-5
___ **Heartburn** by Nora Ephron	$11.00	0-679-76795-9
___ **A Fan's Notes** by Frederick Exley	$13.00	0-679-72076-6
___ **Last Notes from Home** by Frederick Exley	$12.00	0-679-72456-7
___ **Independence Day** by Richard Ford	$13.00	0-679-73518-6
___ **A Piece of My Heart** by Richard Ford	$12.00	0-394-72914-5
___ **Rock Springs** by Richard Ford	$12.00	0-394-75700-9
___ **The Sportswriter** by Richard Ford	$12.00	0-679-76210-8
___ **The Ultimate Good Luck** by Richard Ford	$12.00	0-394-75089-6
___ **Wildlife** by Richard Ford	$11.00	0-679-73447-3
___ **The Chinchilla Farm** by Judith Freeman	$12.00	0-679-73052-4
___ **Catherine Carmier** by Ernest J. Gaines	$11.00	0-679-73891-6
___ **A Gathering of Old Men** by Ernest J. Gaines	$10.00	0-679-73890-8
___ **A Lesson Before Dying** by Ernest J. Gaines	$12.00	0-679-74166-6
___ **In My Father's House** by Ernest J. Gaines	$10.00	0-679-72791-4
___ **Of Love and Dust** by Ernest J. Gaines	$11.00	0-679-75248-X
___ **Bad Behavior** by Mary Gaitskill	$11.00	0-679-72327-7
___ **A Cure For Dreams** by Kaye Gibbons	$10.00	0-679-73672-7
___ **Ellen Foster** by Kaye Gibbons	$ 9.00	0-679-72866-X
___ **A Virtuous Woman** by Kaye Gibbons	$ 9.00	0-679-72844-9
___ **Wild at Heart** by Barry Gifford	$ 8.95	0-679-73439-2
___ **Impossible Vacation** by Spalding Gray	$11.00	0-679-74523-8
___ **The Country Ahead of Us, the Country Behind** by David Guterson	$11.00	0-679-76718-5
___ **Snow Falling on Cedars** by David Guterson	$12.00	0-679-76402-X
___ **Life Estates** by Shelby Hearon	$11.00	0-679-75796-1
___ **Floating in My Mother's Palm** by Ursula Hegi	$10.00	0-679-73115-6

___ The One-Room Schoolhouse by Jim Heynen	$10.00	0-679-74769-9
___ In a Country of Mothers by A. M. Homes	$11.00	0-679-74243-3
___ Jack by A. M. Homes	$10.00	0-679-73221-7
___ The Safety of Objects by A. M. Homes	$11.00	0-679-73629-8
___ Cuba and the Night by Pico Iyer	$12.00	0-679-76075-X
___ Secrets by Kelvin Christopher James	$10.00	0-679-75546-2
___ Let 'Em Eat Cake by Susan Jedren	$14.00	0-679-76805-X
___ Angels by Denis Johnson	$12.00	0-394-75987-7
___ Particles and Luck by Louis B. Jones	$12.00	0-679-74599-8
___ Asa, As I Knew Him by Susanna Kaysen	$12.00	0-679-75377-X
___ Far Afield by Susanna Kaysen	$12.00	0-679-75376-1
___ Girl, Interrupted by Susanna Kaysen	$10.00	0-679-74604-8
___ Ride a Cockhorse by Raymond Kennedy	$11.00	0-679-73835-5
___ Steps by Jerzy Kosinski	$10.00	0-394-75716-5
___ The Fan Man by William Kotzwinkle	$10.00	0-679-75245-5
___ A Guide for the Perplexed by Jonathan Levi	$12.00	0-679-73969-6
___ The Evolution Man by Roy Lewis	$10.00	0-679-75009-6
___ Et Tu, Babe by Mark Leyner	$10.00	0-679-74506-8
___ I Smell Esther Williams by Mark Leyner	$10.00	0-679-75045-2
___ My Cousin, My Gastroenterologist by Mark Leyner	$10.00	0-679-74579-3
___ Tooth Imprints on a Corn Dog by Mark Leyner	$11.00	0-679-74521-1
___ The Chosen Place, the Timeless People Paule Marshall	$14.00	0-394-72633-2
___ Dr. Haggard's Disease by Patrick McGrath	$10.00	0-679-75261-7
___ Spider by Patrick McGrath	$13.00	0-679-73630-1
___ The Bushwhacked Piano by Thomas McGuane	$12.00	0-394-72642-1
___ Keep the Change by Thomas McGuane	$11.00	0-679-73033-8
___ Ninety-two in the Shade by Thomas McGuane	$10.00	0-679-75289-7
___ Nobody's Angel by Thomas McGuane	$11.00	0-394-74738-0
___ Nothing But Blue Skies by Thomas McGuane	$12.00	0-679-74778-8
___ Panama by Thomas McGuane	$10.00	0-679-75291-9
___ Something to Be Desired by Thomas McGuane	$10.00	0-394-73156-5
___ The Sporting Club by Thomas McGuane	$11.00	0-679-75290-0
___ To Skin a Cat by Thomas McGuane	$10.00	0-394-75521-9
___ Bright Lights, Big City by Jay McInerney	$10.00	0-394-72641-3
___ Brightness Falls by Jay McInerney	$12.00	0-679-74532-7
___ Ransom by Jay McInerney	$11.00	0-394-74118-8
___ Story of My Life by Jay McInerney	$10.00	0-679-72257-2
___ Edwin Mullhouse by Steven Millhauser	$12.00	0-679-76652-9
___ Traffic and Laughter by Ted Mooney	$12.00	0-679-73884-3
___ Sleeping Beauties by Susanna Moore	$11.00	0-679-75539-X
___ Homeboy by Seth Morgan	$12.00	0-679-73395-7
___ The Beggar Maid by Alice Munro	$11.00	0-679-73271-3
___ Friend of My Youth by Alice Munro	$11.00	0-679-72957-7
___ The Moons of Jupiter by Alice Munro	$11.00	0-679-73270-5

VINTAGE
CONTEMPORARIES

___	**Open Secrets** by Alice Munro	$13.00	0-679-75562-4
___	**Bailey's Cafe** by Gloria Naylor	$11.00	0-679-74821-0
___	**Mama Day** by Gloria Naylor	$12.00	0-679-72181-9
___	**City of Boys** by Beth Nugent	$11.00	0-679-73351-5
___	**Buffalo Soldiers** by Robert O'Connor	$12.00	0-679-74203-4
___	**Kentucky Straight** by Chris Offutt	$12.00	0-679-73886-X
___	**Littlejohn** by Howard Owen	$10.00	0-679-75001-0
___	**Clea and Zeus Divorce** by Emily Prager	$10.00	0-394-75591-X
___	**Eve's Tattoo** by Emily Prager	$10.00	0-679-74053-8
___	**A Visit From the Footbinder** by Emily Prager	$10.00	0-394-75592-8
___	**A Good Baby** by Leon Rooke	$10.00	0-679-72939-9
___	**Mohawk** by Richard Russo	$13.00	0-679-75382-6
___	**Nobody's Fool** by Richard Russo	$13.00	0-679-75333-8
___	**The Risk Pool** by Richard Russo	$14.00	0-679-75383-4
___	**The Laughing Sutra** by Mark Salzman	$11.00	0-679-73546-1
___	**The Soloist** by Mark Salzman	$11.00	0-679-75926-3
___	**Mile Zero** by Thomas Sanchez	$12.00	0-679-73260-8
___	**Rabbit Boss** by Thomas Sanchez	$12.00	0-679-72621-7
___	**Zoot-Suit Murders** by Thomas Sanchez	$12.00	0-679-73396-5
___	**Anywhere But Here** by Mona Simpson	$12.00	0-679-73738-3
___	**The Lost Father** by Mona Simpson	$12.00	0-679-73303-5
___	**Honey** by Elizabeth Tallent	$11.00	0-679-75511-X
___	**The Joy Luck Club** by Amy Tan	$10.00	0-679-72768-X
___	**The Kitchen God's Wife** by Amy Tan	$12.00	0-679-74808-3
___	**Air & Fire** by Rupert Thomson	$12.00	0-679-74730-3
___	**The Player** by Michael Tolkin	$10.00	0-679-72254-8
___	**Many Things Have Happened Since He Died** by Elizabeth Dewberry Vaughn	$10.00	0-679-73568-2
___	**Myra Breckinridge and Myron** by Gore Vidal	$15.00	0-394-75444-1
___	**Birdy** by William Wharton	$13.00	0-679-73412-0
___	**All Stories Are True** by John Edgar Wideman	$10.00	0-679-73752-9
___	**Philadelphia Fire** by John Edgar Wideman	$10.00	0-679-73650-6
___	**The Final Club** by Geoffrey Wolff	$13.00	0-679-73592-5
___	**Providence** by Geoffrey Wolff	$10.00	0-679-73277-2
___	**The Vintage Book of Contemporary American Short Stories** edited by Tobias Wolff	$13.00	0-679-74513-0

Available at your bookstore or call toll-free to order: 1-800-793-2665.
Credit cards only. Prices subject to change.